MY WIFE, THE SERIAL KILLER

H.J. GARBETT

This is a work of fiction. Names, characters, businesses, places, events and incidents are either the products of the author's imagination or used in a fictitious manner. Any resemblance to actual persons, living or dead, or actual events is purely coincidental.

Copyright © James Garbett, 2025

The moral right of the author has been asserted.

All rights reserved. No part of this book may be reproduced or used in any manner without the prior written permission of the copyright owner. This prohibition includes, but is not limited to, any reproduction or use for the purpose of training artificial intelligence technologies or systems.

To request permissions, contact the publisher at rights@stormpublishing.co

Ebook ISBN: 978-1-83700-132-3
Paperback ISBN: 978-1-83700-134-7

Cover design: Lisa Brewster
Cover images: Shutterstock

Published by Storm Publishing.
For further information, visit:
www.stormpublishing.co

Para o meu amor...

PROLOGUE

His body slumped to the floor instantly, like a marionette with the strings cut. As the blood began to bubble and flow out from the back of his head, it was only his right foot that had any kind of life left in it, rapping repeatedly against the carpeted floorboards.

At a bit of a stretch, it sounded to me like his foot was tapping to the beat of 'Under Pressure' or, of course, 'Ice Ice Baby' – if you are an uncultured swine with no taste in good music.

My brain began to fire on all cylinders. You can't exactly ask Siri where's the best place to hide a dead body – that would surely have the SWAT team ramming my door down in no time. I began to evaluate my options.

1. **Leave the body there. Wait for someone to find it.**

No. That was a recipe for disaster. His carer would find his corpse on Monday, call the police immediately, and forensics would not only discover the method of murder but would turn the whole neighbourhood into a *CSI* episode. An investigation into our house would be inevitable, alibis would have to be concocted, kitchen knives taken away for analysis. That would all be one big ball ache, and I desperately needed as much time between murder and investigation as possible.

2. **Move the body from the house to somewhere more secluded.**

There was no way that I, a five-foot-five woman, would be able to carry a heavyset septuagenarian from his house to my car and then to some deserted spot in the woods at three in the afternoon. Not only would this result in a very strained, if not broken, spine, but realistically, there was no way in hell I would be able to weasel my way out of that one if I got caught in the process.

'I'm sorry, Officer. I just went to go in and check on my neighbour and thought he would love to continue his nap in the back of my Ford Fiesta. Wait, what do you mean there's a knife in his head?'

3. **Alkalise his body.**

That could work. It would be awfully gruesome, but if I chopped his body into several large chunks and treated it with a strong enough drain cleaner, the sodium hydroxide could break his body down, and I could pour him down the sink like a cup of tea, albeit a little lumpier.

I rushed down the stairs and began flinging open cupboard doors to find where O'Neill kept his cleaning products. I found a scratched and scuffed bottle of drain cleaner that felt light to the touch. It was barely half full and certainly not enough to break a whole body down. We had a few substantial wholesale-sized bottles that we'd bought to clean the bathrooms before we moved in. That could do the trick, but the football mums across the road would be off to pick up their little star athletes any second. I would almost certainly be caught running between the two houses and be forced to engage in chit-chat.

4. **Just admit it was me, but change the motive.**

I killed him in self-defence. I just came to see if he wanted any help with his shopping, and when I was inside, he throttled my neck like he was squeezing the last bit of toothpaste out of the tube?

Nope, the knife lodged in his eye was pretty drastic evidence to the contrary. Not only had I taken the blade from *my* kitchen, but I had pierced him so perfectly through his eye socket that there was no way it could have been anything other than hot-blooded murder.

I was racking my brains for option number five. I hadn't realised I was still gripping the knife so tight that my knuckles had turned a pale white against the gold of my wedding ring. I tried to loosen my grip and instead focus on the carton of semi-skimmed milk leaking from his grocery shopping, dribbling across the carpet and mixing with his blood, forming something that resembled the national flag of Bahrain.

So, I stood there, watching over his corpse, wondering why the hell I had decided to be so spontaneous. I remember Gareth had said that he liked that about me when we'd first met.

'You're just *so* spontaneous,' he had said to me amidst the ambience of a grotty student bar, as if he had just realised for the first time that there existed people who wouldn't need an itinerary before taking a casual trip to the local newsagent for a fizzy pop. I think all I'd done was change my order from a soda and lime to a vodka tonic. Not exactly groundbreaking.

I knew that the longer I dithered, the higher the chance I

had of getting caught. Yet, I found that I couldn't stop staring at the body with this strange mixture of repulsion and gratification. The blood and milk concoction that now almost resembled the Japanese flag was dribbling towards O'Neill's little finger on which that god-awful bronze ring was still wedged. I just wished that the Zodiac Killer had managed to write a *Killing for Dummies* before he'd vanished into obscurity. That would have been extremely helpful around now.

I decided to go with one of Angus's old adages: 'A bad plan is better than no plan at all.' I gently placed my thumb and index finger around the ring still lodged onto O'Neill's bloated, chubby finger and yanked it off. I rinsed the viscous, gloopy blood from the metal in the sink of his wet room before rushing back down to the kitchen to grab the stain remover, humming a very particular 90s hip-hop song as I did so.

Well, this was certainly not nearly as easy as the last time.

ONE

FRAN

> Sorry babe will be at work L8 2nite, busy night, c u when I get home. Lyl. Sorry.

I loved that after all this time, Gareth still texted like a grandma getting used to the nuances of predictive text. I also loved how he thought that pretty much any common phrase could be acronymised. Translation: *lyl* stood for 'love you lots'. However, he had some other acronyms that took a lot more deciphering to figure out.

I snatched up the lovely Azulejo plates, popped them back in the worn cardboard box, and then indelicately yanked out a Pyrex dish from the cupboard to replace them. The dish was – admittedly – the only thing we had in the cupboard at this point. Just between my job and Gareth's, we hadn't really had a chance to have dinner together yet. I had created some fake superstition that until Gareth and I finally had dinner together at the house, I couldn't allow the fancy plates, which were a housewarming gift from his mum, to finally rest within their natural home of the right-hand cupboard above the sink. And besides, the dish was microwavable, so it meant that the amount of washing up I had to do was drastically reduced.

I readied the dish and steadily began to pour the risotto in. The minute the first grain of rice touched the glass, Mep hopped on the counter and began his approach. I angled my body to try to block his path.

'Mep, back off, you scab. This isn't for you.'

He did his awful throaty purr in retaliation as he attempted to bounce onto my shoulder, but, unfortunately for him, his old, creaky cat joints wouldn't let him. What was meant as a glorious leap akin to those of his lion ancestors could be more accurately described as a slightly sprained hop.

I mean, look, I got it, of course I got it; it was a new promotion, and Gareth wanted to make a good impression. He had gone on and on and on about working in the CID as a sergeant for God knows how long, but there was still a part of me that wished some nights he would tell the cases to sod off and just come home for an early evening dinner so we could actually spend some time together. Surely, some of them could wait to be solved until another day?

I tossed the portable cutlery cases in the cool-bag and placed it in the passenger seat of my car. I grabbed my phone and texted him back:

> On my way dickhead, get ready for dinner in 10.

If he had ordered takeaway already, I was going to kill that man.

I already knew the desk sergeant at the front, and as always, I waved to her as I came in.

'What is it tonight, Fran?' she asked as I powered through the immensely stiff glass door of the station.

'Mushroom risotto today, Judith.'

'Oooh, sounds lovely,' she exclaimed, pursing her lips and stretching herself over the desk to get a glance. I even noticed one of the men in line, who had his wrists encased in handcuffs, darted his eyes over to the bag. 'I'll buzz you in.'

The metallic door unlocked with a poorly greased squeak and then a high-pitched shrill as I hauled it open. I manifested the bulbous biceps I would have by the time Gareth got his next promotion here with all this heavy door-pulling. I wondered if I could even grab some growth hormone from the contraband section to really try and fuel my progress.

I strolled through the various offices of the police station and eventually found my husband. Almost everyone else had gone home, but lo and behold, there he was, hunched over in his small cubicle, typing away on his crappy desktop. I had always been so bitterly disappointed by how police detectives actually worked; even now, I kept expecting an old crusty cigar smell from the minute I entered, a fedora perching off the side of a wooden chair, and maybe even a half-broken typewriter as the detective pondered who had killed the mayor outside his mistress's home on Fifth Avenue. Instead, it all looked incredibly dull, like Gareth could have been an accountant for a stapler company just as much as a detective sergeant trying to solve some grisly homicide. He hadn't noticed me yet, so I slowly let my arms drape over him and moved my lips closer to nuzzle at his neck.

'Mmm,' he moaned, tilting his head back. 'Vivian, I told you, not at work.'

'Oh, piss off,' I laughed with a cackle, clipping his ear lightly with the back of my hand. I pulled out the office chair from the vacant desk beside me and began to dish out the risotto. I could see the few other stragglers left in the CID begin to peep up from their ergonomic mole holes to investigate the smells.

Gareth slammed his case book shut, placed it onto his desk

and gracefully dipped his nose into the wafts of risotto fumes drifting up from our traditional Sunday-evening dish.

'Oh, my gosh, smells so good,' he crooned as he began to shovel the food in. 'So, who goes first? You first? Me first?'

'I'll go first.'

Gareth gestured for me to go ahead as he began to rapidly inhale his portion.

'Well, you won't believe this. Keith Johnson ran away from home again.'

'Again?!' Gareth groaned in between mouthfuls.

'Yeah, got a call from an officer about it this morning. He's back with his foster family now, but the police caught him a few miles away from the home last night with a bunch of pick 'n' mix stolen from the newsagent's in his hoody pocket.'

'Do you think they'll press charges?'

'Nah, I convinced them it wasn't worth the trouble for a few flying saucers and raspberry bonbons, but I'm speaking with him and the family tomorrow afternoon. That should be a barrel of laughs.'

'It's sad that the lad can't keep himself out of trouble, though. Any more updates on that new strategy thingy?'

'Nope, nothing since last week. Veronica sent me about ten emails changing the dashes to commas, though, but she's got another think coming if she thinks I'm going to do that on my Sunday afternoon. Right, I think that's my time up.'

I should clarify: to prevent ourselves from being the boring couple who only talk about work, Gareth and I had decided to give each other a sixty-second max limit for work talk. I always used to moan that Gareth grumbled way too much about his job, while Gareth said that I never complained enough, so we met in the middle: sixty seconds, no interruptions or off-topic questions from the other party.

'So how about you? Solve any murders?' I asked with my usual impishness.

'A few,' he replied rather nonchalantly.

I had asked him that question without fail almost every day for the past few years. When he was on the beat, he would always laugh it off and just tell me he was doing some mundane task – from investigating who had trodden on some old dear's flowers to settling minor disagreements between two middle-aged, beer-bellied thugs down the pub. But now, he was actually doing the thing I'd always joked about. It made me feel sort of uneasy that homicide had become the standard working day for him.

'Anything you can talk to me about?'

'Not really. They're all pretty much open and shut cases. The CPS has done most of the heavy lifting for them, anyway. We're just there to cross the *t*s and dot the *i*s, really.'

'Urgh, with Isla, I bet,' I said through a scowl. 'Lawyers.'

Gareth gave a wry smile as if he wasn't going to rise to the bait. I wasn't a fan of Isla, and I made it a point to remind him of that every chance I could.

'It's a different criminal lawyer this time, Andrew Shorestone, who's been an absolute pain in my neck recently, drowning me in paperwork.'

'And how are you getting on with the team now?'

'Good, good, they're all good. I think the first month of staying late as a sergeant is kind of the rite of passage though, some weird kind of hazing, I guess.'

'They're still being nice to you?' I said, jabbing my knife vaguely towards where a few of Gareth's colleagues were sitting.

'Yeah, they're a good bunch of blokes,' Gareth mumbled. The way he deflected made me suspicious; I wasn't sure I believed him.

'And how's Vivian?' I asked, knowing it was going to prompt some kind of negative response from him.

He grimaced and took another gulp of the risotto before continuing.

'Won't have much left for continuing the family line the way she's busting my balls at the minute,' he muttered under his breath. 'She's got no...' He bit his lip, which he often did when he couldn't think of the right word. 'So, get this, right?' he said, switching his tone to a hushed whisper and shuffling forward in his chair to speak to me more clandestinely. 'She came in to supervise the questioning of one of my suspects today, and I don't think I even got a word in. Ever since I started, she just always takes over the entire investigation, doesn't let me do any of the job I'm paid to do.'

'But it is *your* investigation, right?'

'According to her, every investigation is her investigation. I know it's only been a month, but she's such a...'

I knew the word circling around my husband's brain was 'bitch'. However, he'd had too much of a strict Roman Catholic upbringing to actually say the word, so instead, he went for something less offensive:

'... bully.'

'Does everyone else think of her the same way you do?' I asked, trying to hide my smirk.

'No, I think they've all got used to her. They say she's become more bitter since the divorce proceedings started last week. Apparently, the kids are fine as they're all over eighteen and doing their own thing. Rumour is it's the blimming cat that they're fighting for custody of.'

'You've got to be joking.'

'I'm not joking. It's ridiculous,' Gareth said, finishing the last of the risotto with a gulp and throwing his fork into the dish like an Olympian launching a javelin. 'If we divorce, you're getting Mep, no questions asked. I don't want that angry void cat any more.'

'Screw that, I don't want Mep. You can keep Mep,' I responded.

'He was your idea.'

'He likes you more.'

'He hates me *the least*,' Gareth corrected.

He was admittedly kind of right there.

Mep, for as long as we'd had him, existed in a permanent state of both senility and hostility. We had rescued him from a shelter as a kind of wedding gift to ourselves. We couldn't afford a honeymoon after spending our limited savings on the wedding, and we'd foolishly assumed we'd only have Mep for a few years before he would tragically pop his clogs, but five and a bit years into our marriage, Mep just kept on trucking. Sometimes, I wondered if it was his sheer hatred for us that gave him life. He seemed to relish being such a constant source of annoyance that maybe he couldn't bear the thought of us living easier lives without him. He relied on us for food, shelter and the occasional pet, and that was about it.

'And no more interaction with the creepy neighbour?' Gareth asked.

The lie rolled off my tongue more smoothly than I expected, likely thanks to the rehearsals I'd had with myself during the drive here.

'Saw him struggling with his shopping yesterday actually, but that was about it. Just packed some stuff away and then watched a bit of crap TV, made dinner, and here I am.'

'You helped him with his shopping? That's awfully Christian of you.'

'The man's about seventy-nine, Gareth. I mean, I debated helping him for sure, before my conscience won out. Stupid conscience.'

'Ah, I see, I see,' Gareth said, nodding his head like one of those bobbing dogs you put in the back of your car.

'However, Mr Donoghue, the real question is: when do you

reckon you'll finish tonight?' I said, changing the subject as subtly and quietly as I could.

'Got about two more hours. Isla is on me for an action plan for this GBH case next week, and of course, the DI from hell still wants Carl's investigation logs done at some point, but then I'll be finished.'

'Okay, but then you come home and wake me up, all right?' I instructed, motioning to my lower area. 'It's *peak* time.'

It took him a minute to register, bless him. I could almost hear the gears clunking and thudding in his brain as he tried to work it out.

'Ooooh,' he said as the penny dropped.

'Yeah,' I said, really extending and enunciating the vowels as I nodded so he would get the message.

'Got you, already on it. I'll have a black coffee before I come home,' he said, hyping himself up.

'No, no, you dummy, don't have a black coffee before you come home, or you'll be up all night, and you'll barely sleep.'

'I will have a green tea.' He squinted his eyes and wiggled his body on his ergonomic office chair. 'With extra matcha,' he assibilated.

God, he was such an idiot. I loved him so much.

'That's better, okay? But just make sure that you wake me up, all right? Don't you dare just come in and go to sleep.'

'I won't, I promise!' he said emphatically. 'You know me, I never break promises!'

I couldn't believe I had to pester my husband for sex. How utterly depressing.

'You seem happier today, my love. It's... nice to see,' Gareth said sincerely, beaming through his warm smile.

'Just realised how lucky I am,' I said, pressing my hand lightly against his cheek.

. . .

I left the station, said goodbye to Judith, got into the car, and headed back to the house. I still had the satnav on; even though I had done this journey more than twenty times now, I still wasn't a hundred per cent on the way to get home. It still felt like we were on a holiday, spending time at this lovely guest house we were renting before we went back to our actual apartment, our actual home.

As I pulled up, I saw a familiar silhouette toddling towards me, waving her arms about madly to get my attention. I groaned as I braced every muscle in my face, trying to muster my absolute best fake smile.

'Oh, Fran, hello, hello, hello!' came her shrill banshee screams from across the street.

'Hi, Beryl,' I said, trying not to let any reluctance show as I got out of the car, and trotted over to meet her on the other side of the road.

Of course, it was nice to have friendly neighbours, but part of me wished that they were more like colleagues who work on a different floor. You'd smile, you'd say hello, but you'd never have to commit to the most grievous of all sins: chit-chat. Beryl was late sixties, and bless her, a lovely old woman who was losing her hearing and had told me her life story approximately forty seconds after I had exited the moving truck. Her husband had tripped, fallen down the stairs and died four years ago, and since then she had thrown herself – poor choice of words, I know – into her knitting. Knitting for homeless dogs, knitting for the neighbours, even knitting hats for children in Kenya to wear to school. I didn't have the heart to tell her that I didn't think children in Kenya would really need thick woolly hats.

'How's it going? I guess you're fully unpacked now?' she asked.

'Not yet, I'm afraid, we still have a lot to go,' I replied.

'Well, if you ever need a hand, you know exactly where I

am – and how's that hard-working husband of yours? I bet he's solving lots of murders.'

God, people loved to ask that question whenever I mentioned my husband was a detective. Now, being on the receiving end of it, I could finally grasp how incredibly annoying it was.

'I just got back from seeing him, actually. He's good, he's well, though I think he's working too hard.'

'Oh, of course he is, of course he is. I remember Trevor...'

This was a good time for me to nod, smile, and wonder what kind of bath bomb I would use tonight. Fairygloss Dreamland or Angel's Heaven?

'... he would work himself to the bone, he would. I hope you don't think I'm being nosy, but I noticed you went into Mr O'Neill's house yesterday afternoon. How is *he* doing?'

Shit.

Shit.

Shit.

'Oh, so I noticed he was struggling a bit with his shopping as he came in from the driveway, so I just thought I'd see if I could give him a hand,' I said, trying not to let any nervousness or hesitation in my voice show.

'Oh, that makes sense. He is a rather... unusual man. I've only spoken to him a few times since we've moved here in '78, but I'm so glad he's taken to you so quickly.'

'Ah, it's the social worker in me, I think,' I said, forcing a polite laugh.

I silently cursed as my eyes clocked Beryl's front door, which had one of those video doorbells that directly faced not only ours, but O'Neill's house, too. I felt a flutter in my chest that I struggled to stifle. 'I can talk to anyone about anything...' I said, but I noticed that my voice was trailing off. Spotting that camera had complicated things.

'Right.' I clapped my hands together and slowly angled my

body towards my house. 'I better be going, lots more unpacking to...'

As I started to gently sidestep towards the house to make my exit, I noticed Beryl wince and groan slightly.

She wanted me to do something. Subtlety was not Beryl's strong suit.

'You okay, Beryl?' I asked, hoping compassion would be the visible emotion and not my internal frustration.

'Yes, yes, I'm fine. Just a pain in my back, I'm afraid. Tony pulled me off so hard today I think he may have done my back in.'

For context: Tony is her Shih Tzu; get your mind out of the gutter.

And just like that, a perfectly formed plan fell right into place, another way I could cover up my tracks.

'I can walk him for a few days if you'd like, Beryl. I have work tomorrow, but I don't mind giving him a walk around the block a bit before and after if it helps you out?'

'Oh, would you? That would be marvellous. I'm sorry to be such a pain, but I just think I need to rest up and let my back heal.'

'You do that, Beryl, okay? I'll come by first thing tomorrow morning and pick him up, all right?'

'That would be just so fantastic. Oh, thank you so much, Fran.'

'Not a problem at all. I'll see you tomorrow, okay?'

I quickly rushed back to the house before Beryl remembered anything else to chat to me about.

When I opened the door, I was instantly greeted by Mep's demonic shrieks. I did like to wonder what he was trying to say sometimes: *Where the hell have you been, cretin? What time do you call this?*

I washed up the risotto dish, dried it with the tea towel Gareth's nana had given us, and popped it away in the cupboard. I sighed as I looked around the house, still cluttered with an array of cardboard boxes. Then I began to unload a few of the 'memory crates' that Gareth and I had been adding to over the past seven years. I was painfully sentimental, and every date with Gareth, I had decided to keep a little something to remember it by. A ticket stub from the arcade, the ripped and worn jacket that I'd been wearing when we had our first kiss, even the pack of cigarettes that I'd confiscated from him three months into dating.

I did what I seemed to do with all of our stuff in the moving process: deposited it from one temporary box into a more permanent one and then promptly deposited it somewhere else out of sight.

I drew myself a bath and realised that with everything that had gone on today, I hadn't checked in with Angus. I typed up a quick text.

> Everything all right today?

> All good

I would tell him about everything with O'Neill later. Angus was the kind of person who preferred to be left alone, but I still liked to check up on him every day. I wondered what he would say to me after I told him about O'Neill – he'd probably be absolutely furious with me, but I figured I'd cross that bridge later.

Mep came to sit with me as I went through a few more reports from my clients in bed before flicking the lights off to sleep.

Gareth came home an hour or so later than he'd said he would, but true to his word, we still had sex, a very simple, bread and butter kind of sex. He finished within two minutes, job done. I considered tucking my legs up, a technique Gareth said his mum had sworn by when conceiving him and his brothers. The nature of the advice seemed problematic, even vaguely

Oedipal, but I decided to give the pregnancy Pilates a miss for now.

'When we have the baby, I'm going to dial it back, I promise,' Gareth murmured, placing an arm around me, and drifting off to sleep.

I was far too drowsy to respond, but I knew Gareth was only half-committing to what he was saying. He would always have three loves in his life: me (obviously), our future children (hopefully), and the police (unequivocally).

As I tried to sleep, I calculated roughly how far away we were from the remains of the corpse, from our bedroom to his wheelie bin. Roughly, I calculated about eleven metres.

TWO

FRAN

Honestly, I kind of hated Tony.

I know, I know, what kind of dickhead hates a dog? Well, the same dickhead that kills her neighbour, I guess.

He was this wiry, vicious little thing that was more teeth than fur. I could already see him sizing me up from the hallway as Beryl led him out to me.

'Here you go,' Beryl said cheerily, stuffing my hands with poo bags and dog treats. 'Now, he can be a bit feisty with the bigger dogs: small-dog syndrome, Trevor used to say, so best to keep him on a short lead and distract him with treats if he does try and go for any of them.'

I wondered if a similar strategy would have worked on Napoleon.

'Keep him away from Dalmatians. Something about their spots gets him all riled up. And thank you again for doing this, Fran. It's so, so appreciated,' Beryl gushed as her face cracked into a relieved smile.

'It's not a problem, Beryl,' I said, desperately attempting not to let my eyes dart to the side of her. My brain felt like it was firing on every available synapse, calculating how much force I would need to muster to break that infuriating piece of cheap imported plastic. I kept talking to Beryl, somewhat aimlessly, but my mind was focused on whether the door at the police station had built up enough muscle in my tricep to be able to break the casing.

'Sorry, my dear, what was that? Can you say that again with a tilt?'

My stomach lurched upwards. Had she rumbled me? Seen my eyes' focus swing between her and the doorbell? Had my mind gone on autopilot while talking to her, and had I accidentally confessed the details of the grisly homicide I had committed?

'What was what?' I asked, trying to keep my composure.

'Could you just angle yourself, dear?'

'Oh, of course,' I said, hoping she wouldn't catch the frantic tone of relief in my voice as I angled my body slightly to the right. Beryl was constantly losing her batteries for her hearing aids, so she had taken to relying more on lip-reading as a way to get by. I repeated myself as I saw her eyes drop down to carefully watch my lips.

'I thought that I might take Tony up around the river. Give him a bit of a walk that way?' I said to Beryl, as I now made direct eye contact with the ominous lens of the doorbell while trying to recall what I had said in somewhat of a foggy conversational haze.

'Okay,' Beryl said ebulliently, after taking a moment to process. 'That sounds like a grand idea. And, oh! One more thing! Just be careful...' Beryl came forward, and her facial muscles shifted into a serious, stoic frown as she leaned her small doddery frame closer to whisper to me. 'Tony does have a tendency to defecate when he's nervous. It doesn't matter where he is, be that in the sewers or the Savoy. I'm just letting you know, but it is rather important that you try not to make him feel ashamed about it.'

What a horrible dog.

'Call me if you need anything. You have my number,' Beryl chirped, transitioning seamlessly back to her friendly tone without missing a beat.

'Thanks, Beryl. I'll be back in half an hour or so.'

She slammed the door shut behind her as I made a purposeful rummage through the poo bags, dropping a few before attempting to stuff them back into my pocket. As I watched her totter away through the glazed door, I slipped on the leather gloves Gareth had given me for Christmas 2023. Then, I took a deep inhale, and in one swift movement, I rotated my heel and thrust my elbow into the video doorbell, simultaneously tossing my body clumsily into the doorframe. I was lucky, it must have been a cheap knock-off, as my elbow crushed the lens instantly on impact, causing flimsy shards of plastic to fall onto the gravel below.

'Oh, bugger, oh, crap!' I yelped.

I put on a good show, trying to fix the camera as I wedged more bits of the broken plastic into the lens to really ensure it was destroyed beyond repair. I got a B in GCSE Drama for my portrayal of a gender-swapped Algernon in our adaptation of *The Importance of Being Earnest*, you know, so I'd like to think I'm pretty good at this kind of thing. I peered inside the exposed mechanics and saw the camera had ruptured inwards on itself. There was no way it would be recording any video after this.

I realised that perhaps overacting might give me away, which was maybe why I'd only got a B, and strolled Tony across the road to the small gap between my house and O'Neill's. I took a quick cursory glance and practised the, 'Oh, I think I accidentally threw away a half bottle of wine' speech in my head, just in case anyone was nosy enough to ask why I was rooting around the rubbish. I pulled open the dustbin we kept in the shelter and hauled out the lightest bag of the two. I had decided to keep his identifiable body parts somewhere I could easily reach, but where others wouldn't go rooting around, and certainly not within our actual house. It wasn't like the new place had a spare cadaver cupboard.

Tony smelt it instantly, perching up onto his hind legs and beginning to whine and beg. I had forgotten how heavy the bag was, and I did my best to keep it suspended above the ground whilst Tony kept incessantly nipping at my heels. It came to mind that, to be fair, this may actually be quite a good nutritious meal for Tony, but I wasn't sure Beryl would approve of this particular kind of raw-food diet.

'Not for you, boy,' I said as I threw the extra-strength bin bag into the back of my car, which was conveniently placed in the gap between O'Neill's house and ours. I placed Tony in the passenger seat with a small plastic bag fitted under his rear end – just in case.

I heard the rubbish truck clunking and some incoherent male shouting a few streets over. I had timed everything perfectly.

Now, you don't need to tell me that what I was doing was pretty gruesome and disgusting, and if there was ever a documentary made about me, this would probably be the point where people lost some sympathy. But let me just state on record, I wasn't a serial killer. Serial killers had to have three murders, and I was currently riding just a little beneath that bracket.

Admittedly, ever since we had moved in, I had been obsessed with killing Mr O'Neill, and that's a pretty *serial killer* thing to think, I know. I had been a terrible wife, and Gareth had noticed. I blamed it all on the move, of course. But truth be told, as soon as I saw O'Neill outside, it was like I had been a sleeper agent, and someone had just told me my trigger phrase. I couldn't help it, every single moment, whether awake or asleep, I was thinking about killing him. It was less the *how* I would do it and more just the *wanting* to do it. My thoughts would drift to his homicide while I was unpacking boxes in the house, working at my computer, or even having sex with my husband. I know it sounds rather serial killer-esque, but I did give O'Neill something of a choice before I killed him.

For the past month, it had been impossible to concentrate on anything else; sleep was elusive and eating felt like a chore. However, today was different. I felt remarkably well rested, and even indulged in the leftover risotto for breakfast, which is scandalous, I know.

This part of the park wasn't the nicest, mostly known for drug addicts and the occasional stabbing. Gareth had always told me to avoid it if I could, but today, I almost hoped someone would try.

'Give us what's in the bag, lady,' some hoodlum would strut over to me and say with gusto.

'Oh yes, of course, here you go, all yours,' I would reply, handing over the bag.

They'd look inside, be petrified, and run away as fast as they could. I'd film it on my phone, put it online, and it would go viral. Such a laugh for us all.

I glanced quickly around me. The nearest dog-walker was a few hundred metres away, and a few kids on their bikes were riding through the field, but they would whiz right past me without even noticing I was there.

I twisted my head back around to the river. The current was flowing at a rapid pace, which was exactly what I needed as I gently pulled out the first of O'Neill's appendages and gripped it tight in my gloved hand. Tony, next to me, squealed and quivered with excitement, little bubbles of saliva forming at the corners of his mouth. They always said that disposal of a corpse via consumption by pig was a good way to go, but I wasn't quite sure that a Shih Tzu would have the appetite for a whole body. I felt like Tony would stop at three fingers before passing out into a food coma with a bloated belly.

I did one last check around me and then, without glancing at its planned trajectory, tossed the hand into the river, holding extra tight onto Tony's lead just in case he didn't think it through and made a suicidal jump after it. When I looked back, it had all but vanished. I could only see the top half of the fingers dancing across the spurting streams of water, as if O'Neill was doing a polite little wave goodbye to me. This part of the river was only half a mile away from the estuary, which was at least a few metres deep. No one would ever find his remains, and even if they did, the amount of time the body parts would have spent immersed in water would wash away any identifiable prints from him. What body parts constituted the other half of Mr O'Neill were currently being crushed in a rubbish truck in several layers of extra-strength bin bags mixed in with all the other non-recyclables and waste, exactly where he belonged. I did make a mental reminder to find out what brand of bin bags O'Neill used, as frankly, they were excellent.

I continued to dispose of nearly everything that was in the bag. I savoured the moment of throwing in his right hand, which had always been adorned with that tacky old ring they all wore. It was just his right foot left, now.

I had waited about thirty seconds between throwing each appendage into the current, aiming to space each of them out. My brain told me this would help disperse the evidence more effectively. Although, in the grand scheme of things, I wasn't sure it would really matter; it was probably more likely superstition on my part.

As I waited, I booted up the notes app on my phone. All the entries were in my little code, of course. Gareth knew my phone's passcode, and I had no other secrets to hide from him. But it would certainly raise red flags if he stumbled upon: 'To-do list: clean up murder'.

- **Clean the wine stain**

Wine was, of course, code for blood. That was done. Warm water and trusty baking soda from O'Neill's pantry had done the trick on the wine/milk concoction that had brutally stained his carpet upstairs. A few minutes of scrubbing and dabbing had made his carpet actually look cleaner than before, if anything.

- **Write the shopping list**

This task had been unexpectedly challenging. I had contemplated staging the scene as a suicide, but I'd known there'd be some detail I'd overlook. My husband's work stories and countless TV shows had taught me that murderers rarely manage to leave absolutely no trace of their crime; there was always something that gave them away.

So, I'd settled on making Mr O'Neill's 'suicide' a mere vague, mysterious disappearance, leaving behind a note about how much he'd loathed his life and had chosen to end it. However, this presented its own set of difficulties. I knew how the man spoke but not how he wrote. I hadn't a clue what his handwriting even looked like, and that could be a dead give-away if he was still in touch with his daughter. So, wearing gloves, I'd searched his home for any handwriting samples to mimic. My efforts were fruitless, save for a handwritten note that simply read:

I'll kill you

Hardly what I was searching for, but it had left me wondering if perhaps I wasn't Mr O'Neill's only enemy.

So, I had to be creative. He was a pretentious prick; I remembered that much about him, so I yanked out a few of his poetry anthologies and swiped to the contents. I didn't know who Penelope Thornfield was, but I wished I could go back in time and kiss her for writing a piece of poetry that fit the bill perfectly for my current predicament. I tore out the piece of paper carefully, as I'm sure he would have, and then really getting into character, I teetered over to the desk in his study and placed it as square centre as I could, trying to mimic his quivering hands. I'd have tried to get his fingerprints all over it, but they were smothered in blood, so opted not to take that risk.

- **Reset the camera**

Of course, this was, in fact, poor Beryl's video doorbell. I did feel bad, and I would own up to it when I got back from walking Tony and offer to pay for a new one, but it would be foolish of me not to expect some police investigation when Mr O'Neill's carer reported him missing. So, if the camera had caught me fishing something out of his bin while walking Tony, that wouldn't help my case. As it stood, the worst I could be accused of was clumsiness. I wasn't entirely sure if the camera had recorded me entering the house in the moments before I killed O'Neill, but if it had, that would only align with my alibi of being a helpful member of the community: helping him with his shopping and taking the bins out for him.

- **Get rid of the rubbish**

Done. One part was halfway to sea, and the other halfway to a godforsaken landfill. Admittedly, I will leave the gory details of chopping him up to the imagination. All I'll say is the knife I'd used had served two purposes, and thank God he had installed a wide, spacious wet room in his old age. It had made everything so much easier – and cleaner.

- **Pack the shopping away**

That wasn't really in code at all. I realised after I'd killed O'Neill that it would be unlikely he would decide to kill himself just after he'd bought a bunch of groceries. I'd debated whether to leave the shopping to go mouldy or not, but then I realised it was a chance to advance my own alibi. I took off the gloves and put my fingertips all over his shopping as I packed it away in his house – mostly just vegetables, sanitary products, and a carton of milk, half of which had spilt across his carpet. The knife I cleaned thoroughly and popped back onto the rack at home. I know, I know, that's incredibly gross, but someone spotting a missing knife from our board during a murder-by-blade investigation would not exactly be great timing for me. It wasn't like I was going to use it when I cooked dinner anyway; it would just have to be purely for display. Shame really, as it was a good quality Nesmuk knife, too.

I was just about to scroll down further on my phone when suddenly I felt my arm jolt backwards like something was attempting to yank it out of its socket. I squealed as this shrill demonic roar began to emanate from the world's angriest Shih Tzu behind me. I quickly got my bearings and jerked Tony back to my ankle. Behind me, a middle-aged man: balding, fat. He held his poodle with the weakest, limpest grip I had ever seen. God damn – his poor wife.

'You got a feisty one there, haven't you?' he said, his face revoltingly plastered with a droopy grin.

Why was everyone in this town so talkative?

'Yeah, he's not mine. I'm just walking him around the block

for my neighbour,' I said, taking a quick, uninterested glimpse at him and tugging Tony back to my side.

'Oh, is that right?' I could feel his eyes darting to the bin bag. 'You dumping up here or what?'

I instinctively clasped my hand tight around the strap of the bin bag which still held the final piece of O'Neill. I had my face turned away from him, but I could feel my jaw ever so slightly start to quiver.

'No, not dumping,' I quickly responded while my mind started racing to concoct a convincing lie. This man was a stranger; he'd think nothing of it if I gave him no reason to. Tony leapt for the poodle again as I lunged forward to yank him back, my hand still firmly gripped on the neck of the bin bag.

'Oh all right, so what are you doing with that bin bag, then?' he asked.

'Nothing special,' I snapped, turning my head to give a genteel smile as compensation for my aloofness. I twisted my body back around to face the river. If I told him anything, he'd want to look. I knew these kinds of middle-aged pre-retirees; their mid-life crises manifested themselves in an incessant need to know *everything*. I'm sure I could tell him I was drowning a bagful of kittens, and he'd ask me what breed they were before trying to intervene.

'Ah, all right then,' he said, confused, as he watched Tony's tiny wet nose eagerly pushing against my wrist, trying to get inside the bag. 'He looks interested in it, whatever it is.'

'Yeah, yeah, I know,' were all the words I managed to say as I attempted to gently push Tony back with my lead-holding hand. It didn't deter him much as he began to nibble at my fingers, piercing the skin with his sharp little teeth.

'You got some dog food or something in there, maybe?'

I knew if I spoke, my voice would quiver from the sheer adrenaline that was coursing through my veins, but I had no idea what to say. Tony, however, had now realised he could work smarter and not harder as he began to tear the outside of the bag with his teeth. The rapid, thunderous beat of my heart had begun to drown out the man's voice as I could see pink, bloody flesh through the rupture of the bag.

If a bad plan was better than no plan, then maybe a bad excuse was better than no excuse?

'It's my mother's ashes, all right? I'm sprinkling them here; this was her favourite spot, so can you leave me alone now, please?' I blurted out. 'This is a... a special moment, and you're ruining it for me.'

The man physically recoiled, and nodded, like that was a satisfactory answer and no further information was needed.

'Oh, very sorry for your loss, sorry to hear that. I'll leave you to... er...'

He was going to say something stupid:

'... sprinkle in peace.'

I knew it.

I kept watching him out of the corner of my eye as he began to walk backwards, retreating to a safe distance from the weird woman by the river. 'But just letting you know, best not to be around these parts for a woman alone, a bit murky if you ask me,' he yelled.

'Duly noted, thanks,' I shouted back.

'And they sell urns, you know?'

Wow. Just wow.

I didn't even wait until he was out of sight before tossing the foot in the river and shoving the blood-soaked liner in the nearest park bin.

When I hopped back into the car, I let myself relax, loosened my shoulders, and practised breathing exercises I had watched on 'Meditation Minute' on trashy daytime TV. It was done. I had to keep reminding myself that Gordon O'Neill was dead, and I was the one who had killed him. Part of me almost wanted to tell Gareth, to accept all the consequences of my actions just to be able to confide in my husband, but my better judgement – or maybe self-preservation – won out.

I smoothed my hands over the steering wheel as if it was giving me some kind of stress relief. I glanced over to Tony in the passenger seat, who was still watching me intently, his little body continuing to tremble.

'I killed him, Tony. I killed Gordon O'Neill, and if you tell anyone, no one will ever believe you,' I said, jabbing my finger in his direction.

Tony just stared back at me vacantly in response, one of his eyes bulging more bulbously than the other. I think he was still irritated that I had thrown away potentially the most delicious thing that could have ever passed his lips.

I realised that there was one person I could tell, and found Angus in my phone.

I hesitated before pressing the call button, comprehending that involving my brother-who-wasn't-really-my-brother might just lead to the world's longest lecture. But before I knew it, the phone was ringing loudly through the car speakers. At the first blare, Tony squealed and scrambled to dash into the footwell.

'Hey, hey, it's okay, buddy,' I said, stretching my arm across in an attempt to console him.

I had told Angus about the last time, and he had managed to keep his mouth shut for seven-odd years, so why would this time be any different? I reasoned to myself.

'Hi,' Angus answered in his usual miserable tone.

'Hi, Angus...'

I paused, knowing I should just hang up or ask him how his day was, but I felt like a hyperactive child trying to hold in a secret about where Mum and Dad had hidden the presents on Christmas Eve.

'I did it,' I said, trying to suppress the triumphant grin that was pushing through my face. 'Gordon O'Neill? I killed him.

Not only can I send you the photo, but I got his goddamn ring too, just like Macleod.'

There was silence on the other end of the line. I could only imagine the look on Angus's face right now. Shock, relief, despair, disappointment?

And then, as if on cue, Tony promptly lifted his rear end and began to explosively spray his shit all over the car seat.

THREE

GARETH

> Just walked Beryl's dog, that was a bucket load of laughs. Going to see Angus for a little bit, babe, how's your day going?

I made a silent 'aww' sound to myself. I loved Tony; he had the sweetest, most adorable face I had ever seen on a dog. I switched over to the messenger app on my phone and started to text back:

> Good. Say hi 2 him from me. Lyl. X.

I almost jumped out of my skin when the door in the cubicle next to me smacked open, reverberating across the flimsy wooden separator. I could tell by the squeal of the cheap shoes that it was Carl. Also, it was past 10 a.m.; he had just had his morning sacrament of Colombian coffee, and that man's whole digestive system was like clockwork.

I shut out any additional jump-inducing noise by cranking up the volume on my earphones. I rested my elbows on my knees and pressed play again on the video, performing a swift scan around my surroundings as I did so. All my secondary school days of kids using the toilet bowl to prop themselves over the separator and take a glance into the next stall had really given me a mild case of PTSD.

And it wasn't that I was embarrassed. It was just that, honestly, I thought I hadn't really been performing that well recently, and I felt like maybe Fran was beginning to notice. I just wanted to see what had worked for other men in similar situations, no harm in that. I just preferred if my colleagues didn't find out about it, because I'd never hear the end of it if they did. The squeeze technique honestly sounded kind of painful, but mental distraction seemed to be the one thing the other people in the comments had said worked well for them, although thinking of my nana and her doilies the whole time seemed like a pretty disgusting thing to do.

The bathroom door slapped open again, jolting me and my heart upwards as I clasped my chest and fumbled to get a grip of my phone before it clattered onto the tiled floor.

'Donoghue, if you're in here, you fat bastard, the DI wants to see you,' I heard Steve yell as he strolled over to occupy the cubicle next to mine.

I groaned silently, closed the incognito tab, and flushed the empty bowl of the toilet. As I walked out, I saw Darren standing by the sinks, swiping his finger across his phone in a variety of directions whilst smoking a cigarette, puffing the excess smoke out of the small gap in the restricted window.

'Did she tell you to come and get me from here?' I asked, trying to make my voice as baritone as possible. I washed my hands using the rather sticky, pretty revolting hand soap which I suspected hadn't been replaced – or even used – since the poll tax riots.

'Yep, she's onto us,' Steve replied, as I heard the very distinctive sound of magazine pages flipping from inside his cubicle.

It made sense; she was a detective, after all.

'Don't rat us out, Donoghue. No one likes a tattletale,' Darren said to me, crooking his head slightly forward and squinting his eyes.

'Snitches get stitches,' Carl hollered from the other cubicle.

'I'll pass that on to internal affairs,' I grumbled with a smirk, turning my head to see if anyone would mirror my smile.

I couldn't see Carl and Steve's faces, but I imagined that, like Darren, they too were simply glaring at me threateningly.

'Oh, come on, guys, it was just a joke,' I said pleadingly as I began to dry my hands.

No one even managed a mild guffaw. Not even Steve, who had always been the least dickish among the officers, made an attempt at an audible smirk from his cubicle.

'Well, wish me luck,' I said to Darren, hoping to get some kind of positive affirmation from him. Darren simply stuck his two fingers up at me. I don't know why I still made an effort with Darren; he was such an arse.

I slowly dawdled across the office as I walked from the toilets, past the empty break room, and into the stairwell. I decided I would take as long and meandering a route as possible and use the time to try and steel myself for the interrogation that was awaiting me.

I kept thinking about my colleagues at the station and wished their general hostility didn't bother me as much as it did. All I wanted was a single invitation to join them for drinks on a Wednesday. Was that too much to ask? Now, let me get this straight, I wasn't one of those people who had a pathological craving to be liked. But at the same time, it felt like there wasn't much that I wouldn't do to be a member of their group. There was a small, tiny part in the darkest corner of my psyche that wanted some kind of traumatic event to happen that would bond us all together. Maybe I would be out with Steve or Carl, we'd witness something crooked and have to take an oath of silence between us all, swearing to never tell anyone what had happened. Not that I'd ever want anything *that* bad to happen, but it would be great to have a little something to bond with them over. I wished I could be like Fran, so self-assuredly introverted and inwards that everyone desperately wanted to be friends with her.

I had thought about messaging Cis and seeing what advice she would have. She was a colleague-turned-friend of mine who I had gone through police training with, but she'd shot up the ranks way faster than anyone else, and she never let anyone forget it – while pretending to be remarkably modest, of course. The woman had somehow managed to command a level of authority and respect amongst everyone she worked with at the station, but I wasn't quite ready to ask for help yet, plus I didn't want Cis's ego to get any bigger. She had been one of the youngest in our station to become a senior, and rumour had it she was already gunning for another promotion.

I knocked twice on Vivian's open door. Without looking up from her work or uttering a word, the detective inspector gestured for me to come in, which actually meant, 'come in and stand until I decide you may sit'. I'd had that rather rude awakening on my first day.

So, I stood there, gazing out of the window whilst waiting for her to finish writing, thinking about how much I disliked Darren and wondering how on earth some of our female colleagues could find the man attractive. He drove a Renault Vel Satis. What kind of girl could truly ever love a man with a Renault Vel Satis?

'Sit down,' Vivian ordered, snapping me out of my trance. I complied, carefully taking a seat to avoid wrinkling my shirt.

'Did you get anything back from forensics on the Paul Lock case?' she asked, her tone blunt.

'Nothing yet,' I replied, mentally bracing myself for the backlash.

'Well, you should probably chase that up. The family and

their lawyer have left me several distressing voicemails.' She paused, sizing me up as if she were a snake about to pounce. 'Maybe I'll forward them onto you. Might make you pick up the pace on finding some sort of conclusion as to how their son died.'

I tried to force myself into a place of empathy, to remember that this was a lady going through a divorce, a very emotional and turbulent time for even the most patient and kindest of people. But my gosh, at that moment – and it pains me to admit this – I did sort of hope she wouldn't get the cat.

'I'll tell them to get right on it,' I said, nodding, trying to remove any hint or trace of venom from my words as I spoke.

'Oh, and some woman rung up 101 today. One of the people she cares for didn't answer the door today. She rang his landline, and there was no answer either. I'd like you to do the welfare check; it's on Campion View.'

Campion View? That was our new address.

'Of course,' I replied, wondering why I had been chosen for this. Out of everyone, I had taken on the most work in an effort to try to show myself as a committed, passionate part of the team, but, in reality, it had seemed that I had more just thrown a 'pin the case on the dumbass detective' sign on myself.

'Number 22. I don't want to waste resources getting one of the uniforms, and I think it's not too far away from your neck of the woods. Go and take a look later after work, so it's off my plate. Break down the door if you must.'

Number 22? Wait a sec, wasn't that the house of the creepy neighbour next door?

'We're going with Sec. 17 of PACE if anyone gives you any bother about it,' Vivian continued. 'I imagine he's probably just popped his clogs in his sleep. Once you're done, call the paramedics, and then you hop home for dinner.'

'Okey dokey. I'll get right on it,' I said. I placed my palms on the edge of the chair to begin pushing myself up, but the dominatrix of doom clicked her fingers and then pressed one finger down against the desk, which I followed the direction of back into the seat.

'Gareth. Is everyone retreating to the gentlemen's bathroom to avoid me? It seems every day when I walk past the breakroom, it has been suspiciously empty. I want to know why.'

Oh, gosh.

'Gareth,' Vivian said, still writing down notes on her pad of paper, still not having the courtesy to actually make any eye contact with her prey. 'I am going to need you to answer the question for me, please.'

I knew that *she* knew that she couldn't go into the men's bathroom to check if this was the case, and of course, she knew that *I* knew the answer to her question. If I told her, she could then act on that information without having HR ringing her up and slapping a bunch of disciplinaries on her wrist.

'I'm not really sure...' I murmured as unintelligibly as I could.

'Don't bullshit me, Gareth,' she snapped, finally glancing up from her notes to lock eyes with me, but her hand was still darting and dancing across the page.

I took a sharp inhale whilst looking into the python's eyes. Suddenly, it felt as if the central heating in the room had been cranked up. I mean, I could lie; I could claim that I didn't know where everyone had gone, or that I hadn't noticed people choosing the bathroom over the breakroom. But that wouldn't be the truth.

'Yes, yes, we do,' I confessed, my face grimacing as I did so.

'I knew it, those little pricks,' she said, smacking her pen against the desk somewhat triumphantly and throwing herself back on the chair, hands behind her head. 'You know, Gareth, if they want to act like school children, they'll be treated as such. You can go.'

In a quiet display of resignation, I rose from the chair

without a word and tried to skulk, in the most professional way possible, out of her office.

'By the way, don't feel bad that the boys haven't asked you out yet,' she reassured me as I wrapped my fingers around the handle of the door to pull it shut behind me. 'They're worse than a bunch of teenage girls. Just... you're too much like a golden retriever, Gareth. I need you to be more...' She made a weird kind of claw with her hand. 'Rottweiler.'

Geez, I wasn't just wishing she wouldn't get the cat now; I was practically rooting for the other guy.

I hurled my fist into the dashboard of my car, and the pain of punching the hardened polyvinyl struck up my arm, which – obviously – only made me angrier, making me punch the dashboard again, as hard as I could this time. Which, of course, began a very brief self-flagellation cycle of pummelling and pounding before wincing and pouting. Rinse and repeat. It was when I could feel my knuckles beginning to bruise that I realised I probably wasn't helping myself feel any better.

I had had my fair share of scowls and intimidating looks for the rest of the day, so I was glad to be leaving the station to avoid any more threatening glares. Vivian had printed a piece of A4 off and pinned it to the bathroom door, saying that only two people were allowed to be in the boys' bathroom at once. She had typed it up in Times New Roman, which I thought was a touch too far in the passive-aggressive scale, although Vivian probably thought default Calibri was too polite.

After driving home, I pulled up outside the house and glanced at my watch. Four thirty. Fran would be meeting with the young boy and his foster family now, I guessed, and would probably be home within the next hour. I had to admit, it was nice to know that I would finally be able to have dinner at home today. I knew the move had been rough on Fran. She had been walking around with her *mad-but-I'm-not-going-to-talk-about-it* face for the past month.

I had been the one who'd asked her to move, after dropping small hints for the last year that our flat really wasn't big enough anymore and my promotion to sergeant would come with a nice pay rise. However, I don't think the gravity of the situation truly hit her until we arrived. She had been pretty content and jolly until the moment we pulled up, started unpacking, and met the neighbours, and then I think the penny dropped. Even though it was only half an hour's drive away from where we had been, it didn't feel like home to her.

I strolled over to Mr O'Neill's house now, and having done a few of these visits before, I crossed my fingers and offered up another prayer to God, hoping not to find another old geezer who had passed away on the loo – just like the last three times on the trot.

I rang the doorbell and waited the standard twenty seconds. Nothing. I repeated the process, still nothing. I pushed open the letterbox, crouched down, and shouted into the house.

'Mr O'Neill, it's the police, we're here checking up on you,' I hollered. I waited in vain, hoping to hear the sound of an old man come hobbling down the stairs, but of course, not a thing.

I pushed down on the door handle, expecting the usual locked clunk, but instead, I heard the metallic crunch of the bolts, and the door slowly creaked open. Unlocked door? Not a positive sign.

I tiptoed precariously into the house, shutting the door behind me softly, and slipped on my gloves as procedure dictated.

'Mr O'Neill,' I called out again as I made my way through the identical house design and structure that Fran and I were getting used to – only this one smelt distinctly of pensioner.

What does that smell like? you ask. Google 'nonanal'.

Approaching the downstairs toilet door cautiously, like a

moment from a horror film, I gently pulled it open and took a quick peek inside the loo. No corpse.

I checked around the downstairs of the house, but there was nothing out of the ordinary. Through a process of elimination, I imagined he had probably passed away in his sleep. I hopped up the stairs and pushed open the bedroom door – but his bed was empty, pristine, in fact, sheets perfectly folded back and made with impeccable placement of the decorative pillows. Strangely, there were no family photos adorning the walls of his home. Instead, the walls were hung with framed poems – a rather unusual choice of décor. As I paused to read a few, I recognised the names – Poe, Tennyson, Cummings – but could not, for the life of me, tell you a single line they had written. Most of the poetry I knew was from nursery.

I checked his upstairs loo and wet room: no body there, either. I could take a little bit of solace in knowing I had broken that particularly macabre streak.

The last place left to check was his study. I walked in, ready to call Vivian as soon as I glimpsed the sight of a dead body hunched in its chair, but the room was empty – except for a lone piece of paper on the desk. I leaned closer to read it.

Left
Penelope Thornfield (1891–1945)

Sharp Days stretch and stretch, for long everlasting grey.
Lone sunrise burns bitter, galls on flaked tongue.
The birdsong aches and rings a mere discord.
Motherly hand beckons my neck
as if to still the noise for me,
A last yearning for silence,
All at once.

I had investigated a few disappearances and suicides in my

time. Never once had I seen a poem left as some kind of note by the victim. Scanning the small study again, my eyes landed on the array of bookshelves fitted into every wall. It was probably a poetry nut's wet dream, each anthology and collection lined up on each shelf amazingly neatly. I didn't need to take a book off to see the obvious care; no dog-eared pages or thick layers of dust to be seen. Someone who treated their books with such reverence wouldn't be the type to rip a page out for a suicide note, surely? I picked up the torn extract again; it looked like someone had tried to be careful but, in the end, had given in to urgency, with obvious jagged edges and some paper residue surrounding the poem's edges.

I called Vivian.

'Where was he? I was wagering on the stairs,' she said.

Most people normally said hello.

'Actually, there's no sign of him. The door was unlocked, house is in pristine condition, no sign of any kind of foul play. The only thing here of any kind of significance is a poem.' I read it out to her, and I could hear a few moments of irritated silence on the other end of the line.

'And...?' she replied.

That woman was truly something else.

'So, I'm thinking something's clearly not right here. We need to get forensics in, see if there's anything we can find, maybe put out a request to the search advisors and see what they find.'

'Donoghue, the old man probably just dawdled off in a dementia-fuelled haze or decided to call it quits early. We'll find his body washed up somewhere in a few days. I've seen plenty of these, hundreds. They're all just the same.'

'But it doesn't make any kind of sense. I—'

'We, as a department, don't have the resources to probe into some old man's suicide,' Vivian cut in callously. 'And I, as a DI do not have the time for the paperwork to approve such a lengthy investigation.' She paused briefly before adding, 'I'm emailing you a revised draft of the Lock case for the CPS. Have a look at it tonight.'

She hung up.

I pushed the phone back into my pocket with an exasperated sigh. I couldn't help but feel like the Lock case was being prioritised just for the significant amount of attention it was getting in the press. But something wasn't right here.

I did one more scan around the house, this time careful not to disturb or touch anything. Three quarters of suicides took place at home, and the other twenty-five per cent were often done in public: high-traffic areas like bridges or train tracks. Very rarely did anyone try to hide their suicide, and if so, why?

Humans weren't like cats, sauntering off to die. Elderly person suicide was more common than you'd expect, but usually, it was through overdoses or self-imposed starvation – not a vanishing act. With one gloved hand, I pulled open the fridge door in Mr O'Neill's spotless kitchen and saw the spotlessness didn't extend to his fridge. It was a mess in there: a half-drunk carton of milk, a selection of meats, and an array of fresh vegetables that hadn't even begun to go off.

My first thought: why buy groceries if you're planning to kill yourself?

My second thought: ginger, garlic, garam masala...

Mr O'Neill had all the ingredients for a tikka masala.

I heard the distinct, archaic mumble of Fran's car engine pull up outside as I crouched down to set the oven to 180 degrees. Mep dawdled over, slinking around my knee as I scratched the back of his neck with my index finger. For the first time in weeks, Fran was starting to feel at home here. But how would she react if I told her something shady had gone on next door with our creepy neighbour? Would she want us to move back to the flat?

The thing is, even though we were only a thirty-minute drive away from where we had been, our old shoebox apartment wouldn't work with a baby, and I couldn't face that awful motorway commute any more.

Deep down, I knew she would love to go back. While she was trying desperately to make the move work, I was terrified that this would be the thing that would tip her over the edge and have her bundling our things into suitcases.

'I cooked!' I shouted as I heard the key turn in the door. 'Curry!'

'You cooked?' Fran yelled back as she jogged through the corridor and gave me a peck on the cheek. Mep greeted Fran in the usual way by making his signature meowing sound of an antique tank breaking down on a cobbled road.

'Well, I wanted to cook, but then went out and bought a curry, but I did pop it in the oven, and I'm not using the microwavable rice this time. So, I did *cook*; I just missed quite a few of the steps along the way.'

Come on, I know what you were thinking: did this idiot really use ingredients from a missing person's house, in the middle of an active case, to make his and his wife's dinner? No, I did not. However, did it give me a hankering for masala? Yes, it did.

'So, go on, update me. Tell me about your day: sixty seconds counting down,' I said as I turned to grab the bowls out of one of the moving boxes.

'Walked that asshole dog in the morning, he – in due course – pooped on the car seat.'

'No, he didn't,' I softly moaned, tilting my head back to curse the heavens. I had spent hours cleaning Fran's car the other day in the pouring rain.

'I had to spend a small fortune to clean that up, saw Angus, visited a few families, including pick 'n' mix kid, and then went into the office to do some paperwork and say hello. I have a new family to work with starting next week, and Beryl is pregnant.'

'Beryl is pregnant?' I exclaimed.

'No, not neighbour Beryl. Co-worker Beryl, the one who's about twenty-five.'

Gosh, who knew the name Beryl was so ubiquitous in this day and age?

'Honestly, a very boring, but a very fine and normal day. How about you? Solve any murders?' Fran asked, as per standard.

'The usual. Had to chase up some people about forensics and go over some interview reports, and then I...'

I hesitated. I knew it was deeply dishonest of me, but I had already had a month of Fran walking around the house looking miserable. She finally seemed quite happy for the first time in a while. Did I really want to ruin that?

'Come on, update me!' Fran pestered, smacking me on the arm while I silently hesitated. 'I want to know about your day!'

Instead of telling her, I recounted my 'Judas moment' in the office, which she found hilarious. I knew keeping Mr O'Neill from her was a lie by omission, and in a court of law, it wouldn't stand as a moral act from me. Yet I couldn't bring myself to tell her about our neighbour. Vivian was probably right; his body would surface at some point in the next few days, and that would be a simple case closed. For now, Fran didn't need to know.

'Well, being a good, honest copper is your *ikiagi*,' she told me reassuringly.

'*Ikiagi*?' I asked. 'What on earth is that?'

She explained to me that *ikiagi* meant 'reason for being' in Japanese, your life's purpose. She later told me she couldn't tell me what her own *ikiagi* was.

We went to bed and had sex, hoping that was the one that did it, but admittedly, my performance was – in my personal opinion– still shockingly poor. I felt like I put my hip out during standard missionary, which then, subsequently, led to the sail dropping to half-mast.

Don't get me wrong, I loved sex, especially with my wife, but when it was every single day in the exact same positioning, it had become a little monotonous. Foreplay was something which I distantly reminisced about. I'd always thought that as soon as Fran got pregnant, we could go back to our normal sex lives. But then I remembered that, once that happened, in less than a year, we would have a slightly bigger problem – I mean – blessing, on our hands.

It was exciting, right? Trying for a baby, having even more sex than we did on our honeymoon. I was thankful for the fact that Fran and I had always been on the same page about kids: four of them, two girls and two boys, if we could choose. We'd said we'd start trying when we moved into a house big enough to begin raising our family, so it had all come together nicely when the promotion had allowed us to move somewhere bigger. We had started... *attempted* procreation a few months before, to get a head start on things, but there had been no real return on investment yet.

I wouldn't say I was nervous about becoming a dad, but I wasn't confident. My dad had been something of a legend to me, so the fear of not living up to his example had made me feel a little intimidated at the idea of having a mini-me. It was hard to find a dad who could be both the stern, decisive voice of reason, and the gentle, kind mentor that you could tell anything to, but my father had somehow managed to be both. He had gone through my entire childhood and adulthood without ever disappointing me. That was a tough act to follow.

Fran drifted off to sleep before I did, but I couldn't stop thinking about Mr O'Neill. Had he been taken? Had he collapsed in his garden? Being so close to a crime scene didn't exactly help me have some boundaries from my work.

Of course, it had occurred to me that there was a possibility Mr O'Neill might still be alive. But all my training as a detective had honed a nauseating gut feeling, telling me when that was no longer a possibility. Every bone in my body was telling me something wasn't right, and I knew I wouldn't be able to leave it alone. Call it my *ikigai*.

I knew I was looking for a killer.

FOUR

GARETH

I took a long sip of my coffee as I walked towards Questioning Room A, readying one of my many personalities as I did so.

I had formed three distinct professional work personas. Office Gareth was an affable, quite charming man; someone you could have a bit of a laugh with. Also known as the colleague who would ask how your weekend anniversary plans had gone on Monday morning or who'd make himself available to look after your pet whilst you were on holiday. Admittedly, that part had become less of Office Gareth after Fran had drawn the line at looking after Isla from CPS's milk snake while she was in the Maldives.

Meanwhile, Tom Selleck Detective Gareth was reserved for suspects or troublemakers. I tried to mimic my Sunday school priest when he was disappointed in me, blended with a gritty 80s cop on a weekday crime procedural that Nana used to force me to watch when she babysat. Both had astonishing moustaches. Arms always folded, unflinching eye contact, voice lowered a few octaves, and at the end of every question, I would rest my index finger against my temple. It worked on first-time offenders, but repeat visitors to the station could easily see through it – probably because I couldn't actually grow a moustache.

Finally, Friendly Neighbourhood Detective Gareth exuded some authority – whilst appearing trustworthy and determined. I would speak succinctly, but listen intently. When talking to a witness, if I just waited for a few moments after they finished speaking, they'd always fill in the silence with seemingly irrelevant details that would often be the info that would bring the case together. Listening and waiting had done me a great deal of good in my career.

I can remember Nana saying 'If God wanted us to do more talking than listening, he'd have given us two mouths and one ear,' in her thick Cork accent, paired with the thick, sweet musk of a pensioner.

The best pieces of verbal evidence rarely come from direct answers to questions. Instead, they're found in the little details, the off-the-cuff remarks that interviewees thought superfluous. A small anecdote about the suspect randomly turning off their phone location or a quick verbal side-note describing recent insurance premiums. That's what I'd hoped for, but fifteen minutes in, I realised that I wasn't going to get that nugget of knowledge with Sofia in Questioning Room A. After a while, I realised this was just some kind of weird game of chicken, waiting for the first person to give in and fill the silence. The last four answers she had given had all been monosyllabic and lacked any of the meaningful detail or information that I was after.

'Any strange behaviour from Mr O'Neill?'
'No.'
'Any signs of dementia from Mr O'Neill?'
'No.'
'Did he have any trips planned?'
'No.'
'Has Mr O'Neill done anything like this before?'

'No.'

I was waiting, desperately hoping that she would just add one little anecdote that would make this whole puzzle slot neatly into place. But instead, she gently licked the tip of her finger and began to gradually rub a smudge off the steel desk in front of her. I thought I saw her mouth 'dirty place', to herself, but I wasn't certain. This small lady – difficult to discern her age, mid-fifties maybe – with thick round-rimmed glasses and a bucket hat perched on her head, was going to drive me to the point of insanity. Considering Sofia was the one who'd called 101, I'd thought it wouldn't hurt to find out if she could enlighten me a little.

'And how have you found Mr O'Neill as a person? What is his personality like?' I asked, giving in and breaking the silence, but rotating in Selleck Detective as the identity at the forefront.

'Very pleasant. Very nice, always very polite,' she said, her eyes still fixated on the small mark in front of her.

This was pointless; all the active listening training that we had been taught was failing me now. The page in my diary which I had allocated for this meeting was obnoxiously blank. So, I activated my contingency plan. I got up from my chair and, without speaking, began to make myself another coffee on the small kitchen counter we had in each questioning room.

I gestured to the kettle to ask if Sofia would like anything, but she lamentably shook her head. I filled the kettle up from the rusty tap, pushed the switch down, and began to drum my finger on the desk. I had to hold out on talking. I had to wait for that info dump that would make this case a little more tangible in my head. Sofia wasn't a suspect, nor was there technically an official case surrounding Mr O'Neill, but Vivian was out of the station today, and what she didn't know and all that. Plus, the questioning room had excellent soundproofing, so it wasn't like anyone could eavesdrop on me disobeying direct orders.

'And no family on the system, no next of kin, emergency

contact, or anything like that?' I said, twisting the top half of my body round to talk to her, trying to embody my hazy memory of Magnum PI while the kettle bubbled away.

She gave an exasperated sigh and buried her face deep into her hands.

'I've told you already,' she said, her voice muffled as she spoke through her palms. 'He didn't give any emergency contacts. He started the care support from the agency after he went to hospital for his knee surgery some five or so years ago. He never said any more than that.'

'So, he didn't mention anything at all?' I asked, persistent. My back was to her now as I began to spoon the coffee granules into one of those mugs you get with Easter eggs. 'No wife, no children, nephews, nieces, cousins, friends?'

'Well, he did *have* a wife. I told you that already, I think,' she said, giving a side-eye glance that even the eyes in the back of my head could see. 'But she died a while ago I think; he only ever mentioned her in past tense.'

As the kettle's switch popped, reaching temperature, a switch flicked off in my brain at the same time. A fourth personality began to percolate and emerge into being as the cheap coffee began to bubble, froth, and rise to the rim of the mug whose cartoon graphic had been worn away over decades of usage.

'Anyway, tell me about you. How long have you been working for the agency, Sofia?' I asked, my voice mechanically rising in pitch.

'I don't really see how that's relevant, Detective...' she began to reply, tilting her head up to peer at me through her glasses. She had clearly forgotten my name.

'I'm not asking about Mr O'Neill. I'm asking about you,' I responded, swatting my hand at her playfully and taking a seat. 'And call me Gareth. I know we're the police and all, but that doesn't mean we need to be quite so formal.'

'Oh,' she replied, readjusting herself in the chair, taken back by my sudden change in mood.

'Now, I want to know all about you, Sofia,' I said, resting my hand over hers for just a second before placing it back on the table, remembering I had just broken official police guidelines. Whoops.

Now, let me be frank. The next forty-seven minutes were pure pain. I asked Sofia about her family, her friends, all the latest gossip at the agency. Turns out, a bunch of people were thinking of quitting after their area manager, Lisa, called a colleague's husband 'a man-slag'. A big walkout, Sofia told me, was going to happen any day now, just as soon as Maggie got over her bad hip.

I'll save the rest of the unnecessary details. But once Sofia got in a chatty mood, she just couldn't stop. I kept shoving more and more coins into the jukebox to the point that I was listening to the same lyrics over and over again. While the active listening training workshop we had undergone had advised us not to use words that the witness could interpret as approval or disapproval ('Avoid using words/phrases such as "Right", "Are you sure?", "Interesting", etc.'), they seemed to actually encourage more relevant information out of Sofia.

'And Mr O'Neill.' She took a sip of her coffee and then clapped her hands together flamboyantly. 'I liked Mr O'Neill a lot, you know. I liked him. I said I liked him not five minutes ago.'

It had been over half an hour since we had mentioned him in passing.

'But, my gosh, he was a strange man. A strange, strange man. All those poetry books. Hundreds of them.'

'Do you know *why* he had so many?' I asked, leaning back in my chair and crossing one leg over the other.

'No,' she said, finishing her third cup of coffee. 'But I'm very good at reading people, Gareth. You know that about me now, I think, and something about that man wasn't quite right. Can't quite put my finger on it, but I think Gordon had a lot of secrets.'

First-name basis, now. Interesting.

'And he would always go on about this community foundation he was a part of, the something somethings. You know he was a successful businessman in his time, right?'

'No,' I said, my pen furiously beginning to scribe, hoping that wouldn't throw her off-kilter. 'His file just said he was self-employed?'

'He had this foundation and another business too, something with accountants...'

Before I could probe more, there was a polite knock, and I saw Darren, of all people, peer around the edge of the door.

'Are you going to be much longer?' he asked coarsely. 'I booked this room out from eleven.'

'Sorry, sorry. I'll be literally two seconds,' I replied, with a brief appearance from Office Gareth. 'Just finishing up and then it's all yours.'

He didn't even acknowledge my response as he slammed the door shut. It wasn't worth the effort of rolling my eyes. I turned back to Sofia.

'You take as long as you like,' I said slowly.

'Well,' she said, leaning forward again, switching her voice to a superfluous whisper. 'I don't know much about that foundation he was a part of. Think it was like a community trust or something. He went on about it a lot, but I was never really sure what exactly they did. Showed me some newspaper clippings of it once, had them building a new hospital clinic or something.'

Interesting.

'You said he had no close family or anything like that?' I asked.

'Now that I think about it, he did mention once, a while back, that he had a daughter, but that was all he said. I don't know what her name was, where she lives, or anything more about her. Gordon wasn't exactly one to open up.'

He had a daughter? So, why wasn't she calling us, asking what had happened to her father? And why was there absolutely no trace of any family in his house? I had seen no family photos or portraits.

'So, there was nothing? No indication, no sign that Mr O'Neill would just up and vanish?'

'You know, Gareth,' Sofia replied, shuffling slightly forward in her seat, 'he once told me, when I brought up the possibility of assisted living, that he would rather die in that house than move to anywhere else in the world. I think the man had too much pride to just randomly vanish or off himself.'

I winced at Sofia's rather abrasive turn of phrase. But at least now I had the gut feeling from another person that Mr O'Neill hadn't just disappeared – something malicious had happened to him. I knew it: I wasn't having some isolated psychotic break.

Part of me wanted to tell Vivian and ask her if we could launch a full investigation, but I had a feeling that without any hard evidence of foul play, this would just end with me bracing for yet another slap on the wrist and a disciplinary meeting scheduled in my calendar.

'Well, would you look at the time?' Sofia said, playfully swiping my hand and rising to her feet. 'I'd better get going; things to do, people to see.'

'Ah, I guess you do have other clients to get to today,' I said, getting up and starting to shake the numbness out of my legs.

'Oh no, Tuesdays are my PhD day,' Sofia said, as if this was common knowledge to me. 'I have to go into the library to complete my research. I told you earlier, remember?'

'Oh,' I said, realising I had zoned out for a lot of her monologue, as she teetered out of the room.

'Lovely meeting you, petal,' she said, closing the door just as

I decided to permanently eliminate Bingo-Girl Gareth from my personality roster.

I knew I had precisely four rings before I'd have to pick up. Four rings to think of an excuse, reason or any kind of plausible deniability for skirting around my slightly maniacal boss's orders. I scrunched my eyes shut for a split second and began to force my mind to think as the first rumbling note echoed and bounced around the speakers of the car. I had to pick up, otherwise there would be a very angry email sent to me, and that would be so much worse. Trust me, so much worse.

Ring.

After talking with Sofia, my research into O'Neill's foundation, Heart of Hope, hadn't exactly been fruitful, only uncovering that they gave a sizable chunk of money to the local community. But following Sofia's tip, I had found Mr O'Neill had previously served as the managing director of a firm called IGN Accountancy from 1974 to 1988. According to Companies House records, IGN Accountancy appeared to have raked in substantial profits until all of a sudden: bankruptcy and liquidation. It seemed as if O'Neill had managed to restore some of his fortune when he set up the Heart of Hope Foundation in 1991.

Ring.

I'd tried to dig a bit deeper to pinpoint the time of O'Neill's disappearance. There was a chain convenience shop at the far end of our road where I'd grabbed some microwave meals before, so I swung by on my way home for lunch and asked them for their external CCTV footage. They'd told me the feed went directly to their corporate headquarters, but they promised to email me the footage by the end of the day. While I didn't expect it to turn up any crucial leads, it had been good to cross another potential source of information off the list.

Ring.

I'd performed one more sweep of O'Neill's house while I was nearby, careful not to disturb anything or move anything a millimetre out of place. I'd thought about asking Steve to give me a hand looking around the house to see if there was any detail I'd missed, but I felt after yesterday's bathroom debacle, it would be a surefire way to get me into Vivian's office again.

Ring.

I had no line or excuse prepared as I indicated into the hard shoulder on my way back to the station to go over some files on another case. I pressed down hard on the answer button like it was the final cable to cut as I attempted to defuse a nuclear bomb.

'Hi, Vivian, how are... things?' I asked, grabbing my tea from the holder and nervously taking a sip – a coping mechanism, I was sure.

'Darren tells me you booked out Questioning Room A for nearly two hours today. It had better have been for one of the cases I assigned you.'

I had an answer prepared for this, but also, I thought: *snitches get stitches – right, Darren?*

'Yep. Spoke to the Lock family this morning to keep them in the loop, forensics sent me the results, files are on your desk. Thought it would save adding any unnecessary weight to your inbox.'

I could hear her pause, a little stunned – and hopefully a little impressed – but I knew that feeling wouldn't last long.

'Why did you book out Questioning Room A for two hours, Gareth?' she asked, barely missing a beat.

I took a glance at my diary, which lay open on the passenger seat. The page I had allocated for Sofia was scribbled with notes and question marks in my signature red ink. Red ink meant 'unconfirmed', black meant the opposite. As you might have guessed, there was a copious amount of red ink sprawling across the page, so much I couldn't seem to make sense of. No matter how much I wanted to, I just couldn't ignore Mr O'Neill's case.

'Look, I know you said not to investigate, but I had some spare time, and I just wanted to see—'

'Gareth. No. You went against orders on this one. I told you not to investigate this, and you did anyway. You couldn't leave well enough alone, could you?'

'No, you told me to focus on the Lock case, and I did. The results are on your desk. But a man is missing. When his daughter calls, worried sick that her dad isn't responding, what are you going to say? Will you tell her that a police detective noticed he was missing and you did nothing, or will this become yet another tabloid story?'

During the silence that followed, I realised that a less aggressive tone might have helped my chances to appease Vivian. I knew the tabloid comment would sting. I'd heard breakroom rumours that our station had featured in various escapades – putting it mildly – in the five years Vivian had been DI and she was under close watch from the commissioner for any more negative front-page publicity.

'So, what exactly are you proposing?' Vivian asked.

Now I was the one stunned. I didn't think Vivian had ever asked me for actual input on a case for the whole time I had been here. Christmas had come remarkably early. This was my chance to not only find the killer who had presumably murdered my next-door neighbour, but also to finally prove myself in the station.

'Donoghue, are you there?' she pressed when I didn't answer right away.

'I propose that we start investigating,' I said, managing to string some words together in a somewhat articulate order. 'Maybe we get a constable also working on the case, and if we can, get forensics to do a sweep of the house. There's a killer here, I'm sure of it.'

There was a silence on the other end of the line, and I winced, hoping that it wasn't all just one big play from her to then backhand me.

'You know the relevant emails. I'll get on the risk assessment paperwork. You let me know what else you need, okay?'

'Thank you, Vivian, so much,' I stuttered, still in a bit of disbelief.

You get more flies with honey than vinegar, that's what I always said to Fran.

'But if you cock this up and he turns up at home safe and sound tomorrow morning, I'll have your head on a spike. And your dick on a kebab.'

Well, she had to go and ruin it, didn't she?

FIVE

FRAN

Do you know how the pregnancy test was invented? In 1927, a perverse pair of German scientists discovered that injecting a pregnant woman's urine into female mice would, in fact, make them ovulate. Part of me does wonder: how the hell did they discover that? Were they just horsing about in a laboratory one day, and decided it would be a hilarious idea to inject some pregnant woman's urine into poor female mice?

'*Ja*, Hans, do it, what a *sehr* funny idea!'

Did they stumble upon that by accident? I sometimes wonder if scientists are paid to think of the craziest and weirdest thing to do – if it yields some kind of useful result to society, then that's just an added bonus. Bunch of sick puppies.

I balanced the stick on the side of the basin and perched on the loo facing away from it, just in case pregnancy tests suffered from any kind of performance anxiety. I waited for the standard three minutes, a frustratingly short period of time, but somehow also not long enough. Not enough time to run down and make a cup of tea, but not long enough just to sit there and do nothing. Instead, I plucked the packaging out of the bathroom bin and read the instructions on the back, this time looking at all the different languages, too. That led me to wonder whether, to the untrained ear, the instructions in French could potentially sound sexy?

Mettez l'embout absorbant directement sous le jet d'urine. Laissez sous le jet pendant au moins 7 à 10 secondes pour avoir un résultat correct.

God, I bet whispering that sensually into Gareth's ears would send him berserk – provided he had no idea what I was actually saying.

I wasn't certain about the test this time, but I was more certain than last time and definitely more certain than the first time, which reassured me a little. I glanced over at Mep, who had trotted into the bathroom like it was just another part of his empire. Since we had moved, he often wandered into our en suite and made himself very comfortable by the towel heater. It might seem a bit weird to go to the loo with your cat there. However, most who'd criticise probably hadn't had a cat like Mep. By the time you'd have finally shooed him out just so you could relieve yourself, you might as well have driven to the local supermarket to use the facilities there. And for those thinking, *Why not just close the door?* – you try urinating while a cat makes a sound resembling metal being thrown into an industrial blender on the other side of the door. It's hardly conducive to a relaxing wee.

I peered up to look at the test. The line had begun to fade in. Line, singular. I snatched it up and in one fluid movement, tossed it in the bin with a clatter to join the others. Mep glanced over and arched his neck forward to sniff it.

'Trust me, Mep, you wouldn't want to try that,' I said to him as I hoisted up my tights, flushed the loo, and brushed out the creases in my dress. I glanced at the mirror, making sure that I still looked somewhat nice and presentable.

I had often been thinking I was pregnant recently. It turns out that basically anything and everything is a sign of pregnancy. Your yoghurt tastes different today? Pregnant. You feel more easily bloated? Pregnant. You're having a really great hair day? Pregnant. I had started to wonder if it would be easier to count the signs that I wasn't pregnant at this point. I knew it had only been a few months, but I just thought it would have happened by now.

It was 19.56; Gareth had four minutes before he was officially late to pick me up for dinner. So far, we'd had no phone calls, no texts, no form of communication since 16.03, when he had given me an update on his late lunch as well as telling me that he wanted to go to IKEA at the weekend. Frankly, he sounded like the epitome of a domestically morbidly basic husband. I, of course, had replied by stating that I didn't think he'd ever had such a good idea in his life.

I paced downstairs, taking a glance at O'Neill's house from our landing window. A light was on; I could just about make out the small beam of illumination stretching across his own landing carpet. Was that his bathroom light? I remembered that I had been incredibly vigilant not to touch anything, so either he must have left it on, and I didn't notice, or perhaps his carer had flicked it when she had presumably gone looking for him around the house. The thought took hold of me for a second. Had it been me? Did I need to go in and turn off the light? Was my fingerprint on the switch?

I closed my eyes and took a small, short breath, trying to calm the anxious and erratic thoughts scrambling over each other in my mind. Most cases were solved within the first forty-eight hours, and here I was, without suspicion, on day five. Last time, I had got away scot-free, so who was to say I couldn't do it again?

I pushed the thoughts out of my head, distracting myself with the anger rising in my gut. I took my phone out of my handbag and keyed in a text as I dawdled into the kitchen downstairs: a very simple, very blunt:

> Where are you?

In the early months of dating Gareth, I'd grown accustomed to his straightforward texts. Gareth, however, had quickly learned that if my text contained only a few words and no smiley faces, I was pretty mad. As I hovered my finger over the 'send' button, I felt like I was gripping onto the pin of a grenade, poised to pull it and brace for the detritus.

But then, out of the corner of my eye, I spotted the blade – *the* blade. My hypothetical fury at my husband began to slowly ebb away as I felt myself being pulled towards the murder weapon that I had hidden in plain sight. I approached the rack tentatively, plucked the Nesmuk knife from it, and carefully studied it in my hands, recalling how it had felt when I'd used it to jam it directly into O'Neill's eye. God, it had felt good. The same kind of satisfaction as pulling a thorn from your skin, but in reverse, I suppose.

I continued to loiter around the kitchen and then went into the hallway, still holding onto the knife, reminiscing as if it were some sweet nostalgia I was reliving. The way it had pierced his skin, the way it had crunched when it collided with the frontal bone of his skull. I imagined just how incredible it would feel to use the same knife to kill Clark, but I guessed O'Neill would have to do for now.

But then something caught my eye for a moment. I had frenziedly washed the knife again and again, but only now did I notice a clear, distinct notch on the top of the blade. A segment of the knife was clearly missing.

Before I could inspect it, my very smartly dressed, patchy-bearded husband swung open the door with a resounding smack,. The knife was quickly tossed into my handbag as subtly as I could, landing neatly in between the moisturiser and the alcohol gel.

'Sorry, my love, am I late? I'm not late, am I?' he said in between his breathy pants.

'No, you're not late,' I said, the frustration vanishing in an instant, my face inadvertently blushing. He gestured for me to follow him. I kept my handbag tightly between my arm and ribs.

'The waiter,' Gareth mumbled somewhat unintelligibly behind his menu, his gaze scurrying across the room and his body slowly sinking deeper into his chair.

'What?' I asked, squinting at him and edging my seat a few inches closer to hear what exactly he was whispering. I followed his eyeline to the waiter who had shown us to our table. I didn't recognise the guy. Maybe he said something weird that I hadn't noticed?

'The waiter,' Gareth maffled again. His gaze bounced downwards, and his face began to lightly redden. I could see him looking around, wondering if anybody had noticed.

'Oh, he's not hitting on me, if that's what you think he's doing,' I said with a scoff, waving my hand dismissively and pushing my handbag a bit further underneath the table.

I had noticed the waiter's wandering eyes, though. He was probably only about twenty-one, and I *had* decided to dress to the nines for date night, so I could hardly fault him for a quick glance.

'No, no, not that. He's wearing the same shirt and tie as me. The *exact* same shirt and tie.'

I looked at Gareth: very light blue pinstripe shirt, navy tie in a Windsor knot. I looked at the waiter: very light blue pinstripe shirt, dark blue tie in a four-in-hand knot. My face of bemused bafflement split into a cackle at poor Gareth, who was trying to see just how small he could make himself in his chair.

'Do you want to borrow my dress?' I asked him, guffawing as I reached across the table and lightly pushed the menu away from his face. 'You may get stopped on your way to the bathroom by someone asking about their soup, though.'

'I'm just going to leave my jacket on,' Gareth grumbled, as he began to sheepishly pull his blazer over his shoulders.

'Did you change at work?' I asked, grabbing a piece of the complimentary bread and popping it into my mouth.

'I did. I had a feeling I wouldn't have time to have a shower at home.'

'And how was work? Give me the rundown, come on,' I said, prompting the sixty-second debrief. 'Solve any murders?'

'Work as usual, really. Vivian, I think, may be slowly warming up to me, but that's a bit of a work in progress.'

'Oh really? What did she say today?' I asked as, despite my very best intentions, my mind started to wander to the contents of my handbag underneath the table. On the drive to the restaurant, I had deliberated if there was any safer place I could stash the blade after we got home. But after much internal back and forth, I had realised that the safest place was still deep at the bottom of the bag. I had no excuse or reasoning planned if someone spotted it, but Gareth had never taken the initiative to look through my bag in seven-odd years, so I was hoping the trend would continue. I couldn't help but wonder whether, after three cycles of 70-degree intensive washes in the dishwasher and multiple baths in boiling hot water, all the traces of O'Neill's optical and brain matter had been removed from the blade, or if there was still some of him lurking onto the metal.

I forced myself to tune back in.

'... I mean, she wasn't a massive fan of me taking the lead on it at first, but I asked her politely, stated my case, and feel like I may have stood up for myself a little bit, maybe. Then she just told me to go for it.'

'That's amazing, my love, just what we like to hear,' I said, somewhat muffled, as my mouth was stuffed with bread. Gareth, though remarkably good at his job, had always been a little bit of a people pleaser when it came to his colleagues. It was always nice to hear stories about him sticking up for himself a little more, especially against people like Vivian. Just a shame it wasn't Isla – or his friend Cecilia, or Cis, as she preferred to be called. I was not Cecilia's biggest fan, nor was she mine. There had always been something scheming about her that I'd never quite trusted. Like there was always something ticking away in her brain.

'What case is it, though? Anything interesting?' I said, switching my tone to a voice-level whisper.

'Oh, just a missing persons case, nothing particularly exciting,' Gareth said as his doppelganger returned with a bottle of wine.

A cold shiver gently tingled up my spine. A missing person case? Could it be O'Neill? No, surely not. If Gareth was investigating the disappearance of our next-door neighbour, he would definitely have mentioned it to me. This was the man who could never resist telling me what my birthday gift was each year. I took another deep breath, letting the thought slip from my mind as quickly as it had entered.

'And you? How was your day today? Anything thrilling happen at social services?' Gareth asked.

'Not really. But I did get those super-strong bin bags you like that don't leak on my lunch break, though. Found a Morrisons that sells them, so small victories, right?'

'Oh, now that is exciting. We can toast to that,' Gareth said, as the waiter finished off pouring our glasses. 'Did you speak to Angus today?'

'No, not today. I think he's having one of his bad mental health days, so he let me know he was all right, but nothing more than that.'

I obviously couldn't delve into the lengthy diatribes Angus had been subjecting me to every time I'd called over the past few days. All he'd done was rant to me about how foolish it had been for me to kill O'Neill, and state that – despite having scarcely left his flat for the past decade or so – he wouldn't help me clean up the mess. Because of course, he was just so helpful last time.

'Ah, that makes sense. He's still taking his meds though, right?'

'To the best of my knowledge, he is. I think he has a lifelong prescription for paroxetine.' I grabbed my glass and took a sip of wine, realising I really needed to send Angus another message before the end of the day to ask him if he was still taking his meds.

'And anything from Beryl today?'

'I mean, today she was talking about how she can already feel her boobs getting bigger.'

'What?' Gareth exclaimed, his mouth agape, aghast.

'No, no, not neighbour Beryl, colleague Beryl – the one who's just got pregnant.'

'Oh, I see,' Gareth said, shaking his head and giving a quick, relieved wheeze. He composed himself and then grinned at me, a huge full-tooth smile that I'd always loved, but which he never liked to show in photos, for some reason. 'I had *so* many questions.'

'God, I'm going to have to say goodbye to so many bras when we get there,' I moaned, taking another swig of wine, realising that I had unconsciously drunk my entire glass.

'Don't say the Lord's name in vain,' Gareth said with a smirk. 'But what about neighbour Beryl? Did you speak to her today? She still looking into our window every chance she gets?'

It was true; Beryl was an exceptionally nosy neighbour. Gareth was convinced she had been spying on us. With her house being opposite us and situated higher on the street's incline, he swore he'd seen her peering down into our kitchen on more than one occasion. The fact that she could lip-read due to her hearing loss didn't ease Gareth's paranoia either.

'Not to my knowledge,' I said. 'I'm still walking that dog though, which is a joy. Though Beryl says that she's feeling better now, so hopefully it won't be too much more of me having to walk Mussolini reincarnate.'

I could see Gareth thinking about something as he scrunched his face up, wondering if he should say it.

'What about grumpy, creepy neighbour? Have you seen him recently?'

I wasn't quite sure why he had hesitated. He had probably clocked on to my revulsion towards O'Neill. No matter how much I'd tried to hide and suppress it, unfortunately, it seemed like my husband knew me too well.

'No, not since I helped him with his shopping. When was it? Saturday, I think, but haven't seen him since. Saw the light was on in his bathroom today.'

Gareth seemed satisfied by that answer, nodding as he reached across the table to grab another piece of the rapidly dwindling pile of bread.

'I do feel we have joined a nice little community here, which is good. You feeling a bit better about the house now? A bit more at home?' Gareth asked, taking a redundant glance at the menu that he had definitely already studied online.

'I do. It's just... moving is just strange, isn't it? You go from knowing about every nook and cranny in your old place to suddenly being somewhere completely new. Like, who's in our old apartment now? Is it a younger, sexier couple than us, who get up to wild stuff and have loads of parties and have shower sex?'

'Have you been thinking about this a lot, Fran?' Gareth asked with a comforting chuckle, reaching his hand across the table to clench mine.

'No, I haven't, because shower sex is actually really hard and wet and cramped and it takes a lot of awkward positioning, but I do think it's a bit bad that we haven't done it in our new place yet.'

'Do you want to have shower sex?' Gareth asked, furrowing his brow.

'Yes, I do want to. And I realise it's been a while since we've had any sex other than normal, standard sex, but I want to,' I said, my lips curving into a precocious pout as I laid out my expectations.

Gareth nodded, as if receiving a directive from his commanding officer. 'Very well, shower sex tonight,' he proclaimed, giving the table a gentle thump with his fist.

The waiter came over to take our orders and already I knew exactly what Gareth was going to get. He ordered the ribeye steak, and I could see his lips mouthing my words as I asked for the cured trout. The waiter didn't carry a notebook. When I'd once asked Gareth why he thought waiters did that, he'd given a very intuitive, detective-style response. 'That way, there's no evidence that they got your order wrong.'

Just as Gareth asked for some tap water for the table, I watched the waiter's eyes suddenly shift to my handbag beneath the table. I noticed a small glint of light had flickered and landed onto his face, reflecting the bright restaurant lights directly above us. The clasp must have come undone and the bag had sagged open. My heart clambered a little further up my chest. Had he seen the knife? As the waiter's eyes flicked upwards to mine, I just smiled as warmly as I could in response. It took him a moment, but after an excruciatingly long beat, he politely nodded and walked away.

'Hey, Gareth,' I began as I tried to quietly breathe yet another inconspicuous sigh of relief, 'what will we do if I, or if we, can't have children?'

Gareth exhaled, pushing his hands across his knees. He had thought about this too. I knew he had, but didn't every couple at some point? I watched him begin to say his prepared answer that he must have run through his head a dozen times.

'There are *so* many options, you know that, right?'

'That's the bullshit answer, you know that, right?' I snapped at him, with probably a lot more bitterness than was needed. Gareth just nodded silently, taking it on the chin. After seven years together, he knew how to deal with my small fits of anger.

'What scares you about not being able to have children?' Gareth asked calmly. 'It's not set, not every couple needs to have children; it doesn't make them any more or any less of a family. Mum and Dad weren't even sure about having me before I blessed their lives unexpectedly.'

'I know, and I agree, but it's always been the plan, hasn't it? You, me, two boys, two girls, two dogs, and Mep, a picture of domestic bliss.'

'Yeah, and if that's what you – *we* – still really want, let's keep trying. We can try IVF or surrogacy, or we can even adopt. And if we don't want to do that, maybe it's just not meant to happen, and that's okay. That's just what life has in store for us. Maybe we'd hate having kids. Maybe they'd be little arseholes.'

'But you've always wanted kids,' I said, wondering if part of me was testing him to make sure he wasn't just saying this to make me feel better about not being pregnant yet.

'I mean, don't get me wrong: being a dad scares the shit out of me. But I want a life with you, Fran, kids or no kids.'

I fake-retched, and Gareth's sincere stoicism cracked into a genuine chuckle. I knew Gareth's feelings about becoming a dad were more complex since his own father had passed away last year, but I couldn't help but melt a little into a smile as he reached out across the table and interlocked his fingers with mine again.

'I love you, my beautiful girl,' he said.

I killed O'Neill. I killed our neighbour next door. You have to believe me when I tell you that he deserved everything that I did to him. But I am terrified I am going to get caught, go to prison for the rest of my life, and lose you and our idea of our perfect life and our perfect family.

I wanted to say that all to Gareth. I wanted to tell him everything, to share every nervous thought in my brain with him. But I knew Gareth wouldn't be up for the old Bonnie and Clyde routine. And I wouldn't make him choose between his dutiful police heart and me. Partly because I wasn't certain what he *would* choose.

'I just wish my dad and your parents were around to see what a great mum you'll be,' Gareth said lovingly.

I tried to smile. It was sweet of him to say, but I wanted to promptly change the subject from my parents.

'Yeah. Me too,' I said. I remembered that a lack of eye contact was a common trait of liars or those who felt uneasy, so I attempted to gaze longingly into my husband's eyes as he softly stroked my hand.

'I need a wee,' he said lovingly.

'Ew, gross.' I snatched my hand away. Gareth got up, took his jacket off, and had just begun walking to the bathroom when a random woman on another table outstretched her arm to him and he turned to speak with her. I saw his face drop into a grimace, and I could just about hear his exasperated cry.

'I don't work here!'

As Gareth made a beeline for the loos, my gaze suddenly locked onto the waiter who had served us. He was at the far side of the restaurant, quietly chatting to a man who I guessed was the manager, occasionally glancing in my direction. I pretended not to notice, instead grabbing the last piece of bread in the basket, tearing it off, and dropping it into my mouth.

As discreetly as possible, I glanced down at my handbag again, checking that the blade was still hidden. Even though the bag had been open I thought it was unlikely he could have seen it – the black handle camouflaged nicely against the dark faux leather of my handbag – but what if he *had* spotted it? What if they wanted to check my bag? Trying to make my façade seem as casual and calm as possible, I snatched up my bag and strolled casually to the loo, quickly analysing my options for hiding the knife. The sanitary bin? No, that wouldn't work; it would be extremely visible against the transparent liner when someone came to remove it. The loo itself? No, surely it would just get clogged up there when I tried to flush. The Nesmuk knife was many things, flushable it was not.

I pushed through the heavy toilet door, realising I yet again needed some sort of last-minute plan. My eyes flicked around, searching for a vent or duct where I could stash the knife. Just as I was observing a small parting that lay in the ceiling tiles, the door behind me began to squeak open, so I hastily slipped into one of the cubicles and jammed the lock across the door. Out of ideas, I quietly lifted up the cistern lid and placed the knife next to the valve. Jabbing my finger into the flush, I watched as the knife rose with the water level before settling back down between the gasket and the valve with an almost inaudible metallic chime. Carefully, I placed the lid back, the heavy, hollow clunk of porcelain reverberating around the cubicle.

I pulled back the lock and emerged from the cubicle, smiling at the lady at the sink as I began to wash my hands, fully aware that she had no idea she was washing her hands next to a murderer who had just hidden their weapon of choice. But as I dried my hands, it dawned on me that perhaps my actions were maybe a stroke of hidden genius. After all, when was the last time anyone had checked their toilet cistern?

SIX

FRAN

Gareth, with his favourite Mr Men mug full to the brim with coffee in one hand and a bag of frozen peas in the other, quietly creaked open the bedroom door and tiptoed in. I watched him place the coffee down as he perched himself on the edge of the bed and softly pulled the bag of frozen crinkle-cut chips from under my head. He unwrapped the tea towel they were placed in, substituted them with the peas, and tenderly put the package back under my bruised temple.

Shower sex – in hindsight – had not been the best idea.

'How are you feeling?' Gareth asked, smoothing his hand along my shoulders whilst taking a small sip of coffee.

'Fine, I think,' I groaned.

I propped myself up in bed on my elbow, slipped my hand around the handle of Gareth's cup of coffee, pulled it over and took a sip.

'Not feeling sick? No dizziness? No headache?'

'None of the above, my love. Although I can't seem to remember my name. Is that a problem?'

He scoffed softly and pushed himself off the bed. Through

my sleepy glaze, I watched him fastening his belt and smoothing any rogue pieces of fluff off his suit trousers as I rummaged the peas around to create a small indentation for my head.

'I can't believe they wanted to check your bag last night. Ridiculous,' Gareth murmured, mostly to himself, as he double-checked that the taps in the en suite were off. 'What did they even think they were going to find?'

'I know, nuts, right?' I grumbled as I tried to make myself comfy in bed. Last night had been a too-close-for-comfort near-miss. I had to be more careful – this was how serial killers got caught: stupid slip-ups. While I had hoped, when stashing the knife, that I could retrieve it at some point, I thought that was an impossibility now. I just had to pray the restaurant wouldn't do a toilet cistern inspection any time soon.

'I'll ring you at lunchtime, okay? Have a good day,' Gareth whispered and gently kissed me on the forehead.

While the pick-up and drop-off sessions with Tony must have been how divorced parents felt picking up their progeny, it was also a good time to receive my daily dose of neighbourhood gossip. Beryl was a reliable, if not exactly discreet, supplier, always giving me the details and filling me in on the politics behind planning permissions and the complex cutthroat machinations of the local Neighbourhood Watch that she was chairwoman of. Whether the people down at Number 28 had finally resolved their feud with Number 7, and the continuing events of the garden-related civil war between Numbers 14 and 16 with the long hornbeam hedge that stretched between their respective gardens acting as their very own DMZ.

Beryl pulled open the door and gave her usual upbeat 'Morning!' as she handed me Tony, who excitedly jumped up on my leg and began whining affectionately. I gave him a small stroke and passed him a treat. Maybe he was growing on me – a small, fractional, almost imperceptible amount.

'So, tell me, Fran, I have a question for you,' Beryl said, leaning against the door frame and crossing her arms as if she was about to drop another juicy load of neighbourhood gossip. 'Have *you* heard anything from Mr O'Neill recently?'

I raised an eyebrow and jutted my bottom lip out, my fake-thinking face. I gave a long 'Hmm,' as I nodded my head, creasing my forehead and glancing casually upwards to the sky as I did so. 'No,' I said, resolutely. 'No, I don't think so. Last time I saw him must have been Saturday afternoon, when I helped him with his shopping. Why do you ask?'

'Well, have you not seen it?' Beryl asked, pointing her finger across the road.

I couldn't believe I had missed it this morning. There was a long line of thin blue police tape wrapped around the perimeter of O'Neill's house, along with a few orange cones for good measure. The police tape was intimidating enough to ward off any potential crime scene intruders, but those bright orange cones sent a terrifying tingle down my spine.

'Oh,' I said, genuinely surprised. My heart had executed a small hop in my chest, and I felt the slightest quiver in my hands as I pretended to process the information like an innocent person. 'Have the police been here?'

'I saw them out there last night when you and your husband went out for dinner. Two police detectives went in at about nine o'clock, came out half an hour later, and then cordoned the whole thing off.'

God, Beryl really didn't need that video doorbell. She was already the Big Brother of the neighbourhood.

'Oh gosh,' I said, still trying to feign surprise as best I could. 'You didn't see them bring a body out?'

'Hmm, well, if the police were going to get involved with anyone on this street, of course, it would be Mr O'Neill. A very peculiar man. Trevor and I tried to invite him round for dinner, but he would only ever grunt when we tried to reach out.'

Beryl gave a long exhale, as if she'd remembered not to speak ill of the dead. 'Well, I reckon everyone will be asked a few questions by investigators at some point or another.'

'Well, what a way to introduce ourselves to the neighbourhood,' I said with a fake titter. My mind was racing again, and I could feel my pulse start to quicken. I gave Tony another stroke as he nuzzled up to me between my legs. I had decided to now commandeer him as my own personal therapy dog.

I had been ultra-careful about everything inside O'Neill's house. I knew I had been. Everything had been triple-checked before I'd left, but a little voice had begun to whisper in my head now that the police were beginning to investigate. Could I have potentially missed something? Like when you check the taps and the oven are off before going out, only to later realise that you didn't lock the door. Why did I *feel* like I'd missed something? Like I was some fiendish murderer who had left some huge great clue right in the middle of the scene of the crime. A great big manifestation of 'Fran did this', right in the centre of O'Neill's blood-stained bedroom.

On one of mine and Gareth's first dates as a couple, in a seedy little bar that did a whopping twenty-five per cent student discount that financially challenged student Gareth had found, he had gushed to me about his criminology course. Most of it had sounded extraordinarily boring, but there was one thing that had always stuck with me. 'It's pretty well accepted,' Gareth had said with some gusto, 'that there are four types of serial killers.'

There were Visionaries, the sick puppies who believed that there was some kind of power or entity commanding them to kill their victims. Most likely, they were suffering from some form of psychosis.

Then there were the Mission-Oriented, the sick puppies

who thought they were doing society a favour by getting rid of a particular certain group.

Then there were the Hedonists, the sick puppies who got off on the thrill of what they were doing.

Finally, there were Power/Control Freaks: those sick puppies for whom it was all about being able to enact their despicable little power fantasises; those who enjoyed dominating and controlling their victims.

So, the question remained: which kind of sick puppy was I?

The problem was, I didn't think I was any one of the four, but also maybe I was a mix of all of them. I did think I was doing society a favour, I had got a bit of a kick out of it, and I had enjoyed the power I'd wielded on O'Neill before – you know – killing him. The look in his eyes when he'd finally realised who I was. I wasn't quite sure how the Visionary part factored in yet, considering I was a dirty little atheist who thought that God and heaven were just elements of a kid's fairy tale that had got out of hand (don't tell my husband that). But, admittedly, the fact that we'd moved in next door to O'Neill had seemed to be just like fate. The universe seemed to have crafted the perfect situation to kill him, just for me. But despite the initial euphoria I had felt, the almost paralytic anxiety which had been festering in my chest since O'Neill's death was beginning to pulsate and grow.

'Do what?!' O'Neill had said, as he'd realised he may only have a few more words left to utter in his life. 'What the hell are you talking about?'

'You can tell the world what you did twenty years ago or I'm going to kill you.'

The look on his face – it had been almost the same as Macleod's, but O'Neill had slightly more integrity. I had seen the small tremor of fear in his eye, yet I'd known it wasn't me he was most afraid of. We both knew who the boss was.

'No,' he'd said with quiet determination, as we both stood there taking in the moment.

Then, of course, I'd killed him.

I swiped my finger through the notes on my phone whilst power walking through the field. It wasn't until I was halfway across that I realised I had been practically dragging poor Tony's body through the grass as I marched, unaware he was being slightly throttled as his tiny legs weren't able to keep up with my aggressive strides. As I forced my feet to slow down to avoid explaining to Beryl how I had choked her beloved Shih Tzu, I kept thinking of any possible way I could be linked to the crime scene, or any kind of evidence of foul play that could be discovered by the police. I wanted to ring Gareth and ask him a million questions. Maybe I could say I was asking for a friend of a friend's cousin's auntie who had just murdered his next-door neighbour and wanted a few small tips and tricks on evading arrest? That would be plausible, right?

I took a deep breath, and my mind gradually began to calm itself. Then a thought would pop into my head, and I would instantly feel an overwhelming sensation of panic. *What if I'd left a strand of hair there that a few tests will instantly verify is mine?* Then I would remember I had my cover story: I was there to help him with his shopping. I put some stuff away, made some polite chit-chat that went on far too long, put his rubbish out and then left an hour or so later. I ran it through my head again and again, trying to think of any inconsistencies or errors I could get caught out on. Most murderers are stupid, but there had to be a few clever ones who got away with it.

Gareth had once told me about a workshop he'd attended, led by one of the senior detectives: a 'lunch and learn', as they called it internally at the station. The session had uncovered some new-wave psychodynamic theory that suggested killers harbour a deep, unconscious feeling of guilt for their crimes. At their core, the murderer wants to be caught, driven by a death drive, or Thanatos, that ensures they can never truly escape the consequences of their misdeeds. Subconsciously, they want to be brought to justice.

So, while I thought this was a massive load of poppycock, I figured if I kept running and rerunning the cover story through my mind, maybe my brain would somehow accept it as fact, and then it wouldn't even feel like lying any more. The only problem was that, despite the anxiety, I still got somewhat of an intense, deplorable dopamine rush when I remembered that I had been the one to kill O'Neill. It had been so long since Macleod that I had forgotten what it felt like. I just couldn't help but let the biggest smile creep across my face whenever I remembered that feeling of clasping my left hand around O'Neill's elderly, saggy throat, gripping, and squeezing it as tight as I could, and then sliding the blade slowly, precisely into his eye...

Hmm, now, that was quite serial killer of me, wasn't it?

I finished the walk, trying to be more aware of my power-walking tendencies for the sake of the five-kilo dog I was meant to be looking after. I gave a small sigh of relief when we turned into our street and saw there were no flashing police cars outside my home, nor a sudden text from Gareth asking where I was as he prepared the handcuffs on our dining room table. Positive thinking, I told myself. I strolled up Beryl's path, knocked on the door, and passed her Tony.

I gave her a warm smile after the exchange we had performed what felt like a million times before, and I turned around to leave.

'Have a good one!' I said as I began to trot down her path.

'Oh, by the way,' she called after me, 'I'm sure you've noticed already, but it seems you may have lost an earring?'

I stopped in my tracks, frozen, and jerked my hands up to

touch my earlobes. On my left, I felt the metal of a small gold hoop. On the other, I just felt the tiny pinprick of a hole. Suddenly, this idea that my superego was out to get me didn't seem so implausible.

'Shit,' I cursed quietly, as out of the corner of my eye, I could see Beryl's mouth drop, aghast.

I searched the whole house. I emptied every drawer; I smoothed my hands along every square inch of the carpet – nothing. I even rang up the restaurant from last night with a fake identity and asked if anyone had handed anything in, but still – nada. There was absolutely no trace of the earring anywhere. I realised that it could be in any one of a hundred different places. It could have plopped into our loo, or be nestled in the long grass in the park where I walked Tony. But the same terrifying image kept popping into my head. A perfect gold hoop, lying right in the middle of O'Neill's bedroom carpet.

I was sure I could add it to my cover story, right? I'd used his en suite loo rather than the downstairs loo, as maybe O'Neill had said that one was clogged. That was why I'd had to go upstairs. Would that work?

But what if a detective went and checked the loo and found out it was working absolutely fine?

Maybe I had to go up and help O'Neill move some things around?

I kept reminding myself that it was now six days since I had killed O'Neill. Surely, I would have noticed a missing earring by now if I'd lost it when I was there? But the fact that I usually left my hair down and seldom took out my earrings only added to my unease.

I texted Gareth to ask if he'd remembered or noticed if I was wearing earrings last night, but he responded with an expected eloquent and helpful answer.

> No. Soz.

I couldn't exactly go into O'Neill's house now to check the place. If the police had been there, they had undoubtedly put some temporary lock and security scheme in place. There was simply nothing I could do now but wait.

I needed to get away with this.

SEVEN

GARETH

'Oh, Gareth, I can't believe I let you talk me into this again,' Cis said to me, out of breath and wiping the dense sweat off her brow.

'I know. I'm sorry,' I said with the biggest grin I could muster, trying to be as charming as humanly possible. I couldn't resist going to her. Cis was the best at what she did. Everyone else just seemed to pale in comparison.

'You know Vivian will find out about this eventually, though? She always finds out,' she said, as I felt my heart rate begin to steadily drop. Cis checked to see how many calories she had burned on her smart watch. 'And then she'll probably get us both disciplined when she does – remember, she's still above me, too, Gareth.'

'Oh, I can handle Vivian. Don't worry about her. What was your final time?'

'Twenty-two minutes, fourteen seconds. You?'

'Twenty-eight minutes and twenty-three seconds.'

'You're getting slower,' Cis said to me with a smirk. 'There used to be days when you'd be done in nineteen minutes flat.'

I walked over to the dewy park bench and began to smooth

my hands over my thighs. I was no longer the young upstart who could run a lean 5k in sub-twenty minutes. When I became a detective, I had found that a perk of the job was that I didn't need to do much running any more. But the best time to be able to catch Cis was when she was doing her morning jog at 6 a.m. around the local park.

'So, nothing more since Vivian green-lighted the case?' Cis asked, regaining her breath much quicker than I did.

'Breadcrumbs. What I really need is a full forensic sweep.'

'So, what are you thinking? We do a double act? You as the officer in charge and investigating officer and me as the crime scene manager?' Cis walked over to the bench, twisted herself around, and began to do dips. I lost my words for a minute, unable to tear my eyes away from her remarkably defined arms, which were reminding me to visit the station gym the next time I had a spare hour.

'I need a forensic team there by the end of the day, really; at least a set-up and a photographer,' I said. 'We've already cordoned it off, but I'm spread too thin with other cases, and I need someone like you to volunteer – someone who knows what they're doing. I can't really ask someone like Phil, now, can I?'

'You know about the toilet seat story?' she inquired, not stopping for breath in between dips.

'Of course I know the toilet seat story. Everyone knows the toilet seat story.'

'A whole case down the pan,' Cis said. 'Literally.' She yanked her water bottle out of her bag, took a swig, and joined me in sitting on the bench overlooking the water as the sun began to creep up from the horizon. There was a short, uneasy stretch of silence between us, which I knew meant she was working up to say something serious to me.

'I am a little worried about you, Gareth.'

Here we go. I jolted my head back slightly. I didn't like the way she said those words, like a teacher who'd asked a kid to stay behind after a lesson.

'Why? What did I do?'

'You're Moby Dicking.'

'What?' This sounded like a weird German sex act.

'Moby Dicking,' she repeated, enunciating the words more slowly as if that would suddenly make me understand what she was saying.

'You've lost me,' I said, squinting at her and trying to follow her eyeline, but her gaze was fixed on the gently moving currents of water. I still wasn't sure what 'Moby Dicking' was, but it irritated me that Cis seemed to be singing from the same hymn sheet as everyone else in the CID. Crazy old Gareth and the case that was blindingly obvious.

'Cases like this, you don't need someone like me, you don't need a forensic team, you don't need hundreds of case files of witnesses and alibis. We both know that people go missing, and sometimes they just don't come back. There's no foul play, no murder. He's just an old man who walked off and didn't come back. He even left a poem. In a few years, someone will find a corpse washed up on some bay on the Thames or somewhere, and that'll be that. Are you sure you need a whole forensic team to get to the bottom of this?'

'He was killed, Cis. I'm certain.'

'How can you be so sure, Gareth?'

'I don't know,' I muttered, somewhat defeated, as Cis reached out and began to rub my shoulder tenderly. 'I just am.'

'Everyone gets burnt out. Look, give yourself a few hours. Sit in the office and mull it over. If you still feel as strongly about this then as you do now, I'll get stuff in order and be right there to set up forensics. Who does Vivian have lined up to be crime scene manager now? Don't say Phil.'

'Phil,' I confirmed in a groan. 'Why do you think I came to you?'

'Oh, my darling,' she said, gently placing her hand against my temple and pulling my head against her shoulder. Laying my head on her deltoid felt like I was resting against one of the rocks at Stonehenge.

'This isn't very comfortable,' I said, realising I was, in fact, in the world's most tender headlock.

'Aren't you relaxing?' she replied.

I paused.

'Yeah, I guess so,' I said, watching a few joggers shoot us the oddest of looks as they ran by.

I realised that I still wasn't particularly liked in the station. As I came into the room after popping my lasagne – lovingly prepared by Fran – in the fridge, I felt all the eyes of the office stop, fix, and glare at me, analysing and scrutinising every single move I made. Men's-toilets-gate had clearly not yet been forgiven.

I sat down at my desk, ignoring the stares as best I could, and went over some of the other cases I had been working on. While I might have wished life was like a police procedural drama, in which murderers were considerate enough to take turns on a week-by-week basis (starting in September and ending around May), real life lacked such security. It seemed that murderers, burglars, and the rest were not a very thoughtful bunch when considering the time management of the people trying to arrest them.

The more I thought about it, the more I realised that maybe Cis was right. Maybe I had overblown this whole case in my mind as some kind of proxy obsession. It wasn't even like there was a missing person's family begging me to bring their loved one home. My attempts to track down Mr O'Neill's daughter had been in vain, so I imagined some estrangement must have taken place. It was like Gordon

O'Neill had vanished into thin air, and no one other than me really cared.

As the hours passed, arduously and slowly, I felt like I was beginning to come to my senses. As Darren and Steve made frequent jokes about how I was wasting police time with this case, I had to accept that if there was something concrete and substantial to the disappearance of O'Neill, they would have found it by now.

Maybe Cis was right. Maybe the move, the new job and all of the baby-making stress had finally got to me, and some mental cracks were beginning to form. I had been trying so hard to stay calm and relaxed, and to not ask myself constant questions about why Fran getting pregnant was taking so long, or why sex now seemed like a chore, or, really, why had it been so long since I had had a blowjob? Just once, I wanted some kind of sexual gratification without it having to result in a chance of conception.

While I really wanted that blowjob, Fran's lasagne was waiting for me in the fridge, and that seemed like the next best thing.

I went to the breakroom and pulled open the fridge, ready to have some Italian commiseration food. Strangely, however, after a quick scan, I realised my lasagne wasn't there. Had someone moved it? I asked some of the other detectives if they had seen it, but they all shrugged their shoulders with genuine ignorance.

I checked my car, I checked my desk, I retraced all my footsteps, and even went to the front desk to ask Judith if she had seen anyone eating it. She said no, and that she would recognise the smells of Fran's cooking anywhere. I was still dead certain I had put the lasagne in the fridge. I came back into the office and checked it over one more time. As I scanned the various desks, out of the corner of my eye, I noticed Darren and Steve sharing what looked like self-satisfied smiles and muffled chuckles.

Trusting my gut, I headed straight for the notorious bad-smelling bin in the breakroom and pressed down on the pedal. As the lid flipped open, glistening Tupperware caught my eye, and the unmistakable fragrance of my favourite of Fran's dishes wafted up, mingled with the less pleasant odours of rubbish.

I sighed, feeling that a few eyes were looking at me right now, waiting eagerly to see my reaction. I rolled up the shirt sleeve on my right arm, slowly popped my hand in the bin, pulled out the Tupperware, emptied it and walked over to the sink. I could have sworn I heard two men doing a terrible job to stifle their laughter behind me as I washed up, scrubbing off the pieces of stuck pasta sheets.

Steve's eyelid swelled red as the fleshy purple began to creep across his face. Blood gushed from Darren's nose as he tried to grimace through shattered teeth. My fist slammed into him again and again, his face becoming more and more unrecognisable. Now, it turned a fluorescent shade of red as my boxing glove slammed into the bag again. The images of physically assaulting my colleagues stuck on replay in my mind offered a strange sense of comfort, even as the other officers in the station gym watched uneasily while the crazed, newly promoted sergeant flailed exhausted punches at the boxing bag.

I knew that in a few days, the anger would subside and wash away, and I would go back to being friendly, charming, and offering them my biscuits during the unofficial mid-morning break, because I knew deep down, I couldn't hold a grudge for more than a week. But right now, I didn't want to be the guy in the office that everyone liked. I wanted to be the guy that they didn't mess with. I wanted to be one of those people who oozed natural authority, with a certain charming charisma to match. Someone for whom, when I walked into a room, everyone would instantly sit up, straighten their chairs, and actually say nice stuff behind my back. I felt like I had been that guy in my last place; why couldn't I be here?

I shifted my feet slightly, bracing myself to deliver another right hook into the bag.

'You know, it's way past your lunch break, and I am sure you have cases that need your attention.'

Ugh, I thought. Who drew a pentagram and summoned her?

I pivoted my body to face Vivian and, without a word, began to yank at the Velcro on my boxing gloves. She raised a hand to stop me.

'You're still frustrated?' she asked, stepping forward.

'You know what they did?'

'Yes. But they threw your lasagne in the bin; they didn't shag your wife. You need to stop being so dramatic, Gareth.'

I thought about explaining that this was more of a straw breaking the camel's back situation, but I didn't think Vivian would care that much for an explanation of my internal feelings.

She pulled off her blazer, hung it on one of the coat racks in the gym, walked over to me, and then wrapped her arms around the bag. I stood there, slightly bemused. I was a six-foot man – or 182 cm, but who's counting – and she was a relatively petite five-foot-nothing woman, presumably wanting to be my bag holder.

'Go on,' she said, slapping her hand against the bag, gesturing for me to start punching.

I hesitated; this was the prelude to one of those scenes that go viral on the internet. I could see it now: 'Punching Bag Fail, Man Sends Boss FLYING'.

'What's stopping you?' Vivian asked.

'With all due respect, Vivian, I don't want to be taking you to A&E. I don't think that would be a good look for my appraisal.'

'You're overestimating yourself. Throw a jab,' Vivian ordered.

It felt rude to underestimate her, so I launched my hand into the bag with moderate power. She wobbled a little, remaining firmly on both feet. She motioned for me to go again, and I began to slam into the bag.

'I got a call this afternoon from Detective Carlota; she said that she's happy to act as CSM on the O'Neill case going forward. Says it came across her desk, and she wants to nominate herself,' Vivian said as I hurled a left hook to the bag.

So, Cis had clearly got my text from an hour ago, the one where I'd rather ungraciously begged her to be my CSM on the case. Maybe this was in fact some weird psycho-overcompensation from me, but I couldn't just let it go, so I thought I may as well lean into it. I knew there had to be a killer hiding somewhere in my neighbourhood, and I was going to be the one to catch him. And all I could think about was the look that would be on Steve and Darren's faces when I did. Maybe then I'd be invited for after-work drinks. Maybe then they'd respect me.

'Ah, right,' I said, trying to moderate my strength as I landed another jab into the bag. 'And you'll let her? Shouldn't it be Phil?'

'I had no reason to reject the request, and Phil is currently in Essex, helping on a case there. But I'll go with you on this one, Gareth: do you still think this case is worth investigating?'

I hesitated. I wish I could say it was a powerful sense of moral justice that motivated me, but in truth, it was a red-hot furious desire to prove Darren and Steve wrong.

'Let's do it.'

EIGHT

GARETH

'Maybe *das unbehagen*? It's a feeling you can't quite put your finger on, that mixture of uneasiness and discomfort all mixed up into one.'

'Ahhh, see, I just knew the Germans, of all people, would have a word for it,' I said, tilting my chin toward the car microphone above me.

I heard Fran chuckle to herself down the other end of the line.

'You know there's literally a word for every kind of weird niche feeling in German,' she said. 'There's *Sehnsucht*, which means like a longing and yearning for something unknown and unsaid. There's *Heimweh*, which is the feeling of homesickness and nostalgia, and of course, my personal favourite: *Backpfeifengesicht*.'

I remembered that one. The literal translation was an insult meaning 'punching-bag face' – particularly apt after yesterday's events.

'So, what now? I guess I'll be interviewed with the rest of the neighbourhood at some point? You can't just bring out a notepad at dinner and ask me some questions then, I suppose?' Fran asked.

'Well, actually we all use recording devices now.'

'Really? Gosh, how the police have moved with the times.'

'What do you mean? We're always modern and up to date in all aspects,' I remarked glibly.

'So, you're not really going to be involved much with this case at all?' Fran asked.

'No, not really,' I said, glancing at Mr O'Neill's house from the car window. I could see the unmistakable clinical white of the forensic team's suits moving around inside, and the long wads of paperwork I had to sign off in the passenger seat.

Deep down in my psyche, I was trying to forget the story of Ananias and Sapphira from Sunday school. Long story short: lying in front of the Holy Spirit strikes you down dead as dead can be.

'Makes sense. Guess it could be considered a conflict of interest or something. So, who will be interviewing me? Please don't say Darren,' Fran groaned.

'Probably Steve, I imagine. Darren isn't allowed to do witness interviews after he had four different complaints about making people cry. One of which was a six-year-old girl.'

I had decided not to tell Fran about the lasagne incident either, for two main reasons. The first was that I didn't want her to worry about me at work. She'd go full lioness and start hunting for balls when really, I kind of just wanted to forget it had ever happened.

The second was, for the sake of my own ego, I didn't want her to think I was unliked at the station. Maybe it was narcissistic, but I wanted to maintain the image that I had worked for years to build up in my last role. It had been a great feeling to have her come to visit the station then. As we'd walk through the hallways, everyone would be saying hi or hello to me.

'Right, I'd better get back to work, my love. So, love you lots, and I'll see you tonight for date night,' I said.

'Amazing, thanks, my love.'

'Did you book in Mep's check-up by the way?'

'Yes, absolutely,' she replied, less than confidently. Fun Detective Observation: no one telling the truth replies with 'absolutely' to a 'did you...' question.

'Okay, just remember we need him on that new prescription,' I said, slightly raising the pitch of my voice to illustrate some sense of urgency to her. I could almost hear the frantic tapping of keys in the background as she scrambled across the web for the vet's telephone number. 'I'll see you tonight at eight. Love you! Enjoy Pilates!'

'Love you more! I won't!'

I took a moment to myself in the car, running my hands through my hair. I hadn't eaten breakfast today, but I still wasn't particularly hungry. Over the past few days, my stomach had been constantly churning and groaning. I wondered if this was the first telltale sign of the mental breakdown that Cis had warned me about or – more likely – if hiding all this from Fran had literally made me sick to my stomach. I couldn't help running the mental litmus test of how I would feel if I were to walk away from the case, and instantly, I could feel my stomach begin to steady. But then again, my late-night shish from Marmaris Kebab last night *had* tasted a little dodgy.

I could recognise Cis's bulky form from the way the muscles seemed to pop out of her unflattering white forensic suit as she opened the door to Mr O'Neill's house, tapping away on her tablet. I realised I should probably stop holding a little pity party for myself and do the work I was paid to do.

Forensics, more than any other department in the police, was somewhat of a circus. After the photographer and the sampling expert had performed their duties, a wide array of people would flood in and begin to check, analyse, and scrutinise everything. From preserving and protecting the crime scene, to capturing fingerprint evidence, DNA samples, and collecting traces, it was all a pandemonic flurry of silent and carefully enacted activity.

For a detective, there was not a whole lot to do other than provide moral support for the forensics team and see if you could find some kind of task that made you look somewhat important. For me, it was bringing the coffee. The only problem I had been grappling with on this particular task was whether to say the coffees were my treat, or to very politely tell each specialist my account code and sort number and ask them to transfer me the required £3.50. I wanted to seem like the cool police detective, but I wasn't made of money. Frankly, being a detective wasn't all that lucrative. I sometimes wondered if I should have followed my dad's advice and joined the navy – better pension, too.

I braced myself, steadied my gurgling stomach, and left the car, snatching up the coffees as I did so. I could see the neighbours congregating in their gardens, moaning about the sudden increased police presence on the street. But I knew that deep down, they all loved that this was happening. I imagined it was the most drama that had occurred in the neighbourhood since some old grandad had put the wrong bin out on rubbish day in 2006. The curtain creepers were murmuring exclamations to themselves in their front gardens while people walking their dogs purposefully slowed down to try and peer inside the house. It was nothing I hadn't seen before; as soon as the white tent went up outside someone's house, it was like the bat symbol to the nosy neighbour brigade.

I walked across Mr O'Neill's front lawn, yanked up the tape, and entered the small tent that had been set up as a base of operations. There was a long, neat row of small transporter cases, where evidence was being hastily packaged and thrown in. The doors to the swab safe were constantly being yanked open and closed as countless samples were tossed inside in a scene of pure organised chaos. Cis, now on her laptop, reviewing footage that her team had recorded earlier in the day, was seated squarely within the madness. I knew better than to disturb her when she was in the focus zone, so I plucked up her latte from the cardboard holder and placed it silently next to her.

'Ahh, Detective, thank you very much,' a specialist said as they trotted over to me and yanked a coffee from the holder without changing their pace. They jerked off their face mask and strolled away, guzzling the drink furiously before I could even open my mouth about the possibility of them paying me back. It was a domineering attempt on their part that had ended any conversation before it had even begun. Lord above, what a power move.

'Ah, Gareth, my darling,' Cis said, finally breaking out of her focus mode, closing the laptop, and standing up to give me a hug. Enveloped in her giant nylon marshmallow, I prayed she wouldn't hug me too hard and cause a devastating accident with the coffee. 'Good morning, nice of you to finally join us.'

'Ah well, I thought it was good for me to show up and make sure that you're not wasting too much time doing whatever forensics do,' I said, gently pulling myself away from her iron grip. 'How is it all going? Found anything?'

Cis looked over each of her shoulders. The tent was still a flurry of activity, so she gestured for me to take a walk down the street with her. Before leaving, she pulled herself out of her disposable white suit to her rather casual gym base-layer as I placed the remaining coffees on the table. As we walked away, I watched out of the corner of my eye as the white-clothed vultures begin to pounce on the coffees I had left behind. That was £24.50 down the drain.

'So, we've been looking a lot at the bedroom, which we've established as the focal point of this whole crime scene,' Cis explained, hands tucked into her armpits as she quickly scanned around the houses to make sure no neighbours could overhear.

'And?'

'Aisha noticed that there had been a recent change to the carpet's texture. When we sent it back to the girls in the lab, they instantly found traces of blood, milk, and some kind of carpet cleaner. We think we also found traces of bicarbonate of soda.'

'Strange,' I remarked, wondering if I was being a hypochondriac or if I could feel a sudden bout of clamminess beginning to emanate from my palms.

'Right,' Cis affirmed. 'So, looking more at the sample analysis, all three of those texture changes happened in the last week or so, which, of course, would place it right at the same time that Mr O'Neill disappeared. Meaning, naturally...'

'Foul play, surely?' I said. 'Blood was spilt. Someone cleaned it up, and it seems awfully convenient for it to be at the same time he goes mysteriously missing without a trace.'

'Also, judging by the stain and clean-up patterns, there was a lot of it. A *lot* lot. At least a litre. This wasn't a simple nick on the neck while shaving. You were right on this one, Gareth, I have to hand it to you,' she said, sounding half impressed, and half slightly vexed. Cis did always like to be right.

Part of me did feel vindicated. So, it was a murder. But I couldn't also shake this nauseous, guilty feeling, as if I was never meant to have this sense of satisfaction – that, in fact, I was delving deeper into a rabbit hole I wasn't meant to go down.

Or then again, maybe it was the kebab.

'But you'll love this,' Cis said, with a wry smile.

Cis passed me her phone. I stopped walking to take a clearer look at the image. A piece of scrappy A4 paper, encased in a plastic pocket. The writing was sketchy and hard to read, but I could just about make it out:

I'll kill you.

'I think you're missing the bit above,' Cis remarked as she extended her fingers to zoom in on the phone screen. Sure enough, above the bolded 'I'll kill you' there was some fainter writing.

Stay away from her or...

'Well, did O'Neill write this to send to someone, or was someone sending it to him?' I asked.

'We haven't found any other handwriting from him yet, so we're looking into it, but it's weird, right?'

Most of the crimes I had been assigned to already had a culprit attached. The hit-and-run had been a joyriding teenager. The petrol station incident had been an unhinged husband who'd finally snapped. As the cliché goes: if you are going to be murdered, you more than likely already know who's going to kill you. But Mr O'Neill didn't seem to have still been in touch with anyone.

'Nothing was taken, so it wasn't a burglary attempt,' I said, trying to make sense of it all by speaking aloud. 'The whole thing feels like a...' I tried to articulate a way to explain it. 'Like a spontaneous act of violence. Like someone just walked in one day and decided they were going to kill poor old Mr O'Neill. Almost like it was some kind of impulse killing.'

I took a glance at Cis, who was currently in a mid–deep inhale.

'What do you think about all of this?' I asked.

'I think it was personal,' Cis said rather bluntly.

We stood there for a bit longer, both processing everything, when a message pinged through on my phone.

'What is it?' Cis asked. I read and reread the message as she waited for me to explain myself.

'Darren says that Beryl – one of our neighbours, she lives just across the street from us – has one of those video doorbells.'

'Oh?' Cis said, her eyes lighting up. 'So, there might be footage of O'Neill's house.'

'There's a chance, but some devices only start recording when they detect someone nearby, so we can't be sure we'll find anything useful. Also' – I couldn't help but scoff – 'Fran, of all people, told me she managed to break it while walking Beryl's dog. And Beryl? She's flipping clueless about where the footage is sent. She doesn't even have the app on her phone. Darren mentioned he's attempting to reach her son, citing high police importance, as he seems to be the only one capable of accessing the video.'

'Christ alive. Even in the suburbs, we're always being watched, right?' Cis muttered, her gaze scanning around to spot any cameras that might be observing us while I tried to ignore that she had taken the Lord's name in vain.

'And don't you feel much safer?' I said flippantly, resting a hand on my stomach, which had begun to feel queasy again. I couldn't help but let out a small guttural belch that was luckily covered by the loud blaring of Cis's phone ringing, which she instantly snatched out of her pocket and slapped against her face. I tried to make out the tinny voice on the other end of the line before she gestured to me to turn around and head back to the house. Cis being Cis meant she went straight into power-walk mode, whereas I was staggering pathetically behind her, hoping the nausea would pass.

A member of the forensic team spotted us as we approached Mr O'Neill's. He motioned us to suit up and enter the house. Theo, who I identified by his name tag (they all wore them, for obvious reasons), led us up the stairs. The house aroma had completely shifted from the scent of pensioner to sterile liquids and fresh-out-of-the-box polyethylene.

'The attic was padlocked, so we used the bolt croppers,'

Theo said to us as he waved to the ladder for us to ascend. 'Can see why he didn't want anyone getting in.'

I clambered up the ladder first, lifting the small compartment door to the side as I raised my torso up onto the flooring and scooted my legs up. I offered a hand to Cis. But Action Woman easily yanked herself up like it was nothing.

'Jesus, Mary, and Joseph, it stinks to high heaven up here,' Cis exclaimed, causing me to yet again grit my teeth at her blasphemy as she carefully began to tiptoe around the attic. Only a small, cheap bulb illuminated the space from total darkness.

'It's mould,' I heard one of the forensic team say. 'Lots and lots of mould.'

At first, I found nothing particularly odd about the attic, but as my eyes adjusted to the darkness I made out countless cardboard boxes sprawled all across the space.

I took a step forward, trying to avoid the attic insulation as Theo scurried up the ladder and joined us.

'Now I'm going to guess, there is a lot of paperwork he didn't want people to see,' he said, 'not many people lock their attics.'

'There I was, imagining Mr O'Neill as this kind old recluse, like that crotchety man from that balloon house film,' Cis said. She turned around to check on me, giving me the thumbs up in the form of a question, to which I replied in kind. I took a glance at one of the boxes. *Finances 1988–1990* was etched in pen on the side, along with furry green mould that reached across the cardboard.

'I read about this,' I said as I began to open up the box. 'Successful businessman, lost it all and then set up a community foundation to give back.' I yanked out a very 80s-looking folder and began to drift through the pages of invoices, receipts, correspondence.

'Ah yes, businessmen and their guilty consciences,' Cis remarked.

'Huh,' I said to myself, as my perusing was cut short by an End-of-Year Report 1988. 'What kind of company goes under when they're making far more money than they're spending?'

'That's just a successful business,' Cis commented.

I flicked over to the next page. A letter with the very clear and unmistakable House of Commons insignia at the top, with the subject line 'Our Burgeoning Partnership', from an Abe Clark. The next page was even more surprising: a handwritten letter whose legibility had been worn away over time, but at the top, the letterhead was the Office of the Metropolitan Police. It was only as I held the paper to the light that I could make out just one phrase in what was quite frankly terrible handwriting:

They'll never suspect a thing, I promise.

A feeling began to creep over me – a feeling that could be best described as dread. As if I had just waded into the deep end before I really knew how to swim.

I felt my throat begin to clench and my stomach to convulse as I crouched down to take a closer look. My stomach lurched, and I found myself charging back down the ladder again to try to expel the kebab and what else was left in my belly.

'Oh Jesus!' I shouted.

Yes, I know, I know.

'Outside! Outside!' I heard one of the forensic team members call after me.

NINE

FRAN

Next time, I would think ahead, I told myself. Next time, I wouldn't act on impulse. Next time, I'd confront the old bastard the minute I got in the door, before he decided to scramble up the stairs, desperately trying to get away from me, still gripping onto the groceries he was in the middle of unpacking. This was something that, next time, would be very important to avoid. I made a strong mental note in my head, before realising that my mind had yet again drifted off mid-conversation in a situation that I had also rushed into without much thought for the consequences.

'This is such a lovely cup of tea,' I said to Mrs Cohens as I took another polite sip. It tasted like arse. Clearly, the woman did not know that the perfect length of time to brew a cup of tea was three minutes. Five minutes in, it started to taste like lukewarm stewed brown water. If you liked brewing it any more than that, then you probably also liked strangling puppies and watching badger porn.

'Oh well, you're very welcome,' she replied, placing both of her hands on her thighs. 'It's just nice to get some company, actually. My son never tells me anything about what happens at work. I'm in the dark all the time!'

'It's these men, Mrs Cohens. They never tell us anything,' I exclaimed with fake exasperation. She gave a knowing guffaw as she took another sip.

'So, when do you reckon your son will be home, Mrs Cohens?' I asked, slightly pushing myself forward on the chair.

'Oh, any time now, I imagine. He's not normally any later than about five on a Thursday. Can I get you another cup of tea, Francesca?'

'Hmm,' I said, pursing my lips. 'I'd better not. I do have a doctor's appointment at six, and a cup of tea will have me in your hair for at least another hour.'

'Oh, don't be silly,' Mrs Cohens said, slapping my hand teasingly. 'It's so nice to meet you, and hopefully, we can do this again sometime.'

I tried not to let my feelings find their way to my face as I watched her get up and start boiling the kettle.

'Of course we can,' I said, with the manufactured grin I'd left hanging on my face, knowing that I was well and truly winning her over.

I vaguely remembered one of the staff at the children's home, a genuinely lovely man named Clive, whose defining feature was that the gap between his eyebrows was always a bright tomato red from plucking the hairs that would otherwise form a thick, bristled monobrow. He would always tell me in the quiet room, where difficult children were exiled, that I had a bit of a tendency to see red, to launch myself straight into a righteous fury. I often thought of him whenever I found myself in situations like this. Wondering if I should have taken the ten deep breaths he used to tell me to take to try to stop myself from doing something stupid.

I heard the front door unlock with a heaving metal clunk

and listened to the footsteps of her piece-of-shit son dawdling towards the kitchen.

'And who the hell are you?' Darren moaned, before he had even fully walked into the room.

'Language!' Mrs Cohens snapped at him, turning from sweet latter-aged lady to feisty dragon within a moment.

'I'm Fran. I'm Gareth's wife,' I said, grinning from ear to ear. It was authentic this time. The piece of shit's eyes suddenly widened, almost bulging as he took a small, almost imperceptible stumble backwards, and I could see him now try to put on an artifice of attempting to look unfazed.

'Well, why are you here?' he grunted as he leaned awkwardly against the doorway and crossed his arms, almost like he was sizing me up.

'Well, let me tell you, here I was, thinking you were the alpha big balls of the station, and it's just so surprising to me that you still live with your mother,' I said to him as he sheepishly lowered his head. 'I mean no offence, Mrs Cohens,' I remarked, reaching out to touch her hand.

She solemnly shook her head as if it was not a problem, but her eyes were still fixed upon her son with equal parts disappointment and anger.

'It's just until I get back on my feet,' he murmured to himself.

'Ah yes, because you were kicked out by your wife after she found the dick pics that you sent to your colleagues, I remember Gareth told me.' I tried to stifle a chuckle as I shook my head, exasperated. 'It's funny because, you know, Darren, my husband would *really* hate for me to be here. He never likes anyone fighting his battles for him, and that's fair enough. I get it, I do.' I rose to my feet and strolled slowly towards him as he cowered in the doorway. I switched to a hushed whisper: 'But my husband cannot lie for the life of him, and I know for a fact that he didn't eat that lasagne that I made for him. And while he'd never admit it, I also know for a fact that you've been giving him bother. Am I wrong?'

Darren's head lowered even further. If he had a tail, he would certainly be tucking it wholly between his legs. The piece of human waste was probably a good foot taller than me, but his sulk and bowed head had brought him down to my eye level, where I glared at his pupils as they tried to glance away from me.

'Am I wrong?' I repeated.

'Nah,' he grumbled, still not making eye contact with me.

I slammed my hand into the door frame behind him. Mrs Cohens jolted with a yelp just as Darren wrenched his head back in surprise, knocking his thick skull against the wood of the frame.

'You bitch,' he hissed, as he clutched the back of his head.

'Don't call me a bitch, you bitch, and if you dare try to mess with my husband again, just remember I know where you live,' I said to him softly, watching his face start to redden in embarrassment, anger, pain – or maybe all of the above. 'I'll come over to your house, and I'll make my cat bite your shrivelled, wart-ridden dick off.'

I could see from his closed fist that Darren just wanted to punch me there and then, lay me out flat on the cold of his mother's kitchen floor, but I could also see that he was a little bit afraid of me and what I could do to him if I tried. God, what a thrill. Part of me even wanted him to throw a punch, just to see what I would do in response. Even I didn't know!

I could see he was beaten. His glare was mostly focused on his mum now. I gently raised my hand away from the door frame behind him and slipped it into my pocket.

'Thanks again for the tea, Mrs Cohens,' I said. 'We really should do this again sometime.'

She was too scared to say yes and too polite to outright refuse. Then again, I had just threatened to castrate her son –

perhaps I had gone a little too far – but the adrenaline of it all had made me deviate from the script I had written in my mind on the way over. The minute that I'd found out who she was during the dreaded small talk at Pilates, I just hadn't been able to help myself. I knew she would probably never talk to me again, would maybe even switch clubs. For me, of course, that would be a win-win.

Well, that was one thing ticked off my 'to do' list for the rest of the day: feed the cat.

I drove to the clinic and ran through everything in my mind again. The blood, the cover story, the evidence. Trying to run through every single possible scenario, trying to avoid a dreaded realisation of Murphy's Law: anything that can go wrong will go wrong, and always at the worst possible time.

The last hurdle with O'Neill, I thought to myself, as I waited outside the clinic for Gareth, was the questioning that would inevitably take place, and I reassured myself by remembering that I had crushed it when they'd interviewed me about Macleod.

'I don't believe this woman has a violent bone in her body,' the inspector had said about me. Whoops, if only she knew what I had just done before my appointment.

Yet, over the past few days, I had not been able to shake the unsettling feeling that Gareth was not telling me everything. Our usual sixty-second updates on each other's day had become shorter, blunter and more abrupt on his end. Was he keeping something from me, or was I just projecting?

I decided to compartmentalise and visit that troubling train of thought later as Gareth rocked up at the clinic with only a few seconds to spare. He jolted out of his car and gave me a quick peck on the cheek as we hurried inside, blurted our names to the receptionist, and then sat down in the most Godforsaken of all places: waiting rooms.

Among those waiting with us were a small toddler and,

presumably, her mum. Not yet fully dexterous, she was playing with one of those wooden bead maze things, trying to push the small, chunky multi-coloured hoops along the track. She realised I was watching her, and her small, innocent face looked up to me. I gave as warm a smile as I could muster under the circumstances, leaning forward a little, but then she just began to splutter-cry and darted away to the safety of her mum. I guessed my maternal instincts still needed some work.

Her mum began to turn around to see what monster had made her baby sob and snot, so, trying to avoid her gaze, I reached out for a magazine to hide behind and then remembered where I was and what kind of tests they did, and decided to maybe hold off in picking up the latest housekeeping edition. I could see that Gareth was thinking the same thing as he motioned to me that he had a bottle of alcohol gel in his coat pocket. The man had come prepared.

'Do you think, like, they'll ask me to do it today?' he whispered in my ear.

'What, have a wank?' I let slip, speaking way too loudly. A few of the other people in the waiting room quickly twisted their heads to give me a passive–aggressive side-eye.

'Whoops,' I said, skulking deeper into my chair as Gareth gave a light slap of discipline on my arm, trying to control his own laughter.

'So, you know, I knew someone who had a girlfriend who worked at one of these places. Said the official name of the room where you tug yourself off is the sample room, but they all call them the wank rooms.'

'Ewww,' I groaned. It was my turn to give him a soft slap as he quietly tried to smirk to himself, only to realise that he may have to venture into the wank rooms himself in only a few minutes.

'He told me that they want to make it look as close to a bedroom as possible,' Gareth continued.

'What, like some kind of Pavlovian trick?'

'Isn't that a dessert?' Gareth said, tilting his head slightly.

I scoffed. Gareth, for someone so finely tuned into the way people worked, lacked so much general knowledge.

'Anyway, that place must just be filthy,' he murmured to me. 'Think of how many babies have started their journey right there in that room.'

I couldn't tell if Gareth was just bored or if he was trying to be his remarkably goofy self to make me feel less anxious about everything. But I also knew that whatever his motivation, this was his personal challenge: to try and gross me out. I wasn't having it. I was un-gross-outable.

'So, they stick up a poster of Pamela Anderson, secret stash of *Nuts* magazine, and maybe a race-car bed to really nail the message home?' I asked.

'Who reads *Nuts* any more, Grandma?'

The mum whose child I had made cry rotated her head slowly, looked us both dead in the eyes, and then changed her gaze to look directly at me as if to say, *Please, control your man.*

'Sorry,' Gareth grunted, even though the mum was still glaring the sharpest of daggers at me. He didn't wait a moment to let the embarrassment subside before turning to whisper to me, like a schoolboy at the back of the class that just couldn't help himself, 'So, what kind of porn do you think they'll have in there?'

'Oh, for goodness' sake, Gareth, will you shut up!' I snarled at him playfully.

'Mr and Mrs Donoghue?' the nurse said, and I could hear the sounds of collective relief from the rest of the room when we stood up to be escorted to the doctor.

We were led through a sterile corridor and into a generic hospital room. The only change they had made was that it had been furnished with a few stock photos of happy families hung up on the walls, which I figured would be salt in the wound if someone left the appointment unhappy.

Dr Patel joined us a few minutes later, and we had polite preliminary discussions. He listened intently as we told him about the many trials and tribulations we had encountered in trying to get pregnant. He did his best to reassure us, but I couldn't help but feel like he said these things to everyone. This was just him reciting lines he had been performing his whole career.

'This happens to a lot of couples.'

Well, duh.

'You're doing the right thing by being here.'

Well, of course. We didn't think worshipping an emu god would be the next logical step.

'There are a lot of solutions to the problems couples face while trying to conceive.'

Yes, we know about IVF, which is not exactly cheap. Just say what you mean, Doc. Enough with all the fluff.

'In twenty-five per cent of couples, fertility problems can't be explained, but don't let that worry you.'

That one *did* hit a little deeper, and made me try to tone down my internal monologue. We must have been his last couple at the end of his day, and he was still taking the time to try and explain all the details and reassure us as much as possible.

'Even if we don't get the result we want, this doesn't mean you can never have kids. A lot of couples receive diagnoses that make them feel like they'll never be able to conceive naturally, and then a year later, *bada bing, bada boom*, we have a little one on the way. So please, do not fret, okay?'

I nodded and reached out for Gareth's hand. The tension of the moment had been overridden by the fact that this well-respected, sixty-something doctor had just uttered the words 'bada bing, bada boom'. Gareth grabbed hold of my hand and wrapped his fingers softly around mine. He wasn't as hyperactive as he had been in the waiting room; the reason we were actually here had slowly begun to sink in.

'Did you bring the sample, Gareth?' the doctor asked with a beam. He was asking for Gareth's cum with the most wholesome of smiles, and somehow, it wasn't creepy. I was in awe of the sheer audacity of this man.

'Oh, I was meant to bring it from home?' Gareth asked.

'Yes, the receptionist should have said. Not to worry, though. I'm sure there will be a sample room going free. I'll just grab someone,' the doctor said as he strolled to the other side of the room to call for a nurse.

'Damn it,' Gareth said to himself, realising he was now about to face the terror of the wank rooms by himself.

'Just think of me in a ponytail,' I said softly to him. 'And a tight sports bra?'

He gave me one last look and nodded, determined to succeed, as a rather attractive, well-proportioned nurse opened the door and escorted Gareth out.

He'd better still be thinking about me as he's tugging it, I thought.

'Shall we get started?' the doctor said, and I gave a silent thumbs up as I hopped onto the seat, pulled up my shirt, and placed my feet on the stirrups while he prepared the probe.

'As you probably know, this will feel a little cold,' the doctor said as he spread the gel across my belly and began to scan. I took a look at the murky grey images that were swirling around on the screen in front of him. I had no idea what he was looking for, so tried to judge by his subtle facial reactions how it was going.

'So, what do you do for a living, Francesca? Anything interesting?'

He was making small talk.

'I'm a social worker in child protection – I mostly deal with foster kids. You?'

The balls on this doctor to just give a gracious and tender laugh back to me, and not look at me as if I hadn't said the most idiotic thing he had heard today.

'I always wanted to be a painter, truth be told, but my mother ushered me into the family profession. Although your work does sound very rewarding.'

'It is,' I said, carefully studying the man to distract myself. He had the most excellent skin. As he squinted his eyes to look more intensely at the monitor, I tried to gauge any nuance from his reactions.

There was a silence, which may have only lasted a few moments, but I felt the need to fill it.

'How are my tubes, Doc?' I asked.

'From what I am looking at here, Francesca, you have very healthy ovaries and your fallopian tubes don't seem to have any abnormalities, which is a very good sign,' he said, removing the probe.

'Oh, I bet you say that to all the girls,' I quipped. As he began to tell me about an HSG – to the layperson: an X-ray to determine if my fallopian tubes were blocked – I heard my phone vibrate on the side. It could be Gareth, maybe needing a bit of motivation, I figured. I tilted the phone up to take a precarious glance at the caller ID. It was Angus.

'I'm so sorry, I need to take this,' I said, and before Dr Patel had a chance to say anything, I scooped up my phone and pressed it to my ear.

'Angus? What's wrong? What's happening?' I asked frantically, trying to yank my shirt down and scramble out of the chair.

'Fran, I'm fine. Don't worry,' Angus said on the other end of the line, cool as a cucumber. 'Calm down. You always panic.'

I wasn't convinced. He never rang me first.

'Angus, tell me what's wrong, right now.'

I heard him take his signature long, exasperated sigh before he began to speak.

'Look, just come over when you can, okay? I have something to tell you.'

Angus was the world's worst communicator, so if he was reaching out to me, it must be something important. 'No, tell me now. What is it?' I snapped. I saw the doctor's eyebrows leap up his forehead, and he scooted off in his chair, making himself busy on the far side of the room.

I heard Angus sigh again, the longest and most elongated sigh I'd ever heard in my entire life, as if he was making sure every little ounce of carbon dioxide was removed from his lungs.

'I was looking through the papers today, and I found Abe. Abraham Clark.'

'What?' A surge of panic, anxiety and glee began to flow around me, my heart beating faster again. It was that same feeling that had coursed through my body when I'd seen O'Neill there on the day we moved in, watching us from his garden as he watered his potted plants. I could still see that image, burnt into the hard drive of my brain, of him attempting a half-smile, half-grimace, as we hauled our stuff into the house. And now I felt overwhelming dread, like it was all going to happen again. An urgency, a deep, crushing kind of panic, that I needed to fix.

The door to the consulting room opened, and there was Gareth, holding the door in one hand, clasping the cup sheepishly in the other. He spotted me just as I put down the phone, and his face dropped to a scowl. The doctor, in all his saintly composure, must have picked up on this as he tried his best to defuse the situation with a smile.

'Record time,' he said, as the door slammed shut with a thud.

TEN

FRAN

It was a silent walk back to our cars. The doctor had told us about the subsequent next steps when Gareth had returned after... depositing. I wasn't really listening. I hated it when Gareth was angry. My own bouts of ferocity consisted mostly of me doing some loud shouting and slamming some doors, before quickly getting over it and being ready to make up. But with Gareth, he would just sit there, seething and marinating in his own rage for a handful of hours at least – sometimes days, if I got really unlucky. The normally optimistic and energetic man became monosyllabic and abrasive, only speaking in grumbles and murmurs. Not even the offer of a blowjob could get him out of his self-imposed funk.

I tried calling him a few times on the drive home, but naturally, he didn't pick up. I got home first and waited for him with Mep on my lap, perched on the steps outside the front door, facing the huge white tent that enveloped O'Neill's house next door. About ten minutes later, he pulled up onto the drive and stayed sitting within his car. I knew he was trying to avoid talking to me by pretending to be busy. This was the classic

Gareth move. 'Men need processing time,' I remembered a uni friend once saying to me.

I watched him pretending to put away his work stuff in the relevant compartments when I knew for a fact he would have already done that meticulously before he left the station.

'You're going to have to get out eventually,' I yelled to him. But he pretended not to hear. He stayed in the car, face neutral, shuffling around the pages in the car manual for the millionth time.

It was only a few minutes later that I decided this was silly, and also, it was far too cold to stay sitting outside. I swung Mep from my lap onto my chest, strutted across the driveway, yanked open the car door, and sat in the passenger seat.

'So, you going to ignore me for the rest of the evening?' I asked him.

'Maybe,' Gareth grumbled contemptuously.

Mep, furious that he was being denied entry to his palace, gave a small growl as he scratched at the car window with his paws.

'Gareth, come on, don't be like this,' I pleaded. 'I'm sorry. Is that what you want me to say? You know what I'm like when it comes to Angus. I'll say it again, okay? I'm sorry. Are we friends now?'

'Just why?' Gareth said, raising his voice, breaking out of his emotionless zombie state. 'Why did you have to take his call right there and then in the bloody fertility clinic? Could it not wait? What was it even about?'

'It was nothing really, I just...' I lied, letting my voice trail off.

'No, go on, tell me. Tell me what happened that was so interesting that it just couldn't wait,' Gareth snapped.

'It was just something he saw in the paper,' I said, as softly as I could, trying to calm the situation. 'He thought it would be of some interest to me, okay?'

Gareth raised his hands up as if to say, 'I was right', and slapped them back down on the steering wheel. We both sat there quietly for a few more moments. Gareth reached his arm out towards me – I thought maybe to grab my hand as a peace gesture, but instead, he pushed his hand underneath Mep and pulled him over the console to place him on his lap. I decided to let it slide. He needed Mep more than I did right now. However, I didn't think Gareth realised quite how hard he was stroking Mep; every time he patted his head, I could see the poor cat's eyeballs bulge out of their sockets.

'I just don't get why you feel the need to drop everything for your brother-who's-not-really-your-brother the very minute he needs you,' Gareth said, as Mep discovered what feline botox would feel like with Gareth rubbing his head maybe slightly more forcefully than he realised.

'Oh, come on, don't be cruel,' I said. He had something of a point, but I couldn't help that I was worried about Angus. He had been through a lot. Well, we both had. But then I remembered it was different for Gareth. He had no idea about Edith, about the fire.

'I'm just frustrated, okay? That's all – I'm frustrated,' Gareth said, more calm and considered now, like he was choosing his words carefully. 'This is something serious that is going on between us – this is our future, as we plan a family together – and I don't get why Angus had to ring you during the time you were getting your... fucking fanny scanned, nor do I understand why you had to pick it up. Could you not have just let him go to voicemail and called him back later?'

There was another little interval of silence, which I wasn't sure was making us calm down or just winding us up more, but I couldn't help myself. I felt my body convulse and shudder as I clasped my hand over my mouth. I burst out a cackle; my Wicked Witch of the West cackle, as Gareth liked to call it.

'What?' Gareth hissed through his pout.

'Getting your fucking fanny scanned?!' I managed to say through the hysterical laughter that was making my whole diaphragm shake uncontrollably. 'Fanny!' I repeated, through my shrieks.

I could see Gareth try not to break. He wanted to laugh; I *knew* he wanted to laugh. He turned his face to try and stare at the wing mirror, but I raised my finger, pointing at him.

'You want to laugh. I can see it in your face!' I managed through the giggles.

'I don't want to laugh,' he retorted, even as the corners of his mouth began to slightly twitch upwards.

'Oh, come on, can I touch you now, hot-head?' I asked with a smile, my cackles beginning to subside, and Gareth gave a snigger. I stretched my arm out and began to stroke the back of his head gently.

'You're right. I'm sorry, okay?' I said. He finally tilted his head to look at me and gave something of a smile, although to me, it looked more like he was passing wind.

'I'm sorry for exploding.'

'It's okay, we all explode sometimes,' I said back. He leaned forward and gave me a kiss as he rested his hand on my thigh.

'For example,' I said as I placed my hand on his cheek, 'you exploded in record time in the wank room today.'

It was the following Monday and I had decided to work most of the morning from home, which worked out well as Gareth had rushed out in the morning and had taken my phone instead of his.

I hadn't really thought much about Clark after we'd got back from the clinic. It had mostly been pushed to the back of my mind as Gareth and I had discussed what Dr Patel had told us. But in the cold light of day, alone with my thoughts and only mundane email admin to distract me, Clark's grotesque face began to slither into my head. I had tried tracking them all down over the years, and it was only Macleod I had ever managed to find. I had thought that maybe Clark had died long ago. But now two of them had turned up in just over a month. It all felt vaguely serendipitous – for me that is, certainly not for them.

I tried to find a way to distract myself. I set countless work targets to keep my mind occupied, but no matter how hard I tried, Clark's smug, gross face kept appearing in my mind. That flash of fear that I hadn't felt for years. More worryingly, the thought of killing him kept pushing its way into my cerebral cortex, attached to a rather uncomfortable feeling of delight. Macleod was like a scratch card, and O'Neill, perhaps, the Thunderball. But Clark? He was the triple rollover Euromillions – the most cruel and sadistic of them all. Suddenly, all I could think about was Clark.

Again, I know this is probably something that psychopaths think, and I know that I've said that I am not one. However, I won't lie to you. The thought of slitting Clark's throat was genuinely indescribable. Like, you must have something that feels like this. I had this intense rush of joy as I thought about the most painful and agonising ways I could do it. I loved the whole piano-wire thing from gangster movies, you know. I could just say something cool like 'Francesca says hello', and then yank it back against his throat as his little old arms and legs flailed about.

I hadn't really thought about the possibility of going to prison until after I had cut up O'Neill, and even then, it was tempered by that weird old feeling of fate lurking in my mind that had propelled me to kill him. This was the universe giving me a chance to correct it, so why would I be punished for acting on the opportunity presented before me?

I started to realise that maybe, in fact, I was perhaps *un poco* psychopathic. Hey, at least I was self-aware.

I decided that not a lot of work was being done, so I would go and see Angus. I thought about picking him up some papers along the way, but knew that would probably only feed his own personal obsessions more, positioning me as some kind of enabler.

I hated where Angus lived, not just because it was about an hour's drive away, but also because it was so incredibly miserable. The whole small estate seemed to be in a constant state of grey, drizzly overcast, and all the high-rise apartment buildings shared the same plain grey concrete exteriors with a small pink neon sign at the top, so over-lit that I couldn't even make out the word it was trying to say. I clambered up to floor eleven, wheezing, as I dared not take the lift that looked about the same age as the Roman lighthouse at Dover Castle. I beat my fist hard on the door six clear and coherent times, counting each knock as I did so. He swung open the door, saw me, and barely reacted.

'Hi,' he said, unbothered by me standing there, still damp from the rain that I had got caught in.

'You good?' I asked somewhat cautiously, with an expectant smile. He stared blankly at me and shrugged his shoulders.

'Guess so,' he replied. 'You want to come in?'

'Nah,' I said.

He just groaned in response to my sarcasm, and turned to walk back into his flat as I followed him in. At least he had done some organising since I had last been here. The newspapers in the hallway, which formed a small tunnel, had all been nicely folded and organised with little multi-coloured markers placed to indicate the date. The other tens of thousands looked a little more erratic in terms of their organisation.

'How long did it take you to arrange this?' I asked, examining the thousands of thin spines of paper that were all placed perfectly on top of each other, no edge even slightly out of place.

'A week or so. There were re-runs of some old Hammer

films on one of the channels, so I watched them whilst I did it. Time flew by.'

'So, what am I looking at here?' I asked, motioning to one of the many eight-foot-tall pillars of newspapers, curious if I could call him out on his knowledge.

'You're looking at... 2009,' Angus said, hands on hips, like he was inspecting a modern art piece. 'Please don't touch it, though.'

'Pfft, you think I'm that brave,' I replied as he led me into his kitchen – also full of papers, as well as plenty of empty food-stained pots from microwaveable ready meals and takeaways.

'Jesus Christ, it's gross in here, Angus,' I said to him, trying to take in the sheer mess he had crafted: pans had been left permanently soaking in their own fat and grease, a wide selection of plastic pop bottles had been tossed on the floor, and a small ecosystem of flies were hovering around a room that served as their all-you-can-eat buffet.

'I'm sorry you feel that way,' he muttered under his breath.

God, Angus really was insufferable sometimes.

'I won't take up too much of your time, okay?' I said, trying to find someplace to sit that wasn't covered with food or newspapers. It was equal parts strange and offensive that he actually looked relieved when I said that. I don't think he had seen anyone since I'd last checked in on him some two weeks ago, and there he was, counting down the minutes until I left him alone again. 'I just want to know more about Clark. I want the paper,' I said, realising it was easier to stand than find somewhere safe to sit.

Angus nodded, spinning himself around to one of the smaller stacks that I guessed he was still building. He filed through the stack for a second, carefully and tenderly dancing his fingertips across the thin spines of the papers, and then yanked one out and passed it to me.

'He's around the midway mark,' he said. 'Please, please don't rip it.'

I scanned through the horrible texture of newspaper, hating the dry, velvety feel of it on my fingertips as I passed through the mundane local journalism. School fair, school play, new community hall, school presents gender-flipped nativity, school faces dozens of complaints, and then I found him. There were some six or so other people in the photo, all pensioners. But there he was on the left, unmistakable. Either the years had been kind to him, or the photo had been put through Photoshop: he was rocking a full, thick head of hair like some kind of wannabe silver fox. It was funny: even in the monochrome paper, I could still make out that bronze ring on his little finger. I bet part of them all felt a little bit pleased that they had managed to get away with it.

I must have let my feelings make their way to my face, as Angus's face shifted into a scowl in response.

'Don't you do it. Don't do it. If you do it, you'll be the stupidest person in the history of the whole planet. So just don't.'

'I'm not going to do it,' I said calmly and serenely back to him. 'Do you really think I'd be that idiotic?'

He waved his hands up in exasperation before slapping them against his face.

'Well, come on, Fran, it's not like you went and killed O'Neill now, is it? With no planning or prep. I could have at least helped.'

'How could you have helped?' I asked, feeling the repressed pangs of infuriation begin to ascend. I had been here two minutes, and I was already fed up with Angus always pretending he was this wise old sage when he barely knew how to work the microwave. 'You could have brought a stack of papers to mop up the blood, right? That would have been your contribution to the whole thing, I bet.'

'Oh, piss off,' Angus said, storming out of the small kitchenette and towards his bedroom, where he slammed the door shut behind him.

Of course we had argued. Every time I'd come over recently, we'd seemed to argue. Maybe we were more like brother and sister than we thought, or maybe if we hadn't gone through so much shared trauma, we would have killed each other ages ago.

'Don't walk away, come on,' I yelled pleadingly. 'I'm only joking.'

I closed the paper and placed it back on the pile as neatly as I could, careful not to add any flame to the fire as I began to walk to his bedroom, ready to execute the whole 'apology' act that I knew he needed. But just as I did that, he marched back in, grabbed the paper, and inserted it into its proper place in the middle of the pile, which I, of course, had failed to do in my foolish ignorance.

'Are you going to get your job back?' I asked after him as he angrily sauntered off again, trying to organise something that clearly bothered him in one of the other stacks.

'No,' he grunted.

'Why not?'

'I'm not going back to cleaning supermarket floors. It's degrading.'

'Oh, come on, you cannot take some kind of high ground here,' I groaned at him. 'There is absolutely nothing wrong with supermarket work.'

He wasn't having it. I knew he didn't actually find the work degrading; it was just another excuse so he could stay inside and not do anything other than get papers delivered, watch TV, eat food, and then go to sleep. Sure, he had trauma to process, but I'd gone through everything he had, and I was a functioning member of society.

Angus was still silent. He just kept on fiddling around with his newspapers, using his index finger and thumb to gently manoeuvre each sheet into its right place, ultra-careful not to crease or rip.

I knew what would get him talking to me, so I slipped my hand into my jeans pocket, closed my fingers around the small plastic bag, and yanked it out. Angus watched me in his peripheral vision, clearly aware of what it was before his eyes had even properly focused on it. He stopped his ameliorating and walked – still with more than a hint of sulk – over to me to inspect.

I passed him the bag that still had a few smudges of blood inside and he felt around the plastic-encased ring. His eyes were transfixed on it, mesmerised.

'You want me to hold this one with Macleod's?'

'Surprisingly, living next door to the murder I committed means it's probably best that I don't have any evidence on me,' I remarked. 'So I would consider it a big personal favour if you could hang onto it for the time being.'

He gave a grunt as he continued to inspect every tiny scratch of the ring through the plastic bag.

'Would you have done it?' I asked him. That stopped his trance. He placed his hands in his pocket with the ring, performed his signature sigh, and pursed his lips together.

'No.'

'What would you have done?'

'I don't know, reported him to the police or something. I wouldn't have killed him in broad daylight like you, you lunatic.'

'I mean, I gave him a choice?' I said, trying to ignore the irritation I felt at being called a lunatic.

'You only did that to make yourself feel better. You really think you wouldn't have still killed him if he said he'd go public with what they did to us?'

'Look, I get it. You're right,' I said to Angus, surrendering to him. I didn't actually mean what I was saying, but I couldn't be arsed to argue with him any more. 'But I don't want anyone else to get hurt. As long as they're walking around out there, they're a threat. We need justice.'

'Bullshit. Justice and vengeance are two different things.'

'Justice and vengeance are like... Flakes and Ripples, basically the same thing!' I justified.

'Oh my... Fran, you're doing it because you're a sadist. You think I couldn't tell how euphoric you were when you told me you'd killed O'Neill on the phone? I mean, you've kept his ring as a memento, despite it being obvious evidence that you slaughtered him. Who does that?!' Angus growled.

Gosh, that hurt even more. Maybe it was because he wasn't too far away from the truth. *Euphoric* did seem a stretch, though. Ecstatic, maybe, but not euphoric.

'They deserve to die, though, right? What, you think they deserve to have their happy little lives? Their happy little endings with their little glasses of homemade lemonade and playing tiddlywinks every other Tuesday. Is that what you want, Angus?' I hissed. This was a different argument to yesterday with Gareth. This felt raw. I wanted my words to hurt Angus. I wanted him to get that kind of inner, surging jolt of pain like he had just given me. 'And you're telling me that every time you think about...'

I paused, bracing myself to say her name aloud.

'... about Edith, you don't think about killing them?'

'I want you not to go to jail, Fran. All of these guys have – what – ten years left, if that, before they pop off? Then that's it, they're dead. You, on the other hand, have a whole life left to lead, and killing Clark – if that's what you're going to do – may just end with you rotting in some prison in Dartmoor or somewhere. It's going to ruin you... and Gareth.'

'Oh, my God!' I shrieked, my anger finally reaching the surface, destroying any composure I had left. 'I am not going to kill him!'

Angus looked at me like I was suddenly being the unreasonable one, his eyebrows launching up his forehead.

'Okay, relax,' he murmured. 'I was just saying. I mean, don't you ever just want to be honest with Gareth? Just tell him everything.'

'No, I don't,' I said without missing a beat. I wished I could, desperately, but I knew, Gareth being Gareth, that if I did, our marriage would crumble in a matter of moments. I knew I could be obstinate at times, but it had become a running joke between me and my uni friends when Gareth and I had first started dating just how law-abiding he was. I once asked him who would care if he watched some bootleg copy of a film online. 'It just wouldn't be right,' was all he said.

Angus and I both sat there in silence for a moment. At first, I thought it was a moment of mutual unspoken understanding; even though we argued and bickered, we would always be there for one another. That was something that didn't need to be verbalised. But then, after a few moments of Angus shifting awkwardly, as if he was getting ready to speak, I knew he was going to say something stupid.

'Have you ever thought about coming forward? Just telling the police everything?'

He was nothing if not consistent.

'With what evidence, Angus? Do you not remember Clive tried going to the police about the fraud they were committing after the fire, and Macleod shut it down so fast? What makes you think it would be different now? We've got no evidence. The police, the system are always going to want to cover up what they did to us.'

He didn't know how to answer that.

'Any chance of justice is screwed because of Clark and his pals,' I murmured. 'He would never get what he deserves.'

'The arc of the moral universe is long, but it bends towards justice,' Angus mused.

Wait a minute, was he quoting MLK?

'It only bends if we pull, Angus,' I clarified.

I offered to make a start on cleaning, but he began to not-so-gently shoo me out of his apartment before I could do so. I tried to argue – the mould festering on his dishes was giving me a tangible level of anxiety – but he kept corralling me to the door.

'Don't do anything stupid, like kill Clark,' Angus grumbled before he slammed the door shut, and I heard the secure clunk of the lock.

Oh, I was definitely going to kill Clark.

ELEVEN

GARETH

I carefully ran my fingers through my hair, before pulling it as hard as I could from the back, and stared at my reflection. The strands jerked, fell back into place, and flattened as I leaned closer to examine my scalp.

'Are you sure?' I repeated, not truly believing what she was saying. Perhaps the stress of last week, with Mr O'Neill and the fertility clinic, had taken a toll on the total density of hairs on my head.

'Yes, I'm sure, just at the front. But I think it would be best if you maybe just relaxed a little bit, Detective?' Isla said to me, softly pushing her elbow against my face.

'Eh, maybe, I don't know,' I said, as I pushed my nose up against the metal to take an even closer inspection at the state of my hairline, my breath fogging up the steel of the coffee machine. 'Just to me, I swear there was a lot more hair there. It looks a little more' – I motioned to my head – 'deserted, now.'

I pulled my hands out of my hair, and it flopped back down unceremoniously as I stood up from my semi-squat, having scrutinised any potential hair recession in the mirrored sheen of the coffee maker. I noticed that the barista had been looking at me, rather unimpressed, as she kept her arm outstretched with my coffee. A long line of people had gathered for their morning caffeine fix in the seemingly short time I had been diligently examining myself. I sheepishly grabbed my coffee from the barista's hand and wandered across the café floor, slumping down in a chair at a window that overlooked the dull concrete courtyard below.

'Honestly, this coffee is absolute bollocks. I have never tasted such – urgh – blandness in my life,' Isla said as she took a hefty gulp.

'Then why are you even drinking it?' I asked.

'Cos what else is there? We've all tried to start a petition to open up a proper concession, but they won't do it. Sorpressa has apparently been here for decades. They have roots going straight into the sewers.'

Isla and I had worked together for the past few years, and her name was often whispered amongst officers with a mix of equal parts fear and respect. Fortunately, I'd discovered that the key to maintaining a good relationship with the prosecution was regularly buying her coffee while updating her on cases. I knew I didn't trust her; she wasn't someone I could rely on to have my back, like Cis. I wasn't sure if I liked her either. She was undeniably outstanding at what she did, but there was always something ruthless and calculating about her that she didn't even attempt to hide.

I plunged my hand into my bag, yanked out my files, and slid them across the table for her to glance at.

'And this is Novik's, right? The same ones from the email? For me to hold on to?' Isla asked, snatching them up to examine.

'It is, indeed. CCTV at 22.34 at the off-licence, very clearly intoxicated, very clearly displaying aggressive tendencies.'

Isla flicked rapidly through the photos, like an addict receiving her long-withheld fix.

'God damn,' she said with a triumphant smile. 'Sometimes I

wish I could just get this out spontaneously in a trial, you know, like a really awesome silver bullet. But no, instead, I have to go through all the boring procedures. Disclosure, let the defence prepare and all that. What an absolute bore. Just once, I wish they'd let me Atticus Finch it.'

'Atticus Finch was the defence in the book, though, right?' I asked, trying to remember it from school. 'Tommy Robinson?'

'Tom Robinson,' Isla said. 'Don't ever call him Tommy again.'

Isla shoved the photos back into the paper folder and pushed it very uncarefully into her handbag as she took her second hefty swig of her coffee, finishing the cup.

'Anything else in the pipeline I need to know about?' she asked. 'I heard you're investigating some old codger gone missing? Sure he didn't just wander off and fall down a drain? That's what happened to Grandad Paul.'

'Yeah, we're looking into that right now,' I said, very careful of the words I chose to say to the lawyer. 'Currently, it's fruitless. But we have forensics studying some samples, so hopefully we'll have some more solid leads over the next few days.'

'Sure, just keep me posted.' Isla's face ever so subtly twitched into a smirk. 'Did hear that you chucked up on some evidence, though.'

This was never going to end, was it?

'I vomited, *outside*, due to food poisoning. It wasn't on any actual *evidence*,' I clarified for the umpteenth millionth time. Isla – obviously – didn't believe it, though, as she mimed spewing vomit into her handbag over the photos I had just given her.

'Hilarious,' I replied, deadpan.

'Oh, don't be such a bloody bore, Gareth. You've always been so serious. Your poor wife,' Isla said with an overdramatic scowl, placing a hand a little too close for comfort on my wrist. I gently pulled away. I was never quite sure if Isla was just overly touchy-feely or if she maybe had a bit of a thing for me. Either way, I had no intention of finding out. 'So, what do you think happened? Some guy comes in, stabs a pensioner for the sheer thrill of it?' she asked, indifferent, as always, to the gory details.

'We think there may have been some premeditation involved, yeah,' I said, my mind flicking back to the removed blood stains on the carpet, and of course, the charming note reading:

> *Stay away from her or I'll kill you.*

Isla slouched back in her chair, only partly satisfied, for now. I knew it was best to keep schtum about what we had found in the attic at this point. She would have had a field day with that. It was all about tiptoeing around the classic lie of omission with Isla.

I did, however, feel that small prick in my chest and slight gurgle in my stomach as the memory from last week went through my mind again. My pulse ever so slightly began to quicken, and the words began to spill out as quickly as the kebab had a few days ago.

'Imagine someone truly vile ends up murdered, like a real A-tier bastard. Would you ever struggle to prosecute the guy that killed them?'

'How vile are we talking?' Isla asked.

'Pretty bloody vile.'

Isla leaned in, her voice dropping to a hushed whisper, tinged with palpable excitement. 'Intriguing,' she mused, clearly fascinated by what I was asking her. 'But no, the law is the law. You can't simply take lives, regardless of how awful a person is. That's precisely why they pay me – to ensure that "justice" prevails and those found guilty find their way to a cot at Berwyn.'

'But, come on, sometimes people are driven to extremes to

protect others. Right? Like, surely justice isn't always just what the law dictates?'

Her response was cold and uncaring. 'If I didn't prosecute, Gareth, I wouldn't have been able to have my honeymoon in the Maldives.'

You know, I didn't think I actually liked Isla at all. She'd never even thanked me for looking after her milk snake.

I went back into the office. The stares from other detectives had now seemingly subsided, but I still felt a little like a gazelle in the lion enclosure. Steve and Darren had mostly kept to themselves ever since I'd started, but over the past few days, Darren had seemed to make a conscious effort at communicating with me. Telling me how the case was progressing, updating me every chance he got. He'd even offered to get me a drink from the cafeteria. I didn't want to commend myself, but I did wonder if my personable efforts with him had finally paid off in some way. Maybe he felt bad about the lasagne; maybe he'd realised I wasn't such a bad guy after all. I walked across the office and sat down at my desk, though any pleasant, warming feeling of potentially being liked by a colleague was swiftly cut down by the thick wad of case files in front of me. From gleaning through the notes, it seemed that there were three points of information that had emerged over the past few days.

Number one: they had recovered the doorbell footage from Beryl's son, who had all the video streamed right into his laptop, and sure enough, we had video confirming that Fran was the last person to go and see Mr O'Neill. Just before, he had exited a taxi with his grocery shopping, which had set off the motion detector on the doorbell. She had followed behind him as he entered his house only a few moments later. They had both gone in at around 3pm, but only Fran had come out, an hour and a half later, carrying some enormous bin bags.

Which was longer than Fran had implied she had helped him for. Darren and Steve had combed through the rest of the footage, before contacting the taxi driver in question to ask some questions about Mr O'Neill, but had found nothing of interest.

Fran had smashed the doorbell camera a few days later in quite an impressive form of clumsiness, meaning that any footage after that point was through a shattered, iridescent lens. However, O'Neill hadn't been picked up by the camera between returning with his shopping and Fran's accident. Although he could easily have left his house without the motion-detector picking it up. We had been told by Beryl herself that the camera was extraordinarily incompetent.

Number two: they had begun conducting very casual interviews with a few of the neighbours, and it had all come back that Mr O'Neill was – to put it mildly – a bit of a weirdo. There had been repeated stories of Mr O'Neill being antisocial, reclusive and aggressive, often shouting obscenities at the small children who lived on the other side of his house if they ever built up enough courage to trespass one inch onto his property on their bikes.

Number three: they had done a little digging on his business, but the fact that the Heart of Hope records were close to half a century old had meant a lot of it had got stuck through hard-copy bureaucracy, with a bunch having been ravaged by the festering mould that made O'Neill's attic smell like a dog's armpit. Nevertheless, it was understood that O'Neill's business hadn't gone under because of financial difficulties; there had been something else at play there. My assumption: not something that was exactly legal.

I spotted more case work and paperwork on my desk to sign off. On the top of it was a handwritten note:

Vivian wants to see you at some point. Good luck, darling. C.

Archives had sent through everything they could find on O'Neill. Most of it was records of his various charity works. Pictures of him donating books to schools, opening community centres. I was surprised there weren't pictures of him healing the sick at this rate.

When I'd finally gathered enough courage, I took a big breath, put on my big-boy pants, and walked across the office. I executed the classic two knocks on Vivian's office door. She was seated at her desk, gazing slack-jawed at her computer, and gestured me in without even attempting to acknowledge me or generally try and look in my direction.

'Are you okay, Gareth?' she asked in a monotone as I skulked into her office and slumped into the chair that I felt must have gained an imprint of me by now. Her words may sound nice on paper, but her voice didn't have one iota of empathy. It was as if she was passively analysing how much spark I had left in the tank before becoming a complete crash, the way you'd ask a mechanic how many more miles you've got left in your Toyota Aygo before it breaks down on the M4.

'I'm okay,' I muttered, trying to rally my energetic, work-efficient self. 'Just cracking on, you know.'

'Okay,' she said slowly, repeating my word but elongating the vowels to indicate that she clearly didn't believe what I was saying. She shuffled some papers in front of her and began to speak, her eyes not even bouncing up to meet mine.

'I spoke to the chief superintendent last night about the way this case was progressing. We think there is a high chance that we may have only just uncovered the tip of the iceberg, and for a case like this, where there is a particular... set of circumstances behind it, we've decided to go in hard.'

I didn't want to feel any more smug, but I had begged and begged for Vivian to investigate this case, and now it had the attention of the chief superintendent. Although, that did seem peculiar – those at such high levels never normally got involved in cases like this. Was this because of the letter from the police chief that I had found in O'Neill's attic? How were they connected to this?

Vivian paused and looked upwards, still avoiding my gaze, but I saw her eyes rapidly scanning left to right. She had memorised this whole speech already. This was simply a monologue she was reciting, that I was being forced to listen to.

'With this case, Gareth, I think you're too closely connected...'

True.

'... and I believe it goes above your experience level.'

Dick.

'Not only has this happened right on your doorstep, but there is also a likelihood that your wife could be brought in as a suspect.'

What? Fran? They thought Fran could have killed him? Were they on crack?

'I want you to have complete and utter ignorance to this case. Darren, Steve and Cecilia will be briefed this morning about not involving you in any aspect of it. Let me say that if you do try and get involved, it may be grounds for severe disciplinary action. Do I make myself clear?'

I stared back at her for a moment. She was ready for a fight. I could see her fingers drumming on the pen nervously, and I could just about make out the vibrations that her tapping foot was causing across the carpet floor. This was all completely ridiculous, but little did Vivian know, I was a total and utter people-pleaser.

'Absolutely,' I said, trying to muster something of a polite and understanding smile. 'Not a problem.'

Vivian leaned back on her chair, folding her arms and slipping her hands against her ribs as if she was trying to hug herself in a weird kind of comfort embrace. I hadn't known her long, but she looked nervous, as if she was the one in the wrong about doing this.

'You're not going to fight me on this?' she asked, somewhat in disbelief.

'I could put up more of a fight if you'd like?' I replied. 'I can get a little mad, maybe storm out and slam the door as hard as I can?'

She didn't even attempt to crack a smile at my comedy attempt. I'd thought five years of marriage with Fran had given me some great sarcasm skills or, as Fran would describe it, 'elegant sardonic wit'. And here it was, being used on people who didn't even appreciate it.

'I do have one question,' I said as I edged towards the door, speaking against my better judgement. 'If O'Neill was doing something a little shady, how did he get away with it for so long? No one picked up on it? Not at all?'

I spun around to see if Vivian was still looking at her computer, but she was looking directly at me for the first time today. For a fraction of a moment, her eyes flashed with something that – to me – looked like a bit of pride. Or maybe it was trapped wind; I couldn't be sure.

'All I know is he was *known* to the police well before this case,' Vivian emphasised, lifting both of her palms as if she was surrendering to me. 'That's all I know.'

So, I walked back to my desk, slid my hand underneath the collections of files, documents and folders, and balanced them precariously as I slowly strode over to Darren and dropped the pile in front of him. He jolted at the smack of the small forest's-worth of paper hitting the table.

'Good luck, mate,' I said blankly.

I knew I needed to somehow find a way to clear Fran from the investigation before she got dragged in. But if the superintendent was getting involved, maybe there was far more going on than I had originally thought.

I felt my phone vibrate in my trouser pocket, and pulled it out to see 'Husband Hunk' had texted me.

Husband Hunk?

It took a second for the neurons in my brain to connect. I had accidentally taken Fran's phone with me, a fact reinforced by the message preview on the phone screen:

> You took the wrong phone, you plonker.

I scoffed to myself as I offered a small prayer that I hadn't left any tabs open about how to be an alpha male in the bedroom. I typed in the pass code and swiped up on Fran's phone to unlock and text back, but the notes section opened:

- Clean the wine stain
- Write the shopping list
- Reset the camera
- Get rid of the rubbish
- Pack the shopping away
- Feed the cat

TWELVE

GARETH

'So, say that word again, but a bit slower?' I asked Fran as I leaned as far back in the car seat as I could, scraping the tips of my fingers across the roof. Across the quiet road, I watched a woman carefully watering the plants in her front garden.

'Progesterone,' Fran said to me, sounding out the word. 'It's a hormone test that checks if I'm ovulating.'

'And they just take your blood?'

'Yep. Easy as pie, so hopefully we'll have a few more answers when those results come back. How's your day going?'

'It's... fine,' I said, as I kept stretching until I finally felt the satisfying crunch of my spine clicking into place. 'I just feel... cream crackered. Vivian has got me doing this admin work rather than my actual job.'

'Why's that, my love?' I could hear the concern in her voice.

'I don't know. I *think* that she *thinks* I'm burnt out or something. Maybe this trying-for-a-baby thing is having more of an impact than I thought,' I lied. I didn't want to ruin her peace of mind any further with the news that she could be a suspect.

'Yeah, I know, it's tough,' Fran said. I heard her pause as a thought must have drifted into her mind. 'Hey, why don't we just press stop for a little bit after the tests today? We can take a minute to just let ourselves recuperate. It's not like we have to race this. We have plenty of time.'

'That is a... great idea,' I said, pushing my palm across my face and into my hair. 'I love you so much, my beautiful girl.'

'I love you, too, my handsome man. Look, I'd better go, but just come home early tonight, okay? Let's go to the cinema or something. We need to do something to take our minds off things. It's been kind of non-stop. I've got to go, but I love you, okay?' Fran made some vague kissing sounds before hanging up.

I smiled to myself as I pushed Fran's phone back deep into my pocket. I didn't ask her about the notes app, but the fact that it would be easy to connect the list there to the current situation with Mr O'Neill had to just be one of those weird coincidences, didn't it? Clean the wine stain? Fran was the clumsiest person around; she'd probably just spilt something and corrected it before I'd even realised. I was always nagging her about not drinking red on the living room sofa. Reset the camera? That may have just been an autocorrect about fixing Beryl's; maybe 'replace' was what she'd meant to write. It was probably all just vaguely connected, but it didn't incriminate Fran in any way. I knew I was overthinking this hugely.

But my mind still found itself thinking: *what if?* But, look, Fran hadn't killed O'Neill. I knew it, and deep down, I just felt it. This was the woman I'd married, the woman I was trying to have a child with. And she had no reason to do it. No one just wakes up one day and decides to kill their neighbour. Besides which, Fran always told me literally everything, from the grossest details about her bodily functions to the most embarrassing and humiliating stories at university. There was no way she could ever keep anything like that from me.

I sighed, and turned my attention back to the woman carefully tending to her daffodils. She was middle-aged with long, mousey-blonde hair, glasses and a thick woolly cardigan. She looked like the type of secondary school English teacher who'd force-feed you *Of Mice and Men*. I knew this wasn't exactly in line with official police regulations, but I thought it couldn't hurt to at least talk to her. I had stumbled upon her details in the reams of paper we'd found in O'Neill's attic – a small scrap of paper that simply said 'Maeve', followed by this address. I had my hunch about who this could be. But more importantly, she might have something that could lead me to the killer and get Fran out of Vivian's crosshairs before they found their way over to her.

I gently got out of the car and waved as I approached her. The woman shot me a suspicious glance as I drew closer.

'Hello,' I said, doing my best to channel friendly Neighbourhood Gareth. 'Sorry for disturbing you. Are you Maeve Chatterly?'

She didn't answer right away, just glared at me, narrowing her eyes slightly. 'Who's asking?' she said, not entirely hostile, but certainly not friendly either.

'My name's Detective Donoghue. I'm just here to ask a few questions, if that would be all right.'

'About David?'

I shook my head, assuming David to be her son or partner. The way she asked me made me think that David was an individual who often found himself in trouble with the law; I'd probably arrested him before.

'No, about your father: Gordon O'Neill.'

She scoffed and then abruptly picked up her watering can and stormed back inside, slamming the door shut behind her. I knew better than to follow her. Safe to say O'Neill's daughter was firmly a dead end.

As I was driving back from Maeve Chatterly's, feeling slightly defeated, an alert pinged through on my phone. It was a message from Cis, asking to meet in the station car park ASAP. It was a slightly peculiar message to receive from her; we were local police detectives, not rogue MI6 operatives. Nevertheless, when I finally pulled into the station, I spotted her straight away, leaning against her car near the back of the basement, arms folded, as if she'd been waiting for me for hours.

'I heard you're kicked off the case,' she said, glancing over each of her shoulders, vigilantly scanning for eavesdroppers.

'Yeah, something like that,' I murmured, exiting the car and slamming the door shut behind me. 'This feels like a very poor attempt to be clandestine, Cis. Is this the part where you tell me we need to go off-grid? Throw in our badges and become vigilantes in the police station car park?' I said in the best Dirty Harry accent I could attempt.

Cis sheepishly looked downwards, focusing on a loose thread in her trousers. She fiddled with it, still not turning her head up to look at me. A lot of people didn't want to make eye contact with me today.

'I'm telling you this as a friend, but they're calling in your wife for official questioning,' she said, still not meeting my eyes. 'Not arresting her, just under the guise of a witness statement. Vivian thinks she could be a suspect, so has asked Darren and Steve to go and get some answers from her.'

I felt a deep, cold rage begin to bubble and froth inside me as Cis spoke, but I just did my best to look pensive in response.

'Right,' was all I could manage to say, biting back everything else I wanted to yell at her. I knew Cis was just the messenger, but still, part of me was mad at her for even being the one saying it to me. I ran my hands nervously through my hair again, tugging on tight to the back of it. It may have been my imagination, but I could have sworn I felt at least ten hairs leap off my scalp to their deaths. 'So why? On what grounds, exactly?'

Cis didn't say anything. Her eyes now seemed transfixed on the ground.

'Tell me,' I said, still trying – but not really succeeding – to control the tone of my voice.

'Forensics have found a lot. We found bone cartilage and the remains of organs in O'Neill's shower drain. We think he was murdered in his bedroom and then cut up in his shower, and his remains were disposed of somehow.'

'Shit,' I groaned, placing my hands on my face. 'But nothing that directly incriminates Fran?'

'No. This is the thing, Gareth. Nothing that directly incriminates her at all.'

'And no motive?'

'No motive whatsoever. But look, they have something else too that I think you should know about. Off the record, but I think this could help the case.'

'You mean, that could lead to the arrest of my wife.'

Cis shot me an exasperated and frustrated look, her eyes meeting mine for the first time in this conversation.

'You know that's the last thing I want, Gareth, and I believe just as much as you that Fran didn't do this. But we need to stop seeing this as Fran being incriminated, and rather as a chance to get her vindicated. She tells her story, proves her innocence, and all this goes away. This is that opportunity, okay, darling?' she said, grabbing both my arms and giving me a light, reassuring shake.

I forgot how good Cis was in a crisis, the right kind of calm and collected person you needed by your side.

'What's the other thing you need to tell me?'

'Now *this* you can't tell anyone, but I need to get ahead of the curve.'

'Okay, sure, fine, whatever,' I mumbled as she reached into her bag and yanked out a file, passing it to me. She did another quick spin of her head, scanning the park for any colleagues who may walk into this secretive rendezvous.

It was a screenshot from Beryl's video doorbell, dated a few weeks before Mr O'Neill's disappearance but about a week after Fran and I moved in. It was a Wednesday, midday, so both Fran and I were away at work. It was a blurry, distorted image of a car pulled up outside our house. Another taxi. I moved my eyes up the image and saw a man walking towards Mr O'Neill's house. The picture was pixelated and grainy, so it was hard to make out any real defining characteristics.

'Do you recognise this figure?' Cis asked. 'You may not, and that's fine, but I need to know.'

I squinted and looked at the body more closely. I didn't know him well, but I certainly recognised him.

THIRTEEN

FRAN

'So, what you're actually saying is that I'm a suspect,' I blurted out. Gareth had droned on and on about police procedure and the overly complex ways that their cases are conducted for the whole car journey. He'd insisted that I shouldn't worry and just treat the interview as a conversation between me and a friend.

'No, no, that's not what I'm saying,' he said, glancing away from the road he was driving along to look at me. Lying wasn't my husband's forte, which was ironic considering his job revolved around being at skilled at detecting deceit in others. His tell was a slight pause before speaking, a dead giveaway he wasn't being entirely truthful. 'Look, you were the last person we know of who saw Gordon O'Neill alive,' he continued. 'So you may have the critical piece of information that could solve this whole case, even if you don't think so right now.'

'I just packed away his shopping, had some chit-chat that went on too long, and took out his rubbish. He grumbled something to me as I left, but that's about it,' I said. I had replayed my fake memories now so many times that they did almost feel real. 'I don't know what more I can add at this point.'

'Okay? See, so that could line up with something else

they've discovered or what someone else has said to them. The truth of the matter, Fran, is that you didn't kill him, so you really don't need to worry.' Gareth spoke softly, trying to reassure me whilst we turned another corner on our way back home. 'Although, I wish he'd died before we bought the house. We could've got it so much cheaper that way.'

I didn't find his joke funny.

'Truth of the matter is, I'm a suspect. I just have to find a way to prove to them it wasn't me,' I said matter-of-factly, feeling reassured, not by Gareth, but by my own self confidence.

Gareth opened his mouth to speak as if he had some retort planned, but he jutted his bottom lip out and just bobbed his head up and down instead. He was stalling.

'Well... kind of, yeah. Everyone is a suspect. But you didn't kill him, so you're fine.'

'But what if they think I killed him?'

He paused again. 'They won't. It will all work out, and it will all be okay,' he said, comforting me one last time. 'And like I say, you didn't kill him, so you don't need to worry.'

'OKAY!' I yelled, smashing my hands down onto the dashboard. Gareth jolted in shock and the car weaved across the road for a second, but he quickly regained control.

The car went eerily silent.

I didn't mean to shout, but in a millisecond after the umpteenth time Gareth had paused and then told me that I didn't kill O'Neill and not to worry, what had become something of a mild, irksome annoyance suddenly festered into anger, which evolved into a fearsome rage, which expressed itself in me abruptly and spontaneously combusting. The idea that Gareth, even for a moment, could entertain the idea I might be a murderer filled me with a feeling I didn't think I could even name.

Gareth carried on driving silently as I crossed my arms and twisted my body to look out the window.

'Sorry, Beryl,' Gareth said.

We had both admittedly forgotten that Beryl was still in the car, holding onto Tony, who had just come back from the vet's. We had seen her walking through the torrential rain as we were driving back from the cinema and had offered her a lift. We didn't want to ask what was wrong with Tony, but through careful eye contact that we had refined over the years of marriage, we thought that it may have been a broken penis since he had a strangely shaped cast around that general area.

'Not a worry at all,' Beryl said, her voice clearly a little shaken by the quick shift in tone on my part. 'It is a bit stressful, isn't it? A murder in our neighbourhood. Like something you'd watch on telly.'

We pulled into the driveway as Gareth, ever the gentleman, opened the car door for Beryl. Cradling Tony tenderly like a newborn, she slowly began to amble across the road towards her house.

I lurched out of the car, closing the door behind me swiftly to get some space from my husband, but found myself spinning around and jogging after Beryl.

'Hey, Beryl,' I said, calling after her. 'Is Tony... okay?'

Okay, all right, I'll admit it. Maybe I liked Tony a little bit. Maybe there was a small part of my being that actually cared for the well-being of the world's most vicious and horny dog.

'Well, we always thought that he hated Dalmatians. Turns out, he was quite physically attracted to them.'

'Was?' I asked.

'He attempted to consummate his relationship with one, and it all ended rather painfully, shall we say,' Beryl said politely, and then, as subtly as she could – for the sake of Tony's pride, I'm sure – motioned her finger towards his man parts.

'Enough said. Well, thanks, Beryl,' I answered. I didn't need to know any more. She wished us good night and walked across the road and into her house.

I paced into the house silently, walking into the kitchen, filling up the kettle, and as violently as I could, slamming down the switch to set it to boil. Gareth walked in behind me and gently placed his hand around my arm.

'Hey, my love, are you okay? I'm sorry I went on about the whole thing for too long. I'm really sorry,' he said, rotating me around to pull me in for an embrace. 'I know between my job, the pregnancy thing, O'Neill, this has all been so stressful.'

He wrapped his arms around me, and I felt the anger in my body melt as I lifted my arms up around his shoulders and squeezed him tight. I was sure that it was just that he didn't want me to worry, but I couldn't help but think that maybe, deep down, Gareth thought I was the murderer. Of course, I was. But maybe it wasn't so much about not wanting Gareth to know I'd killed O'Neill, but more about the lens of a murderer I feared he'd see me through if he knew the truth about everything.

'I'm sorry,' he said again, muffled, as he pressed his face into my shoulder.

'It's okay,' I said, my fury beginning to dissipate. I squeezed him tighter. 'You don't think I did it, do you?'

I just wanted him to still see me as *his* Fran, his wife, not as a suspect in a case.

Gareth gave a chortle, placed both of his hands tenderly on my cheeks, and gently pushed his forehead against mine.

'I've known you for years. Do you think I'd ever believe you could ever even hurt a fly?'

Somehow, the elation of knowing that Gareth loved me outweighed any kind of guilt I had lurking around in my subconscious. It was nice to pretend that I didn't have this weighing over me for a brief moment. We held each other in the kitchen for a little while longer, both of us not wanting to be the first to let go.

'Just remember, you're not guilty, so there's nothing to worry about, darling,' Cecilia said as she walked out of the cubicle and joined me in washing her hands in the sink. I refused to call her 'Cis', the nickname Gareth had coined for her during training camp.

'Yeah, thanks,' I said, disinterested as we both stood uncomfortably at the sink, the sound of our hands squelching the ancient hand soap echoing around the bathroom. I was grateful to use the absurdly loud hand dryer, its mechanical roar cutting sharply through the awkward silence. One of the many uneasy moments Cecilia and I had experienced together since Gareth had first introduced us at a very tense board game night.

I left the toilets and hoped I might have lost her while she took the time to use Zeus's almighty hand dryer, but alas, she suddenly reappeared behind me before I had a chance to get my bearings in the corridor.

'Interview Room B, right? I'll show you the way.'

I didn't even have a moment to respond before she placed a still-damp hand on the small of my back and gently but firmly steered me down the police hallway. Interesting technique, but I'd be damned if I let Cecilia get any sort of power play over me.

'So, has Gareth been investigating this case?' I asked her point-blank.

She may have been shocked by the question, but she didn't really show it. She just tilted her head to the side, trying to articulate an answer.

'I think this is the kind of case a lot of us have had some sort of involvement in, but Gareth isn't leading the investigation, for obvious reasons.'

'Why?' I asked, playing the fool.

Cecilia shot me a glance that did make me feel slightly idiotic. In all honesty, I don't think she meant it as such, but I decided I would add this to my ever-growing list of why I disliked her. Part of me felt a tiny prick of doubt after what she'd said. Had Gareth been involved in the investigation earlier on, but not told me? Surely, he wouldn't have kept that from me?

'Here we are,' Cecilia said, gesturing me to the wooden door adorned with a long piece of masking tape covering up a broken sign that presumably read INTERVIEW ROOM B.

'Cool, thanks, see you around,' I said, plonking myself down on one of the small benches outside the room. Cecilia gave a wry laugh as she pushed open the door and motioned for me to enter whilst holding on to the handle.

'We're ready for you,' she said playfully.

God, was this meant to be another of her power plays? I couldn't tell. What she'd done wasn't particularly mean or cruel, but there was just something about the way she did it. I pushed myself off the bench, trying to appear unfazed as I walked in, ignoring that stupid smile of hers that I could see out of the corner of my eye. Steve was already there, awkwardly munching on a chocolate bar, his expression fixed like he had just been caught in the act of some secret vice.

'Sorry,' he tried to say, spraying small chocolate flakes everywhere in the process. I twisted my head to avoid having to witness the unflattering sight.

Cecilia took a seat next to him, opposite me, with a longer-than-average desk between us. She offered me a glass of water and I politely declined, as Steve was scrambling frantically to get the recorder working. He repeatedly pushed a button, but I could see a small logo flashing on the opposite side of the device.

I didn't want Cecilia to think I was scared, so I just continued to half-heartedly smile in her general direction. Lord,

I'd forgotten how much I disliked her. Everything about her reeked of a Machiavellian character. Even on the dreadful board game night Gareth and I had attempted with her and her partner at the time a few years ago, everything from her comments on the food to the way she'd won at Risk had felt cunning and duplicitous. But just covert enough for her actions to come across as genuine. She was someone I could never really get my finger on.

'How's Mep?' Cecilia asked, sensing that my mind was elsewhere.

'Oh, Mep? The cat. His consistent screeching makes every day an absolute delight,' I remarked, avoiding her gaze as I kept my eyes fixed on the lone window in the interrogation room.

'I've always meant to ask: what does Mep mean, as a name?'

'It's a nickname,' I said, not willing to expand.

'Of?'

'Mephistopheles.'

'The demon?'

'Yeah.'

'From *Doctor Faustus*?'

'Well, he was from German folklore first.'

'Yeah, but you know, he's more generally known from *Doctor Faustus*.'

'Ah, well, tell a German that,' I fired back. Who did she think she was, trying to tell me who I'd named my cat after? I mean, it *was* after the demon from *Doctor Faustus*, but she shouldn't make those kinds of assumptions.

'It's working!' Steve said proudly, holding his trophy aloft before quietly placing it back down on the table.

They gave me the spiel that Gareth had already briefed me on. That I wasn't here as a suspect; I was here as a person of interest. There was no evidence against me that would implicate me as a potential suspect, and that I would need to sign some form at the end that may be used in court. Just when I thought Cecilia was done talking, she then went on to tell me I could walk out and leave at any time, and I didn't *have* to answer any questions, and they just wanted for it to be a friendly chat to find out a bit more about the case.

'So, Fran,' Cecilia said after they had finished the preamble. 'Why don't you tell us the events of Saturday the tenth, as accurately as you can.'

Listen. I am not a psychopath, sociopath or any other kind of crazy murderer freak. This is something I feel I've been quite transparent about. That being said, I know what I am about to explain to you is very much full psycho-killer, so please bear me with on this.

'Sure, of course. It was a few weeks ago now, so I apologise if I get anything wrong. But we had only moved in for about a month or so at that point, and I had met Gordon a few times. He's a quiet and reserved man.'

I made sure to refer to him in the present tense, to cover all my bases. I let my voice quiver just a little bit. I'd leave the tears for now; last time, it had worked a treat, but I had to work my audience. I interlaced my hands the same way Cecilia had and made sure to count five seconds of eye contact in my head for each person before switching to the other.

'Then that Saturday, I was doing some bits in the kitchen, and I saw him get out of the taxi he'd taken to the supermarket, and I could see from my window he was struggling with his shopping. So, I offered to help. Thought it might be a gesture of goodwill, you know? He said something that sounded like a yes when I went out to ask him, so I did. I carried the bags in, we took a few bags upstairs, left a few in the kitchen. Then we had a chat that seemed to go on forever about the price of semi-skimmed milk, and then I took his rubbish out for him as I left.'

In between that, I also drove a knife through his eye socket and cut his body up into pieces and disposed of it in the rubbish.

My mouth twitched. Like someone had just farted at a

funeral. *Don't smile, Fran. For the love of God, don't fucking smile.*

'And that was the extent of your interaction with Mr O'Neill?' Steve asked.

'I chatted to him for ages, it was just small talk. I wanted to make sure he was okay.' I had my doe eyes deployed now; they always worked a treat. I let them well up a bit, to really drive the message home, still fighting the battle with my face to not let the smile make an appearance.

I could see both Cecilia and Steve were unconvinced. The doe eyes were not having the impact I wanted. I'd thought Steve would be a doddle, but he seemed very unmoved by my act. Maybe I was losing my edge as I approached my thirties.

'Oh, and I cleaned up some milk, too, that he said he'd spilt the night before. He asked me if I wouldn't mind as he didn't have the knees for it.'

Was that a really bad move? It felt like a bad move. I don't know why I felt the impulse to say it, but I just did. I begged and prayed they would buy it.

Steve just nodded. The way his eyes had flared when I mentioned the milk meant there was some recognition there, and I carefully watched him as he glanced downwards and shifted his body towards Cecilia, who took a big sigh inward and crossed her legs, placing her interlaced fingers upon her knee.

Gareth had told me about this interrogation technique. They would wait and wait and wait until the witness continued to talk and babble, which would be when everything would come tumbling out. No one can stand silences, not even guilty people. But I could wait all day. I had daydreams and fantasies all prepared in my head for these very situations that I could get myself lost in.

'Anything else happen while you were with O'Neill? Anything of note he mentioned to you, even offhandedly?'

Cecilia asked, following about thirty seconds of silence during which I was quite happily wondering if I could rent four cars to quarter and dismember Clark and the exact logistics involved with doing that.

'You know an hour and a half is a long time to be in a house with a stranger, what else did you talk about?' Cecilia asked.

Maybe Gareth thought this was just going to be a case of simple witness questioning. Maybe Cecilia thought differently.

'Oh, well you should have heard him talk about the Neighbourhood Watch and besides, you ever tried to clean up milk out of Berber carpet?' I asked. 'Give it a go and get back to me.'

That was probably more aggressive than I'd intended, as I could see Cecilia almost wince at my response.

'Fran. We feel like there may be more to this story than what you're telling us.'

Gareth had told me this was a technique that they used. Even if the witness was saying everything they knew, the interviewers would always throw that one out there to see if it would garner any kind of result. But my body began to shift into survival mode again, the pumps in my brain churning out the adrenaline at a record rate, my limbic system was fully going buckaroo. What if I said O'Neill had tried to touch me, maybe rape me, even, and then I had pushed him off me in a fit of rage and run back to my house, and then in all of his regret, he had killed himself? That didn't seem smart. Who would kill themselves by knife through the eye? *Stick to the plan*, I kept thinking to myself. *Stick to the story that you've revisited and relived a hundred times at this point, and also don't fucking smile.*

'I... did find him to be quite odd. Quite strange. But I've told you everything about my encounter with him. I helped him with his shopping, spoke to him for a bit, cleaned up some milk, put his bins out, and then left.'

'And he said nothing to you about any travels or trips? Were there any signs he may have been planning to make a journey?' Cecilia queried.

'No.'

'And you hadn't seen him since then?'

'No, I don't think so.'

'And there was no suggestion that he was planning to hurt himself or put himself in any kind of danger?'

Not from himself.

'Not that I can think of. I mean, you're asking me all these questions, but I didn't know the guy,' I said, trying to really make sure I was looking both of them in the eye.

The two of them turned to look at each other and seemed to nod – some kind of small signal – as Cecilia reached deep into a briefcase and pulled out an A4 sheet with an image printed on it. She slid it across the table to me.

'Do you recognise this person?'

I felt I could breathe a little easier when I saw from the shape of the figure that it definitely wasn't me. It was the shape of a man – a small, frail man. I looked around the edges of the image and realised it was a screen capture from the video doorbell. Beryl's, I thought, the same one that I had obliterated, but the picture here was untainted by any shards of glass in the lens. I squinted my eyes to try and work out who the figure was that was walking into O'Neill's house, but I still couldn't make it out.

'I'm sorry, I can't make out who it is from this,' I said apologetically, moving the picture back across the table.

'Look again,' Cecilia said, gliding the paper back to me before I had even removed my hand. 'Really take a long, hard look and see if it could be anyone you know.'

What was she getting at? What was she trying to get me to see? I dragged the photo back to look at it again as decisively as I could. Black jacket, small frame, dark hair. I pushed my face closer to the image until all I could see was my nose, wondering if this mysterious man was the suspected killer at the moment, my knight in shining armour?

Then it clicked, and I had to summon all the acting prowess that I could recall from GCSE Drama to push the photo back across the table one more time.

'No, afraid I really don't know who this is. I'm sorry.'

'So, you really have no idea who may have wanted to cause harm to Mr O'Neill? You don't know anyone who would have been happy that he was killed?' Cecilia asked with a deeply mistrustful glare plastered on her face. I could see from her eyes that she knew I was bullshitting, and I was starting to wonder if maybe I didn't like Cecilia *because* she was a fantastic judge of character. Did she know I killed O'Neill? Did she know I was the one they were after? The one who had deviously killed the waste of human flesh and removed any trace of him. Surely no one was that good a detective to have realised that little old me was the one to have slaughtered Gordon O'Neill?

Suddenly, Cecilia and Steve's faces dropped, both slightly aghast, their expressions seeming to wrinkle up like they were disgusted by me. Did I have a bogey? I lifted my hand to the small groove below my nose, but it was dry. I followed their gaze, in case the problem was something behind me, but nothing.

Suddenly, it clicked.

I didn't need to look in the mirror to see that, despite my best efforts, a sly smile had crept along my face.

FOURTEEN
FRAN

This was all very bad.

It had been going remarkably well to begin with – no evidence, no body, no investigation, but now everything was spiralling out of control, and fast. The calculated, methodical part of my brain was rapidly being overtaken by the side that was screaming pure, utter panic.

And the smile – I know, I know, it was so unbelievably stupid. But it was completely involuntary. Surely, it had happened to other innocent people before. It was like when you start laughing when you're being scolded by some kind of superior; it's precisely because you know it's the worst thing you can possibly do under the circumstances.

Angus hadn't returned any of my calls; I had set an alarm on my phone every hour and twelve minutes to remind me to ring him, leave a message, and repeat until he answered, but there had been no such luck so far. The same boring generic answerphone greeted me every time, so I'd put the phone down, set the timer, and waited. The additional twelve minutes were more so that he wouldn't catch on that it wasn't being done on an hourly basis; I'd hoped he'd feel a little more urgency if I seemed to be more sporadic in my communications.

Mind you, I didn't think Angus had felt much urgency at all for the last twenty-odd years. I thought he spent most of his days masturbating, watching TV, and collecting newspapers. Not exactly strenuous, I imagined. But nevertheless, although I knew his phone had probably run out of charge or had been lost down the side of the sofa, that wasn't going to stop me from trying everything I could before I'd finally just drive to his shitty apartment and break the door down.

God, I had a lot of questions to ask that bastard.

But what had been more curious for me this morning was that I had realised I was late. In all the pandemonium, I hadn't been tracking my periods as stringently as normal. It was now I realised that it had been a week and a half since I was due. I knew that high levels of stress could impact your cycle – I remembered that revising for my A levels in a foster home had disrupted my usual pattern. But it did seem a little peculiar that the doctor had rung me, only a few moments after I'd realised, to ask if I had a spare hour for Gareth and I to come in and see him. There was something important he needed to discuss, he told me.

I didn't want to get excited or even to do a pregnancy test. One step at a time, I had to keep telling myself. I pushed any optimism out of my head before it could even take root. At the same time, part of me was wondering if I even really wanted a baby. I had to remind myself that that was just the nerves talking and that I didn't even know for a fact I was pregnant yet. This could all just be for Dr Patel to inform me that Gareth had spunked in the wrong petri dish.

A small, anxious part of my brain started to simmer and hint at the idea that maybe Gareth already knew, consciously or subconsciously, that I was the suspect the police were looking for. I shook it off. This was Gareth. He wouldn't be able to keep *that* from me. The only thing that had really made me question what he thought about me was the red pen.

Okay, should I have looked through his diary while he was sleeping? No. That was a big breach of trust and privacy, which are important things in a relationship, but I just couldn't help myself. He must have been adjacent to the O'Neill case, as there were a few words I could make out that alluded to it:

Knife, Beryl, Doorbell – but the main one being *Fran* – all scribed in red writing.

I know that sounds strange, but Gareth's notes were usually just scribbled with black biro, words running into each other, overlapping, smaller words underlining other, bolder words. It was an absolute mess of a diary. Occasionally, a small doodle of Batman would also make an appearance, but never in red pen. Why had he written my name in red ink?

I checked over the house, and we didn't have any red pens, so he must have done it at the office. Had he reached for it in a eureka moment? Maybe he'd simply borrowed it when one of his pens had run out of ink? Or maybe he'd gone to Staples to get a red pen just to write in his diary as a moment of significance? That would be silly, right? But there was something to me about that glaring red ink that made me want to crawl inside Gareth's head and find out what he was thinking about me.

I knew I probably should have told Gareth, but he clearly wasn't checking his phone and I really couldn't wait any longer. But when I got to the clinic, I quickly realised it wasn't nearly as fun being in the waiting room without my husband thinking out loud about the state of the wank rooms, or what kind of porn there would be. Dr Patel gave me his lovely smile and then led me into his office. He sat me down, and we exchanged the classic small talk.

'Could your husband not make it?' he asked as he wheeled himself on his chair from one end of the room to the other.

'He's working, I'm afraid.'

'Ah, okay, busy man,' he said with his signature warm smile, which suddenly began to deflate as if someone had just popped a pin in his cheek and squeezed out all of the joy from the man's face. He pushed himself forward on the chair, a loud squeak echoing around the room as he waddled towards me. He furrowed his eyebrows and interlocked his hands.

'I'm just going to come out with it. I've been looking at your ultrasound results and spoken to some of the embryologists, and I'm afraid that with this particular case, I think it is going to be very hard for you to conceive naturally with your husband.'

Oh.

'I know this may seem shocking, but it's important for you to know—'

'Whose fault is it?' was all I could manage to say in a half-whisper, half-croak.

'Well, it's no one's fault. No one is to blame here.'

I didn't really listen to the rest of what he said, his voice kind of faded out after a while and was replaced by the loud thumping of my heartbeat and a shrieking, high-pitched ringing thundering in my ears. Dr Patel kept talking and I tried my best to acknowledge his suggestion for us to try IVF. He told us our local council was very good at paying for it, and that if that didn't work, our journey to have children didn't have to end here. Adoption was always on the cards, and several other factors, such as stress and anxiety, were also variables in trying for a baby. He also said that he would need to do a lot more tests. He gave me a booklet, told me he'd be in touch, and tried to give my arm a comforting touch. It didn't work.

I walked out of the clinic and somehow managed to stumble across the tarmac and make it to my car. I yanked open the door, slid into the seat, locked the doors, and sat there for a little bit with my forehead pushed against the top of the steering wheel.

It could be the stress, I thought to myself. It could be the stress of this whole charade that had just affected my menstrual cycle badly. That could mean that when this had all blown over, a baby was still on the cards. Even if it wasn't the traditional way, IVF was still an option, right? But I couldn't get that stupid doctor's face out of my head. I bet Gareth's swimmers were all little Michael Phelpses. I was the problem. I was the one who couldn't get pregnant. My body was unable to do the one thing that it had evolved to do. It all felt just a little bit shameful, really.

It then began to dawn on me that I had absolutely no one to talk to. Gareth wasn't answering his texts. I couldn't get through to Angus. I didn't really want to bother any of my friends, most of whom I hadn't properly spoken to since the move. I was quite simply on my own. It was at times like this, I wished I had parents I could talk to about this kind of thing.

I didn't want to stay in the surgery parking space any longer, so I began to drive. I drove out of the surgery car park, through the city, and onto the motorway. I decided I would keep driving until my tank hit half, and then I would turn around and come back. Thoughts kept stumbling through my head. Was this fate punishing me? I'd taken a life – well, two lives – and now God wasn't giving me one in return. If I had just done nothing, would I be pregnant? Would we be starting our family?

Suddenly, Gareth finding out about me murdering someone didn't seem so bad. It was the moment when he found out I couldn't have children that I was terrified of.

I'd gone to church with Gareth once, when we were newly engaged. Classic Gareth, of course, he'd wanted to get married in a church like the good Christian boy he is, so we'd had to go every other Sunday to show our faces, and all the change we had scraped together for saving would go straight into the collection tin. The vicar had adored the sound of his own voice. Maybe he should have considered a career as a podcast host. I couldn't remember many of the sermons, but I did remember one in which he'd told us how, in those Old Testament times, when a woman was barren, she could be compelled to share her husband with a fertile rival. Often, it turned out that their infertility was associated with sin. When Rachel had pled with Jacob, 'Give me children or else I die,' her husband had only responded with, 'Am I in the place of God who has withheld from you the fruit of the womb?'

An omnibenevolent God, indeed.

A car blared its horn at me as I got lost deeper and deeper into my thoughts and began to drift onto the right-most lane. I yanked the wheel to the left, and an elderly man cursed at me as he drove past.

I clocked that the small needle on my dashboard had hit halfway, and I glanced up from the road to look at the signs. My subconscious had known where I was driving before I had even realised.

I left the motorway, drove down the pothole riddled A-road and parked up around a few other cars. It was a classic rural car park with no real lines or rules, and a Land Rover which had blocked in a number of cars already. I saw a young couple opposite me also just pull up. A broad and bearded man opened the door for his partner. The woman hopped out, laughing at some joke he made. They exchanged a few words to one another before she pecked him on the cheek and laid a hand on his chest. Then, grabbing a pink harness, the woman reached into the backseat of the car to pull a small creature out.

Had it been a baby, I may have just gone and offed myself right there and then. But it was just a Chihuahua, one that the man hoisted up and then slid into the front carrier on the woman's chest. The Chihuahua's line of sight met mine for a minute, and I could almost hear his croaky, gravelly voice calling out to me.

'End meeeee.'

I started walking across the field. It was abandoned now, of course. Moss and ivy had only just begun to slither their way across the walls, and a long, thick line of red graffiti which simply read BALLS was spraypainted onto one wall of the building. I'd thought it would have been turned into something by now, but maybe it was beyond repair. There was no door, no windows. Not even the flooring had survived. I smoothed my hands over the dull beige brick as I tried to forget what my home had looked like twenty years ago.

I wasn't sure why I'd chosen to subject myself to this, feeling the worst I'd felt in years and then opting to only deepen that pain by coming here. Maybe it was because I'd realised that I couldn't feel any worse than I did now. I remembered just how hungry I would feel in the evenings as a child, hoping that the clawing in my stomach would subside for long enough that I could go to sleep and have my one hot meal at school. Edith and her annoying pal, Angus, were always bothering and pestering me with their questions when all I really wanted to do was go to sleep so the hunger wouldn't feel quite so ravenous.

And of course, I remember the fire. I remember the smoke, so thick you could barely make out your hand in front of your face, and Clive bursting into our room in the middle of the night, shouting to get us out. The air so hot it burned the passageways of your throat just to breathe, and despite that, still trying to scream Edith's name at the top of my lungs. I remember being eleven years old and learning that they made coffins children-sized. How old would she be now? Twenty-seven? Christ, would she be married now? Would she have children?

I traced my fingers along the faded, burnt lettering – ST NICHOLAS'S CHILDREN'S HOME – that lingered on the scorched brick. How ironic. St Nicholas: the patron saint of protecting children.

I decided to drive back, and the thoughts of my useless womb began to subside. Instead, something else was beginning to take over: Clark. I just needed to find him and drive a knife across his throat, or maybe through his scalp. I think the scalp has more nerve endings.

Again, just to reiterate: not a psychopath.

I was getting hungry, so I decided to stop by a small gimmicky American-style diner a few miles off the motorway. I hopped in one of the booths in the corner and ordered a steak sandwich and a cup of tea. I flicked through the pamphlet Dr Patel had given me as the waitress delivered my order, drawing small moustaches and glasses on the faces of happy families to make myself feel better.

Using the steak knife, I rehearsed my grip on the blade's handle a few times. I hoped no other customers would look over in my general direction, watching as I repeatedly stabbed my knife into the sandwich again and again without even taking a single bite.

This was perhaps quite an effective coping strategy for thinking about Clark. It did take my mind off everything. But I knew I had to be smarter about this one, less impulsive, and more strategic. I doubted I would get away with the same approach for the third. But after going back to St Nicholas's and the memories of the fire coming back so vividly, for the first time in my life, I realised I could actually be the one to kill all three of them – the trifecta. It was ironic, really. Three kills would officially make me a serial killer.

FIFTEEN
GARETH

'So, it's my first day on the beat, I'm helping out as a community support officer – you know, the usual – when I see a man, drunk like a fish, passed out in a wheelie bin,' I said, trying not to notice the vacant expressions barely looking in my direction. 'And I asked him where he lived and if I could walk him home and the guy was absolutely passed out, right? So, I tried to get him to his feet. I'd grab him, pin him against the wall, but then he'd slide right back down onto the ground again. So, the officer I was with, Linda I think her name was, we both hoisted him up and dragged him home, one arm each over our shoulders. He would mumble and groan instructions every so often about where his house was. It was this lovely cottage. We thought we'd just leave him there, let him walk in, but when we tried to unhoist him from our shoulders he collapsed right back down again. So, we literally dragged him to the door, rang the doorbell. Both of us wondering, how can you get so pissed that you can't even walk? But then his wife opens the door, and she says, "Well, where's his wheelchair?"'

I waited for anyone to laugh but they just continued to glare at me, dumbfounded. Normally, that story absolutely killed whenever I told it. I confess it wasn't actually true; it was adapted from a joke I had heard somewhere, but it made for a good icebreaker when people asked if I had any funny police stories.

I suppose they were only nine. But not even any of the other officers in the classroom laughed; their looks, too, were treacherously vacant.

'Tough crowd,' I heard one of the others say at the back of the classroom.

Lord above. I hated Schools Outreach Day.

'Okay, well, thank you so much for that interesting story, Detective Donoghue. Class 4B, let's give him a big round of applause,' the teacher said, laden with fake zest.

I wandered ruefully to the back of the classroom as the pupils gave me very scattered and broken applause.

'Nice job,' Cis whispered patronisingly, as we both leaned against an iridescent wall display of how photosynthesis happens.

'Ha, good one!' I retorted sarcastically in a hushed tone as we half-watched one of the other officers from the station invite a child up to put handcuffs on a dummy.

'So...' she muttered. 'I don't think you answered my question.'

Urgh, I had forgotten she had asked me that on the way here. How the hell was I supposed to answer that?

'Yes, if it came to it, yes, I would, of course,' I said as quietly as I could, while trying to hide my irritation with her. I didn't think there was the slightest possibility of it ever seeming likely that Fran had killed Mr O'Neill; that the loving wife I had been with for a quarter of my life had murdered this old man in cold blood.

'You sure? You know spousal bias is a thing, right?' Cis responded.

'If I truly believed that my wife killed Mr O'Neill, I'd bring her in myself, I promise you,' I said to Cis quietly yet sternly, and I believed what I said. I wouldn't make a promise I couldn't keep. But Cis had been asking me this kind of stuff all week since Fran had given her statement, and all it had achieved was to make me feel even more distant from her, like I was betraying her by even being involved in the case. 'So, can we just... drop it now, please?'

I didn't really want to discuss this when I still hadn't found a meaningful way to exonerate Fran from the investigation. My research into O'Neill and his Heart of Hope foundation had continued to be frustratingly unfruitful. But those notes on her phone... something about them was still bothering me. I told myself it was nothing, but I knew I'd have to ask her about them when the investigation wrapped up.

'Well, department policy means it couldn't be you arresting her, but it's still good to know.'

One of the teaching assistants spun rapidly around in her chair and hushed us. We both lowered our volume again, feeling as if we had regressed a few years, and obediently cowered our heads in shame.

'Do *you* believe I'd arrest my wife?' I asked after a minute or so had passed, and the assistant had gone to help some kid yank a pen he had got stuck up his nose.

'Gareth, do you remember that time you turned over a Twix from a witness when you thought it could be considered bribery? I have no doubts that you, sir, would turn over your own wife in an instant,' Cis said. 'If Fran did kill O'Neill, she covered her steps well. But there won't be any kind of footage or evidence that would incriminate her. This is the problem.'

'Okay. Can you just... not?' I said to Cis while folding my arms, starting to feel she was pushing my patience a little too far. 'I don't particularly want to talk about this. The idea of my wife being a murder suspect doesn't fill me with joy.'

'I get it, sorry, that's on me, darling,' Cis admitted as she placed what was meant to be a comforting hand on my shoulder. Both of our eyes snapped to watch the 'drugs are bad' part of the presentation that Steve took over to lead.

'Well, this is painfully ironic,' Cis murmured as Steve drastically dumbed down the UK's war on drugs for primary school kids. Didn't quite know what Cis meant by that, but I was afraid to talk any more or face the wrath of the teaching assistant. Part of me wanted to shout out: 'Don't listen, kids, they say cocaine only makes you party harder!' but I decided that potentially being suspended probably wasn't worth the embarrassment it would cause Steve.

'So, Angus? Have you brought him in?' I asked, breaking the silence that had steadily built up between Cis and I as we'd left the classroom and walked through the school corridor after Steve's sermon had come to a close.

'Well, we went to him to talk, he refused to leave his house, so we set up there to ask him some questions. God damn, the place was piled high with crap and reeked to high heaven. Have you been round there recently?'

'No... no, I've never been,' I said.

'You've never been round to Fran's brother's house?' Cis asked, not even trying to mask her surprise.

'I've met him two, maybe three times, and he's said about that many words to me, too,' I explained, realising it would seem a bit crazy to someone who didn't know about Angus. 'The guy is a recluse, he barely comes out of his house and doesn't seem to ever let anyone in. Normally Fran goes alone, every few weeks.' I paused, realising there were several nuances and layers to Angus. 'You do know he's not Fran's biological brother, right?'

'Yeah, the records said. So, what actually is the relationship there?'

'Fran never really speaks about it much. Well, she never really speaks about her childhood at all. But from the small breadcrumbs that she's mentioned, she and Angus grew up together in the same children's home.'

There was another brief, uncomfortable pause between us as we walked through the school corridor that was littered with shoddy art exhibits from the children. We signed out at the desk and returned our visitor passes. I felt like Cis bringing this up meant she had something up her sleeve. I was a pawn in some part of a plan I couldn't quite fathom yet. Somehow, she needed me to connect the dots. Some people at training had called her 'The Puppet Master' after she used to play the pretend-witnesses off each other during questioning, causing them to accidentally incriminate one another in the process.

I liked Cis, but Fran had always said something about her just rubbed the wrong way. 'Machiavellian' or something was the word she often used. I always dismissed Fran when she said that or when her face turned into a scowl whenever I mentioned Cis's name. But now, I was starting to wonder if my wife had more intuition than I realised. If your friend's wife was a suspect in a murder case, would you really quiz him about it so nonchalantly?

'This whole case, Gareth, it's all completely baffling to me. I honestly believe you when you say you don't think Fran did it,' Cis said as we strolled back to the car.

Now, I knew that was an out-and-out lie.

'What do you want, Cis? Just...' I said in a half scoff, half groan, stopping in my tracks in the middle of the car park. 'Just get on with it, please.'

'Look, I didn't want to get into this here,' she said with a murmur, 'but I need your help.'

Ah, Puppet Master, we meet again.

. . .

'If Vivian finds out I'm letting you do this, so help me God,' Cis said as we walked through the Criminal Investigation Department.

'God help us all,' I corrected as I marched into Cis's office and saw the reams and reams of paper strewn and pinned all across the small three-by-three-metre room. There was a clear lack of any positive feng shui in here. How did she manage to get anything done in this rubbish tip?

'And this is everything from O'Neill's attic, too, right?' I said, gesturing to one of the many clutters of case files.

'Correct,' she affirmed. 'Other than the stuff the director's office took.'

That didn't surprise me; there was something else going on here with O'Neill that the head honchos at the police were clearly concerned about.

'But let me be perfectly clear, Cis, the only reason I'm helping you with this is to prove Fran didn't do it. Someone killed O'Neill, but I'd bet my career that it wasn't her.'

By now I was realising that I wished I hadn't followed my gut in the first place, but Cis was relentless. My passive attempts at any kind of placation with her had failed, so I had to do something to protect Fran from her. I was just still hoping it was a random stranger who had offed O'Neill. I was going to be in trouble if it ended up being Angus.

'Crystal clear,' Cis repeated.

I stopped for a moment, trying to make sense of all the mess Cis worked in. Did she not have any kind of organising system? No colour-coded markers to signify importance?

'Well, I need to find the transcript somehow,' I said, waving my hands at the sheer amount of chaos rammed into the tiny room.

Cis quickly walked over to one of the many jumbles, pulled out a document, and passed it to me.

Why did you visit Gordon O'Neill a few weeks before he was murdered? Cis had asked Angus.

He'd apparently just given a grunt at that; Steve had annotated on the script that it sounded most like an 'I don't know' after he had slowed it down on the recording.

Do you know Gordon O'Neill?

Apparently, Angus had just mumbled again.

Do you know anything that could help us find Mr O'Neill?

Apparently, that 'no' had been more audible than his previous answers.

The whole conversation had seemed pointless, and considering they had nothing on Angus at the moment, they were unable to arrest or charge him with anything, nor search his apartment, which would have required hundreds of police man-hours. I wondered if Fran knew that Angus had been questioned. It wasn't like he was the world's best communicator.

I knew that Angus's life had involved moving between various foster families, where he'd struggled to adapt, frequently experiencing violent outbursts and emotional breakdowns. Most of this I had gathered from dribs and drabs that Fran had told me over our relationship. What I hadn't known, as I scanned his profile now, was that seven years ago, when he was twenty-two, he had tried to rob a Tesco Metro. I had not known he had a criminal record...

A question began to percolate deep within my mind, something that I had been wondering for the longest time.

'Cis?' I asked, peering up from my document. 'What's the difference between a Tesco Metro and a Tesco Express?'

Cis, who had begun to chug on a protein shake, paused and gently placed the bottle down on a column of papers.

'You know what? I don't know. Let me google it.'

As I continued reading, I tried to push aside the ethical qualms I had about delving into such confidential information, especially considering this was a part of Fran's history she had actively decide not to share with me. The reports from Angus's social care worker, forwarded to Cis, detailed him as a recluse battling severe agoraphobia. Exposure to the external environment would trigger intense anxiety and behaviour bordering on schizophrenic. Intriguingly, his ill-fated robbery at Tesco Metro had involved him dialling the police before even entering the store and holding the cashier at knife point with no real demands. Charged with attempted robbery, Angus's guilty plea had met a sympathetic response from both the jury and judge, resulting in mandated therapy and several hundred hours of community service. How he'd avoided any prison time was a mystery to me – probably because Isla wasn't on the prosecution team that day.

'So, what do you think, darling?' Cis asked. 'Please tell me your brilliant detective mind can make more sense of it than I can. I feel like my head is about to explode.'

I rubbed the palm of my hand across the soft stubble on my chin as I thought it over, trying not to let Cis's poorly disguised flattery get to me as I inspected the transcript one more time, making sure there was nothing I missed. She puckered her lips as if she was trying to stop herself from saying something.

'Just say it,' I said to her, exhausted of her performance. 'Seriously, just say it.'

'It won't show up on the transcript but... Fran was too good in the questioning. She was *too* good, Gareth. She did the little shaky voice, the little teary concerned eyes, she came across as a saint. But the woman started to smile at some points. I mean, who does that?'

'Oh, come on, it could have just been nerves, like people who laugh at funerals.'

'Seriously, Gareth, that's your excuse for her?'

'She had been preparing the whole night before for it,' I reasoned peevishly. 'We forget, but it's incredibly nerve-wracking for the people on the other side of the desk. Come on, stop being an eejit.'

Cis nonchalantly shrugged her bulky shoulders.

'Maybe,' she said, clearly not believing anything I was saying.

I spread the papers across her desk and began breaking them apart and analysing them as quickly as I could, finally digesting all the information I'd not had a chance to look at before I'd been yanked off the case. There was something I was missing, something I had overlooked about O'Neill from the very beginning. Why did we all assume that his charity had been altruistic?

'You're looking at it wrong,' I grumbled, before quickly adding, 'sorry,' knowing that Cis would be slightly offended by my harsh but honest critique. I extended out a few more sheets across her desk. 'I was looking at it wrong, too,' I said, more reassuringly. 'You have his personal accounts, right?'

'In one of the folders, yeah?' Cis said, pointing at one of the boxes. I lunged for it, sending the various papers into the air like confetti.

'We gave O'Neill too much credit, thinking he was this golden boy Robin Hood. He wasn't, not at all. How best to get a tax-free return on a profit as a kind of organisational entity?'

'Set up a non-profit,' Cis answered in response.

'Right? So, you close down your business in its best fiscal year yet and then begin to funnel money through that. Because look, that business may have closed, but he set himself up as an independent contractor not three months later; he was still making money on the side. It says so here.' I pointed to one of the records. 'Who buys a second home the year after you close down your business?'

'But the man had a non-profit, Gareth. We have evidence of him investing in the community,' Cis responded, like she was talking to a mad man, while I held another business file aloft in my hands.

'No, no, no. We have evidence that he *said* he would,' I corrected, jabbing my hand at one of the many photos we had received from archives. 'What have we been finding? Pictures of him making pledges, announcing funding, launching scholarships, but all these initiatives ended before they were off the ground. Look at these Heart of Hope Foundation projects here,' I said as I began to slap the pictures on the table like they were tenners at a strip club – not that I had ever gone to one, of course. 'The community centre that never finished construction, the children's home that had to close down after a fire, the scholarships that no one actually was awarded. I would bet my pension that these schools and town halls only saw fractions of the money they were promised. Imagine it: countless local council grants, government funds, big donations, all becoming one big income stream that can't be taxed, plus being an independent contractor to keep up appearances.'

I reached across the desk, snatched yet another piece of paper, and smoothed it out under my palm. Lord above, I despised the way Cis organised her work.

'Just look at this,' I said, jabbing my finger on the paper. 'In 1995, £150,000 from a local council grant, and another £50,000 donation from a tech company for corporate social responsibility. All of it earmarked to renovate a sports centre for local communities based in Southampton. And now? Want to guess what that sports centre is today?' I didn't wait for an answer from the slack-jawed Cis, practically hurling my body into the nearest pile of papers to search for the relevant file.

'Here,' I exclaimed, holding up one of the files. 'See this? Six hundred pounds, a measly six hundred pounds! That's what they claimed they spent on bringing in a surveyor, and that's it. And the so-called sports centre now?' I quickly searched for it on my phone before holding it up for her to see. 'Renovated into luxury apartments.'

Cis took a step back and raised her hands triumphantly above her head.

'That's it. That has to be it,' she said, as I could see the spark of excitement behind her eyes.

'He was a common fraudster, of course he made enemies,' I explained, as the fog of the case seemed to dissipate ever so slightly. 'I mean, he didn't deserve to die, don't get me wrong. But the man leeched money off the state, had some friends in high places, probably split it a few ways and got rich doing it. Maybe he conned the wrong person on a really bad day, and it finally caught up with him after all these years. The axe forgets, the tree remembers.'

'Oh my, Vivian is going to be so happy,' Cis exclaimed, the glee visibly beaming from her face.

A folder caught my eye with a name I recognised: Francesca Donoghue.

'Is Fran's file here? Have you got her history?'

'Yeah. You know she was involved in an investigation before?'

'She was?'

'You didn't know?' Cis said. I thought I saw her face twist and break into concern, perhaps the first time I had seen her exhibit a genuine emotion today.

'Well, shit,' I remarked. I had never even thought to search Fran up in the database in the years I'd had access as a police officer. It had crossed my mind a few times, sure, but part of me felt like doing that would not only be using my police privileges unethically, but also admitting to myself that I didn't trust Fran to tell me everything. At what point do you stop taking people at their word? Fran was a social worker who had never been in trouble with the police, a law-abiding citizen as long as I had known her. But then again, weren't you supposed to tell your partner everything? Why hadn't she told me was involved with a police investigation before?

'You read it, right? Her file,' I asked Cis.

'Well, of course I did.'

'Anything in there that directly implicates her in this?'

'No,' Cis said, somewhat gently. 'If there was, she'd be in a cell already.' She realised the bluntness of her words. 'Sorry.'

Now I knew she didn't mean that apology, but I decided that I could call her out on being a bad friend when I'd finally found the sick murderer that had killed old man O'Neill.

'I didn't know that she grew up in a children's home, though, St Nicholas's?'

'Fran doesn't like to talk about it much, I don't think it was easy for her,' I replied with the same brusqueness that Fran would speak with when talking about her childhood.

There was a short, uneasy silence between us.

'Look, take that, and considering you're meant to be off the case,' Cis said, cutting through the silence, 'I'll give you access to my email – off the record, of course, or you'll cost me my whole career,' Cis hurriedly added, her words picking up pace towards the end of the sentence as though she wanted to minimise the time they hung in the air. 'Look through the file and then look at what forensics sent me and what Vivian forwarded on to me. See if anything clicks. I need you, Gareth, to help me put all this together.'

She quickly scribbled down the details on a piece of paper and passed it to me as I casually slipped it into my pocket.

Not very cyber-security friendly of Cis to give me her email password, but there might be something within those emails capable of completely exonerating Fran – something Cis had overlooked and she wanted me to be the one to find it for her. That's likely why Cis and I were such a good team during training; she excelled with talking to people, and I excelled at information, seeing how it all fitted together.

'Let me make this clear again, Cis, I'm doing this to find out who killed O'Neill and to get Fran out of your crosshairs, do you understand? I'm not doing this to help you put her away.'

'Yes, Gareth, I get it,' Cis responded, like a child tired of her mum's nagging. 'Just... be careful with my email, don't send Vivian a picture of your balls or anything.'

'And is there anything else that I don't know?' I asked, ignoring her comment.

Cis took in a big inhale and crossed her arms.

'Tesco Express are smaller shops for office workers, whereas Tesco Metro is more for the everyday consumer.'

I stayed for another hour at the station, my bright red highlighter like a knife as I circled every small breakthrough that confirmed my theory. Inflated invoices, extortionate supply costs, donated money from corporates that had gone missing, fake salaries, bogus consulting fees, it all clicked. After a while, I ran like a man possessed to my desk and logged into my account to access the database.

I typed 'Thomas Macleod' into the search bar, the man Fran had been investigated for murdering some seven or so years ago.

I read the digital version of the file. He had died in suspicious circumstances when Fran and I had been in our early days of being together at university. I sifted through the reports on the internal system, but nothing jumped out as directly relevant or enlightening to our current situation. My search led me to Macleod's obituary on a local news website, which featured a cheerful photo of him on a fishing trip with his son. And there, prominently displayed on one of his hands, was a bronze ring. Lower down, there was another photo, this one a decade or so later. Sure enough, there was it again, the ring still lodged tight on his finger.

I grabbed my phone and opened the message app. The data and records of messages had been stored for years across various devices, despite having had two different phones since then. Fran and I had hundreds of thousands of messages that went back to the start of our relationship, so I wouldn't be able to keep swiping. I searched online how to go back to a specific date, and then, using my computer, found what she had been doing on 3 September, seven years ago.

When I asked her when she was next free, she told me over text that she was away that weekend on a girls' trip. If only I had known what she was really up to. I hadn't questioned her honesty for even a moment. From the early days of our relationship, I had always trusted her implicitly.

I glanced through the records of the previous detective.

Fran had been a tenuous suspect, but a suspect, nevertheless. She had been visiting the village by herself on what she called a peaceful getaway, when a woman of her description was spotted on a chicken shop security camera walking back from the direction of Macleod's house in the early hours of the morning. The police had questioned her but found nothing incriminating or suspicious. Macleod's death was, perhaps, ghastlier than O'Neill's. Forensics and post-mortem had found that he had been assaulted in the doorway, and his throat cut from the front whilst he had been struggling to get on his feet. Apparently, the whole thing stank of amateur hour, since the cut lines were all over his neck. The use of a knife matched up with Mr O'Neill – but knives and blades were the number one weapon for murder in the UK. That wasn't enough to link Fran.

I read over her questioning report. Apparently, Fran had sobbed so much throughout the interrogation that they had taken a brief pause to console her, ultimately refusing to let her back in to finish the interview despite her demands to be treated like any other suspect.

The interviewing officer had said that he thought there was

no way in hell a young woman would have been capable of a murder as gruesome as that.

Yeah, you and me both, mate. Even at the time, she had been vague about what they had actually done on their girls' trip.

I read further down the report, searching for any kind of link between O'Neill and this Macleod guy. There was nothing obvious until I popped his name into the archives. Then his name appeared thousands of times, but not as any kind of perpetuator. He had been an employee at the Met once, but he had been promoted since then. Thomas Macleod, Director of the Serious Fraud Office.

Oh dear, oh dear, oh dear.

SIXTEEN

GARETH

I pushed down on the handle of the door as hard as I could until I heard it clank. I caught a small glimpse of Mep darting away at the air-splitting sound as I stormed through the door, hurling it shut behind me as hard as I could. I thought I heard something snap and break, but I didn't go back and check. I simply marched around the corner and into the kitchen, hurling my bag onto the table as I did so.

'What the hell, Gareth!?' Fran exclaimed, jolting backwards, knocking the pot she had been stirring. It spilt all over the floor and down her top, drenching the top half of her body with thick red Bolognese. She looked like a girl who had just won Prom Queen, before she murdered her classmates.

'What haven't you told me?!' I snapped back at her.

'What are you talking about, Gareth?' she said to me, more flummoxed than angry.

'Are you a murderer?' I said, staring her down.

I couldn't ask her if she'd killed O'Neill or Macleod specifically; I didn't want to know the answer to that one at the moment. But I had to hear her say something.

Fran glared up at me, the thick red pasta sauce still racing down the side of her face and congealing on her chin. She carefully and purposefully placed the wooden spoon on the worktop counter, then stepped a little closer to look me dead in the eyes. She placed both of her hands on my arms, as if trying to calm me down.

'No,' she said, surprisingly calmly.

We both inhaled, sucking all of the available oxygen out of the room at once.

'Liar,' I replied softly.

'I'm not lying,' she hissed, her words gradually becoming more venomous. 'Where is this coming from? You talking to Cis? Is that it? She's telling you I did it? Cis going on and on about how I'm an awful wife and all that?'

'This isn't about Cis,' I retorted.

'I can promise you it is. You believe her over your own wife? Is that it? Is that it?' Fran came right to my face. 'Fuck,' she said again. 'I can't even talk to you right now. I'm so furious with you.'

She swung around and stormed out of the kitchen, traipsing the Bolognese across our recently fitted cream carpet in the hallway. I could see Mep had taken sanctuary from all the shouting in the living room. Seeing Fran come marching towards him made him quickly dart upstairs as fast as his legs could carry him.

'No, no, no, don't just run away from me,' I demanded, following her. 'Come on, if you didn't murder O'Neill, who did? Angus?'

'Why are you bringing Angus into this?' Fran hissed at me, her hands extending and repeatedly clenching into fists.

'You tell me?' I replied, wanting to see her reaction, to survey and examine, to see how she would respond.

'It's lost on me, Gareth. I don't know what you're getting at?'

'Angus. He was at the house a few weeks before O'Neill

was murdered. And by the way, I know all about his little *robbery* stint.'

I never saw Fran's eyes ignite with such fury before. I almost felt the living room lights flicker and begin to dim.

'How do you know about the robbery?' she said, so slowly and enunciating every word, like she was about to fling herself at me any second.

'Oh, you know, I'm not sure if you've realised, but I am in fact a police detective. And he did in fact commit a crime. He tried to rob a Tesco Express.'

'He robbed a Tesco Metro,' Fran spat at me, instinctively grabbing a coaster off one of our stands and pelting it at me. It smacked into my elbow and ricocheted onto the wall.

'Nice,' was all I said. 'Nice work, Fran. Hope that's not how you killed O'Neill.'

'You... absolute...' Fran said to me through gritted teeth, the red Bolognese now staining into her clothes and marking her skin, '... dick. What the hell is wrong with you? You think I murdered O'Neill? Do you even understand what you're accusing your wife of, or are you too pigged-up to tell the difference between me and a suspect?'

'Don't say that!'

'What?!'

'You know what you're saying.'

Fran stared back at me, goading me on to say it.

'Don't,' I said, forcing my eyes to stay open as I uttered every word. 'Don't say that. I've told you how much I hate that word.'

I thought I saw Fran almost mouth the word 'sorry', but she was still too angry to put her voice behind it. We continued to glare at each other. But I knew my wife well enough to see that though her eyes were practically aflame with hot-blooded rage, there was something a little bit fearful behind it. Fear of me?

No, certainly not. Fran didn't seem to be scared of anything. This must be something else.

'What are you afraid of, Fran?' I asked, in as soft a tone I could manage.

'What am I afraid of?' she repeated, taken back, her voice breaking momentarily.

'Because I have this crazy fear that you've killed O'Neill, although I can't for the life of me figure out why you would have done it. And I'm afraid you're going to tear our family apart before it even properly starts,' I stuttered, struggling to get the words out in a coherent flow. 'I'm afraid that you've done something stupid and you're going to go to prison and I'm going to be left here. How would we ever come back from that, Fran?'

Fran wiped away a tear before it had even left her eye, and I watched her visibly swallow a lump in her throat.

'Well, I'm afraid that you're going to leave me, and I'm still going to love you afterwards. I'm terrified that you'll leave me, and you won't even give me a good reason to hate you afterwards. Do you know how selfish that would be, Gareth?'

We were both silent again for a minute, ten minutes, maybe an hour. Time seemed to go a little askew. The silence lured Mep back; he began to slowly creep into the living room, thinking the chaos was over.

But I couldn't help myself. I had to know what really happened.

'Did you kill O'Neill, and did you kill Macleod?' I asked, as slowly and calmly as I could.

I dodged the book that came hurtling towards me and Mep swiftly drifted around the corner, doing a 180 again to flee the shouting.

'Why... why would you say that?!' Fran screamed at me, pushing her face towards mine. 'Why did I have to marry such a pig?'

'What did you just say, Fran?'

Fran's eyes didn't show any remorse. She meant this.

'I said you're pigged up,' she said, doubling down on the insult. 'You absolute idiot.'

Lord above. She knew how to push my buttons. To anyone else, I knew this would sound like such a ridiculous kind of argument. But every couple has that *thing*, that *word* that may seem absolutely bonkers to everyone else but goes off like mints in a fizzy Coke can between them. My mind was racing, fuelled by rage, searching for an insult that could hurt her as much as what she'd just said hurt me.

'Whatever you say.'

I paused before speaking again, hoping I would be able to stop myself.

'Murderer,' I grumbled.

What happened next was something of a blur. All I saw was her charging towards me, slamming me against the wall, her forearm against my neck, pushing down with life-threatening pressure. I tried to look in her eyes and I didn't see Fran any more. Her gaze was fixed on my neck and she was continuing to push down tight. I knew I had enough strength to push her off, but I didn't know what to do. The shock of it had made my limbs go lifeless. My throat was closing in and tightening up, but I watched as she slowly realised what she was doing and lurched herself back. I glared at her in disbelief. Her skin went the palest shade of white, crimson sauce still moving down her body.

'Hey,' I said, reaching out to her. I knew she didn't know what she was doing. Something else had taken over; she hadn't meant to do that.

But she simply got up and walked out the door, closing it shut. I heard her car drive off before I even managed to move myself away from the wall.

. . .

I tried calling Fran what must have been a thousand times. Ringing and ringing until I didn't hear any ringing any more. Just a cold, emotionless voice telling me that she wasn't available, and to please try again later.

I found Mep, who had retreated into the cupboard upstairs, scooped him out and stroked him and held him until he stopped quivering.

'It's okay, buddy,' I said, gently holding him against my chest and running one hand down his back. By the time I had finished petting him, he seemed more infuriated than scared by the evening's events. I wasn't sure if Fran had fed him, so poured him some food. He took a few mouthfuls, still looking trepidatious that the shouting could suddenly interrupt him again at any moment.

I cleaned up the kitchen as best as I could. The Bolognese came easily off the countertops and cupboard doors with a few wipes. The carpet was more difficult. I filled a bucket of water with bicarbonate of soda and a squeeze of detergent and began scrubbing away. I put the TV on in the living room to whatever channel seemed best to take my mind off this evening's events, and spent the next few hours pushing my arm back and forth until my wrist physically couldn't take it any more. I would experience an occasional pang of hope whenever I heard a car go past the window, darting my head up like a meerkat at the zoo, only to see it shoot past the house. It didn't take long to dawn on me that Fran probably wasn't coming home tonight.

Why hadn't she told me that she had been a suspect for murder before? Let go after questioning – but still, the case had never been solved.

I was now realising that my wife wasn't who I thought she was. Not because of her not having told me about being a suspect previously. And not because of anything she had said, or how she'd reacted to any of the questions. Hell, it wasn't even because of how she'd attacked me. It was because of that look in her eyes when she'd stared at me, with her arm pushing down my throat. That wasn't Fran. That was someone else, someone I absolutely did not recognise.

By the time I had finished cleaning the carpet and listening to the entirety of some dull talk show, I decided to go into the station. I wasn't going to stay here and wait for Fran. It was killing me.

I grabbed a piece of paper from my book and wrote a note.

I'm sorry. This was a stupid fight. I shouldn't have asked you that...

I stopped writing halfway through. I wasn't sure about Fran any more. I wasn't sure who she was. This wasn't an ordinary argument; this felt cataclysmic. I scrunched up the piece of paper and tossed it in the bin, then began writing a new note.

I'm at the station if you need me. Please let me know if you're home, okay? My phone is fully charged.

I gave Mep another cuddle, unsure whether it was for his benefit or for mine. Then, in what was now the early hours of the morning, I made my way to the station. The place was usually a busy and bustling hubbub twenty-four hours a day, but as I made my way through the building, it began to get quieter and quieter the closer I got to the CID. I sat down at my desk and placed my phone smack bang in the centre. If Fran rang, I would hear it straight away.

More than anything, I just wanted to know if she was okay. I also wanted some clarification of what kind of fight we'd just had. Had this been a verbal shouting match that got really out of hand, or was this the kind of thing where you took a trip to a family law solicitor to see what your options were?

The more sickening realisation to me was that I knew I couldn't just let it go. If Fran had killed someone, she needed to be held accountable. The law was the law, and there was no bending it just because your wife was the suspect.

Or maybe she was protecting someone. Maybe she was being blackmailed or threatened, and that was why she wasn't thinking straight. Could Angus be involved in this somehow?

I opened her report on my computer and went back to scanning over the selection of documents on my screen. I felt like, maybe from the beginning, I had known deep down she might have had a part to play in this. The cryptic notes on her phone, her unease at the mention of O'Neill, maybe now it was all beginning to make sense.

I heard the office door creak and my head shot up, foolishly expecting that I might see Fran. But unless she had undergone some pretty radical physical changes in the last few hours, including but not limited to male pattern baldness, the person I saw was definitely my colleague Steve.

He looked tired, exhausted even, with big black bags underneath his eyes and his hairline seeming to have jumped back a few inches since I had last seen him. Oh Lord, I hoped mine would never look that bad.

'Hey, Gareth,' he said, in a monotone.

'Hey,' I replied apathetically, before returning to focus on my wife's questioning report on my computer, making sure Steve wasn't positioned at an angle where he could see my screen, full of confidential emails that Cis really shouldn't have given me access to.

'Toddlers, you know?' Steve said, replying to a question that I'd not asked. Reluctantly and arduously, I raised my head to meet his gaze, finding only dead eyes that seemed to show no spark of life. 'Single dad life? Yeah, it's hard,' he continued, again answering his own question.

Just a few days ago, I would have been elated at the idea of Steve initiating a conversation with me. However, given the current circumstances, the last thing I wanted was to engage in any kind of dialogue, especially with someone who had been at the very least an accomplice in discarding my lasagne. So, with a tilt of my head that silently conveyed a dispassionate 'well, what are you going to do?' I sought to politely conclude any kind of conversation. I lowered my head again beneath the cubicle divider, attempting to re-immerse myself in whatever else I could find out about Fran.

'Umm, hey, Olive, my wife – well, my ex-wife actually – gave me some coffee and walnut cake,' Steve said, timidly approaching my desk as he tenderly unwrapped a tinfoil package. 'Would you like to share some with me?'

Screw your cake. That was what I wanted to say. I didn't say it, of course. For whatever reason, Steve was actually trying with me. Maybe Cis had told him to play nice, or maybe even Vivian had given him a slap on the wrist. I checked just to make sure it wasn't actually a piece of faeces he'd squeezed out, wrapped up and was presenting to me.

'All right,' I said, recognising that what lay in front of me was indeed a visually unappetising, but nevertheless genuine, coffee and walnut cake. Feeling somewhat defeated in my attempts to dodge the conversation entirely, I acquiesced, 'That would be nice.'

Steve smiled and gently placed the cake on the table, cutting a haphazard slice with a crappy plastic knife. He passed it to me using a torn-off piece of foil as a placeholder plate, before grabbing a chair and wheeling it over to my cubicle.

'So, Angus. Any updates?' I asked.

Steve took a moment to process, knowing he probably

shouldn't tell me anything about the case, but clearly too tired to resist or care.

'Not a crumb,' he said, only lowering his voice slightly. 'We brought him in for questioning, but he barely spoke a peep. Don't tell Vivian I said that, though.' Steve glanced in the direction of her domain. Even when she was absent, her malevolent spirit still lingered.

This was all information I already knew, and did nothing to help get Fran off the hook.

'Sweat him more, then,' I stated matter-of-factly.

'Oh,' Steve said, clearly surprised by my tone. 'I mean, I don't think we should really be speaking about this...'

'He knows something. So, get him in again, apply a bit of pressure and you'll get some answers, I guarantee it. He'll cave in in a jiff, especially if you raise your voice a few decibels.' This was something Fran had told me a few times about Angus. He was bit of a nervous soul, so it didn't take much for him to piss his pants. My current feeling was Angus had been the one to do the deed, but why? I had no idea. But I knew that whenever Angus messed up, Fran was always there to clean up his messes, and I knew this would be no exception.

'Okay, Gareth, but do you really think that's the best way? You're sounding like Darren at this rate. They'll ban you from the primary school visits,' Steve said with an uneasy titter.

'He knows something, and I bet you and Cis went far too easy on him. Personally, I'd go a bit harder and see what you can find,' I said, finishing off the cake, rolling up the tinfoil and tossing it in the bin. 'Trust me.'

I realised I was being somewhat cruel. The moral argument around me telling my colleague to sweat my brother-in-law-who-wasn't-really-my-brother-in-law was rather dubious. But if applying some extra pressure to Angus meant keeping Fran from life in prison, then surely the ends justified the means?

'Anything else?' I asked, my patience draining.

Steve looked tense. His eyes seemed to glance downwards, and he shuffled awkwardly in his seat. For as long as I had worked with him, I had desperately wanted his respect, to be treated as a colleague, a professional. Had I realised that adopting a brusque tone was all it took, I'd have been an arsehole to him much sooner.

'You know, Gareth, the other boys may joke around, but we think you're all right,' Steve said, through his last mouthful of cake.

Despite this having been probably the worst night of the close to thirty-odd years I had spent on God's green earth, I'd have been lying if I said that didn't make me feel a tiny bit better, just a little.

I was never one for seeing the whole case like a puzzle, as if it would all come together, like a neat painting of a picturesque scene, by the end of the investigation. It was really more like Sudoku – a big mess that, even when finished and all the numbers were in the right spots, didn't make any real sense or fit together nicely.

I'd not heard even a peep from Fran, which was more than a little unsettling, but I had spammed her phone with messages and got no response, so what else could I do but keep going?

I waited as patiently as I could for the CID clock to hit 8 a.m., and as soon as the hand brushed past the 8, I hopped back into my car and drove to the address that was still listed in my recently searched locations. I wasn't quite sure why I was doing this, if I was being honest with myself. Chances were, if someone connected to the case didn't want to talk to you, waiting for a few days wouldn't really change that, but I had to give it one more try to understand what exactly Fran was involved in.

After managing to miss most of the morning rush hour traffic, I pulled up outside Maeve's house, hoping she was home so I wouldn't have trekked all this way for nothing. I gently knocked on the door and a few moments later, she yanked it open, clearly expecting someone else. The mysterious David she had mentioned last time, I imagined.

'You again,' she murmured viciously, moving fast to shut the door.

'Whoa, whoa,' I said, trying to politely stop her from slamming the door in my face. 'It's about your father—' I blurted out, throwing my face into the fast-narrowing gap between door and frame.

The door paused, less than an inch from closing.

'I haven't spoken to my father in thirty years. Why would I care if he's in any danger?' Maeve muttered. Her voice seemed indifferent, but I could see she was feeling a small fleck of concern.

'Because he's still your dad?' I said, appealing to any small shred of familial love left in Maeve's heart. 'That's something you can't change, no matter how hard you try.'

'He probably finally pissed off the wrong guy and got what was coming to him. Is he dead, then?'

'We're... in the middle of an investigation.' I wasn't sure how best to answer that question. *We think your dad has been carved up, chopped up and disposed of* didn't seem to be a response that would help me here.

'What makes you think he's in danger?'

'He's gone missing.'

The door crept open a few more inches, and I finally got a proper look at the woman in front of me.

'Five minutes. I need to focus on repairing my oven so I can eat tonight.'

She didn't offer me any tea or coffee but she did lead me to the small kitchen table, which was cluttered with various parts of some sort of machine. 'Just replacing the oven igniter,' she explained, probably noticing my puzzled look as I tried to make sense of the scattered pieces of machinery.

'Look, my father was an entrepreneur, but he ran his businesses' – she struggled to find the suitable word – 'immorally,' she continued, crouching down to fiddle with the oven. 'The way he operated meant we moved around a lot – usually packing up shop before people realised that they'd been conned.'

'Has anyone ever tried to hurt him before?' I asked, trying to inconspicuously pull out my notebook, hoping the smallest of my body movements wouldn't disrupt her; the way I had to sit perfectly still when Mep finally came to sit on my lap.

'That man could make you madder than you've ever been in your life, then convince you punching him wasn't in your best interests,' Maeve said, a small twinkle of sentimentality in her tone as I heard the oven clunk as she fiddled with some device. 'Even when I was young, I thought that maybe one day his luck would run out, which is probably what has happened now.'

I thought back to yesterday, standing in Cis's office looking over the wads of purchase orders, invoices and statements that belonged to the Heart of Hope Foundation.

'Do you know anything else about this foundation he was a part of?' I asked.

'Oh, that... It was his little way to give back to the community, he said. They donated to schools, museums, art projects, things like that. If my father wasn't home, that's where he'd be. I remember he and his friends all wore these little bronze rings. It meant they were "brothers in blood" or something, that they had made a promise to help others, but it was clear the whole "guild" thing was just one big ruse.'

Rings? Just like the one Macleod wore. I jotted that down in my notebook before glancing back up at her.

'What do you mean?' I asked, trying not to make it blatantly obvious that I was playing a bit clueless.

'Did you not listen to a word I just said, mate?' she laughed. 'My father was a con artist. Do you really think he suddenly had this gracious change of heart and decided to give back to the needy? The man just saw a new opportunity.'

Interesting: the same theory that I'd come to.

'And when was the last time you saw your father?'

Maeve stood up from repairing the oven and began washing her sooty hands in the sink. 'One night, out of the blue, my mother told me to stay in bed until late the next morning. Told me I didn't even need to go to school the next day – so I didn't.'

She stopped when her voice cracked, muttered a quiet apology, collecting herself before continuing.

'Take all the time you need,' I offered. But her face creased with frustration, as if my words had disrupted the flow of her memory.

'We stayed home,' she went on, pretending she hadn't heard me. 'He went to work, and then my mum bundled me into her car and we drove to my grandparents' house in Manchester. We never came back.'

'Did your dad ever find you?'

'No, but I also don't think he tried.'

'And did you ever find out why your mum had decided to leave all of a sudden?'

'I tried to ask my mum about it – I was only thirteen when it happened – but she never spoke of him again. She met another man and settled down, but she couldn't even be in the same room if anyone mentioned my father. I always assumed we had left because he'd finally conned the wrong man – you know, the kind of man who comes back to give you a bit of a punching. Or maybe my mother realised she couldn't stay with a man who stole from hardworking people for his own gain. I never found out why we left that night.'

'And you never saw him again?' I asked. 'You never tried to reach out?'

I could see Maeve trying to hide the sadness in her face, still drying her hands on the tea towel, even though they were perfectly dry by now.

'My mother never wanted to speak to my father again, but she never forbade me from talking to him. But he never even reached out. He never made an effort. Do you know what that does to the mind of a thirteen year old?'

I didn't. I had loved my dad; now I just missed him.

'Gordon O'Neill is a name that's followed me my whole life. I've had people track me down and ask me for the money he still owes them, even after I changed my surname, but I've never heard even a whisper from him.'

She stopped drying her hands and sat down across from me at the kitchen table, letting out a long and mighty sigh as she settled into the chair. While she took a moment, I did the mental mapping in my head about how best I could un-implicate Fran from this.

'Maeve, this might sound strange, but do you have any photos of your father?'

'Why?'

'It may just be useful to the investigation, if that's okay.'

She gave a giant huff and begrudgingly trotted out of the room. I waited, unsure if she was even going to come back. I was lost in a swirl of my thoughts about Fran when, out of nowhere, a handful of photos were slapped down onto the table in front of me, startling me. Maeve had re-entered the room.

I picked them up. The first was of O'Neill – decades younger – holding a baby I assumed to be Maeve. He looked extraordinarily cheery, smiling widely as he cradled the newborn in his arms. The next photo was O'Neill again, flanked by two people who I assumed were his friends. They stood outside some building, grinning at the camera and holding an oversized cheque with the 'Heart of Hope' insignia plastered on the front. O'Neill was unmistakable in the middle. I didn't recognise the face on his left, but on his right stood Thomas Macleod, identified easily as the Director of the SFO from his uniform and the insignia on his badge. Sure enough, all three of them wore the ornate bronze rings on their little fingers.

I looked at the name of the building, St Nicholas's Children's Home, and the headline: 'Children's home receives £100,000 grant for renovations and support'.

'Thank you, Maeve,' I managed to say, my words stumbling over each other as I tried to rise to my feet, everything beginning to make sense. 'St Nicholas's...' I murmured, recognising the name from Fran's report. Surely, I couldn't be thinking right? But as hard as I tried to resist, I believe I had stumbled upon what, in our line of work, you would call a motive.

SEVENTEEN

FRAN

'This place smells like the inside of Florence Nightingale's vagina,' said Angus, pushing himself back on the chair, placing himself in the corner, where he'd feel the safest.

'How do you even know what Florence Nightingale's vagina smells like?' I asked. 'And also, that is deeply offensive.'

'I can just imagine it smells like this whole aura. Death, decay, dysentery.'

'Oh, piss off, and don't speak ill of Florence Nightingale. Just keep looking out, all right?' I quipped to him playfully. 'You're just moaning and groaning, and it's giving me a bit of a headache if I'm being honest with you.' I inhaled to raise my voice to the highest pitch I could. *'Oh, I'm Angus, and the outside scares me, ooh no. It's so scary.'*

'Hah hah, you're hilarious. When's your stand-up special coming out? Never!' Angus snapped back.

Once again, the longer we spent together, the more we had regressed into children. Even back at St Nicholas's, we had never really bonded like Angus had with Edith. The inseparable little boy and girl who'd spend their days laughing and leaping around the house. Edith was the soft, kind-hearted one;

I was the one that would force them to watch zombie B-movies when everyone else had gone to bed.

'When was the last time you were even outside? Like, you know London has had an Olympics now?' I said, eyeing a silver-haired man across the street. I scowled when he turned around and I saw he was very clearly not our man.

Angus, still infuriated with me, pushed his hand across the beer-drenched table, so his middle finger was only an inch away from my face. I slapped it away, then saw him jolt his other hand towards me to do the gesture again.

'Piss off, seriously,' I shrieked as Angus's amused glance snapped to the door. A man in his mid-fifties deftly dipped his head beneath the low-hanging beam as he stepped into the pub. I saw Angus's hands clench into fists as he watched the presumed regular go to the bar and order his usual.

'You okay?' I asked, trying to mask my concern. He had got worse since I had last dragged him out of the house.

'Yeah. You going to text your husband back yet or not?' Angus asked, swiftly changing the subject. 'Going to let the poor guy just think that you've upped and vanished and run off to Argentinia or something?'

'Argentina,' I corrected.

'No, Argentinia. You can say it two different ways; it's the emphasis of the vowel – it's like scone and scone.'

'No, you're adding an extra syllable, Angus. It's Argentina, not Argentinia. Look it up.'

Angus whipped his crappy phone out of his pocket and began to tap furiously on the keys.

'You're going to be *so* upset with me when you find out I'm right,' he murmured.

While I waited for the penny to drop on Angus's clueless face, I tentatively picked up my phone and stared again at the response I had drafted, ready to send, the cursor blinking like a countdown to some kind of time bomb.

> I'm fine. Just think we need some time apart right now.

'Is this too, you know, divorce-y?' I asked, holding the text up to Angus for him to inspect. He didn't look up, and I saw a look of disappointment and regret flash across his eyes as the search results on his phone slowly began to load.

'No Wi-Fi,' he murmured to me as he slammed his phone, almost definitely connected to the Wi-Fi, against the table, face down. He glanced at my text, holding my hand to steady the screen.

'It's divorce adjacent, I won't lie to you. It's a few messages away from, "check your post – the papers are on their way". Like Mep is going to have two Christmases this year, you know?'

I didn't really know why I was asking Angus for his opinion. The boy didn't speak to anyone, so had no idea how to have a meaningful human interaction, especially within the nuances of being a couple. But it was still good to use him as a sounding board, I supposed, even if I was going to completely ignore all of his advice. Maybe that was how I knew I was on the right track.

'So, like, what do you think you and him will do? You nearly choked out the poor guy,' Angus said. 'Do you think he'll even want to get back with you? How do we know *he's* not divorcing you?'

I ignored the last bit of his sentence.

'I'm going to get some therapy. I think that would be the best thing to do, going forward.'

I didn't even remember what had happened. One minute, we'd been arguing. The next second, this burning white-hot rage had washed over me, so intense it was almost like a physical heat consuming my body. Then, in what felt like a blink of an eye, I'd found my arm pressed against Gareth's throat. I wouldn't actually have hurt him, though. I swear I wouldn't. As soon as I'd realised what I was doing, I had got out of there as quickly as I could.

'That's if he doesn't leave you first,' Angus remarked.

'Again, very helpful, Angus. Thank you.'

'And *you* going to therapy? That's like Genghis Khan going to anger management classes. Like, good intentions, but is it going to work? Probably not. You're more messed up than me.'

Had Angus become more sarcastic recently?

'At least I can pretend to be somewhat normal. Which, let's be honest, is not really your forte.' I groaned. 'How are you helping me right now, Angus?'

Angus shrugged his shoulders, somewhat agreeing with my point while appearing to care very little. He then took another glance around him as a pair of men entered the pub. I watched his eyeline as he once again scanned and surveyed all the possible entrances and exits. I was surprised that he had said yes to coming with me to this village in the middle of nowhere. Although I imagined he didn't love the idea of me being in his apartment either. He must have realised this was the path of least resistance.

'So, are you actually going to tell me why you were at O'Neill's?' I asked, reminded that this wasn't the first time Angus had left the house in the past few months.

'What? I've told you already.'

'I don't think "I got the wrong house" is really the most truthful of answers, Angus. You've never visited us.'

Angus groaned melodramatically and rolled his eyes.

'After you told me when you first moved in that O'Neill was next door to you, I got angry, I guess. I just remembered everything: the mould, the broken radiators, the taps that didn't work – obviously, the fire.' I could see him relive the experience briefly, a small film of pain glazed over his eyes as he said that. 'I just thought that if he remembered you, he might try something stupid, so I wanted to scare him.'

Angus must have seen my surprise at the idea of him being able to physically intimidate anyone, as his face instantly twisted into a scowl, ready for a retort. But suddenly, something made his eyes bulge. He smacked my hand and gestured for me to look. I had to be casual about this. Slowly and calmly, I rotated my head to see, through the pub window, a man begin to leave the church opposite, carefully waiting for cars to pass, before crossing the road and heading towards our pub. That was our guy.

Angus looked at me and then at him, and then at me again and then back at him. I took another swig of my beer, which mingled nicely with the four Lorazepam already in my system. My life may be crumbling apart, but at least I couldn't feel it much.

'You'll pay for these, right?' I said, my eyes still fixed on the old man plodding in our direction.

'Don't do it now. Please don't do it now,' Angus said, his voice almost whimpering. I noticed his hands under the table, clenching and unclenching.

I threw my debit card onto the table and darted out of the pub. I thought I heard Angus call after me, but knew he wouldn't chase. I followed the pensioner as he strolled down the street, beaming hello to at least three people like the has-been celebrity I knew he was. Clark had got much fatter since I had last seen him some twenty-odd years ago, a huge pot belly protruding beneath the shaky hands with which he unwound the awning from his shop.

I had only seen him in the flesh a handful of times – once was when he'd come to the home with a few others and one of those stupidly big cheques. That was the day that Clive had gone up to speak to him after they had had their sickening photo opportunity in front of the home, telling him that the faulty, outdated wiring in the home was a literal time bomb and needed to be fixed yesterday. Clark had simply placed a hand on Clive's shoulder and promised he would fix it as soon as possible; he would make sure of it. But I remember the wiring never got fixed that week, or the week after that, and all it had taken was Edith and Angus playing with the half-broken heater for the fire to start.

It was hilarious, really. The notoriously feisty Leader of the Opposition now ran a DIY shop – how quaint. I kept my distance, looking uncaringly across a few windows and pretending to check my phone as I slowly sauntered towards him. I saw his hands shake as he jammed the keys into the door and pushed it open using his excess weight. Clearly, he didn't have much strength left. I waited for a moment, taking extra care to ensure there were no CCTV cameras or video doorbells nearby before following him in.

'Oh, I'm just opening up,' Clark said to me. God, I had forgotten how awfully shrill his voice was.

'Okay, no worries,' I said, closing the door behind me and flipping his CLOSED sign to OPEN as I ambled in and looked at all the tat he had assembled. It had the familiar, very distinct smell of *old*. I didn't want to look at his face, but I was hoping that my coming in had frustrated him. I tried to put salt in the wound by touching and inspecting all of the crap he had in his shop, smoothing my hands over everything I could, praying that he was cursing me silently as he watched from the counter.

'Anything you're looking for, Miss?' he said as I took a glance at the diaries still dated for this year. Somewhat ironic, given that it was October.

'Oh, not really, just browsing,' I said, giving him an obviously plastic smile as he set up the till. I took a moment to take a really good look at him. There was no denying the man looked good for his eighties. His skin still glowed, wrapped tight around his face; crystal blue eyes; his thick white hair was slicked back. No wonder he was popular with the OAPs in the village. As he pushed his hand up to his lips to wet his fingers to turn the page of a catalogue in front of him, I saw the bronze ring, glistening in the daylight. It was the complete lack of shame shown by them continuing to wear the rings that really made my blood boil. Like there was no repentance for what they had been a part of.

I grabbed a huge pink glitter pen with a tuft of tiny artificial feathers at the end, presumably this would catch the attention of whatever young girl had been dragged along on her father's errands. I walked up to the counter and slid it across to him, curious to see if he would recognise me up close.

'Aren't you a bit too old for that?' he said, half smirking, unveiling his unusually pearly white teeth.

'No,' I said, staring at him, dumbfounded. 'What makes you say that?'

Clark, who didn't recognise me in the slightest, wasn't going to miss the chance to make a woman feel stupid.

'That pen sells very well with our primary-school demographic. Good to know that there's a market with yours, too.'

I faked a playful 'oh you' expression as he began to tap on the keys on the till, still amused by his own comment.

'One pound, please,' he said.

I showed him my credit card to gesture for him to do contactless, watching him groan as he picked up the card reader. The banks would rob him for just this purchase in transaction fees. It gave me a tremendous amount of glee to know he would be barely turning a profit with this sale.

I exhaled, stretching my arms out wide before settling them in my pockets. I felt comforted by the small pocketknife resting there, curling my fingers around it like a stress ball, realising how easy it would be to swipe it across his neck and watch him clutch and claw at the gaping wound before bleeding out on the counter. Knowing the knife would only need to leave my pocket for a couple of seconds, before I could nestle it back in there.

God, I knew I was going to enjoy killing him the most. Far

more than Macleod and O'Neill. Clark had always been the ringleader of the gang. I was sure everything that had happened had been his idea from the start. After all, it was his career that had helped them all to get away with it for so long.

I wanted to kill him so desperately, yet I found myself hesitating. As I pushed my card firm against the reader, I realised that Clark had a hold on me that none of the others did.

'That's all done for you,' he said as the card machine began to vomit up a receipt.

I snatched up the pen and examined it in front of him. He watched me scornfully, clearly wondering why this city girl was still even in his shop. I wished that my purchase would have been a good murder tool, death by pink sparkle-bedazzled pen would be a wonderful way for Clark to depart the mortal coil.

I knew this was only supposed to be a reconnaissance mission, but my fear was fast obliterating any restraint I had left. The thought of allowing a man who could instil such terror within me to continue living for a second longer was unthinkable.

'Tell me, Abe, do you remember a place called St Nicholas's?' I asked him.

His old, sagging face slowly crumpled in shock. He remembered.

As my heart hammered against my ribs, I grabbed the handle of the blade in one hand, placed the other on the counter to steady myself, and, planning a clean route up to his neck, yanked the knife out of my pocket.

'Hey, Grandad.'

A young lad, no older than about fourteen, gently pushed open the door. He smiled at me through his braces. I stopped. The knife was out of my pocket, but Clark was distracted as he glanced towards the door. I shoved the blade back in, piercing myself in the hip a little in the process.

'Hello, son, how are you?' Clark said, clearly relieved as he gently lifted his hands up in the air as a salutation.

'I'm all right. Do you want me to start unpacking some of the stock out the back?' the boy asked whilst pulling off his hoodie, folding it, and placing it by the door.

I felt the sensation of blood begin to dribble and drip down my hip. I just had to wait long enough for the boy to go into the back of the shop, then I could still strike and kill Clark. The boy would be scarred, of course, but I'd seen worse by the time I was half his age. With some therapy, he would be absolutely fine. Ten to fifteen years, maybe.

'That would be great. Just start with rearranging some of the boxes this side of the shop though, please.'

Shit.

The boy gently and courteously excused himself by me as I tried not to let my leg tremble or shudder, the prick of the edge of the blade still wedged firmly in my skin.

'So, are you sure there's nothing else I can do you for?' Clark asked, his slack jowls growing ever more taut.

'I'm fine, thank you,' I said, struggling to keep it together as I gave a small wave goodbye and awkwardly began to limp out of the shop, hoping that I wasn't leaving a long trail of blood behind me. For whatever reason, fate wasn't going to let me kill the bastard today.

'Oh, you forgot your pen,' I heard the boy call.

I began formulating and streamlining the plan to kill Clark on the way home. It excited me, like the moment before you drop on a rollercoaster. Killing him outright in the shop would be too obvious. Anyone could walk in. And as much as a stabbing would give me an extortionate amount of joy, the connotations of murder would be too obvious. It would need to look like either a suicide, or an accident. Considering how difficult staging a suicide had turned out to be, I figured an accident would be both easier *and* more plausible.

I rewound and replayed the morning in my mind. There was a small alcove at the back of the shop where Clark kept a load of boxes. What would happen if one accidently fell on his head, giving him a concussion? Or what if, perhaps, he happened to slip on an uneven surface? I made a mental note to research the most fatal kind of accident and see how difficult it would be to recreate it.

After I dropped off Angus, who had decided he wasn't on speaking terms with me after I'd left him in the pub, I reached the house, passing a police car in the driveway. After a quick inspection of the number plate, I saw that it was Gareth's. He was home. I hadn't sent any messages to him in the end; I thought it was just best to talk to him and try to save my marriage through good old communication. At least, I hoped I could save it. I knew he was wondering if I actually was a murderer.

I hopped out of the car and braced myself. I could see Gareth inside through the window. His eyes looked up to somewhat acknowledge me and then back down to the kitchen table. So, it was time for the talk.

I took a deep breath to steel myself. I was ready to apologise, to take the blame. Gareth was the best thing in my life, and I needed to be as honest as I could be with him. I would tell him about what the doctor had said about my fertility; he had an absolute right to know about that. I didn't think I would tell him about my childhood, though, about St Nicholas's and Edith. I didn't think I'd ever be ready to do that.

I walked slowly into the house, as if going the wrong way on a moving walkway, and glanced up again at Gareth in the window. He looked borderline depressed. The window was obviously accentuating his crow's feet and pale skin, but the man looked like he had just caught the plague.

A figure skulked past the window – bulky, tall, and imposing. I froze as I realised the silhouette was in fact, a reflection from someone behind me. Whirling around, I came face to face with Cecilia, whose presence seemed to loom particularly menacingly above me today. I recoiled, stepping back as another officer flung open my front door and descended the steps towards me, the distinct sound of handcuffs rattling in his hand.

'Francesa Donoghue, I am Detective Steve Norton. I am arresting you on suspicion of the murder of...'

Steve stuttered as the words seemed to get stuck in his throat. His eyes, panicking, looked to Cecilia as I stood there, frozen to the spot, unsure if now was the best time to run or to object, or what even exactly the best thing to do in a situation like this was.

'I forgot his name,' Steve murmured. 'Damn.'

Cecilia jerked Steve out of the way, shaking her head, and placed a hand on the small of my back, guiding me towards the police car. Cecilia recited the rest of the rights to me, but I didn't really listen. I realised this was what people would refer to as an out of body experience. I felt completely detached from my own movements as they placed me into the back seat of the car. I just kept my eyes focused on Gareth, through the window. He didn't even glance up from the kitchen table to look at me.

EIGHTEEN
FRAN

'It's not prison yet, actually. You're going to be held at a police custody suite.'

That's what Steve told me, unperturbed, as he and Cecilia led me out of the car, each placing a hand around one of my arms as we walked towards the entrance of the station.

'You're not going to handcuff me?'

'Only if you try to run,' Cecilia snapped facetiously. I didn't find that even a little bit funny.

I walked past Judith at the front desk, who did a double take. Here I was, the lady who was always bringing in food for her husband, now flanked by two police officers.

'Afternoon, Judith,' Steve said as we walked past her.

Judith didn't say anything back, just looked at me slack jawed as I was walked through the lobby.

They led me down the staircase into the station basement. I tried to fool myself into thinking that this was me booking myself into a really shitty hotel, but just for the night. Like a really old Travelodge, or an Ibis found on a last-minute booking website. We entered a large, fluorescent-lit suite with peeling, faded cream walls. There was another policeman sitting behind a long grey barricade for a desk. He tucked his lips inwards and gave the same non-smile I had seen reserved for work colleagues and fake friends.

'Afternoon, Paul.'

'Afternoon, Steve.'

Paul looked like something out of a rogues' gallery. He had a small, weaselly face with tiny eyes, protruding front teeth and a long nose. But the minute he opened his mouth, a soft, thick south Welsh accent emerged. I could barely take the man seriously. I almost wanted to compliment him on how terrifying he looked, yet how wonderful he sounded. The man could narrate the dictionary to me, and I would be hooked on every word.

Paul, who informed me he was the custody sergeant, began to go on about the duty scheme where a lawyer would be provided for me if I did not have one. He then handed me a leaflet regarding my rights while I was detained here, going deep into the minutiae. He must have recited all this a thousand times before. I let his words fade into the sound of the loud droning hum of the lights, telling myself that this was just a brief overview of the packages available during my stay. It was an awful shame they didn't have Wi-Fi. The price you paid for a cheap room, I guess.

A flurry of questions was asked, but after a while I realised I could just use *no* as the default answer.

'Have you got any medical conditions?'

'No.'

'Are you currently on any medication?'

'No.'

'Have you ever been a member of the armed forces?'

'No.'

'Have you ever tried to harm yourself?'

'No.'

'How are you feeling now?'

'Like I want to yank out my long intestine and hang myself with it.'

I said the joke more for my benefit than Paul's, just to break the monotony. He only frowned and wrinkled his forehead.

'Ooh, a joker, are you? We have a lot of them.'

I thought about retorting back to him. I had approximately nine up my sleeve. But then I reminded myself where I was. This would be the guy bringing me my meals for at least the next day, so it seemed easier to just play nice with him.

He told me I would be in room number eight. The nicest, according to Paul, though I wasn't so sure. Cecilia and Steve left just after Paul took my phone and purse, the only things I had left on me. He showed me into suite number eight, and I was given a buzzer to ring the front desk.

'You want to press,' he said, pausing for a moment, 'and hold. Look at me, look at me, please. You press and hold, and that will call right through to the front desk if you have any urgent problems or concerns.'

'What counts as a problem or concern? Poo won't flush?'

Paul sighed and scowled again, a now-signature Paul expression. We were going to be pals, I just knew it.

'Like you're puking up and going to die. That would be a more appropriate time to ring the buzzer.'

Paul left, telling me he would be back soon, heaving the thick steel door shut with a clank. There I was, alone, in a three-by-three-metre room in the basement of the police station.

The suite was tiled in the same cream as the reception. The one long blue accent tile strip circling it was a chic touch. Have you ever sat on a bed in jail? It felt like the kind of crash mats you used to throw yourself around on in Key Stage 2 PE. I tried to get comfortable, but I began to think that the floor may be less scratchy against my skin.

I wondered what Gareth was thinking right now. Was he still at home? I knew he liked to *play* the grizzled cop at work, but there was some rage in him when we argued that I had never seen before, it was like I didn't recognise the man who looked like my husband roaring at me. Would he be fixed, frozen in the same position that I'd last seen him, or maybe sobbing to himself in the corner of the living room? Maybe he wasn't thinking anything. Or maybe he just thought: *case closed, done and dusted.* It just so happened that his wife was the murderer this time.

Why had he not even looked at me?

Being arrested and my marriage probably coming to an end within a single day certainly marked one of my worst on record, not to mention the recent revelation of my near-barren state – a fact still unknown to my soon-to-be-ex-husband. In an attempt to find some relaxation, I pushed myself back onto a mattress that felt like I was lying on frozen marble.

I tried to get back into my happy place. It was important at times like these not to give in to melancholy, and to concentrate on manifesting a brilliant future. For example, how was I going to kill Clark?

Presumably, bail would be coming up for me. That seemed the perfect time to strike. If Gareth was done with me and I was going to prison, then it didn't really matter if it was on one, two or three counts of murder. I would probably be in there until the arthritis started kicking in anyway. I had to find a way to kill Clark that would be quick and easy, but not too fast. That had been the problem with Macleod and O'Neill's deaths. I didn't think they'd even really had time to register what was happening to them. To be honest, neither had I.

Again, essential reminder for you: not a psychopath.

I refused to let myself cry or sob or feel self-pity. The survival instinct had kicked in at this point. So instead, I sat on the cold floor, running through the murders of Macleod and O'Neill, and how I could use what I'd learned from them to take out Clark. It must have been a few hours into me being lost in my thoughts when I heard Paul's beautiful voice echo through the room.

'What would you like for dinner, Mrs Donoghue? The people in suites four and five want korma and tikka masala. Be great if you could get some Indian, too.'

Was he for real? Was this the moment where Paul would then spit in my porridge and fling it through the hatch? Did you get takeaway in remanded custody?

'Ummm, I'll have the jalfrezi, please?' I said hesitantly, waiting for the punchline.

'Oh, that's brave,' Paul replied. 'Glad you have your own toilet.'

An hour or so later, the hatch on the door opened and a jalfrezi emerged, with a paper napkin that Paul had neatly placed a knife and fork on. I wasn't really hungry, but if I kept fooling myself into thinking that this was just for the night, I thought I could maybe get something down. It was a vile, disgusting excuse for a jalfrezi. Rather than being from the local takeaway, it had clearly just been ordered in bulk from a wholesaler. I wished I'd asked Paul what the other options were.

I didn't remember falling asleep, but I woke up to Paul asking me to stand away from the door. He waddled in with a tray containing a protein bar, banana and a carton of orange juice. It was too few items for the space on the tray, so they had been spread out across it.

'Can't eat bananas,' was the first thing I said.

Paul recoiled his head, exasperated.

'Well, how the hell do you get your potassium, then?'

I shrugged my shoulders nonchalantly as I snatched the orange juice carton, plucked up the straw, and pretended to stab myself in the wrist.

Any sympathy that Paul may have had for me with my potassium deficiency was quickly squashed. He just shook his head disappointedly.

'You really think you're the first one to make that joke?' Paul said with sheer, utter, unadulterated disappointment. 'Eat up and drink up. Your lawyer is here.'

I tried to connect myself to the reality of the situation, but, starting from my arrest, this whole process had felt like some kind of haunted house ride. Paul led me into a glorified broom cupboard as another man – slicked-back black hair, mid-fifties, a little short and slightly overweight – snatched my hand up and shook it.

'Francesca, nice to meet you. Andrew Shorestone, Bark & Moore solicitors.'

'You're not one of those duty solicitors, are you?'

'No, I'm not. Your husband called me yesterday afternoon, told me that you had just been brought in, and arranged to have me meet you here.'

I didn't quite know how to feel about all this. Was it a good or bad sign that Gareth was doing this for me?

'First of all, have you been offered a phone call, or is there anybody you need me to ring on your behalf?'

'No. To both.'

Andrew stopped shuffling through his papers, surprised at my answer.

'You sure? Your husband? Mum? Dad? Siblings?'

All things I did not have.

'No, I'm okay,' I said, as indifferently as I could.

'Right, well. I obtained the disclosure from the police. They've arrested you on suspicion of the murder of Gordon O'Neill on what the police are estimating as the date of death to be the tenth of September. The good news is that they don't have anything concrete against you. It's what I like to call a finger-food case: lots of little crumbs, but nothing really substantial.'

I nodded. I was sure this was something he told all the girls.

'From what I can see, Fran, you've been the model defendant. Your last encounter with Gordon O'Neill was you trying to help him. There's no motive for you to attack him, no criminal record, nothing for you to gain from Gordon's death. There's no trace of a murder weapon. I mean, you put the man's bins out, for crying out loud. What kind of murderer does that?'

'So, what do they have on me? Why have I been arrested? Must be more than a reasonable doubt?'

'Between you and me, sounds like the police needed to make an arrest for the case. Superiors were afraid of the media frenzy that could be drummed up. Not sure if you knew this, but this O'Neill guy? Man was a fraudster. What they're going to try and charge you with is the video footage of your last visit to O'Neill, traces of you in the house, and a passer-by that claims to have seen a woman matching your description throwing body parts in the river. That last one is the clincher. So, to conclude: you're not the one who did it, but you're the one they think is most *likely* to have done it.'

I scoffed, somewhat relieved. One, he hadn't mentioned Angus or his 'I'll kill you' note, which was one of the many worries I had floating around my head. Two, he had been paid to believe me. It may have been delusional, but it was slightly comforting to have someone on my side. Three, it looks like they hadn't discovered any of O'Neill's appendages; that was probably a nice aperitif for a school of trout.

'Well, that's barely anything. How can they pin this on me?'

'I'm sure you remember Thomas Macleod, that man who died seven or so years ago –nasty murder. Well, he and O'Neill were friends, which makes you a link to the two murders. Definition of wrong place, wrong time, if you ask me. But that doesn't make you guilty. Just very unlucky.'

'So, how will you spin it?' I asked, hoping I was using the lingo right.

'I think an act of neighbourly goodwill shouldn't make you a suspect to murder,' said Andrew, leaning back in his chair casually and tapping his pencil against the edge of the desk like a kid in class. 'But your past isn't ideal. Raised in the system – being in care generally predicts higher adult criminality. You're the perfect scapegoat for the CPS, I'm afraid.'

What a lovely way to put it. I felt so glad I wasn't being pigeonholed.

'Do I get bail?'

Andrew looked solemn. He took a sharp breath and then grew increasingly shamefaced as he began to speak, like he was about to tell me Fluffy the dog had died right before Christmas.

'No. I'm sorry to say that you'll be held at a prison on remand until the trial. Bear in mind, this is only if they charge you. They could be looking through their notes now and realising they don't have enough to pin this on you. So, let's just cross our fingers.'

They charged me.

We were led into another room, where Andrew and I sat on one end of the desk, and Cecilia and this CPS lawyer sat on the other. I wondered if she was Isla: a slim, beautiful, tall brunette with a stunning balayage, sitting quietly as Cecilia recounted the allegations.

Andrew, and the woman I presumed to be Isla, seemed to have some history. They sparred verbally for a bit, my confidence only knocked when Andrew abruptly backed down as the woman began listing all the times she had won cases against him. I wasn't listening to most of what was being said, but I knew the features of an *oh shit* face all too well. Andrew had told me that mentally shutting down may actually be a good thing, and that I should respond with a 'no comment' unless it was a name, date of birth, or address question. Those, I could answer.

'It lets us get our ducks in a row,' he said to me, an expression he was repeating with grating regularity.

I saw maybe-Isla and Cecilia whispering to each other in the hallway, after the interview. They stopped as soon as they spotted me being led out of the room by Paul. Both of them looked on with part sneers, part pity as I was steered across the hallway and back into my cell – I mean, suite. My very, very nice suite.

The magistrates' hearing the next day was quick. I gave my name, my date of birth and then my address – the new one, although it did make me wonder if I had changed it on my banking statement. I was told by the clerk that I was charged with the murder of Gordon O'Neill on 10 September. I was then told I would be remanded in custody. The whole thing only took two minutes before I was led back out again.

I wasn't sure, but I thought I might have spotted Gareth in the gallery, nestled right at the back. The figure was too far up and too obscured in shadow for me to really see. It was then that I realised that I had almost completely disconnected from any kind of reality. I couldn't tell what day it was, where I was, or where even I was going next. But it was probably better this way. Besides, Gareth hadn't even been able to look at me when I'd been arrested; clearly he had gone beyond any kind of care for me.

I looked down at my wedding ring, thinking about the vows we had said to each other five years ago, and wondered if he was still wearing his.

NINETEEN

GARETH

I didn't want to look. Instead, I just rolled my wedding ring around my finger, while Mep made a small, pained squeal as the vet laid his blue-rubber-gloved hand around his spine, clutching it tight and using his other hand to feel around his ribs. I hated hearing him in pain.

Mep looked up at me, his one working eye a mixture of anger and self-pity. The vet continued to feel around.

'Every time?' he asked.

I didn't understand at first. The vet must have read in my expression that I didn't really register what he was saying.

'Every time he eats, he throws up?'

'Oh, yeah, yeah, it's every time he eats. I thought he'd managed to keep it down today, but after I got back from walking my neighbour's dog, he had just spewed it all up again.'

The vet seemed to fill his body with every ounce of air he could before talking.

'And you say Mep is very old, is that correct?'

'Yeah, we didn't know his age when we adopted him about five years ago. But we imagine he's about seventeen or so now.'

The vet crossed his arms and leaned back against the countertop, peeling off his gloves with some kind of swagger, as if he hadn't had them up a cat's rectum sixty seconds ago.

'To me, this sounds like kidney failure. I'll give you a prescription for some medication, as well as advice for a diet. This may work, in which case you'll have a few more years of Mep. That being said, if he keeps throwing up his food, I'm afraid we're going to have to look at the best and kindest option for him.'

At first, I thought the vet was referring to his diet, but instead he maintained his gaze until I realised exactly what he was talking about.

'Well, then, I'll keep a close eye on him,' I said, trying to hide the breaking of my voice. I gently laid a hand across Mep, who arched his spine up to my palm. He gave a purr, which sounded more like a small explosion at a tile factory.

I placed Mep back in his carrier, paid the extortionate bill, and walked out. I then passed by the local drive-thru, grabbed a double cheeseburger, and sobbed whilst I ate it in the car park, taking breaks between weeping and biting down on the greasy, salty mess in my hands.

Occasionally, Mep would push his face through the grating on his carrier, his small tongue protruding through the bars to try and have a taste of the burger. I would slip a piece of beef onto his tongue, which took him a solid few minutes to munch down. I wondered if maybe fast food would be the key to Mep keeping his food down. We might have to inject insulin into him four times a day, but I could deal with that. A boneless bucket every day keeps the vet away, right?

I carefully removed Mep from the cage, my vision blurred by the tears, and tucked him into my arms. I wondered what Fran was doing right now. If I just turned up at the prison, would she even want to see me? People at the station had told me that Bronzefield inmates could call once a day. I took my silent phone as a sign: she would ring if she actually wanted to see me. They said that those on remanded custody had better treatment than those serving their sentences.

I was still trying to get my head around the precise reason why Fran had killed O'Neill. I knew deep down it couldn't have been a spur-of-the-moment thing, that it hadn't been spontaneous. I'd like to think I still knew my wife a little bit, despite everything, and I knew she had a tendency to mull over things before committing to a big decision. What exactly had her grudge been with O'Neill? I couldn't help feeling like it was connected to Fran's life at St Nicholas's before me but whenever we spoke about her childhood, she would always throw the conversation topic away.

'It's not trauma if you don't remember it,' was her favourite sarcastic remark if it ever came up in conversation, and I'd just accepted that. I felt like such a fool now for ever believing she was innocent: all the warning signs had been there and I had chosen to ignore them. But the moment I handed over that photo to Cis, I knew exactly what was going to happen to Fran, but I did it anyway.

Mep craned his head up to get another bite, so I lowered the burger as he bit into another piece and dragged it back, chomping his way through it.

I still kept trying to make sense of it. The girl I had met nearly eight years ago, the biggest animal lover, the kindest and most caring person, had shoved a knife through the head of an OAP.

My mum had rung a few times, asking very generically how Fran and I were. She knew that I knew she had seen the headlines. It seemed like everyone in the country had seen the papers, as texts from people I hadn't heard from for years began to bounce onto my phone. I knew that every time I'd pulled up in my car for the night this week, the whole neighbourhood had covertly peeled back their curtains to see if they could glean any details about Fran in my ten-metre walk from car to house.

What I was really going to have to come to terms with, perhaps for the rest of my life, was simple. It was me who had turned Fran in.

'What are we going to do, Mep?' I asked as the sun started to peek through the clouds, a small ray hitting my face. It almost made me feel a fraction better, before Mep dribbled his vomit across my arm.

I decided it was time to return to the station. I left Mep at home, keeping the radio on for him, and swiftly changed my shirt to one featuring less vomit. I then drove on autopilot back to the office.

It was like the time I had shat myself in PE in primary school all over again. As I walked through the station corridors, conversations suddenly became silent, numerous pairs of eyes locking onto me and tracking my every move. I could swear I saw a few of them turn their noses up, as if they could smell that aeons-ago poop, echoing through the ages. This was the guy who not only had a murderer for a wife, but was the one who had turned her in. What a bastard.

'Hey, Gareth,' I heard a voice say at the end of the hall. The tone was too cheery, too fake, drenched in self-satisfaction. I had been played by her. Of course I had. I had just been too dumb, too naïve to see it.

'Hi, Cis, how are you?' I asked, wondering if I could get away with punching a woman that was nine times stronger than me. In my periphery, I saw everyone's head lean towards us, trying to eavesdrop on our forced niceties.

'Oh, not too bad. Busy as ever. I've missed you, haven't seen you for a little while. How are you holding up?'

She placed a hand on my shoulder. The self-restraint it took me not to grab and violently twist it around her back was almost impressive.

Keep it together, I kept telling myself. *Keep it together*.

'Oh, you know, as good as I can be under the current circumstances,' I said, matching her artificial saccharine tone. 'Look, I'd probably best be going, I'm dying for a cup of coffee.' The sheer anger I felt writhing around in my gut was nauseating. I gave as warm an expression as I could muster and began to walk away.

Christ forgive me, I hated her. Like truly, deeply, all of my heart just despised her. It hadn't helped my feelings that I had heard that, after taking most of the credit for Fran's arrest, she had been offered the very prestigious promotion she had worked so hard for. I noticed she had changed her email password, too, so I no longer had access to her inbox. Although, luckily, I had saved a few email chains onto a spare USB just in case I needed them again.

'Oh, and by the way, Vivian would like to see you,' Cis said.

I didn't wait for Vivian to summon me into the room this time, though I noticed that she was still trying her luck with the signature finger commands. A click to come in, a finger pointing downwards to sit.

I slumped down in the chair, rolling up my sleeves as she continued to read through her documents. I kept waiting for her. Her eyes tracked across the pages. I wondered what was so important that it couldn't wait a few minutes.

I continued to tap my foot, hoping she would pick up on my impatience and that I really didn't care for her power-play games, but she just seemed to ignore me, lifting one piece of paper aloft and blocking my face from her view.

'Can't that wait?' I said, exasperated.

Shit. I should not have said that.

Her head shifted upwards, her eyes chilled, and I saw her cheeks suck sharply inwards as she clenched her jaw, every facial muscle tense.

'What did you just say?'

I had to pick my next words very carefully.

'This whole – you know, pretending to read documents just to keep me waiting. It's as clear as day what you're doing. Just stop wasting my time and get on with it.'

Double shit. Should definitely have not said that.

I could now see the anger in my boss's face as she stretched her jaw, turned her head away from me, and stared up at the ceiling for a moment, gathering her composure.

Part of me wanted to fill in the silence with another shitty comment, but my mouth couldn't exactly be trusted at this current time, so I just used all my internal strength to keep my gob shut.

Vivan interlocked her hands, her elbows resting on the desk, and leaned forward.

'Gareth, I am reading a document from HR about how to deal with an employee whose significant other has been arrested,' she said calmly. 'They actually typed it up especially for me this morning. I have never been in this situation before, so I was just making sure I was well versed on how best to discuss this with you. I do sincerely apologise for keeping you waiting.'

'Ah,' I said, shuffling uncomfortably in the chair. 'That makes sense.'

'See?' she said, holding up an A4 sheet of paper with the relevant subject line before slapping it back down on her desk. 'I just wanted to ask you if you're okay – if there's anything we can do to support you, going forward, with your workload, or anything. If you need some time off, or some counselling?'

I pushed myself up a little on the chair, digging my nails into some of the flaking rubber in the handle.

'I heard through the grapevine that all the way up the Met

food chain, they were putting the pressure on you to make an arrest. You know, a bureaucratic fraud syndicate right under their noses would be a horrendous bit of PR for the police, considering our default public opinion is usually negative.'

I saw Vivian brace herself, like I was an insolent child playing up. But I also caught the slightest, almost unnoticeable, bit of nervousness as she needlessly arranged some of the paperweights on her desk. No one fidgeted quite like Vivian. She twisted a glass apple to one side before pushing it back to its original position.

'Gareth, I do understand that you're upset—'

I groaned, scrunching my nose and flicking a little bit more of the innards of the chair handle onto the carpet, watching Vivian's eyes as she tracked its descent. I could see she was getting agitated. Part of me was enjoying it, forgetting that my wife was a murderer awaiting trial with potential life imprisonment on the table. Only last week we had still been happily married, trying for a baby to complete our vision of domestic bliss... Shit, what if Fran was already pregnant? I hadn't thought about that.

'Gareth, I think you may need a few more days off. I feel like you can't be expected to...' Vivian began, breaking my quick brain spiral of wondering how I would raise a baby on my own.

'Okay,' I said, nonchalantly rising from the seat as if I didn't have a care in the world. 'But I guess everything about this whole fraud syndicate is all going to have its day in the sun.'

Vivian winced as if I had just struck an uppercut to her face. I'd hit a nerve. Oh, maybe this was the reason the superintendent was getting involved with the case? Another corruption scandal would be the last thing they needed, even if it was from decades ago. I had handed the evidence over to Cis and Steve, initially thinking Fran might have killed the two men for the money or something. Bunch of rich guys who liked to flaunt their cash made for high-value murder targets. But maybe not. Maybe this went a lot deeper than I'd ever realised.

'You know how we work, Gareth,' Vivian said after a pause. 'And you know that we wouldn't have arrested Fran if we didn't have enough evidence against her. Do you think that maybe your feelings right now are coming from a place of... guilt?'

'What do you mean?'

'Gareth, come on. I know you were the one that gave Cis the photograph of the two men outside the children's home, connecting Fran to the murders, and I know you two worked together on this case. Do you think I'm stupid? That gave us evidence beyond reasonable doubt. I mean, Fran is suspected of killing two men, and both men happen to be linked as benefactors to the children's home she grew up in. Both men are murdered and somehow Fran is a likely suspect in both. That's no coincidence.'

Vivian's reaction to the way my face must have shifted told me that she instantly regretted her remarks to a husband who was going through a lot right now. Was she saying I was to blame for his? Her mouth dropped a little before she caught herself, straightening her back against her office chair. I could see that, out of the corner of her eye, she was trying to skim-read the piece of paper, refreshing herself on the best thing to say next.

'Are you aware of our Employee Assistance Programme?'

I saw myself out.

I glanced again at the copy of the photo Maeve had let me take away, comparing it to the Wikipedia image on my phone. For what was probably the eighteenth time today, I scanned between the two images. It was definitely him – Abe Clark, MP, wildcard Leader of the Opposition some forty-odd years ago.

I could see Vivian standing sentinel, watching me from the office to make sure I was leaving the building. I gave her a wave, gesturing to all the necessary work equipment I was leaving behind on the desk. Her face wore an expression of both suspicion and relief. I didn't much care what she thought any more. I walked across the office, still feeling the stares, their gazes following me into the bathroom. I pushed open one of the stalls and flicked out my phone to have a look through Clark's file in private. Unfortunately, I couldn't print out Clark's record or email it to myself: that would send alarm bells across our very secure network. The man's file was pretty standard for a pensioner: no police record of convictions, cautions, warnings, or reprimands.

Before I even had time to process the discovery, I heard a loud noise coming from the cubicle next to me – a long sniff that evolved into a hearty cough. I knew that sound. It was the sound of a very particular type of substance being insufflated as it lined the nasal passages.

I flushed the loo, left the stall and waited as I washed my hands, looking at the shadow of the person still inside in the cubicle.

He coughed heartily again.

'You all right in there?' I asked.

No answer.

I finished washing my hands and waited for a few moments longer.

'You sure you're all right, buddy?'

Still no answer.

I stepped away from the sink and towards the door, opening it and letting it go as I kept my feet planted to the same spot within the small alcove by the door.

I heard that long, loud sniffing again as I watched the lock on the cubicle door flick open and Steve timidly strolled out, his nostrils flared and red. His eyes expanded in panic as he saw me waiting by the door.

'Come on, man,' was all I could say, a little crestfallen.

Steve was too shocked to see me to even think of some kind of excuse. Instead, we both stood there, looking at each other. I wasn't so far gone in my police career that I could be apathetic to a man sniffing up the very stuff we were policing.

'Don't tell Vivian,' he muttered softly, his lips barely moving as his limbs stayed frozen to that position. 'It's just been really hard with everything going on.'

I didn't have any words to say to him, so I just shook my head and yanked open the bathroom door, leaving him standing there. I wondered how long he would remain stuck in that position.

The radio continued to crackle and screech, offering little more than static as I drove down the never-ending, winding country lanes towards the town. My only option in the old CD player was one of Adele's early albums, which – while lovely – wasn't exactly the vibe I needed to pull me out of my mental health crisis.

When I arrived, it didn't take me long to find the shop. It sat not too far up the high street. I pushed open the door, which was suitably festooned with leaflets and adverts for events that went as far back as the early 2010s. The small, cramped interior was piled high to the ceiling with useless nonsense, the kind of place you could spend a fortune without actually purchasing anything worthwhile. Chad Dangerfield was the identity I was about to inhabit; a private eye who investigated cases out of his own moral obligations. But not only did it sound a little porny, it had also turned out to be very close to the name of a fictional Lego character when I'd googled it. So, I had decided to keep my name secret if anyone asked. After all, it was something of a legally grey area I was currently operating in.

A young lad poked his head up at the far end of the shop, smiling at me courteously as I raised a hand and began to stroll around. There was no sign of 'Abe' at the moment, so I continued walking around, looking at the copious amounts of sealant.

Spotting a pink fluffy pen, my lips involuntarily curved into a smile. It was exactly the kind of thing Fran would adore – uber-garish and ridiculous. She'd claim to hate it, yet I knew if she owned it, she would never part with it. As much as I tried to suppress the thoughts, memories of Fran seemed to keep flooding in. I missed her, and the gnawing uncertainty of whether our marriage had reached its end kept swirling around my mind. Every time the thought crossed my mind that the last time I might have ever looked into her eyes was when she had pinned me against the wall with her elbow, a sharp, icy pang of pain came to my chest.

I thought about the potential minimum sentence she might face, wondering if a skilled lawyer could argue 'belief in imminent attack' in her favour. Yet, even with a strong defence, she could still face a lifetime behind bars. The law rarely showed leniency for taking a life, even when it might be considered self-defence.

'Oh, hello there,' I heard a voice say. Lo and behold, there he was: Abraham Clark, now aged about forty-odd years since that photo. 'Cool shades,' he said. I had forgotten they were still on. I wasn't a hundred per cent sure if he was being sarcastic or not.

'Sorry, you may get this a lot, but has anyone ever told you, you look like Abe Clark, the politician?'

The man gave what I think he thought was a humble smile as he swished back a loose lock of his hair.

'From a long time ago, yes,' he replied, with a kind of fake modesty that felt sort of sickening, honestly. You could tell the man was obviously enjoying being recognised. Like he was realising he wouldn't need to touch his Viagra tonight.

'So, tell me,' I said, summoning Chad Dangerfield, 'the hotshot bad boy of politics is now running a DIY shop? Shouldn't you be coasting off that sweet, sweet parliament pension fund?'

'Well, everyone needs a hobby,' he replied. 'And this was my father's shop, so I was keen to make sure it stayed in the family.'

I was done with the artificial affability. He seemed at ease, which made it the perfect time to strike.

'Mr Clark, I'm an investigator for a case that's currently unfolding, and wanted to ask you some questions, if that's all right.'

He tilted his head back, an ever-so-small tremble on his lips. I could see from the way his face shifted that he was still a little bit proud that someone had come to find him. 'Do you have five minutes?' I asked.

'Of course, but only if you buy some bin liners,' he said with a simper and an old wrinkly finger pointed towards me.

'Gordon O'Neill. You knew him?' I asked, ignoring his Sunday matinee stand-up routine.

That name struck a chord. The smile on his face vanished, and I could see him become guarded. He asked the boy in the shop to go and check some of the stock in the back, while I examined his wrinkly hands clutching the edges of the counter.

'A long time ago, we were friends. Part of the same charity.'

'Are you aware that he's dead?'

I watched carefully as I saw Mr Clark look visibly jolted by the revelation, his thick, wiry eyebrows shooting up his face, jaw dropping open.

'I was not, no. That's a shame. I haven't spoken to him for quite some time.'

'You used to be quite close, correct?'

'We did, but again, a long time ago.'

'And am I correct in thinking you were close with a Mr Macleod too? Thomas Macleod?'

'Yeah, he was part of the charity, too. But that was decades ago. We all went our own separate ways, after a while. I mean, I briefly saw Gordon at Thomas's funeral, but haven't seen him since then.'

'And I take it you're aware that Mr O'Neill was murdered?'

I watched carefully as I saw Mr Clark's face sort of collapse with disbelief, like someone had instantly sucked the smugness out of it, his expression morphing into shock then quickly into fear. His hand started to tremble. He pushed it into his pocket, attempting to hide the tremor, but I had already spotted the bronze ring on his finger.

'That's horrible,' he murmured. 'Do I need protection? Police protection? Should I call the police?'

'Why would you need to call the police?'

'Well, I was friends with both of these men, and both of these men were murdered; that seems awfully coincidental. What if I'm next?' His voice was rasping now, frantic, his hand scratching the inside of his leg from his pocket.

'Why would you be next?' I asked stoically.

'What was your name again? Why are you here? Telling me this?' Mr Clark said, raising his voice now. In the internal reflection of my sunglasses, I could see who I presumed to be his grandson emerge from the back. He quickly scuttled away when he noticed his grandfather's fury.

'Please, don't get upset,' I said. Though in my experience, that always made people more upset.

'Get out of my shop, please. I don't want to talk to you,' Clark said, pulling his hands out of his pockets and belligerently waving me away. I knew I wasn't going to get anything more out of him, so I pivoted around and wandered out, taking one glance behind me to see the man with his head in his hands, slapping away at his grandson as he tried to get closer to his grandfather.

I may have been on the verge of a nervous breakdown, but my detective senses were still intact and were tingling away. One thing I knew for sure was that this Clark guy was central to all of this. The way he'd reacted, like an infant having a tantrum, confirmed to me that Fran was somehow involved. Only she could make someone go quite that crazy.

TWENTY

GARETH

I'd thought that maybe having a wank would make me feel better. In hindsight, it actually made me feel quite a bit worse.

There I was, thinking it would release some magical endorphins that would miraculously improve things. Instead, it just made me want to cry while I sat on the edge of the toilet seat.

I knew I was slowly deteriorating: the idea of food made me want to throw up just like Mep, I felt consistently drained, and it was hard to muster enough energy to even take a shower. It had been exactly eighty days since everything had happened and it still felt so wrong to sleep in our bed without Fran, so I crashed on the sofa and watched the weird teleshopping channels until the early morning. I half expected the little girl playing noughts and crosses with the clown to pop up.

Mep hadn't got much better; all of his food now had to be liquidised for him to ingest anything. While I think the cat found it quite a novelty to have me sleeping downstairs, curling himself up against my chest on the sofa, it was at least a daily occurrence that he would throw up either on or near me. But he seemed to be digesting just enough to keep himself alive.

Mum had come round to clean a few times, and I felt like

we had both regressed twenty years; her asking me how I could live in such a dive whilst I yelled at her to get out of my room. I knew she meant well, but the real problem was that she would not stop asking me if I had spoken to Fran.

Lord above, I wondered what would my dad have done if this had happened to him.

Despite it having been two and a half months since the arrest, and despite all the legal, by-the-book investigation, I was no closer to understanding why Fran had done what she did.

Worse, I still had no idea how she was doing. I had received nothing from her. Not a letter, phone call, or even a text from some kind of smuggled burner phone. It had to be intentional. Surely it wasn't through a lack of means? I was tempted to just turn up at Bronzefield and ask to see her, but what if she didn't want to see me? What would I do then? Halloween, Christmas, and New Year's had all come and gone without Fran as I'd tried to distract myself as much as possible with the most mundane cases that came across my desk, but Vivian had given me carte blanche to work from home, mostly just doing the admin and paperwork for the other detectives.

I knew the truth, of course. Fran never wanted to speak to me again, and why would she? What kind of husband snitches on his wife, and gets her sent to prison? And what kind of pathetic cretin can't even look at her while it happens? It wasn't lost on me that a normal reaction would be some kind of repulsion at what my wife had done. But somehow, I didn't even feel any kind of cognitive dissonance, I knew my wife and I knew she would have had her reasons.

Between Christmas and New Year, Steve had come to the house carrying a knife wrapped in a plastic bag to ask me if I recognised the blade. I had tried to keep any hint of recognition from showing in my eyes, but I knew instantly it was the Nesmuk knife Fran had cherished so much. I hadn't even noticed it had been missing from the rack for months, Fran had always been the better chef. But the added element was now that I noticed a significant notch was missing from the tip of the blade, and I instantly knew that it had been her murder weapon. I lied to Steve of course, telling him I didn't think I'd seen it before, but I wasn't convinced he believed me. But God strike me down if I incriminated my wife any further.

I rallied as much as I could as I went over the road to walk Tony for Beryl. I had often spotted her watching me from across the way over the past few weeks, just staring from the window before I'd look in her general direction, at which point she'd promptly vanish into thin air. I was still pretty certain she could lip-read any conversation I was having, so I made sure not to stand close to the windows when talking to my mum or Andrew about the case.

'Hi, Gareth,' Beryl said, opening the door that was still adorned with a Christmas wreath, pulling me into her bosom and wrapping her arms around me tight. She did this every day I walked Tony. 'How are you?' she asked, still holding me close to her bosom, rubbing her hand up and down my back.

I had already prepared the default response.

'I'm surviving.'

'Oh yes, you are,' Beryl said as she loosened her grip around my lower chest – which was all she could reach – and I took the chance to gently pull myself away from her.

As usual, we exchanged the brief pleasantries, though her occasional glances to my mouth to read my lips continued to unsettle me. I was just about to leave to walk Tony when a text pinged through on my phone.

> Just been told I'm subbing in as the lead on the prosecution against Fran. I'm sorry, but I have to block your number. I appreciate we won't be friends after this. Been a pleasure. Isla.

Normally, this might have been upsetting, but the way the

year was going, it didn't even faze me. I was almost surprised the news wasn't shittier. It all felt like water off a duck's back at this point. After I had walked Tony and passed him back to Beryl, I came back to the house. Still cold and feeling empty, I averted my eyeline from any photos of Fran and me, including the huge one of our wedding day, which took up most of our hallway wall. I strolled into the living room, ready to collapse on the sofa, when I found Mep there, sprawled out on the floor. He wasn't breathing.

My brain went into panic mode. I snatched up my phone and scrambled for a YouTube video for CAT CPR, rapidly tapping the 'skip ad' button before following an annoying American lady blowing air into a stuffed cat. '100 to 120 times a minute,' she said.

With one hand on Mep's sternum and the other over his heart, I started compressions, but I didn't know how long to do it, so I just kept going, whispering, 'Please, Mep,' with each desperate press. Eventually, after about five minutes, I felt a pulse, very faint, and very slow. Mep's eyes were just open enough to recognise me, as he tried to let out a tiny, helpless mew.

I sprinted to the car, holding him in my arms and gently placing him in my lap as I began to reverse like a madman out of the driveway. Unfortunately, there was no law that allowed you to drive through red lights when your animal was sick. So, every pause at a traffic light had me frantically checking that small pulse was still pumping, before shouting obscenities at the inanimate lights above me.

I pulled up at the vet's, straight into the disabled space, slammed the car door without locking it, and rushed inside. I saw a small girl with her mum at the counter, holding onto her tortoise and probably engaging in some very pleasant chat with the receptionist. I ran through the sliding doors and hurled myself across the waiting area. I was so out of breath and my voice so raspy with worry that all I could do was hold Mep aloft. My unconscious cat, with its fur moist with his own sick. It looked like some really messed-up scene from *The Lion King*. Luckily, the receptionist understood the strange charade, seized Mep from me and charged into the vet's office, gesturing for me to wait outside.

It was a few hours later when the slight arsehole of a vet from last time gestured me to come into the room. He spoke with a little more sympathy this time. Mep was likely suffering with heart disease, as well as kidney problems; they had managed to keep him stable for now, and had got some nutrients inside him, but they weren't sure how long he would have left.

'He's a very old cat, Mr Donoghue. He's had a great life, but his body isn't what it used to be.'

'Is there a chance he'll recover? At all?'

'A slim chance. Medication and diuretics could help with the kidneys and heart to give Mep a good quality of life. But he may just slip away tonight, Mr Donoghue. He's very weak. Take him home, make him comfy. Maybe he'll rally, but he may also just be content to take his last breath.'

My first thought was: should I tell Fran? What could she do? As much as I wanted to, I couldn't bring a cat to prison for her to see at a reasonable distance. If anything, telling her Mep was dying – and that there was nothing we could do – might break her heart even more than her husband having been responsible for her being arrested. But would she want to know all the same?

The vet kept looking at me, his fingers interlaced, his eyes showing an understanding only a pet owner could know. A kind of gut-wrenching awfulness that was hard to put into words.

'Would you like to pay now, or we can invoice you later?'

. . .

I just held Mep again in my lap in the driver's seat, using one hand to stroke him when I could. Occasionally, I rested my hand against his chest, just to make sure his heart was still beating.

'Please don't go, my man,' I whispered to him as we stopped at a red light. 'Please don't go.'

When we got home, I wrapped Mep up in blankets and placed him in his favourite spot on the sofa. I gave him a quick kiss on the forehead as I heard the quiet murmur of a contented meow. I then sat next to him, booted up my laptop, and looked at what daytime TV had to offer.

Cis had sent me an email. I did a quick skim, but lacked the mental fortitude to read any more. She had clearly spent some solid time on it, probably with the trial about to begin she knew I'd be struggling with it all. Something along the lines that she was very sorry about what I was going through, and she'd always be my friend, but her job – and justice – had to take precedence. I knew it was all artifice, and I pressed the delete button as soon as I saw the words 'You know deep down what she did' flash up on one of the paragraphs, sending the message vanishing into cyberspace.

I was now feeling more and more of a slow-digesting rage. Cis and I had only just scratched the surface of how many lives the Heart of Hope Foundation had indirectly ruined in our initial investigation. Heart of Hope was meant to be a crucial lifeline to so many people, offering key services that the government had outsourced to them. Yet help never arrived to the people who needed it.

Furthermore, the closest I had come to a concrete motive for Fran was that they had been the ones to invest in the same children's home she had lived at. But it still didn't explain how that had propelled her to kill them. I had tried to investigate as much as I could under Vivian's radar, but nothing really explained why Fran had killed O'Neill.

I knew Cis and Isla were sure as hell ready to recruit Clark to position him against Fran, but weren't even thinking about rummaging through the mountains of dirty laundry of decades-long police cover-ups they had been told to ignore by the mysterious people above Vivian. How had an organisation like that existed for so long without anyone knowing about it? Well, a high-ranking policeman, the Leader of the Opposition and a successful businessman/fraudster made for quite a team, all with the sick façade of actually working on giving back to the community while they installed home hot tubs and went on all-expenses-paid holidays.

Mep and I were right in the middle of *Cash in the Attic* when I heard the doorbell go. I wondered if maybe a reporter had finally found out where I lived. I walked towards the door, ready to slam it shut just as quickly as I opened it. But as the door pulled back, I saw a man there, hair slicked back, and well dressed in an expensive designer suit. He looked as if he was about to ask me about the kingdom of Jehovah.

'Mr Donoghue? Andrew Shorestone, from Bark & Moore, just wondered if you had a few minutes to chat?'

'Oh,' I said, surprised, realising that I had only spoken to the gentleman representing Fran over the phone before. I didn't really know what I'd expected him to look like, but his general appearance had taken me aback, most notably because the man barely scratched five foot. He was the result of the several thousand pounds I had withdrawn from the secret fund I had been building to take Fran on a very belated honeymoon. I gestured for him to come in and take a seat in the living room.

'Can I make anything for you? A tea or a coffee or anything?' I asked as Andrew placed his briefcase down by the door, trying to ignore the complete tip the house was in.

'Not for me, thank you. I shan't be long,' he said as he took a seat on the very edge of the sofa, glancing to look at the cat next to him. Mep was still staring vacantly at the TV, refusing to acknowledge the new presence in the house.

'He's ill,' I explained as I took a seat on the ottoman opposite Andrew.

'Oh,' Andrew said, alarmed, inspecting Mep, seemingly unable to take his eyes off him. Maybe he thought I was harbouring a taxidermised cat in my living room; perhaps he thought I was having a psychotic episode. He seemed to move past it. 'Well, I just want to give you an update on the trial, with court proceedings starting in two weeks.'

I groaned, feeling my intestinal knot tighten.

'How is she doing though, Fran?'

'Urgh...' he said, considering his answer, trying to hide the grinding of his teeth together. 'CPS and the police are really pushing this case as hard as they can. They're dead set on declaring it cold-blooded murder on your wife's part.'

'And... you're certain I won't be called up to testify?' I asked nervously – a question that had been lingering in my mind ever since Fran was arrested.

'No. As I said, we thought about it, but it doesn't help our defence in any meaningful way. The prosecution will simply claim that you're biased.'

Andrew took another look at Mep, who must have felt his stare, the cat gradually rotating his head to glare blankly right back at him. Andrew quickly averted his gaze, pushing his hands through his greasy hair again. I wasn't sure, but I thought he felt intimidated by the cat.

'Okay, and how's the case looking overall?'

'Well,' said Andrew, stretching back onto the sofa, 'I can't lie, we're up against the wall. All the evidence points to Fran, and there's not a whole lot we can outwardly refute or deny. Fran is still denying killing him, point blank, telling the story that she went in, helped him with his shopping bags, cleared up some milk from his carpet and walked out again, but she's also the only one with any evidence that puts her there at the time of death—'

'But if she says she didn't do it, then maybe she didn't do it,' I said, perhaps deluding myself a little.

No, you're right, I was deluding myself a lot.

'Yeah, that would be the logical thing to think. But the evidence paints a clear picture,' Andrew stated, matter-of-factly. 'An elderly man vanishes suddenly, leaving no trace, yet they discover evidence of fresh blood loss and bone cartilage and organs in his shower drain. And the last person to see him is a woman who was also suspected of the murder of a close friend of his.' He grimaced, pushing back his hair again. 'You can see how that sounds, can't you?'

'So, what we're looking for is a miracle?' I asked.

'If someone came forward and confessed to killing O'Neill, that would be...'

Andrew paused, and his eyes widened. 'Fantastic,' he muttered. He looked slightly deranged as he said that, which made me realise that Fran was giving him a run for our money. 'Without that, there's no chance she gets away with this without prison, Gareth. I told her this this morning, but she didn't seem to get it. I'm sorry.'

'So, why are you telling me this?' I said coldly, pushing my head back against the cold surface of the wall behind me. I had somehow hoped he was here for good news.

'Because I've seen this all before and just want to prepare you for the worst face to face. The spouse doesn't think their loved one did it, but they did. Fran's going to go to prison for a while and even when she gets out, things won't snap back to the way they were. You know the statistics on divorce after one party gets out of prison, I presume?'

'I would like for you to leave, please,' I said as politely as I could.

Andrew saw that he had struck a very tender nerve and rose sharply from his seat.

'Before I go, though, I'm quite sorry, but I'm afraid I'm going to need some smart clothes for your wife.'

'Of course,' I said with a groan, contemplating the strongly worded email I would send to Andrew's employer as I fished my best guess out of Fran's wardrobe.

In the two weeks leading up to the trial, no matter how hard I tried to push it out of my mind, to convince myself I'd done the right thing, I knew I couldn't take back what I had done. I was the one who had turned my wife in; there was nobody else I could blame for my wife being in prison. I wished I'd just destroyed the evidence, stashed it away under some papers in my desk, or, better yet, never investigated Mr O'Neill's disappearance at all. Slowly, I skulked over to the last box left from our move. I knew that what I was about to do would only make everything worse, but I couldn't stop myself. I just wanted to feel something, anything, that was painful and sharp enough to break through the numbness.

The one box left unpacked held our photo albums. Carefully, I opened up the flaps, peeled back the layers of padding Fran had so meticulously placed around our wedding album, and pulled it free. I hadn't looked at them since they were printed. Somehow, they felt too special for just a casual glance. I flicked open the cover and there we were: five years younger in the church – my one condition for getting married: a proper church wedding, where we'd say our vows in front of God. I hadn't minded about anything else, that was just the one thing I'd asked for.

For better, for worse, in sickness and in health. I'd meant every word at the time, but now I couldn't help feeling that I'd gone back on those vows. I was supposed to protect Fran. But here I was. Alone in the house we'd bought to raise a family in.

Suddenly, I felt my phone buzz violently against my thigh. Snatching it out of my pocket, I glanced at the screen. It was a number I didn't recognise, but that had been a common occurrence lately. Every time I'd ignored a call when I'd thought it was just a scammer, it had always turned out to be an important party.

Maybe it was someone from Andrew's office before the trial started on Monday. 'Hello?' I said, answering quickly.

'This call is from a person currently in a prison in England or Wales,' the automated voice spoke. 'All calls are logged and recorded and may be listened to by a member of prison staff. If you do not wish to accept this call, please hang up now.'

My heart jolted with a kind of nervous excitement, like when the notification came through that your crush had liked your profile photo on Facebook. Fran? Could it be Fran? What the hell was I even going to say to her?

Before I could spiral into any kind of overthinking, the automated voice ended abruptly, replaced by the hum and buzz of what I could only guess was prison ambience.

'Gareth? Are you there?'

It was her. The sound of her voice sent a shiver through me; it was almost nostalgic hearing it again as I noticed the skin on my arm begin to erupt with tiny bumps. Lord, that hadn't happened for a while.

'Hi, Fran, yeah it's... it's me.'

'Hey,' she replied.

I don't know why, but it surprised me at first that this wasn't like our old phone calls. Her voice was obviously different, more monotone and distant. I mean, I suppose she was speaking to the person who had turned her in to the police, the one who hadn't even been able to look her in the eye as they'd taken her away.

'Look, there's so much to say,' she continued. Her words were steady but still glaringly hollow of any kind of emotion; she had rehearsed what she was saying to me. 'There's still so much we need to talk about, but I just... I really wanted to hear your voice before the trial begins as I don't know if I'll have a chance again. And I wanted to say I'm sorry for everything. I don't know if that means anything to you now, but I wanted to say it...'

I could have sobbed like a baby there and then. Fran's voice may have been empty of any emotion, but I hadn't heard it for so long. A brutal combination of emotions churned inside me: relief, happiness, sadness, guilt. It was nauseating, as if no human was ever meant to feel so many things so strongly all at once.

'I'm... so sorry too,' I said, trying not to let my voice quiver. 'I'm so sorry I didn't even look at you, I was just so... ashamed and all of this is my fault, and... I wish I could take it all back. I wish there was something I could do.'

'There isn't, okay?' she replied, her words brusque, but still not purposefully cruel. She paused, and her tone softened ever so slightly. 'God, I have to admit, it's so nice to hear your voice again. How's Mep?'

I glanced over at the cat, who looked like someone had stuck googly eyes on a mound of mangled fur. He ambled closer to investigate who I was talking to.

'He's okay,' I lied. 'He misses you.'

'Good.' Her voice wavered before she corrected herself. 'Look, I've got to go now, but... just thanks, I guess, for the last few years and just... take care of yourself, okay?'

'Okay,' I repeated, my throat tightening and my eyes watering. Then something else took over. 'Fran, I just want to say... I love you?'

'Okay,' she echoed softly. Then the line went dead.

My mum had always told me she wished she had known

her last conversation with dad would be the final time she would ever speak to him. She'd told me there was so much she wished she had said. But there I was, knowing I had maybe just spoken to my wife for the last time and still thinking of things I wanted to tell her.

It had almost become something of a routine now, trying to drift off to sleep with teleshopping in the background.

It was the same lady on again. Very prim and very proper, but clearly not loving her job as she walked around the overly saturated set with a dead-eyed look. I imagine the viewing figures for teleshopping weren't exactly high.

She presented a product, the price and number flashing on screen. The easy trim, at-home haircut set. If I called the number now, they'd throw in a free comb as well.

I shuffled around on the sofa, but no matter what I did, I couldn't seem to get comfortable, so I got to my feet and yanked out the cushions to flip them over. That was when I saw a gold sparkle shoot into the air and land with a small clink right on the carpet. Mep hopped over to sniff it, but I quickly reached down and snatched it up before he could swallow it. I certainly didn't want to deal with the opposite problem Mep was currently having. It was an earring: Fran's. I gripped it tightly to my chest, exhaled deeply, and then settled back down on the sofa. God, I missed her, I missed her so much. I missed her bringing me risotto at work, I missed the boring bread-and-butter sex, I missed the stupid arguments, and most of all, I missed talking to her. I missed everything about her. I knew she loved me too, but I still just didn't understand why she'd done what she had.

I stretched my arm out to feel Mep, but couldn't find him there.

'Mep?' I called, propping myself up on my elbow and

squinting through the dark to make him out. I could just about see his slim silhouette below me, his glowing eyes glinting. I watched him slowly gobble the leftovers of my microwaved mac and cheese I had abandoned by the sofa. I leaned forward, carefully, cautious not to make any kind of noise or movement that could throw him off as he chomped on each bite. To my astonishment, he didn't puke it straight up over the carpet. I listened closely to every single audible gulp he made.

'Good boy,' I whispered, leaning back into my indented spot on the sofa. I continued watching the telemarketing lady on TV, attempting to sell the easy trim, but any good insomniac could tell that she wasn't having it tonight. Maybe she'd had a rough day with the kids. There was so little zing behind her tonight, deep crow's feet stretched from her eyes as she snatched up the easy trim and held it upward. She seemed almost lost for words in the majesty of something so... cheap.

'Look, level me with here,' the lady said with a half-groan. 'You know sometimes, when you have really stupid ideas, and you know they're stupid. You know they're foolish, and you know that you're probably going to regret it and that it's probably not a good move,' she said to the camera, clearly in response to her producer begging her to try something, anything through her earpiece. 'But something within you compels you to just do it anyway. To act.'

She paused.

'That's what the easy trim is, so don't waste time in picking one up today.'

TWENTY-ONE

FRAN

Surprisingly, I'd been given my own room or prison cell or whatever exactly I was meant to call it. Something about remanded prison rule seven, saying that I didn't have to share with another prisoner until I was officially found guilty. But it was harder to keep up the façade that this was all part of my budget weekend away when there were literal thick cast iron bars now outside my window.

I had a desk, a small flatscreen TV, and some surprisingly nice patterned curtains to cover up the avant-garde design of exposed metal. The cell even featured a lime green accent wall to contrast the dull beige I had in my custodial suite.

Although, I had to admit, I not only felt like the new girl at school – but also the new girl that had her arm in a cast, so couldn't do PE. I didn't need to go to inmate education or work, and the guards didn't treat me with quite the same animosity as the others. They mostly just left me to do my own thing between roll calls. One of them even asked me about the book I was reading, and we engaged in some light small talk, although he was no Paul.

I got to meet some new people, which was nice; a different

type of people from my usual neighbourhood, though I felt like I was doing a good job of the head-down-low thing. I had made no nemeses yet, no one trying to shiv me during recreation, which I was taking as a good sign. A lot of the stereotypes I'd had about prison were already eroding away.

But while I was projecting the whole unfazed, strong-but-silent type around the rest of the inmates, truth be told, I was terrified. Not of *them*, of course. Sure, there were probably some other killers in here too, but I bet I could win against them in a one-on-one fistfight easily; I had killed scarier people than them, even if some of them looked pretty damn scary. What I was truly petrified of was that the rest of my life could be like this. To the rest of the inmates, remanded custody seemed to carry something of a stigma, like I was a baby-faced infant about to have my bliss shattered at any moment. Word was, a lot of those on remand just pleaded guilty to get some control of their lives back, and not live in constant anxiety. A bunch of inmates in the lunch queue had casually told me to get used to my new home for the next few years.

I had made a friend, though, Lucy. She had killed her sister over a row about inheritance, but had told me in good faith that her sister was a bit of a bitch, so I was going to take her word for it. I tried to stay on the good side of the guards, so they could put me with Lucy as a roommate if I was found guilty and had to be stuck here until my teeth started falling out.

'I hear you had your lawyer coming in today?' Lucy asked me at lunch, as she dipped her bread into the mayo. An interesting cuisine choice.

'Yeah, to bring some clothes and to brief me before it all kicks off tomorrow.'

'Oh yeah, when is your trial again?'

'Tomorrow,' I repeated, hoping I wouldn't make Lucy feel stupid.

'Awhhh, that'll be nice,' said Lucy, as if we were talking

about a cream tea at a country estate. She took a big bite of her bread before returning it to dip into the mayo. 'It will be good to get out for a bit and get some fresh air, I guess. How come you never have any visitors?' she asked, dropping her bread with a thud against the plastic tray and crossing her arms. 'You don't get anybody. You haven't got a boyfriend or a husband or a girlfriend?'

'Oh, I have a husband,' I said, before reconsidering. 'I have a husband technically, but for complicated reasons, he's a lot of the reason I'm in here.'

'Ohh, I see,' Lucy said, tapping her nose. 'Pimp?'

'What?! No, he's a police officer.'

'Oh, that makes more sense. He arrested you?'

'No, but he helped.'

Ooh, that hurt more than I thought it would, to say it aloud.

'Not much of a husband then, is he?' Lucy said, using the last teeny bit of crust to mop up the remaining modicum of mayo.

'No. Well, he isn't exactly...' I didn't want to complete the sentence. I guess I hadn't ended up being much of a wife. Whatever way you cut it, I had killed our neighbour – I cut him up in quite a few ways actually.

I kept thinking about the phone call, remembering how good it had felt to hear Gareth's voice again. God, just hearing him speak again, I'd wanted him to tell me we had a dinner reservation at Positano's tonight, to wear the dress he liked and that he'd swing by at eight.

Like most of my major life decisions, I'd been mulling this one over for a while before finally taking the plunge. I'd often lingered by the phones in the block, debating whether to be the one to make the call, but I'd figured this was probably going to be my last chance before the trial. Andrew had already warned me I had homework for tonight to prepare for.

I hoped Gareth wouldn't feel too upset by the fact I hadn't said that I loved him back. Thing was, it wasn't because I didn't – as hard as I tried to deny it, I knew I did. It was just too agonising to say it aloud. Despite everything – the arrest, him not visiting for the past three months – I still loved him.

Lucy went to go and meet her boyfriend, who I had heard an annoyingly large amount about, and I decided to go back to my journal, my *ikiagi*. I couldn't really make a mind map in prison about how to kill Clark, so I instead drew random doodles to mark ideas and plans. Like my own personal language of hieroglyphics, I made it up as I went along. Getting away with it would be the difficult part.

Look, at this point, you might be thinking, 'So what? You had a tough childhood because some men stole money from the children's home you grew up in, big deal. But until a few months ago, you had a great life, Fran, so all of this is completely self-inflicted. Why are you living in the past?'

To that I say: maybe you had a rough childhood, even a terrible one. But I'm guessing you've never been eleven years old, with the house on fire, desperately trying to open the door to the next room. The wood's swollen from the heat, so it won't budge, and you keep frying your hands on the doorknob, unable to shift it even a little bit as you begin to hear your sister Edith's terrified screams from inside. Tell me then if you wouldn't want to kill the people responsible for that.

I thought about what Angus said, about waiting until Clark had popped his clogs of old age. But that was part of the problem. I didn't *want* Clark to have a peaceful death, where he tripped over in the night whilst trying to take a piss and died on a carpet that hadn't been vacuumed for twenty years. I wanted him to look into my eyes and remember me as I killed him. I wanted to see the same flash of recognition that I had in O'Neill as he'd slipped away before tumbling down onto the carpet.

However, I was starting to think that could be quite unlikely considering a life in prison was looming over me.

About an hour into my strategizing, I heard a knock at the door. I swivelled around, trying to give the body language of a woman that definitely was not planning to kill again.

It was one of the guards.

'Hey, Donoghue, there's someone here to see you.'

The meeting room looked like some weird university meet and greet, with big fluorescent foam chairs. I was wondering what I would say to Gareth. If I'd refuse to talk, or if I'd maybe just break down, kiss him, and jump his bones right there and then. It was anyone's guess; I didn't even know myself. I had spent weeks building up the courage to call him before I'd finally ripped off the plaster yesterday, but I hadn't thought he would come in to see me.

As the guard led me across the room I saw Lucy in a corner, whose boyfriend was not-so-subtly slipping something into her hand that she crammed fast into her pocket. I kept my eyes peeled across the room, looking for my husband, but I couldn't spot Gareth at all. Instead, I saw someone with their hood up, their back to the wall and hands scratching rhythmically on the bright red fabric of the chair.

'Angus? What are you doing here?'

'Hey,' Angus said, appearing happy to see me, but all the symptoms of his anxiety remaining on his face. 'Hey, how are you?'

I shot him a concerned glance before sitting down on the green foam chair.

'You know I'm in prison, right? I'm not exactly excelling in life at the moment.'

'Yeah, of course, sorry,' he said remorsefully, the joke missing him by a country mile.

'It's fine, don't worry about it. Are you okay?'

Angus nodded, gulping, shuffling again in his chair. I was still getting over the fact that he had even made it here. I hadn't seen Angus leave his house for years, and now the last two times I had seen him, he had been somewhere new. I could tell that prison wasn't exactly a great place for him to visit and test his boundaries, though. He was wearing the red felt on the chair away to reveal the grey scalp of the fabric beneath.

'Yeah, yeah, of course, I was just... worried about you, is all,' Angus stuttered.

'Is Gareth okay?' he asked after a moment. It almost unnerved me to hear Angus ask this many questions. It made me wonder if I should have checked in to prison sooner, to push my brother out of his comfort zone. Maybe he'd actually be worried about *me*, for a change.

'He's doing okay,' I lied.

Angus seemed to accept the answer as he did another survey of his surroundings before talking.

'What do you think people talk about in here? Like, what's there to say? Do you get to watch TV?'

'We do, but it's restricted. We can't watch it all the time, and I try to stay away from the news as much as possible. I don't need to be any more depressed than I already am. What are you going to tell me? Am I famous?'

'Moderately. You're not in all the papers and you haven't made it to any front pages, but you got an article in the *Daily Mail* that was like...' Angus uncomfortably shuffled around in his chair. '"Psycho Sexy Neighbour",' he recalled, it almost paining him to repeat the headline.

'Psycho Sexy Neighbour, eh?' I said, feeling the teeniest glimpse of a smile creeping along my lips. Now, that was a moniker.

'Oh, God, please don't ask me to bring in the paper.'

'No, but just please keep a copy.' I inhaled excitedly. 'I might get a sexy prison pen pal.'

I heard Angus's throat close up as he stifled a gag, but I could tell that even if he didn't want to admit it, he found that a little funny.

'It had an interview from your neighbour, too, the annoying one.'

'Who?'

'Beryl, I think her name was.'

'Ah, shit.'

'She actually said she didn't believe it could be you. Said you and Gareth were one of the sweetest couples she had ever met and she would be "blown down" if a jury found you guilty. Which I suppose is good. Yes?' He paused for a second, gearing up to ask a question he wasn't sure he wanted the answer to. 'What do you think your chances are tomorrow?'

I had the urge to lie to Angus, to protect him from the reality of the situation. But being realistic would be better for him in the long run. With me in prison, he would have no one to check up on him, no one to make sure he was still somewhat connected to society. I supposed that it was important I used the small amount of time I had left to prepare him for the worst.

'Not good. I think I have a small chance with the jury if I turn on the classy waterworks.'

'What's the classy waterworks?'

'Like, you know, the full waterworks is full-on blubbering, drooling, little bits of snot running down your face. Classy waterworks is like a single tear rolling down your face and a little bit of quiver in your voice, but very, very subtle. It's meant to work a treat. I watched a video about it on the internet.'

'God, you're such a...' Angus searched for the words. 'Such a psychopath, sometimes.'

I hated that word, but maybe it was time to accept it a little. I was, in fact, a bit of a psychopath.

Angus chuckled, which turned into a laugh. It had been years since I had heard Angus laugh. Maybe it was the nerves, but to see him smile almost made me want to cry. God, what was wrong with me?

I almost wanted my last day in prison before my trial to drag. I wanted the long, drawn-out hours to give me enough time to emotionally prepare and just think of something or anything that would somehow exonerate me. But I had a feeling that there was no hail Mary, no eureka moment, no miracle coming my way.

As hard as I tried, I could barely eat anything on Sunday evening. I chased peas around my plastic tray as Lucy watched me.

I sat in bed long after lights out, wondering what Gareth was doing at that precise moment, how he was feeling after that phone call. I didn't know what I wanted him to feel, as essentially, I didn't know what I was feeling.

I knew some people longed to relive those romantic days where they'd had their first kiss with their partner, their proposal, their wedding – but all I could keep thinking about was Gareth coming home, slouching onto the sofa, and the way he would wrap his arm around me, kiss me on the forehead, and pull me close. That was what I missed. I guessed that was what I'd given up.

I threw up almost five times before 5 a.m. and a few more after that – so much so that my cell neighbour even hollered for me to shut up and to vomit more quietly. Which, attempting to be a nice future prison inmate, I did try to. It was about utilising your jaw muscles, I learnt. I'm not sure if you've ever tried to expel your bodily contents in a silent manner, but it turns out it's actually quite difficult.

I was woken up before roll call, allowed to change into the

clothes that Andrew had brought for me, presumably chosen by Gareth, and pushed into a police van where I sat for a few hours as we drove to the court.

I couldn't really make out where we were for the whole journey, never sure if we were stopping because of a traffic light or because we were outside the courts. It was only when I heard the crank of the handbrake that I had realised we had arrived. Judgement Day.

I was escorted in. A few journalists were there snapping photos, but it was not exactly the huge crowds of paparazzi or furious sign-waving citizens I had imagined. I thought I was Psycho Sexy Neighbour?

They led me through the corridors of the court, the atrium filling up with people, a police officer on either side as I was guided into the dock. It was somewhat reassuring to know there was nothing left to throw up, my innards continuing to writhe and tense as I sat on the poorly padded wooden stall. I saw Andrew enter with his assistant, wearing their funny wigs, and then Isla coming in wearing the same.

Isla. There were a few times where I'd thought she wanted to shag Gareth, so I'd always kept her at arm's length and had asked for Gareth to tell me only the breadcrumbs of any workday which involved her. But he had told me how barbaric she was in court, and her track record as the prosecution was pretty much perfect.

The judge walked in and took her seat at her bench. I glanced at the twelve members of the jury that all took their respective seats, and wondered how many could potentially be won over by my charm; I needed some allies. There were a few middle-aged men who I could barely tell apart; balding, pot-bellied folks who looked like their perfect Sunday would be football, beer, and then a good shag with their missus doing cowgirl. If I did the classic defenceless fawn act, I wondered whether they'd maybe have my back. I needed those big, brave men to get me off a big nasty murder charge. There were two people who looked like they had no idea what they were doing, two mid-thirties professionals who were almost certainly sleeping together, and a lovely looking old lady towards the front. She had perfectly round glasses and the most innocent face I had ever seen, a face of pure unabashed neutrality. No pursed lips of a resting bitch face, no scowling eyes, no fake smile. A decent, genuine face if I had ever seen one. I was hoping that even if the others thought I was guilty, she'd be my guardian angel in the deliberation room, fighting my case, arguing that I should be completely absolved of any wrongdoing – for just how virtuous I seemed. The rest of the jury I couldn't work out yet: a pretty diverse group of faces that I just hoped I could make something of a good impression on.

I took a glance at the gallery near the back of the court room: all of them faces I didn't recognise, apart from one right at the back. I had to stare for at it for a while, but it was unmistakably Gareth, although his patchy facial hair had begun to grow in, and his features seemed gaunt, as if he hadn't eaten or slept in weeks. He was looking in my direction, but he was too far away to see if he was making any actual eye contact with me.

My eyes glanced away as I saw Isla rise in her seat, my heart almost lurching in my stomach as I heard someone say with a big booming voice, 'All rise.'

Andrew had told me that no one was stupid enough not to stand up at that part. I almost saw that as a bit of a challenge, but decided that maybe this would be a better experiment for when I was at court for an overdue parking ticket, rather than murder.

'Francesca Donoghue lived next door to Gordon O'Neill, a retired pensioner, who enjoyed a quiet and solitary life,' Isla began. She turned to the jury. 'You, the jury, will hear about the troubled upbringing of Francesca Donoghue, as well as the various eyewitness and video evidence that puts her at the scene of the crime during the estimated time that Gordon O'Neill is suspected to have been murdered. You will hear from an eyewitness who saw a woman of Mrs Donoghue's description disposing of what looked like body parts in the river, a knife found at a restaurant that Francesca frequented with her husband, as well as a statement from a member of the forensics team which will provide further proof to you, the jury, that Francesca Donoghue murdered Gordon O'Neill.'

I watched the prosecution assistant hand out neatly laminated pieces of paper to the jury. Andrew told me that this would be a copy of the indictment, whatever the hell that was. I hadn't really been listening when he'd explained the rather tedious particulars of a criminal trial.

'It is well known that O'Neill was something of a philanthropist in his community, even donating to the children's home Mrs Donoghue was a part of as a child. He had no record of criminality, no convicted charges, and was an upstanding member of society. A loving father and grandfather.'

Last I heard, his wife abandoned him and took their daughter with her, so I wasn't sure why Isla was painting him as some kind of saint beloved within the community. Well, actually, I knew exactly why.

'Ladies and gentlemen of the jury,' Isla said, glancing over to the jury members. 'We believe the charitable endeavours of Mr O'Neill were why Mrs Donoghue killed him; that this was an act of someone angry at the system, killing someone she wrongly thought was responsible for her pain. This is the case that the Crown will prove to you, leaving no doubt in your minds that Francesca Donoghue is guilty of murder.'

Isla sat back down, looking pleased with herself, as she leaned over to see what one of her team was writing on a very ostentatious leather-bound notepad. She nodded in agreement. The few of them were crowded around like girls at secondary school, gossiping about the slutty geography teacher.

'Thank you, Mrs Thorne,' said the judge, leaning towards the mic on her stand. 'Ladies and gentlemen of the jury, you have now heard the opening speech for the prosecution. Mr Shorestone, you would also like to make a speech for the defence?'

Andrew rose. I half expected him to tuck in his shirt as he did so, but he seemed comfortable, remarkably at ease in the courtroom. The man who I had thought was going to collapse from a coronary at any minute, seemed somewhat... confident. This chubby, boorish, and remarkably short gentleman had changed into a captivating, enigmatic man – who I now realised was actually quite handsome for his age.

'Ladies and gentlemen of the jury, some of what Mrs Thorne has said is true. My client was indeed seen with Mr O'Neill around the time of his disappearance. She also has a troubled history within the social care system. However, what Mrs Thorne failed to add was that this history shaped Francesca Donoghue into a compassionate member of society. My client, Francesca, was helping O'Neill with his shopping at one point in time within the forty-eight-hour period in which his suspected murder may have taken place. Let me ask you this: what kind of murderer helps someone with their groceries before stabbing them in the eye? I hope we can understand the rather drastic and dramatic leaps in logic the prosecution is trying to convey.'

Andrew twisted himself to address his next point directly to Isla in a way that oozed with confidence.

'Further to that, I hadn't realised that in this country, being brought up in the care system predetermined your future within society. My client has had a reputable career within the social services and does a great deal to help children who have been in the same position as her. I am looking forward to hearing what the prosecution has to say what someone like Mrs Donoghue has to gain by killing her next-door neighbour.'

He had her there.

A few hours ago, I had been half expecting Andrew to just throw the towel in right there and then and tell Gareth to keep the money, but now I thought that perhaps there was some minuscule chance for me yet.

TWENTY-TWO

GARETH

I checked one more time in the mirror, poring over my hairline again. It had definitely shifted in the past few months. I did wonder if that was due to the days of no showering, insane levels of stress, and a diet consisting mostly of microwaveable macaroni and cheese from the shitty store at the end of the street just to not die of starvation along with Mep.

Needless to say, I had certainly looked better. In my defence, it had been a long day, and seeing your wife on trial after you'd been the one who'd turned her in was a pretty stressful situation, especially when the reasons why she'd had a penchant for the odd murder had become all the clearer. I was just about to google the cost of a hair transplant in Turkey when my phone – which was teetering on the edge of the sink – began to aggressively buzz. I snatched it up before it decided to end it all and leap off the side.

The number wasn't one I recognised. But nevertheless, I decided to pick up.

'Hello?'

'Ah, hello, Mr Donoghue, I hope you're okay. It's Dr Patel. I've tried ringing this number a few times as I couldn't reach your wife. I was calling to talk a bit more about when you'd like another appointment to discuss further options regarding fertility treatment.'

It took me a second to click who it was. Our appointment with Dr Patel felt like a lifetime ago.

'Oh, Dr Patel,' I said, straightening my back as if I had to stand to attention. 'I thought that we were waiting on you to call us back?'

'Ahhh, may I ask if you've spoken to your wife about this recently, Mr Donoghue?'

I steadied myself by placing a hand around the rim of the sink. *Oh, Fran, what else haven't you told me?*

'Ahh, now I understand. Sorry, it's been a bit of a long day,' I said, hoping he wouldn't sense any uncertainty or lack of confidence in my voice. 'This is about the test results, yes? She did tell me about them. So, we need to come in for some more tests?'

It was a wild guess, but I knew he wouldn't tell me anything if I showed I was ignorant.

'Yes, that's it, so just find a time with your wife when you can call reception and we can get you booked in to discuss the next options. I know it can be quite distressing and concerning at times like this, and it can be easy to be pessimistic about your chances of conceiving. But this isn't an opportunity to give up all hope. There are options, even if it isn't the news we were maybe hoping for.'

I didn't know what to say. Fran would tell me that I was buffering right now, as I racked my brain to figure out why she would keep this from me too. When had she found out? Presumably, before the arrest? But a more concerning question kept wrangling its way into my head.

Was she keeping anything else from me?

'Well, I was just checking up on you,' the doctor remarked, filling in the uncomfortable silence between us. 'How about you find some time to talk to your wife about when you could next come in, and we can go from there?'

'Off the record, though, doc, what are our chances?' I muttered, running my hand back and forth through my scraggly hair, trying to ignore the various strands that were breaking off and floating down towards the sink.

'I wouldn't like to guess, Mr Donoghue. How about we just run some more tests, and then we'll discuss that if and when we come to it?'

'Sounds great. Thank you, doctor.' I didn't know what else to say. 'Ch... cheerio,' I said with a vocal flourish, like some posh aristocrat, cringing at myself as I hung up the phone.

Why had I said 'cheerio'?

Up until three months ago, I'd felt like my marriage with Fran had lasted where others had failed because of our commitment, courtesy and communication. That was, after all, what was in *How to Make Your Marriage Work*, which I had read cover to cover leading up to our wedding. It was what I always told people when they asked me why we looked so content with each other, why we always stared lovingly into each other's eyes, and why we seemed to still... well... like each other.

After a final glance at my hairline, I took a deep breath and steeled myself. To enact this plan, I knew I needed unwavering focus and confidence. If I hesitated, it could all come crumbling down.

'Oh, Gareth, are you even meant to be here?' A pause. 'You look like shit.'

'What did you just say?' I grunted, before fully distinguishing whose gruff London accent it was.

I turned around to see it was Darren, standing there with this weird look on his face like he didn't know if he should say something cocky, or not say anything else at all. Probably only the third thought he'd ever had in his life, poor bloke.

'Nothing, just... have a good day, man,' he said, his voice trailing off as he strutted over to the urinals.

I felt a deep urge to hiss something venomous to Darren, to finally call him out on his bullshit. But the smallest, tiniest iota of patience I had told me it was best to keep my mouth shut and walk away.

'Heard your wife's chances aren't looking good,' Darren muttered as he approached the urinal. 'And did you hear we found a knife? She really was a crazy bitch.'

'Don't you dare speak about my wife, you piece of shit.'

Darren froze just as he finished fiddling with his fly. His dick was already out, but he was so clearly stunned that he spun 180 degrees, cock swaying with him. I thought maybe it would be tiny, justifying all his ultra-machoism, but there it was, flaccid – actually somewhat average – not as small and misshapen as I'd previously expected.

But no one calls my wife a bitch, although Darren's tone suggested he was speaking about Fran from first-hand experience.

'What did you just say to me?' Darren asked.

I stood my ground, Impulsive, Tired, Depressed Gareth taking control, edging myself closer to Darren, trying to maintain eye contact. But admittedly it was quite hard to be threatening when someone had their cock out.

'You know what I said. What are you going to do about it?' I said, lightly pushing my hand into his chest. That sounded like something someone who knew what they were doing would say. I hoped in execution it came across as assertive as I hoped. I wanted Darren to throw the first punch. I knew I could take it, and I'd been waiting desperately for months to throw a clenched fist back, straight into his jaw.

I saw his eyes flash with fury before he realised his appendage was still unsheathed: I had a one-up on him. I bet that wouldn't do great for his mobility in a fist fight.

I pushed Darren again, doing my best to provoke him as I saw his hand begin to contract into a fist.

'What are you going to do? What are you going to do?' I goaded, continuing to barge him. His back slapped against the tiled bathroom wall as he desperately struggled to put his dick back in his trousers in order to throw a punch.

'What's going on here?' another voice behind me asked.

This one was easy to recognise: Steve. I couldn't glance at him as that would mean breaking the macho stare-down, but I did wonder what was going through his brain, seeing this situation. I wondered what was going through Darren's brain too, actually. To be fair, I wondered what was going through my own brain as I stood there, eyes locked with one of the people I resented most in the world, still with his dick out, desperately trying to tuck it away.

'Go on then, Darren, I'll let you throw the first one for free,' I muttered, genuinely wanting him to – just so I'd finally have the chance to sock him back, right in his skull.

'To hell with this,' Darren murmured, successfully placing his penis back in his pants, zipping up his fly, and marching past Steve out of the bathroom.

'Gareth?' said Steve, clearly shocked at both my presence and appearance as I rotated towards him. 'What... what are you doing here? You know you can't be here. Vivian said you couldn't come in while Fran's trial was happening!'

I followed Darren's lead and barged past Steve, out the door and along the office floor as he shifted into a half-walk, half-jog after me. I reckoned I had about three minutes to prepare the email, and then five minutes to talk to Vivian. I could be in and out in no time, before there was a chance for any officers to escort me out.

'Gareth? Gareth? Talk to me,' Steve snapped, nipping at my heels like an overexcited terrier as I navigated through the winding maze of desks and office booths. A few confused faces peeped over the separators to inspect whatever kind of commotion was occurring.

'What's there to say, Steve?' I said back to him as I sharply turned a corner, hoping I would lose him, but he only smacked into a notice board before promptly continuing his high-speed pursuit.

'Urgh, I don't know, like, why you're still at the station when you should still be on compassionate leave?' Steve asked, frantic.

I reached my desk, strolled over to my desktop, and powered it on as Steve reached out, trying to push the off button before I slapped his hand away with a fair deal of force.

'Ouch,' he said, almost sounding offended that I had actually hit him.

But I ignored him, turning his incessant nagging into background noise as I logged into my account and waited for it to boot up. I think it was safe to say that I was becoming a touch unhinged. I realised I just didn't care any more.

Steve attempted a softer approach, placing a hand on my shoulder. 'Look, I know you're having a tough time, Gareth. But you can't just barge into the station like this. You need to go home.'

'Steve,' I said, swivelling my head to look him dead in the eyes whilst my fingers hovered over the computer keyboard, ready to put in my password. 'Do you really think that you, of all people, can lecture me about what I can and can't do?'

'What do you...' he began, before the penny dropped. He brushed his wrist across his nose instinctively before his face transformed into a mild snarl. I heard the computer start-up sound and snapped my head back to enter my password as Steve's footsteps receded, probably to get the station security to escort me out and make sure they cancelled all of my entry ID.

When my computer had fully loaded, I slipped the USB into the docking station, typed the case number, and whacked the 'schedule send' button before strolling over to Vivian's office. I hoped she hadn't just gone to the bathroom, or I'd really be screwed with this plan I had concocted whilst in a half-daze watching teleshopping last night.

I pressed 'record' on my phone before slipping it into my pocket. I pushed open Vivian's door as gently as all the adrenaline coursing through my veins would allow, and plonked myself down in the seat before Vivian had even looked up from her paperwork. After a solid ten seconds, she finally did a double-take, noticing it was me.

'Gareth? Should you be here? And you know the rules about knocking into my office, I—'

'Vivian. Let's not play games,' I said, remembering what I had read about how to be intimidating. Intense eye contact, short sentences, strong posture, and consistent voice tone. 'I want the name of the man who saw Fran throwing limbs into the river, and I want the full unredacted version of the case files about O'Neill and Clark. Give me that, and I'll be on my way.'

She swirled her tongue across her front teeth before speaking, sounding slightly bemused. 'Say that again for me, please? I didn't hear you.' She seemed almost enchanted by my gall.

'You heard me the first time.'

Vivian smiled, appearing to enjoy this newfound confidence I possessed, as if she couldn't wait to crush it in the palm of her hand.

'Or what, exactly, Gareth? What are you going to do?'

This was the uppercut. This was where my plan could all go disastrously wrong.

'Or I forward an email chain between you and Cis about the police wanting to keep this whole thing under wraps because of Macleod.'

Vivian's face dropped far faster than I was expecting, but I was too into the flow of my monologue to stop. I had practised to

Mep as my audience too many times. I had to keep going, or I'd lose the rhythm and have to start all over again.

'You know, I don't think Cis thought I'd see it, but I had a lot of time on my hands. I read how your predecessors protected Macleod to save yet another Met Police corruption scandal, how they turned a blind eye to his and his friends' activities because he was the Director of the SFO. How O'Neill was already known to the police for all his past embezzlement and they had done absolutely nothing about it. I've compiled it all in a nice, tidy email, ready to release to a hundred news outlets. I've had a lot of spare time over the past few months. Now, how do you think that would affect Fran's trial? Or the police's public standing? Or your standing?' I said, lifting the piece of paper Cis had given me a few weeks ago with her login details.

Vivian's face transformed before my eyes from cold, mocking indifference to a nervous, bubbling anger. She snatched the paper out of my hands to verify.

'You wouldn't dare...' she murmured, skimming over the paper to make sure what I was saying was legit.

'You got me – it's only ninety-two news outlets. I thought the *Financial Times* wouldn't really want to report on it. It's all just the gross tabloids and snotty broadsheets that you're so afraid of, with all the details about O'Neill, the Heart of Hope Foundation, the embezzlement – I particularly liked your quote to Cis in your email of the twelfth of November: "It's best we just find someone we can throw to CPS for them to eat." How charming.'

I inched my chair closer to her. 'You were told to make this all go away by the chief superintendent. They're worried Fran might spill all their secrets, and what, you think if she confesses "guilty" as part of a plea bargain, she'll keep quiet? Is that what you're banking on? Or better yet, she says nothing so as to not incriminate herself? You make me sick, Vivian.'

Vivian launched herself out of her chair and charged

towards me. I thought she was going to knock me out in one swift punch to the face, but she rocketed past me, slamming the door to her office shut just as I saw Steve and a few security officers turning around the corner to chuck me out.

'Piss off,' she yelled at them through the door, before shoving her face right into mine, teeth bared, nostrils flared.

'Do you know what you're doing? I gave you a break after everything with your wife, but this is a new level of stupid,' she growled.

Crikey, she really was quite scary. I tried to look as unbothered by it as possible. Telling myself to maintain eye contact, confident tone, relaxed hand movements to show that it was me who was in control of the situation.

'You have four minutes before it schedule-sends, by the way,' I remarked, edging my head slightly closer to hers, trying not to seem the least bit frightened.

I saw her eyes practically launch upwards. She twisted her feet again towards the door, ready to charge across the office towards my desk and bust my desktop to smithereens.

'Oh, only I can stop it, you know. It's in the cloud,' I remarked.

I had no idea if that was actually how the cloud worked, but Vivian seemed to believe it, slamming her palm against the body of the door in frustration and then throwing another kick into it for good measure. Through the foggy glass, I saw a few people careening over, including Steve and security, wondering what I had said to piss her off this much.

'It was a clever crime, really,' I rambled on. 'There are so many local council grants, donations from big corporations, government sponsored funding... And when you assemble the dream team of the master financial fraudster, the Director of SFO at the Met, and some household-name political chap who probably dines with all the bigwigs with the cash and the connections, you've got a business that just flows money. All with the perfect image of actually being three men giving back to the community they love so dearly. You want to know how much they lined their own pockets with, Vivian? Over the 90s, they pocketed £4.2 million for themselves. Just think how much that would be in today's money.'

Vivian just shook her head at me. It was like she was aghast at my actions but not at those of her predecessors or superiors.

'But of course, that's not just it, is it?' I asked rhetorically as I yanked a few of the other files I had stolen from Cis's office out of my bag and slapped them onto the table. They were copies, of course; I needed to cover my back somehow. 'See, maybe it would be forgivable if the police had let this slip past them once, maybe even twice. But no. There wasn't just one children's home, there were three. Three children's homes across London that didn't get the funding they needed for vital repairs and work. And it wasn't just children's homes. Hospital clinics. Soup kitchens for the homeless. Housing for the vulnerable... and all those people came forward. All those people tried to take legal action, and through the power of police and politics, somehow it never made it to any courthouse.'

I leaned forward, fixing her with a cold hard stare, determined to drive the point home.

'These community funds, grants and donations were created to help people, and Macleod, O'Neill and Clark used them as a way to line their own pockets. Nothing more to it than that. There was no political motive, no social objective; they did it purely out of greed. So, they could sit on a portion of the proceeds, while the world showered them with praise for being the good men they were.'

I thought I had maybe broken Vivian. I stared at the woman with her head firmly sat in her hands. She was partly to blame for all of this. She had taken the police oath just like everyone else at the station, and had betrayed a good portion of the vows she'd sworn by keeping all of Macleod's corruption under wraps.

'You really think you're going to have a career in any police station after this, Gareth?' she murmured, head still in hands.

'I don't want a career in the police. I want those two things, the name of the witness and the unredacted case files. Agree to them, and I'll cancel the emails and go.'

Vivian repeatedly exhaled, puffing out small bursts of air as she walked back to her chair, clutching onto her dry, clumped strands of hair. I didn't really have a contingency plan for what would happen if she had a heart attack.

'How long do I have?' she asked, almost pleadingly now.

'Two minutes. I scheduled it to go out at 11.55, unless – of course – I cancel it from my phone.'

'And why should I believe you?'

'I mean, give it two minutes if you want. I'm sure your phone will be ringing off the hook after that, and then you'll have your answer about whether I'm telling the truth.'

I could see her weighing up the options, small beads of sweat beginning to form on her forehead as she stood with her arms planted on the surface of her desk.

'How do I know that you won't just send it to the press after you've got what you want?' she asked, going through all the possible options in her head.

'Why would I do that? How would that help me? After this, you'll have my letter of resignation on your desk, and you'll never see me again.'

'Even if Fran is still found guilty?'

'A deal's a deal.'

I let Vivian think it over for a minute. I knew I was throwing Cis in hot water, too, but I had this pretty certain feeling that she would be more than willing to screw both Fran and I over for herself. After all, what a great career move this had been for her. It'd surely put her in the good graces of the powers that be. But she really never should have given me her email login.

I looked back to Vivian. She was still making what looked like bad attempts at breathing exercises, pursing her lips and panting small pumps of air, gulping and swallowing before attempting to push the air back out again.

'Just wanted to let you know it's 11.54,' I remarked.

'I know what time it is,' she barked at me, and took a few more breaths before shaking her head, considering her options between the devil and the deep blue sea.

'Stop the emails,' she said, hanging her head in defeat. 'I'll give you the name of the man, along with his address, and I'll send you the full unredacted case files of what we have on O'Neill, Clark, and the rest of them. But I'll only give them to you in print. I don't want any digital footprint leading back to me.'

I did a small nod, as if that was acceptable terms. Vivian's eyes widened as she glanced towards the clock, the colour completely drained from her face. Her stare then focused a few degrees downwards, straight towards the phone nestled in my pocket. I thought it would be cruel to keep her in suspense any longer.

'Oh, the email was only scheduled to go to you,' I said as I pulled my phone out of my pocket and pressed the pause button on the audio recording. 'It should come through any minute now.'

Vivian looked more baffled than angry as she heard the ring of new email rattle through her antique computer. She squinted, somewhat bemused, somewhat saddened, but absolutely furious with me.

'Just remember, if at any time you decide to try anything stupid: I have copies,' I said, with what I hoped was a threatening look.

'You know, Fran will still probably go to prison. Maybe now

you can help her get a few less years, but even with what you have, Fran is still a pretty convincing suspect for a jury,' said Vivian. She didn't sound vengeful, oddly enough. It almost came across as if she understood why I'd done what I had.

'Maybe,' I replied, somewhat coolly. 'But I still have to try.'

Vivian dragged her hand across her face, stretching her dark bags beneath her eyes as she tilted her head up to the ceiling.

'Or maybe you've just cost us both of our careers,' she said contemplatively, sounding slightly mad with despair.

'Oh, you'll be fine,' I said reassuringly, tucking my phone into my pocket and lifting myself off the chair without Vivian's permission for the first and last time. 'You have my word, you won't see me around here again. I'll hand in my resignation in a few days' time, no matter the verdict, and we can blame it all on the stress of the job and the trial. No one will bat an eyelid.'

I realised that this whole time I hadn't felt that red-hot scorching need to tell the truth. For years, I hadn't been able to litter a can on the ground without having a moral crisis. Yet here I was, having just blackmailed a senior member of the police force, and I didn't feel an ounce of guilt.

'Thanks,' I said, smiling through the pain as I strolled out of Vivian's office. Steve and the security guards looked bemused, unsure whether to lunge at me or let me go as I yanked open the door. 'I'll let you know if I need anything else.'

'You were such a good detective,' was the last thing I thought I heard Vivian say before I left.

I woke up with a start as I heard yet another series of whacks against my front door. Mep bolted up to locate the noise as I desperately attempted to clamber out from the sofa hole I seemed to have sunk deeper into each night.

'Shush,' I said, lightly running my hand along Mep's arched

back, then drowsily stumbling my way into the corridor to place my eye against the peephole.

I groaned, wondering: if I left her out there for long enough, would she go away? I then remembered that this was somewhat unlikely for a woman with an inhuman amount of drive and determination. I unlocked the latch and Cis was stomping into the house before I had even fully opened the door, traipsing mud and rain across the floor of our home.

'You threatened the witness, didn't you?'

'What?' I mumbled, still groggy and disorientated.

'You did, didn't you? You threatened the witness.'

'What makes you say that?' I said, rubbing the sleep out of my eyes as I swung the door shut.

'He pulls out of the trial the day before and suddenly wants to retract his entire testimony. He's now saying he's not a hundred per cent sure what he saw, or if it even was Fran throwing body parts into a river. Seems awfully inconvenient for the prosecution, doesn't it?'

'I have no idea what you're talking about,' I said, leaving Cis in the hallway as I strolled back to the living room, closing the lid of my laptop. It was still open on an email from Andrew, thanking me for sending him Vivian's case files on O'Neill and the rest of the funky bunch.

Technically, I knew this broke my promise to Vivian, but if it helped Fran's defence, I wasn't going to deny him evidence that could help her.

'Maybe he strolled into a large sum of money which made him change his mind? Who's to say?' I whispered to myself.

I was going to be paying off that overdraft for years. But there was no way this guy would testify about seeing Fran toss body parts into the river now; that should make her defence stronger.

'And I can't believe you used my login to leak information. I mean, do you have *any* idea how much trouble you could have got me into?'

'Shouldn't have given it to me then,' I said with a vicious laugh.

Cis gave out a small shriek, full to the brim with rage as she threw her hands out in front of her.

'Gareth, I don't know what you're trying to accomplish here. But I know it and I know you know it: your wife murdered someone. Why is that so hard for you to accept?'

'I don't know that, and you don't know that I know that,' I said, trying to not to confuse myself with the mixture of words in the process. 'Neither of us saw Fran kill anyone, Fran hasn't admitted she's killed anyone, and the last time I checked, the law says innocent until proven guilty.'

'You really believe what you're telling yourself right now?' Cis said, scrunching up her nose and looking at me, disgusted.

I shrugged my shoulders and embarked back onto the sofa, hoping that the me-shaped indentation was still there to sink into. Cis paced around my living room, thoroughly incandescent with anger.

'You're throwing your career away. You're throwing my career away. You're purposely disrupting the course of justice. Do you know what that could mean for you?'

'Cis, I'm going to be honest with you,' I groaned as I pulled the sofa throw over my chest. 'I can't tell you how little I care about what you're saying right now. But if you really do want to talk about this more, just give me your phone and then we can talk.'

She almost instantly froze up.

'What? Why?' she asked, immediately defensive.

'Because I know your tricks, and I know what you're like. If you want to talk about this more, then give me your phone,' I said, outstretching my hand.

Cis tried to hide a grimace as she red-handedly pulled her phone out of her pocket, cupping it away from me as she pressed a few buttons before passing it over. I wasn't going to be fooled by my own trick.

I held it in my hand and watched her eyes fixed on me handling the device.

'Are we live on air right now?' I asked with a sly grin, lifting the phone's microphone to my mouth. She reached across and snatched it away from me. 'What are you trying to gain here, Cis? What's your goal?' I called after her as she walked out of the living room. 'Is it justice or what?'

Cis exhaled in the hallway before strolling back across our living room to glance at the photos of Fran and me from our wedding day. The first ones we'd put up in our new home.

'Y'know, for a little while, I thought there was a chance you might actually testify against her,' Cis mumbled, mostly to herself.

That was enough to wake me up a little from my drowsiness.

'What, why?' I said, bewildered.

'Because I thought that you were Detective Whistle-blower. You've always been so rigid, I thought even this wouldn't make you change your ways. Even if she is your wife.'

I didn't quite know how to respond to that. Surely even the most rational person would pervert all the courses of justice in the world if it meant saving someone they loved, right? It had just taken me a minute – or a few months – to realise that.

'I can see you haven't been married, Cis,' I stated. 'Or, of course, been in a relationship that's lasted longer than a few months.'

I should have taken more care with what I said, a recurring theme for me over the past few days. Cis – like many police officers – found it difficult to establish a work-life balance, with new relationships often fizzling out swiftly.

'Yeah, maybe,' Cis whispered, lacking any anger that I thought she would have in her voice. She pulled up a seat. The rage of her poor cyber security skills inside her seemed to be slowly dissipating as Mep strutted towards her. The cat did his usual knife-stuck-in-a-lawnmower meow before twisting his way around her leg. I watched Cis as her face sagged. For the second time today, I had made someone look morbidly depressed.

'Just humour me, Gareth,' Cis said, her eyes still looking lifelessly at the ground. 'So, let's say, whatever game you're playing, whatever plan you're concocting, works, and somehow Fran is released from prison. What then? You live and spend the rest of your life with a murderer? I may not have been married, but I have a feeling that it's not a great sign if your spouse makes you give up on your dream career. And has also – y'know – killed someone.'

She made a good point, but I couldn't say I was particularly sad to see people like Macleod and O'Neill removed from the world.

'We'll see,' I said, not letting her detect the doubt in my voice. 'But whatever happens, Cis, I want you to know that I'm not going to regret it, any of it. I'll confess to the damn murder myself before I let Fran go to prison.'

'Well, that may be difficult. We've got her pinned dead to rights, Gareth, and I'm not saying this to hurt you. I'm saying this as a friend. I don't want you getting any hope that she can get out of this.'

'Cis, what more can we say to each other? We're not going to forgive one another, and neither of us is sorry for what we did, so what's the point in even talking? Neither of us is going to change.'

'I'm not here because I'm angry at what you've done Gareth, I'm angry because of why you've done it. Everything you've worked so hard for is being thrown out the window for... her.'

I had no idea any more if Cis was lying or not, or if she still saw me as one of her chess pieces. I tried analysing her, watching her face shift and her body language change like we'd done back when we'd first sat next to each other in the classroom at training. I couldn't tell any more; she just looked void of anything, really.

'I just wanted to stop you from making a mistake. A big one,' Cis continued, her tone now resigned. 'I feel like, deep down, you've succumbed to this idea that I did this to get one over on you, to advance my career and become Commissioner by fifty or something. But that's really not what I wanted. I didn't want Fran to be the killer, Gareth. I want you to know that. But don't think I'm an arsehole because I want to see a murderer behind bars.'

'But you're testifying tomorrow, right? Against her?'

Cis scowled, infuriated that she wasn't getting through to me. It made me wonder if she was actually being sincere, so I decided to tone down the animosity. 'I appreciate that,' I said, as authentically as I could. 'I do, but this is my decision. No one else is forcing me to make it.'

Cis gently patted Mep as she rose to her feet, not even looking in my general direction as she readied herself to leave.

'Ten years from now, wherever you're working – and maybe you're still married to Fran and maybe you have kids – just remember that there were people who tried to stop you from living that life. I just think...'

I almost could hear her hesitate over what to say next.

'I just think someone who loves you wouldn't make you do this.'

I heard the door slam shut before I even realised that Cis had left the living room. I couldn't bring myself to fully digest what Cis had said. It felt as though my brain couldn't handle any more heavy feelings of guilt, confusion and/or remorse. I distracted myself by grabbing Mep, who was looking stronger by the day, and flicking back onto teleshopping, wondering which wares would be offered to me tonight.

TWENTY-THREE

FRAN

What they don't tell you about court cases is there isn't a whole lot of time for toilet breaks. When you're a very well-hydrated person, like I try to be, you find yourself needing to use the ladies' at quite regular intervals. However, you can't really excuse yourself to spend a penny when you are literally the one on trial. I spoke to Andrew about my concerns early on in the case, and he said it was the first time he had ever been asked that in his twenty-five years of being a criminal defence lawyer. Which I thought was somewhat strange. It could be hours between breaks, and he was telling me that no one had ever asked what their loo policy was?

I thought maybe one of the boring statements, like Cecilia's endless ramble on evidence being objective and her self-praise for guessing I'd chopped O'Neill up in his wet room, could be my chance. That would be the perfect time to tiptoe out, go for a wee, and return before she'd finished her monologue on the lacerations.

But no, I had to stay there, legs crossed, and listen to people go and on and on about me. I thought I had been pretty smart with covering up the murder – more so than others, but, evidently, the police had been smarter. They had correctly guessed that I had disposed of the main husk of O'Neill's body in the bins and the identifiable body parts in the river. I wondered what they were doing now? Probably drifting along the seabed of the English Channel.

Meanwhile, Isla and Cecilia were catching up like old friends on a coffee date. Cecilia said I exhibited all the telltale signs of a psychopath during the questioning – cold, manipulative and narcissistic – and that I knew how to work detectives to make myself appear the victim. What I found more interesting was that Cecilia couldn't even bear to look in my general direction. She seemed composed and graceful to Isla, but pretended I wasn't even in the box for most of her statement. She only glanced at me for a moment when Isla asked her to confirm it was me she was talking about.

They brought up poor Beryl first, who could also barely even look in my direction, though I wondered if that was more out of the pressure than any kind of embarrassment or shame. I saw the poor lady fight any kind of outward emotion, wrestling with herself to try and keep some poise, as Isla approached her. The more I observed Isla in the courtroom, the more she seemed closer to a vulture than a human. Picking on the carrion of the poor people speaking in the box, wearing them down until any defence had been pecked away.

Problem was, Beryl started out strong, saying that I was a great neighbour and there was no way I could have committed so heinous a crime. But when Isla pointed out that she had only known me for a few months, the whole thing fell apart.

Isla noted that Beryl had had her doorbell camera for two years, and it seemed rather coincidental that it was broken not forty-eight hours after O'Neill's suspected murder. Beryl was forced to admit that she had never seen me help O'Neill previously – and nor had I ever expressed an affinity for the man –

with Beryl revealing that we'd both found him to be the strange old senex of the neighbourhood.

Isla managed to tell a quick anecdote about how she'd dated one of her neighbours when she was a graduate, only to find out he was married with family and kids up near Yorkshire. 'You never truly know who your neighbours are,' she said, with a sly hint of a sneer.

Andrew did his best to salvage the situation by questioning Beryl about how I walked Tony every day, and my (rather exaggerated) involvement in the community, but there was no coming back from Isla's questioning. Everything seemed far too coincidental for me not to be guilty.

O'Neill's carer didn't help my cause. I was hoping that she might have outed him as a creepy old man – maybe she had been groped by him, or had walked in on him pleasuring himself to a picture of Charles Manson or something. But instead she said that while he was a crotchety old git, he had never been verbally or physically abusive to her.

We had a quick recess, and the police led me to yet another small, dimly lit room just above the court. Andrew came in with a cup of coffee and a sandwich for me, wiping his brow like it was halftime at a football game, psyching himself up for the next forty-five minutes. I realised Lawyer Andrew must only be reserved for a select few moments in his career. Most of the time, I got the schlub.

Sorry, that was mean; forgive me, I am very stressed.

'So, how is it going, coach? Good? Bad?' I asked. I glanced down at the sandwich. 'Oh?'

'What is it?' Andrew asked, puckering his brows.

'Oh, it's just, I don't really like tuna,' I mumbled. 'But that's beside the point, sorry, tell me how's it going?'

'But I asked what you wanted, and you said "anything",' Andrew responded, half-defensively. He wasn't going to let this one go easily.

'Yeah, but I just didn't think you'd go for tuna, that's all. I thought you'd pick something like a BLT or a ham and cheese. But not tuna. Just – I don't care, just tell me what you think of the case so far.'

I could see Andrew wanted to argue more about the sandwich, but he abandoned the topic and pulled up the chair.

'Too hard to tell right now,' Andrew said, like he was analysing the opposing team's every move. 'Isla works the jury, that's what she does, so even if they don't openly realise it, she's got you in their heads as a cold, smart, violent murderer and O'Neill as a sweet old man who wouldn't hurt a fly.'

'Fantastic,' I murmured, not quite matching Andrew's zest and zeal. I think I was becoming a little more resigned to everything the more the trial progressed.

'But don't worry. We prepared for this; I have some leaked docs that will get the jury thinking about the police's obsession on blaming this case all on you. That's going to change things. I'm sure of it. If that doesn't work, we can leak them to the press tomorrow.'

'What, how?' I stammered, but Andrew had clearly already moved on, scrawling some notes in his diary.

'And who have they got coming up next?' I asked as Andrew tapped his pen against his temples.

'Urgh, well, the upside is that, despite their efforts, they still don't have a strong motive for you. They're trying to suggest you had a reason, but they don't actually know what that is, and we need to use that to support our case. Right now, they're just trying to convince the jury there's a connection. So they have a Clark something or other, friend of O'Neill. But I can't imagine he's going to be much trouble,' Andrew said indifferently, with a wave of his hand.

The world could have ended right there and then and my first primary emotion about the sudden cataclysm would have been complete, serotonin-laden relief.

'You didn't tell me about him,' was all I could say, hoping it wouldn't be too unlikely that the world might swallow me up.

'I must have, surely? The friend, the friend of O'Neill, they went way back together. He used to be Leader of the Opposition, like, forty years ago,' Andrew said, still jotting down notes into his diary.

'No, no, no, I can't...' I stammered, launching myself up from the chair and walking towards the door, forgetting I was still technically in police custody.

The air suddenly vanished from my lungs and all the muscles in my body shrank and weakened as I clasped at my chest.

Andrew rushed over and grabbed me as I began to keel over. My back arched as I retched, dribbling saliva onto the floor.

'Whoa whoa whoa, easy, Fran, easy,' he said, patting and rubbing my back.

I'm not a damn horse, Andrew.

'Do you know him? Who is this guy?' Andrew said, as I moved from all fours to a decrepit slouch, my back against the wall. I yanked off my blazer and slid it across the floor. 'I just assumed he was some random friend of O'Neill's. Is he connected?'

'O'Neill and he were part of the... organisation, thing, charity, something. Clark was the master of the whole operation, kept them all in line through fear.'

I wasn't sure how I would muster any strength to confront Clark in court, knowing my life would be in his hands – a life that had been shaped by this man's greed and cruelty.

Andrew's eyes shifted from worry to confusion as he transitioned from the squat he had assumed to grab me when I'd first dropped to the floor, to a slump as he sat down next to me, both our backs leaning against the cold tiled wall.

'Fran, I need you to be completely honest with me now. What's going on here?'

I placed both my hands against my face, which was extraordinarily moist with sweat, so I moved them to my abdomen, where I could still feel moisture seeping through the fabric.

'Get me some new clothes, and I can tell you everything.'

I couldn't bear to look at him again. The very thought of him knowing that my life was in his hands was, simply put, *unbeschreiblich*: not just indescribable, but also some sort of unspeakable. The amount of power that this wretch of a man now yielded over me must have made him nurse some kind of semi as he approached the witness box. I'm sure when he'd got the call, it had all come together for him: who I was, Macleod and O'Neill, and how he was now the one who could put me away for good. He hadn't even had the decency to take that bronze ring off his finger. He still wanted the world to think of him as a gracious philanthropist.

After the fire had ravaged St Nicholas's, Clark had visited while the firefighters had let us see what little we could salvage. I still remembered Clive glaring at him, furious, as someone explained that the small trinkets I called toys had been completely burnt to ash. I couldn't take it in, I was just wondering where Edith's body was being carried away to, and how I had so utterly failed to save her.

I have no real memory of when and how we were taken away from my parents by social services, but for as long as I could remember, protecting Edith had always been *my* responsibility. Wasn't that what older sisters did? You don't want to know how devastating failing at that would feel for a little girl.

But a memory I can recall even more vividly, was looking up at Clark, who stood there like some kind of aristocrat gazing down at a street urchin. The man who had promised us that everything was going to be all right, that we wouldn't be going to bed cold or hungry anymore. He had sworn to us he was going to fix everything for us at St Nicholas's. Yet of course, he and his powerful friends had covered it all up as a freak accident so that no one would even remember what happened to Edith.

Even then, I was old enough to know that this man and cronies had let this happen. He had let my little sister die, and I remember thinking how good it would feel to kill him. Right there and then, I made a vow to myself that if I ever got the chance to in the future, I would take it.

Predictably, the St Nicholas's fire was traced by investigators to an electrical fault caused by outdated wiring, apparently completely unforeseen by everyone. But not to Clark. He'd known full well about it.

My skin throbbed with a deep, anxious energy now as I watched that same man give a warm smile to the judge, shake the bailiff's hand, and swear vivaciously on the Bible. He and Isla exchanged what seemed like polite greetings as she approached him.

'Mr Clark, thank you for being able to join us today.'

'Oh, it's my pleasure.' He rethought the word. 'My honour,' he amended.

'You knew Gordon O'Neill well, is that correct?'

'I knew him very well for fifty or so years, although we did fall out of touch in the past fifteen years or so. He lived some hundred miles or so away and we just... lost touch.'

That was a lie. They all stayed in touch; that was why they wore the rings.

'As is prone to happen to good friends,' Isla said warmly as she looked through her notes. 'Could you describe Gordon O'Neill to me, please?'

'As nice and as human as they come. A really warm, nice fellow who was nothing but sweet, generous and kind. He was part of our Heart of Hope Foundation, a little group of us middle-aged men in the community who wanted to give back, make a difference to those less fortunate.'

The way he described it made me want to projectile vomit onto the people sitting below me, right then and there.

'And the late Thomas Macleod?'

'Thomas, a fine fellow, real salt of the earth kind of chap. Don't have a bad word to say about him, God rest his soul.'

My fingers wrapped around my thighs to give them something to squeeze, my leg tapping against the carpeted floor of the dock. In my peripheral vision, I could see one of the officers glance at me, bewildered by my shift from existential boredom to sheer, unadulterated fear. Clark wouldn't incriminate himself now, surely? He couldn't truly say how we were connected. In doing that, everything would come spilling out, right?

'Were there any other connections between the three of you? Anyone else who knew you three at all?' Isla asked.

'Not really, other than our family and friends, but it's not like we all went to work in the office together. We mostly had our other lives to get on with, but we would come together once a week or so to do good work for our community.'

'Thank you, Mr Clark. Would you now be able to clarify to the jury if you have seen the woman on the stand before?'

A hot shiver pulsed through my body as Clark's head rotated and his eyes fixed on me. He'd always had a flair for the dramatic, and he trembled now as he leaned forward.

'I have. She came into my shop a few weeks ago.'

I gulped.

'And how would you describe her? How did she come across?' Isla questioned. 'And please remember that you are under oath, so be as honest and candid as possible.'

'An abrupt, cold lady, to tell the honest truth. Savage, I thought. I honestly thought she was going to kill me, especially when I saw that she was holding onto a knife.'

I almost heard the full-time whistle. That was it. The jig was up.

The rest of the trial was white noise. There was no coming

back from this. No way could Andrew describe *that* as a pure coincidence. Macleod, O'Neill, and how serendipitous it was that I had driven a hundred miles from my home to see the final member of the trinity. The only thing they didn't have from me was a motive, but Andrew and I both understood that if Clark further elaborated on the connection between me and the three of them, it would only give Isla more ammunition to prove that I'd killed O'Neill. It wouldn't matter how awful we painted O'Neill as being, it would only give the jury more reason to think I killed him.

I couldn't even bear to look in the direction of Gareth in the gallery. How could I? I had thrown everything away, but the worst part of it all – the rotting feeling gobbling away inside of me – was that I still didn't regret anything I'd done.

I think I would have done it again.

The trial was done for the day, and after the judge banged her gavel, the crowd slowly began to disperse and filter out, most glancing in my direction to see how low I was hanging my head. I looked for Gareth, but he wasn't there any more. I expected he'd left a while ago, and I couldn't say I blamed the man; he'd made his exit for good. I guess I could expect the divorce papers in prison.

I had hated omitting major sections of my life over the course of our marriage, but what else could I have done? Let him see me for how fucked up I truly was? How was anyone meant to make a partner out of someone like me? I mean, don't get me wrong, Gareth was still a prick for getting me arrested, but he didn't have to say sorry for me to forgive him. He didn't know who I was any more.

'Time to go,' one of the policemen said as I finally relieved myself of the numbness in my legs. They led me through the various clandestine hallways of the courthouse before leading me outside and down the courtroom steps. They didn't even ask if I needed a wee.

As they forcefully guided me through yet another set of grand corridors with spotless marble floors and vast, cavernous ceilings, the crowd gushed and surged around us. Some yanked their phones from their pockets and began filming, while those who I assumed were members of the press hurled questions that I couldn't make out through the steady refrain of the police officers: 'Keep moving, don't stop, keep moving.'

But then, as if yanked by some invisible force, my eyes fixed on a single face within the horde of people. A scruffy, gaunt, bearded man. It took only a moment, a heartbeat, to realise it was Gareth. My Gareth.

Wait, was he still my Gareth?

Before we even had a moment to lock eyes like a scene from a cheesy rom-com where the female love interest gets arrested for brutally killing her neighbour, I was dragged away by one of the burly officers. I tried to twist my neck at a precarious angle to get another sight of him, but he was already lost in the throng. I hadn't realised how much it would hurt to see him again. I wondered if he was feeling the same kind of hurt.

When they led me outside, the sun was falling just below the skyline, a few people around us enjoying the last bit of golden hour. I took a fraction of a second to enjoy the sun beaming on my face one last time without it being obscured by a wire fence. I opened my eyes again as I watched my feet, careful not to trip on the stone court steps leading down to the van. But there he was. Not twenty feet away from me. Clark.

He hadn't seen me. He was shaking, bumbling as he tried to talk to Isla, but she was too busy tapping away on her phone to really take much notice of him, both of them standing next to my ride.

I could do it.

The policeman's grip around my arm was limp. With

enough swift force, I could easily slip out of it. They hadn't made me wear handcuffs, which was something of a double-edged sword – handcuffs would have probably been the easiest way to snap his neck.

I had seconds to formulate a plan. Isla and Clark had barely noticed me approach them. One of the officers took his hand off me for a second to grab the keys to the back door of the van.

I knew how I was going to do it. I would charge into him as fast as I could, to knock him into the road. A car might take both of us out, which would be the best scenario, but if it didn't, I would pummel into him with my fists again and again until his skull was crushed. I would have about three seconds to do it, so I predicted I had about three strong punches to kill the man stone cold dead, right there and then. I didn't have time to scan my surroundings, but I hoped and prayed that Gareth wasn't here to see this.

I yanked my arm out of the officer's grip.

'MADAM,' he shouted.

I planned my trajectory, launched off with my legs and leapt towards Clark, but someone caught me mid-flight.

'Let me go!' I screamed.

The strong hands clasped me tight as the officers quickly snatched my upper arms and dragged me back, people erupting into chaos amongst the flash of phones and cameras.

The hands gently released me, as the two officers behind began to ferociously haul me towards the van.

Through the kicking and shouting, I saw it was Andrew who had caught me. He stayed close to me as I was towed, still flailing my limbs around and screaming, into the van, the officers' firm grip cutting off any circulation to my arms.

'Fran,' Andrew hissed. 'Stop, stop, stop, stop.'

'Get away from the woman please, mate,' the officer said to Andrew.

'Just a second, I'm her lawyer!' Andrew snapped back as the

officers, ignoring him, opened the door and began to shove me inside. I tried to crane my neck back as Andrew leaned his face as near to mine as possible. 'Fran, please, play nice for twenty-four hours. That's all I need, twenty-four hours.'

Andrew was still trying to say something as the officers pushed me onto the bench, closed the cage door, and slammed it shut. Through the grills, I could see Clark looking my way, still firmly planted on his feet, Isla reassuringly stroking his back. I watched his face shift into one of smug satisfaction as we drove away.

God, I wanted to kill him so badly.

I stayed awake almost all night, furious that Andrew had robbed me of my one last chance to kill Clark. I only briefly spoke to Lucy when I got in, as everyone was heading to bed for lights out, but didn't really get to expand on my trainwreck of a day. I considered letting the prison guards know that I hadn't actually had dinner, due to all the commotion, but I thought of Andrew's words about playing nice. I had heard that prison officers could be a fickle bunch. Considering I would be getting quite familiar with them, it was probably best to play on the side of compliant for now.

Play nice for twenty-four hours.

To Andrew, I'm sure it was a chance to try and even the odds and actually simmer up a little hope, maybe by talking to Isla or the judge, or even trying to find another witness who may turn out to be my deus ex machina. Best-case scenario, I imagined, was some kind of plea bargain. He'd mentioned he had those leaked documents– maybe that was a part of it? I guessed if I went for guilty, I would get a few years knocked off my sentence, but I'd still probably be in my fifties or sixties by the time I got out. Gareth's children, with his new wife, would be adults themselves by then.

The next morning, they got me up early, just like the day before. I followed the routine, got into the same nice smart clothes, and prepared myself to be led out to the van. This time I was certain they would handcuff me. I imagined my arm would be bruised black by the time I got to the courthouse, through all the manhandling about to occur.

But they didn't. Instead, rather than taking me to the exit, they yanked me to the other side of the prison.

'Ummm, where are we going?' I asked.

They didn't answer.

I winced prematurely. I knew I was probably only seconds away from the beating of my life. I imagined some of the police would be waiting for me in one of the meeting rooms, ready to show me what happened to people who embarrassed them publicly like I had yesterday.

The guard led me to Meeting Room A, hauled open the door and indelicately shoved me inside. I quickly scanned my surroundings, but there was no gang of thugs waiting to punch the crap out of me. Instead, it was Andrew, leaning against the wall, his fingers wrapped tightly around a cup of coffee.

'Andrew? What?! Why are you here? We have the trial...'

Andrew inhaled sharply.

'Well, Fran, this is the thing: no, we don't.'

'What?' I was guessing they must have moved it or shifted it after my attempted murder of Clark.

'After the trial yesterday, there were a few occurrences that took place. I didn't have my phone on me, so I only found out about it all after we were dismissed,' said Andrew, strolling around the small perimeter of the room. 'Someone went into the police station at around seven p.m. last night, and took all the blame for Macleod and O'Neill's death, with evidence that implicated himself and also – rather miraculously – seemed to somewhat exonerate you. Somewhat, that is. I've been speaking to Isla and the judge, and we have decided not to continue with the trial at this time – until we have a bit more information on next steps.'

'What?!' I said again, my mind failing to think of any witty quip in response. Was this some incredibly lucid dream? This hadn't happened, right? And if it had, *how* the hell had it happened, and why did Andrew look so uneasy telling me about it? 'So, who was it?'

Andrew took a big gulp of coffee before speaking, bracing himself. I could tell he wished it was something stronger.

'You idiot,' I was going to say to him. That was the sentence that had been circling around my brain as soon as Andrew had told me what happened. After they'd organised my release, I'd got a taxi and then a train and then a taxi again and then arrived at the station, waited impatiently for visiting hours, and then finally went into the custody suite. I said a quick hello to Paul – it was genuinely nice to see him again – who led me into the meeting room, to see him sitting there, having somehow found a way to get his newspaper crossword. 'You big fucking idiot.' I ripped the paper from underneath him.

'You're welcome,' Angus grunted.

'Just... explain this to me? What? Why? When? How?'

'Does it even really matter, Fran? What matters is you're out, I'm in. You can now go on with your life and play all little happy families with Gareth. Just what you always wanted.'

'You actually think I'm just going to let you take the fall for this? It's my word against yours, buddy, and I can go right back into that courtroom and confess. It ain't over until I say it's over.'

'I told them everything, Fran,' Angus said, with a strange amount of calm. 'I told them about how I murdered Macleod and O'Neill, and how I was manipulating and blackmailing you into doing some of my dirty work, but I was still the one who delivered the killing blows.'

'They won't believe that.'

'Hmmm – the Crown Prosecution Service, who are they going to gun for? The woman who they're not one hundred per cent sure they can convince the jury is a murderer, or the guy with a criminal record who's literally confessing that he did it with a motive and evidence?'

'But surely, they won't just drop everything? Someone saw me throwing limbs in the river. They were going to put him on the stand later on in the trial. That still must make me an accessory, at the very least.'

'Well...' Angus started his sentence, but didn't finish. 'I think you should really talk to your husband.'

'What do you mean?' A quick flash of anger made me lurch forward. 'He made you do this? Gareth?'

'No,' Angus scoffed, almost with an air of incredulity. 'He didn't make me do this, this is all of my decision, but I mean, I hadn't realised what sort of man Gareth was at all.'

'What do you mean?' I questioned, trying to find some sense in all the new information that was being thrown at me. 'Angus, this is prison we're talking about here. You're not going to be able to collect papers and watch old films, you know? This is some real shit.'

'Yeah, but my meals will be made for me, I can do a lot of reading, I guess, and I've always wanted to try making toilet wine.'

I knew he was putting on a brave face. I knew deep down that he was petrified of what he had just committed himself to.

'I... I can't let you do this, Angus. I'm sorry, I just can't,' I said, massaging my neck where decades-worth of tension had wrapped thick, tight knots under my skin. '*I* look after *you*. This is how it works. This is how it's worked since you, me and Edith.'

'Okay. So, you don't let me do this, and then we both go to prison, and who's that going to help?' Angus said, slowing his words to try and drive the point home about how idiotic he thought I was being.

I had been on my feet since barging into the custody suite, stomping around the cell, but I felt like my legs could barely take it anymore. I slouched down against a corner of the room, not exactly sure what this cocktail of emotions was inside of me. Guilt? Shock? Relief?

'So, the police and the CPS, they just... withdrew their whole case against me?' I said, holding my head in my hands. 'Just like that?'

'Well, I'm sure you'll be called as a witness in my trial, you're probably guilty of something, but I guess we'll cross that bridge when we come to it,' Angus stated, unsuccessfully trying to hide the quiver of fear in his voice. 'But I want everything they did to come to light. I know you killed two of them already, but I want the world to know what they did to us, to Edith.'

I gave a quick glance around the cell to just make sure there were no clandestine CCTV cameras fitted in shadowy corners.

'Do you not see why I had to do this?' Angus asked.

I gave a grunt. That was all my body had left as a response now. I couldn't argue or fight any more, I couldn't debate or shout or get mad. All I had the emotional and physical capacity to do was to sit with Angus in silence – me stooped on the floor, Angus sitting at the desk in the cold, lonely, steel vacuum of the custody suite.

'Clark,' I uttered, the word I knew Angus wouldn't want to hear.

I waited for him to shush me, to tell me to shut up and not throw my life away again, to tell me he had just sacrificed his life to keep me out of prison and here I was thinking about leaping back into the murdering pensioners business.

But instead, he just kept staring blankly at the desk in front of him, his hands interlocked, and did one of his trademark deep sighs, inflating his diaphragm fully before sinking back into his chair with the exhale.

'I'm not going to tell you what you can do with your life. I guess some people dream of being astronauts or scientists or models. Some people dream about murdering people.'

My ikiagi, I thought to myself silently.

'You just... you have to understand what you're giving up, is all.'

'But... but... just how?' I stammered. 'How has all this happened?'

'Like I said, I think you really need to talk to your husband.'

TWENTY-FOUR

GARETH

Twenty-Four Hours Earlier

I had been to a few hoarders' houses in my years of police work. Each one had a different smell, depending on that individual's particularities. Some would have the pungency of days-old rubbish, festering in the bin, while others would carry a delicate aroma of rot and mould. So when it came to Angus's apartment, I was somewhat surprised. Fran had told me that he wasn't the most fastidious of individuals, but did have a tidy streak. I braced myself for the *eau de accapareur*, but as Angus cautiously opened the door, I found that he had actually invested in a few different electronic heavy duty air fresheners that had been strategically placed around the flat.

'Angus,' I said, greeting him. 'You called?'

'Gareth,' he replied. We had never really acknowledged each other before, so two words in, we were already breaking new ground.

'So, ummm, have you been well?' I asked as Angus led me into his apartment, guiding me through the sacred columns of newspaper I had heard so much about. I sat down precariously on the sofa, having placed some stacks of broadsheets – as neatly as I could – onto the light grey cord carpet. Fran had complained to me about Angus and his obsessions, but I almost felt she'd undersold it. While I'd imagined these glorious word pictures of newspaper skyscrapers that stretched up to the ceiling, she really hadn't been joking: the whole place felt like the bunker of a post-apocalyptic kleptomaniac.

I could feel Angus's glare, watching every movement of every one of my fingers that touched his papers. I sat softly against the sofa, being very careful not to move a muscle out of place, for fear of accidently knocking a tower over. His face didn't seem to shift into panic or rage, so I presumed that this particular spot was acceptable.

'You just came from the trial?'

'I have,' I responded.

'How was Fran?'

'Well, only an hour ago, I did see her get sort of thrown into a police van and dragged away, so that wasn't a particularly lovely image.'

'Okay. Let's cut the crap. You know my sister killed Macleod and O'Neill, right?' Angus said.

I was blindsided by his bluntness. It took me a second to find the right words to respond.

'I had a medium-to-strong assumption that Fran did kill Macleod and O'Neill, yes,' I said, followed by a deep sigh. Angus looked somewhat impressed by my answer. His eyebrows leapt up, as if taken aback by how not-in-denial I was.

I could've asked him if he had known about Fran's penchant for murdering old guys all this time, but I had a feeling that the answer wouldn't do much for my mental state.

'I have O'Neill and Macleod's rings in my drawer. Do you want to see them?' he asked brusquely.

'Why the hell would I want to see that?' I said slowly, exasperated.

'As proof that she did it. More for her than me, I think. She wanted to have little mementos to remind her.'

These past few days would never cease to amaze me. Angus, the mysterious brother-but-not-really-a-brother, was an accomplice to my wife, the serial killer. Fantastic. This would make Christmas so exciting this year. If there was a Christmas...

'Why even did they wear the rings?' I asked.

'Do you really believe they weren't still in contact? You should know, Detective, those who think they're in high society need some way to recognise each other,'

'That's true, I guess,' I remarked. I supposed what they did wasn't shameful to them: it was smart, it was clever.

'Why haven't you seen her at the prison yet?' Angus asked just as bluntly as he'd admitted that my wife had a predilection for death.

'I've been a coward,' I said, matching his abruptness in fear that if I waited a second longer to respond, he'd offer another brain-breaking revelation.

Angus nodded, somewhat assured by the answer and further impressed by my no-bullshit attitude.

'I went to see her. She told me that if you tried to call, I should pick up. So, I just thought I'd ring you instead. I was fed up with waiting around and thought you might be being a pussy.'

He really didn't mince words, did he?

'Have you spoken to her lawyer?' asked Angus.

'Yeah.'

'How's her chances?'

'Bad.'

Angus didn't even seem to react, replying only with a sharp snort. He took a second to process, and then got up to intricately reorganise one of the countless newspaper stacks. These few words we had exchanged were more than we had spoken in the entirety of Fran's and my marriage. Having only ever said 'hi' to each other in brief moments of passing, here we were shattering records – it was just that, unfortunately, I wished it had been under better circumstances.

'How was Fran, when you went to see her?' I asked.

'She was okay. Scared, I think, which is new for her. She was pretending to be all brave, but it wasn't hard to see through it.' Angus scratched his scraggly facial hair as if pondering some big philosophical problem. 'Do you think there's anything else we could do for her?'

'No. I've tried to bend some rules.' I played down my descent into police corruption to Angus. 'But I think the prosecution have a pretty damning case against her.'

'Nothing that could be done to get her out of this? Nothing at all?'

'No,' I said, sedately. 'Not unless O'Neill suddenly returns from the dead and decides to absolve Fran of all wrongdoing or – I don't know – someone stepped up and magically took all responsibility for the crime,' I murmured forlornly, thinking of what Andrew had said to me a few days ago. Even putting my career on the line hadn't done much to change the tide of Fran's trial now it was underway.

I had just noticed Angus's eyes shift. Up to this point, they had been wandering all across the room, but they had now suddenly focused and narrowed. I caught his gaze as he took one of his famous trademark inhales that I had heard about.

'Could I?'

'What do you mean?' I asked, not sure what Angus was asking.

'Could I say I did it? I killed O'Neill and Macleod?'

My brain went into hyperdrive. The selfish part of me realised that Angus taking the fall for this murder could be a literal 'get out of jail card' for Fran. But he hadn't even committed these crimes. He was barely an accessory, but if he said he'd killed them, he'd get a life sentence at the very least.

What was left of my moral conscience fought against the words coming out of my mouth.

'Angus, no, come on. Don't do that.'

'If I came forward and assumed all responsibility, do you think that would give Fran a better chance?'

I ground my teeth, unsure of the right thing to do or say. What would Jesus do? But Jesus would never have gotten himself into this situation. Instead, I thought about what Fran would want me to do. Here Angus was waiting on me as some kind of arbiter, to tell him if he should take the fall for his sister.

'That's a loaded question, bro,' I said. I don't know why I used 'bro', but the context seemed right. 'Is it going to help her chances? Yes. Would it mean imprisonment for you? Also, yes. But you have to remember that even if you took the fall, it's not a dead guarantee that Fran would walk away. She could still be seen as an accessory to the case, CPS may not believe you, and you could maybe both end up going to prison.'

'Well, then. I'd need your help to get my story straight, I suppose. You know the case – every detail, every alibi. We could find a way to explain it. I mean, you must know that I visited O'Neill, right? A few weeks before Fran decided to off him.'

'I do. Although the officers interrogating you had a hard time getting that out of you.'

'Yeah, because I didn't want to incriminate Fran,' Angus said plainly, like it was obvious information. 'But I told O'Neill to stay away from her, and that if he tried anything, I'd kill him.'

A missing gear slid and then clicked perfectly into place.

'The note. You wrote O'Neill a note after you went to visit him, didn't you? The one that threatened to kill him.'

'Yeah. So, being honest, I never actually spoke to him. I chickened out in the end, so I put the note under his door instead.'

I mean, that was noble, but stupid. Really, really stupid.

I slumped my face into my hands, still jarred by what Angus was telling me, and gave an extended groan.

'I think I can prove I wrote it, too. I have a bunch of different drafts I did. I was trying to get my handwriting as unfamiliar as possible,' Angus stated. Through my fingers, I could see him yanking out various versions of the warning note from a cabinet to show to me. 'That must be a motive, right?'

It remained insanely jarring to me that Angus, a man poised to sacrifice his freedom for his sister, was now driven by an inexplicable surge of giddy excitement, a newfound burst of energy propelling him forwards.

'What the hell is going on?' I moaned through my fingers.

There was a beat between us as I went through each revelation in my mind. I had wondered for weeks what enemies O'Neill had had at the start of this case, when there had been two of them right in front of me the whole time.

'You know, though, that Clark will try and make a run for it, and that my sister is going to try and kill him before he vanishes?' added Angus, stacking the pieces of paper neatly on the oak surface of the cabinet.

It pained me to hear him say that. That Angus could take the fall and go to prison, only for Fran to be thrown in there again a few days later. It gave me a queasy feeling to realise I knew very well how my wife's brain worked. She couldn't leave a job unfinished. She had to complete the set.

'Surely, he could just disappear, and she'd never find him? The world is a big place,' I theorised.

'Let's not fool ourselves, Gareth.'

I let another loud, defeated groan reverberate out of me as I tried to process everything.

'Angus, before we go any further with this conversation, I need you to really carefully consider your actions. Like, really think about it. Both the best and worst-case scenarios of this end up with you going to prison.'

'But would it help Fran?'

'It's not certain, Angus...'

'Would it help Fran?' he interrupted, clearly irritated by my attempts to get him to evaluate how drastically his life would change if he went through with this.

'To be completely honest, it wouldn't exactly harm her case. Given our current situation, it's hard to imagine things getting much worse for her.'

I didn't need to say any more than that for him to stay the course. But if we were going to do this, we'd need a detailed story for Angus to stick to from his confession, all the way up to his trial. We'd have to make notes on any discrepancy, any slight inconsistency that could incriminate all three of us, and Angus would have to stick to it like gospel. He would need to paint himself as a villain – that was for sure – while Fran would have to have been blackmailed or threatened to cover up the murders and dispose of all the various evidence. Sadly, I thought a jury would buy that part of the story. Two kids raised by the system would make easy targets.

'Before we do anything,' I said calmly, 'let me make a few calls and see the lay of the land.'

'What do you mean?' Angus asked, clearly frustrated by the lack of a straightforward solution and obviously unaware of how low my morals had stooped.

'If you're set on going to prison, then let me check if a psychiatric unit or something similar is an option. You'd have more protection and better treatment there, because' – I felt like I didn't need to mince my words around him, either – 'I don't know if you'd last a day in a Category A prison, Angus.'

I wasn't trying to be mean; I was attempting to help him, although I couldn't shake the feeling I was semi-reluctantly leading a lamb to the slaughter.

Quietly, I pulled out my phone, ready to ask Vivian for one last favour.

'So, are you sure?' I asked Angus one more time for good measure as the phone began ringing.

'Absolutely. Fran would do the same for me in a heartbeat.'

'I'm just,' I said, one hand on the ringing phone and the other pulling through my hair and watching countless strands float down to the floor, 'trying to think of any legal way we could get justice for Fran, for you, after everything they did.'

'You think we can rely on the justice system for people to get what they deserve?'

I was desperately trying to stay awake while I drove Angus to the bus stop in silence. I couldn't remember the last time I had properly slept since Fran's arrest. We went through every line of his testimony and every detail of his story, racking our brains to make sure there was nothing we'd missed. The history Fran had always hidden from me, the 'it's not trauma if you don't remember it' comments, it had all been so vague and unclear before. But now I knew exactly what Fran and Angus had gone through, and I finally understood why Fran had done it. I didn't agree with it, of course, but I understood why.

While I told Angus that it would probably be fine for me to drop him to the police station, he pointed out that we didn't want anything that could insinuate a conspiracy between us. We went over his story a few more times in the car, and I told him to keep details sparse, and not elaborate on anything until he had a lawyer. Angus would take the fall for everything; he was the one that had killed Macleod and O'Neill, but couldn't let his sister go down for his crimes. A last-minute confession. It was tenuous at best, but a guilty plea with a tenuous story was a far stronger case than declaring not guilty and flirting with the burden of proof.

As for evidence, Angus already had O'Neill and Macleod's

rings, still with traces of their blood, which would probably do the trick.

I had spoken to Vivian, who had answered the phone almost instantly when I called, probably thinking I had changed the terms of our deal, which I guess I sort of had. I told her that she was about to have a new patsy and that when she was called to testify in Angus's trial, she would recommend a psychiatric unit for Angus to serve out his sentence, otherwise an incriminating email may just find its way into a reporter's inbox. While she was quick to remind me that she had no power over that decision, I knew her words would carry weight in court. It was something, at least, to make what was left of my conscience feel a little reassured about letting Angus go through with this, but all of it felt morally dubious at best.

'Just keep to the main bullet points. They're going to search all over it to try and find a weak spot, but if you stay succinct and keep your words short, there's less for them to pull apart, okay?' I instructed as we approached the bus stop.

'Okay,' was all Angus said to me. Like he was a teenager I had just finished nagging about his homework.

'It's not that much of a plan, really,' I murmured, mostly to myself.

'A bad plan is better than no plan,' Angus quietly said back to me. His initial hope and excitement had faded, as if he was now realising what he was actually committing to.

I don't even know why I was expecting more than the simple 'Thanks' he said before getting out the car and then sitting on the small bench at the bus stop, his hands resting neatly on his thighs. I had expected a handshake, or maybe even a hug. But no, he just sat there in silence, avoiding any eye contact while I wrestled to find the bite of the clutch. As I drove back, part of me wondered if Angus would actually go through with it. Another part wondered if the Germans had thought of a word to sum up shared feelings of both guilt and hope. But I figured that my situation seemed too niche for any language.

The next morning, I rallied enough strength to have a shower. Perhaps it was the fact that I finally had something to feel moderately positive about, as minuscule an opportunity as it might be. It felt slightly emasculating to be sitting down in the shower the whole time, but standing up seemed sort of superfluous anyway. I no longer had the energy to be on my feet for long without feeling lethargic.

My hair, which had become matted, knotty and greasy, seemed that it would never become clean, no matter how much shampoo I slapped on and swirled around my scalp. Although I tried to resist, I kept thinking about Angus and what was happening right now, whilst scrubbing myself to the bone. Had Angus really turned himself in? Was he now in custody? What was even the procedure in cases like this? Did they just stop the trial completely?

After a while, I realised that I had spent close to twenty minutes letting myself catastrophise. The hot water was quickly becoming cool, so I exited the shower, towelled myself off and walked out the bathroom to the bedroom.

I had had several voicemails from Andrew in the last half hour, telling me there had been a drastic change in the case, and that he would keep me posted and let me know ASAP if it was good news. He had something of an upbeat tone, which made my heart flutter a little. Did he think there was a chance? Had mine and Angus's plan actually worked?

Only ten minutes later, he sent me a text:

> She's out.

Before I had a moment to process, Mep, who had been

continuously getting stronger over the past few days, emitted a small, rattly mew to let me know someone was approaching the door. Sure enough, I heard the doorbell ring a few seconds later.

Surely that wasn't Fran already?

I threw on Fran's pink fluffy dressing gown, the only clothing that I had within my reach, dragged it over my chest, tied up the ribbon and quickly trudged my way downstairs to throw open the door.

But as I jerked the handle down and swung the door open, I didn't see my wife, but a balding, middle-aged man. Steve.

He must have seen how my face dropped in disappointment, as he seemed to almost recoil at my change of expression. His eyes then glanced down to the rather vibrant shade of pink I had wrapped around me.

'Hello, Steve.' I tried to keep my face as stern as possible, not letting it turn into the same colour as I was wearing.

His face almost cracked into a laugh, but he stopped and steadied himself, as if he had suddenly remembered the seriousness of the situation. Deep down, I could tell he wanted to make some kind of wisecrack, but instead, he silently passed me a supermarket carrier bag. Inside, in a Ziplock bag, was the Nesmuk knife that Fran and I had received as our wedding present. The potential murder weapon. Wait, let's not kid ourselves – the murder weapon.

'I called up some of our friends and asked around. CCTV spotted a car coming to pick Clark up. He's gone up north. The car is registered to this address.'

Steve reached out and passed me a small, folded-up piece of paper that was *Dora the Explorer* branded.

He must have seen the confusion washing over my face.

'It was the only paper I had available,' he justified, looking at me as if I was one to talk. 'I'm going to give this information to Vivian at 9 a.m. tomorrow, which gives you the rest of the day to do what you need to do.'

I unfurled the piece of paper to look at the address. I didn't even recognise the post code, but knew if it began with a D, chances were it was past Birmingham. At least a two-hour drive away.

Steve took an unsteady step back from my doorway as I crumpled the paper in my hand, not quite sure how to deal with the weight of it. I saw Steve take a fast glance over at O'Neill's house. The police tape and white tents were gone; now it was just an empty house someone had died in a few months ago.

'And now we're even?' Steve asked.

'We're even. Just... best not to do snow in the police station, Steve,' I advised. 'Where you work.'

I could see that Steve almost found that amusing. I wasn't really sure why. Perhaps he was laughing at the ridiculousness of the situation or maybe laughing at how blissfully green I was. Maybe they were all doing it, and it was just Steve I had caught.

'None of us thought you'd stick around,' Steve said. 'We gave it a year. Glad that you were gone in less than half of that, for my sake.'

I rolled my eyes, letting a smirk creep across my face, and shook my head as if it was playground talk.

Steve took a few steps backwards, maintaining eye contact, which was probably him trying to psych me out a little. But after a small stumble on a raised bit of the pavement, he spun around and paced back to his car. Head down, he risked one last glance at me in my pink dressing gown, perhaps to preserve as one of his more peculiar memories.

You know, though, that Clark will try and make a run for it, and that my sister is going to try and kill him before he vanishes? Angus's words circled endlessly in my mind as I began sorting all of my police memories and paraphernalia into a small shoebox to lodge at the back of the cupboard.

Deep in my gut, I knew the police weren't going to arrest Clark, even if everything he and his friends had done came to light during Angus's trial. Why would they? They'd let him get away with it, just like they had done fifteen years ago.

But Fran wouldn't. I was certain of that. She needed justice for everything she'd gone through. For Angus, for Edith. Strange, how someone who had been such a massive part of my wife's life, I had never even known existed.

I was lost in thought when my phone buzzed for probably the eighteenth time today. I'd never been so popular in my life. Who could it be this time? Cis? Vivian? Andrew?

No. The caller ID showed a name I hadn't seen for months: Fran. She was calling from her personal mobile.

I picked up instantly, but found myself simply at a loss for words. The pause stretched on as I scrambled for something to say, finally just saying her name in what could only be described as a high-pitched breathy pant.

'Hey, dickhead,' she responded, her voice a little lighter than when we'd last spoke, but I could still feel the distance between us. 'I guess you heard the news?'

'Yeah, I did,' I replied with a small, awkward chuckle. 'It's great news.'

'Look, I'm with Angus right now at the station. I know this is going to sound really weird, but please tell me you've kept... my pants?'

Somehow, it felt weird to say yes. As if I thought she might think I was holding onto them for some creepy perverted purpose.

'Yeah.'

'Good, I just really need a pair of pants that are not from prison. I know that's strange, but the detergent they use is the worst detergent. I just want a fresh pair of pants, my pants. Can you come drop some off to the station?'

'Yes, yes of course, I'll be right there.'

. . .

It felt weird to be driving back to the station, but this time just as a civilian, not an employee; I almost had to stop myself from turning right into the police entrance. Instead, I decided to pull up a few streets away, worried that Vivian would call the special weapons team if she saw my car approaching. I walked to the small grassy park across the road from the station and texted Fran to let her know I was here. I felt like giving the Met Police a wide berth would probably be in the best interests of everyone else.

Fran emerged about five minutes later, still wearing the clothes they had arrested her in all those months ago. It felt strange to see her again in the cold light of day; she had changed, clearly. Her clothes almost looked a little too baggy for her now, her skin was paler, and her hair was so much longer and messier, yet she still walked with an air of grace that ever so delicately and politely crushed my heart into smithereens. The past few months of trauma hadn't taken away even an ounce of her beauty.

'Hey,' she said with a guarded smile, as she walked over to the grassy patch and stopped a few feet away from me. No embrace, no peck on the cheek, she just planted her feet down as if she had no intention of moving any further towards me.

'Hi,' I replied, staying in position.

'Hi,' she said back. Her eyes, to me, almost looked a little bit wistful.

Wordlessly, mostly because I didn't know what to say, I lifted the supermarket carrier bag stocked full of pants. She half groaned, half smirked as she took a step forward to take the bag from me.

'Thank you,' she replied, nonplussed.

'There are some T-shirts and leggings in there, too, if you need a change,' I remarked.

'Thank you,' she repeated, still bemused for some reason.

'And a bottle of water. I imagine you haven't had time to drink much today.'

'You're right,' she said again, stopping herself from laughing while her eyes glanced at the grass beneath her feet. 'I haven't. But you know, you and I, we still have...' She sighed. 'So much to talk about.'

'We do, we do,' I agreed. Divorce proceedings would surely be one of those things; no couple could go through what we had and survive, but I couldn't bear to think about that right now. 'Look, I know we need to sort things out between us. I get that,' I continued. 'But I just want to say... I'm sorry. I'm sorry for everything I did. I'm sorry for everything you went through at St Nicholas's, everything with Edith, everything with Dr Patel. I had no idea, and if I did...'

'Whoa, whoa, whoa, Gareth. Slow down a second,' Fran interrupted, her face scrunched up as it always did when she was baffled by something I had said. Admittedly, it had been a lot to unload on her at once, though no more than she'd kept hidden from me over the years. 'How do you even know about any of this?'

'It's been a very busy few days. I mean, Lord above, Fran, why didn't you tell me about any of this?'

'What could you have done about it, Gareth?' she said, resignedly. She paused for a second, as I waited tentatively on every word she said. 'I mean, there's nothing in our wedding vows about being truthful, you know, just having and holding,' she added.

'Oh, piss off,' I replied with a nervous laugh. I thought I could see Fran chuckle, too, but I wasn't sure if maybe it was just a gurn. 'God, I thought I knew you better than you knew yourself, Fran.' I gave a long sigh. 'I was so wrong. I had no idea what you went through.'

'I guess I tried not to think about it all too hard,' she said, stumbling over the words as she spoke, like it was some kind of rusty memory she was still trying to unearth. 'I was only a little girl, Gareth. I think... doing what I did made me think that somehow it wouldn't happen again to anyone else. No more Ediths would have to experience what my Edith did. Look, I know that's ridiculous to say, but...'

'No, no,' I said as assuredly as I could. The image of Fran having to go through all that as a child – losing her sister – it stirred something in me. A fury? A rage? I wasn't totally sure what it was, especially standing outside the place that had let the organisation get away with it.

'I didn't know you had a sister, Fran,' I said. 'You know, I could always picture you as an older sister.'

'I know,' she said mournfully. 'I don't even like talking about her with Angus.'

'I get it, I do. I... I just can't even imagine how painful it must be,' I said.

'Yeah,' she said, glancing to the ground again. Clearly even this whole conversation was agony for her.

She walked over to the lone, rather miserable-looking swing set in the park and perched herself down on one of the seats, wrapping her hands around the rusty chains as I gingerly approached and sat down on the seat next to her, hoping she wouldn't scream at me to make myself scarce.

'I get it, Fran, I really do,' I said after a moment of silence. 'Why didn't you tell me about the fertility problems, though? We could have worked through that together?'

'Honestly, I could tell you that it was because when the investigation heated up I didn't have a chance, but if I'm being honest with myself, it's because I thought... I thought that you'd leave me if you ever found out.'

I couldn't help the minuscule smile that escaped my lips when she said that. How could she be so smart and so silly at the same time? How did she ever think I would leave her because of that?

'Look, the idea of having children terrifies the shit out of me, Fran, but it's all less terrifying with you. I would never leave you, not in a hundred years. I thought you knew that?'

'You would arrest me, though?'

I genuinely belly laughed in shock and disbelief. 'Whoooa,' I bellowed as a few passers-by glanced at us, baffled at what these two grown adults were doing sitting on the swing set.

'Too soon?' she asked. 'Too soon,' she affirmed to herself. 'I am glad you know everything now. There are no more secrets I need to worry over. I had always wanted to tell you everything, but thought it would somehow change things between us and we'd fall apart. Look, for what it's worth, I spent a lot of my time doubtful I would ever let anyone in again, and I guess when we met and then got married, what I'm trying to say is...' Her voice softened for a moment before she began a new train of thought. This whole conversation was just discombobulated people trying to articulate their innermost feelings and failing miserably. 'Look, I need to go and talk to my idiot brother again,' she said, rising to her feet. 'But I need some time to decompress, so I'm going to check into a hotel and maybe we can find a time to talk properly in the next few days?'

'Of course, sure,' I said, though I couldn't shake the feeling she didn't really mean it. 'Let's... just stay in touch, okay?'

'Okay,' Fran replied with a slight laugh, amused by my formality. 'I'll talk to you soon, okay? Bye.'

'Bye,' I said, resisting the impulse to say 'I love you' before letting her walk back to the station.

I had already made up my mind before she had even crossed the road.

It was three hours of near-constant motorway driving. After what felt like a small eternity, I finally arrived, pulling up a little distance away from the lone house on the street. I turned off the engine and curled my gloved hand around the knife, whilst tilting the cap further down my face. I checked the crumpled piece of paper in my hand again. It was definitely here. I listened out for anyone else nearby – anyone walking their dog, any teenagers smoking a joint – but it was dead quiet. No cameras, no witnesses. I didn't know how many were inside, but if it was meant to be some kind of safe house, I could practically guarantee it would be under three, including Clark. Two, most likely. He was probably in the process of trying to flee the country to escape, nervous his actions with Heart of Hope were about to be fished out of the sewers.

I waited for thirty minutes or so in the darkened car. After a while, I saw a small glimpse of light as a figure left the house and shut the door behind him. I watched him bumble and stumble across the front garden, and then begin doddering in my direction. Leaving the keys in the ignition, I pulled my fingers around the inside door handle, and carefully opened it up, placing the knife in the pocket of my coat. Silently pulling myself out of the car, I crouched down, gently pushing the door shut. As I eased myself closer to the bonnet to keep watch, my eyes remained fixed on the figure moving towards me. He had a newsboy cap fitted to his head, and a thick winter coat wrapped around him, but I could tell by his stature that this was definitely Clark.

One strike to the head would be enough to take him out, not a doubt in my mind. Once he passed the car I would leap out of my position, launch the knife down onto his skull, watch the man fall, and then drive away within twenty seconds. I planned my trajectory as I adjusted my hands and feet. In this moment of adrenaline, I was suddenly unsure whether I was left or right-handed. Was this how Fran had felt before she'd murdered Macleod and O'Neill?

He still hadn't seen me yet, but he continued walking painfully slowly along the grass directly ahead of me, illuminated by the street's one barely working lamppost. I had to keep reminding myself that this was an evil, horrible man, who had leeched everything he could from the system, and the world would be better without him in it. I knew I *wanted* to kill Clark. At least, I thought I wanted to kill him. But for some reason, the blade wasn't leaving my pocket.

I had told myself this was all for Fran, that I was racing to get to Clark before she could, making sure she didn't spend the rest of her life in a prison cell. But a small, sharp thought now began to seep into my subconscious: was I doing this, at least in part, for myself? These men had ruined hundreds, maybe even thousands of lives, all to line their already fat pockets. And now, here the last one was. I'd made my police oath several years ago, 'upholding fundamental human rights and equal respect to all people'. What kind of oath would it be if I just let him run away scot-free?

He was only a few metres away from me now. It was now or never; I pushed my body up to spring out of my position and deliver the killing blow – but I couldn't help opening my mouth.

'Evening,' I blurted out, instead of killing him.

I thought I had given him a heart attack. Clark jumped upwards, grabbed his chest, and shouted some indistinguishable mixture of curse words as he lurched downwards and keeled over. I just stood there, like a kid about to tell his parents he had thrown up in the middle of the night. As I stood over the man, watching him flail about on the pavement, I pondered how my body had taken control and blatantly revealed itself when I'd had the perfect opportunity to kill him. Strangely, I was now fighting the urge to actually help him up.

'Bastard,' he spat at me. I could make that word out. He took a glance at me. I presumed he could only make out my vague outline, given the cataracts or macular degeneration of most pensioners.

'Are you going to kill me?' he asked with a spitty snarl, as he managed to prop himself up onto his elbow against the pavement. 'Make it quick, then, you scum.'

At this exact moment in time, there was no way anyone could accuse Fran of killing Clark. There would be no way that the timelines would ever match up. I could end her spree before she did.

'I know what you did,' I murmured quietly.

'I thought it would be her,' Clark hissed. 'Guess she didn't have the guts.'

That should have been enough for me to do it right there; a good old prick on the head and he'd be out like a light. But maybe it was the years of police training, or maybe it just wasn't in me. Maybe I was weak.

'Go on then, do it. Kill me,' Clark goaded. It had only just occurred to me that he thought this was an intimidation technique. Like I was dragging out every last little bit of terror from the man when, really, I was just being dreadfully indecisive. He snarled at me again and raised his hand to throw a punch into my shins. I grabbed his wrist before he could deliver the blow, when I spotted the glint of the ring on his hand. I stared at it, making out the small symbols etched across the metal surface, and realised I knew exactly what I was going to do.

'I don't want to kill you, Abe. It's just that I really don't want her to.'

'So, what are you going to do?' he asked, his voice panicking.

I knew I'd brought the knife for something.

EPILOGUE

Look, I know it was in fact quite nosy of me, but I must confess I did keep peeking out of the window to see if Gareth's car had arrived back at the house yet. Not every second, mind you. Just every so often, I would gander past the window and just have a glance between the split in the curtains. It wasn't my fault that I had quite an advantageous view of their kitchen from my house. It had made for some quite interesting viewing over the past few months, to see them moving in, their canoodling, their arguing, or even the moment the police had arrested Fran when she returned to the house. Now *that* was particularly shocking for a Thursday afternoon.

So, I went back to knitting my jumpers. I had no idea how Fran had managed to get out of prison, get back to her house, and sit with a cup of tea at her kitchen table. She had a risotto cooking away behind her and a lovely set of Azulejo plates I hadn't seen before laid out on the table. Gosh, it only felt like only yesterday that I was testifying in her trial. But I was certainly glad she was home. Of course, it didn't take a genius to figure out that she was the one who had murdered Gordon O'Neill. That much was obvious. I had seen Fran enter

O'Neill's on that Saturday morning in September and come out a long while later, hauling two heavy bin bags that had almost certainly contained what was left of him.

Tony had just finished his dinner when I saw what was unmistakably Gareth's car slowing down to turn into our street, and then park up into his driveway. He looked somewhat forlorn as he got out of the car and walked up to his house. But he suddenly stopped dead in his tracks when I saw him notice the kitchen light was on. I had never seen a man so quickly launch up the steps and yank open the door.

I watched Fran's face light up when she saw him, but she didn't move to him straight away. The two just stood there, staring at each other.

'So, who goes first?' I read his lips saying. 'Me first? You first?'

'What?' Fran asked.

'Sixty seconds. How was your day?'

She shrugged her shoulders.

'How about you? Solve any murders?'

'A few,' he replied.

She charged over to him and wrapped her arms around him tight in such a way I thought she may never let him go. She slowly pulled her head away from his chest and placed her hands on his cheeks. The two looked at each other for a while, staring longingly into each other's eyes with relief. I couldn't make out for sure if tears were streaming down their faces, but it certainly looked like both of them had a case of the waterworks. I noticed their elderly cat slowly creeping into the room, tenderly beginning to nudge and nuzzle Fran's leg while the two embraced.

They kissed, and then embraced again. But then I watched Gareth, with Fran still planted into his torso, reach into his back pocket and slowly bring something out. I watched Fran push herself away, a little concerned, as he placed the item on the kitchen table.

She seemed in shock, at first. Her eyes bulged and her mouth dropped as she stared at the blood-stained bronze ring that Gareth had dispassionately dropped onto the table, a small stream of clotted blood dropping onto the veneer. Then it turned to a look of recognition, as if there was some meaning to this. She didn't say anything to him, didn't burst into a frenzy or launch into an interrogation. He said nothing, as if he didn't know how to explain to his partner what he had done. Instead, she looked up at her husband, he looked down at his wife, and she gently and silently reached out to slip her hand into his.

A LETTER FROM THE AUTHOR

To the reader who has finished *My Wife, the Serial Killer*, an enormous, gargantuan thank you from me. I truly hope you enjoyed the book and found yourself drawn into Gareth and Fran's world and dynamic. Believe it or not, this entire story was crafted with *you* in mind, and I hope it made you feel everything I hoped for.

If you'd like to stay updated on my new releases and bonus content, you can join other readers by signing up for my newsletter.

www.stormpublishing.co/hj-garbett

If you enjoyed this book and have a few moments to spare, leaving a review would mean the world to me. Even a short review can make a huge difference in helping new readers discover *My Wife, the Serial Killer*. So, if you loved it (or even if you didn't—but hopefully you did, if you made it this far!), please consider sharing your thoughts and telling your friends.

Thank you again for choosing to read *My Wife, the Serial Killer*. I hope you'll stay in touch – I have so many more stories to share with you!

H.J. Garbett

KEEP IN TOUCH WITH THE AUTHOR

www.hjgarbett.co.uk

instagram.com/onemoresubplot

ACKNOWLEDGEMENTS

I've never particularly enjoyed reading the acknowledgements at the end of a book, almost as if they shatter the illusion that the story didn't actually just happen, and expose the unromantic reality: that what you just read was the result of countless hours of work, most of it spent hunched over a keyboard, hundreds of emails, an abundance of coffees, and many, many late nights. However, now, as an author, I finally understand the importance of acknowledgements, as this has truly been a marathon effort, and I am truly indebted to so many people for the fortunate opportunity to write these words.

To begin, a heartfelt thank you to my family. To my parents, who sparked my love of reading from the time I was a toddler. There aren't many mundane childhood memories I hold close to my heart, but the memory of them reading an endless selection of books to me is one I cherish dearly. If you're a parent, please take this random author's unsolicited advice: read to your children. I couldn't be more grateful for all the stories they shared with me some twenty-odd years later.

To my sister, Hollie, and to my friend Fiona, who were the first to read the full manuscript. Hollie, for her invaluable insights into the intricacies of fertility treatment as an OB/GYN. And Fiona, for being the first person to read the book when it was unagented, unpublished, and potentially destined to gather dust, and for telling me – despite my own doubts – that it was, in fact, not shit.

To Emily, who has rooted for me and my writing from the

early days of university putting on my first play at the M&D Room at Exeter. To Harry, who endured the slog of words to provide his ever-helpful grammar thoughts. And to Tom, for a multitude of reasons, but most of all, for letting me text him late at night with thoughts and ideas, most of the texts starting with: 'Okay, so tell me if this is corny, but...' Another big thank you to Lucie, Claudia, and Gloria for checking the French, police terminology, and German, respectively.

While I think every family member and close friend I have has played a part in the creation of this book (I could write an entirely separate novel about how much your support has meant to me), a special thank you to Louise Sharland, who so kindly gave up her time to advise me on getting an agent, shared her thoughts on the manuscript, and set me on the right course. I don't know if I would be writing these acknowledgements today without her.

This book has been through two agents – first, the amazing Katie Salvo, who took a chance on an unpublished author and made me believe that other people might actually want to read about Fran. And then, of course, the outstanding Kate Rizzo, who, after Katie's retirement, decided to pick up the baton and give Fran and Gareth a chance at life. I couldn't be more grateful to her and the rest of the team at Greene & Heaton. I once told Kate that I needed a cheerleader for an agent due to my frequent self-doubt about the book, and she has been nothing but the absolute best at every single step of this journey.

Emily Gowers and the team at Storm Publishing have been incredible to work with, continuously shaping and supporting this novel into the best it can possibly be. Emily is everything I could have wished for in an editor and I'd not be as proud of *My Wife, the Serial Killer* were it not for her.

So many people have taken risks by believing in me and this book, despite my lack of prior published works, and I couldn't be more grateful. To paraphrase the iconic Lady Gaga: there can be a hundred people in a room, but you only need one – or two in my case – to take a chance on you.

And finally, to *meu amor*, who endured my long, drawn-out moans when I was in crisis mode about how I actually didn't want to be an author at all and actually had always hated writing – I couldn't be more thankful for your unwavering love and support throughout all of this. For grabbing me by the hands, telling me it's all going to be okay, and reminding me to get back to work. Thank you for bringing me coffee and letting me use the comfy chair, *Eu amo-te*.

Printed in Dunstable, United Kingdom